"I still need to add the sugar…"

"You're telling me," Marshall replied. His voice came out in a strangled croak and he began to cough again.

Lovey pointed at him with her spoon. "Sorry. Though my *mam* did teach me to make lemonade so you could taste the lemons."

"Did she?" He laughed. He was captivated by the pretty young woman's eyes, her smile. "Your *mam* would approve of this batch for certain."

"I *am* sorry," she repeated. Then she giggled again.

Marshall watched her. "I can see I'll have to be more careful about reading signs literally when I come in here."

"Maybe you should." She smiled to herself, adding the sugar to the pitcher.

He couldn't take his eyes off her. There was something so familiar about her.

This girl w̶a̶s̶ ̶i̶n̶ ̶t̶h̶e̶ Amish clothing of every other local girl b̶u̶t̶ ̶t̶h̶e̶r̶e̶ ̶w̶a̶s̶ ̶s̶o̶m̶e̶t̶h̶ing remarkab̶l̶e̶ ... ̶h̶e̶r…as though h̶e̶ ... ̶uddenly he wanted t̶o̶ ...e.

Emma Miller lives quietly in her old farmhouse in rural Delaware. Fortunate enough to be born into a family of strong faith, she grew up on a dairy farm surrounded by loving parents, siblings, grandparents, aunts, uncles and cousins. Emma was educated in local schools and once taught in an Amish schoolhouse. When she's not caring for her large family, reading and writing are her favorite pastimes.

Carrie Lighte lives in Massachusetts, where her neighbors include several Mennonite farming families. She loves traveling and first learned about Amish culture when she visited Lancaster County, Pennsylvania, as a young girl. When she isn't writing or reading, she enjoys baking bread, playing word games and hiking, but her all-time favorite activity is bodyboarding with her loved ones when the surf's up at Coast Guard Beach on Cape Cod.

EMMA MILLER

The Amish Spinster's Courtship

&

CARRIE LIGHTE

Her New Amish Family

LOVE INSPIRED
INSPIRATIONAL ROMANCE

LOVE INSPIRED®
INSPIRATIONAL ROMANCE

ISBN-13: 978-1-335-22987-8

The Amish Spinster's Courtship and Her New Amish Family

Copyright © 2020 by Harlequin Books S.A.

The Amish Spinster's Courtship
First published in 2019. This edition published in 2020.
Copyright © 2019 by Emma Miller

Her New Amish Family
First published in 2019. This edition published in 2020.
Copyright © 2019 by Carrie Lighte

This edition published by arrangement with Harlequin Books S.A.

For questions and comments about the quality of this book, please contact us at CustomerService@Harlequin.com.

Harlequin Enterprises ULC
22 Adelaide St. West, 40th Floor
Toronto, Ontario M5H 4E3, Canada
www.Harlequin.com

Printed in U.S.A.

CONTENTS

THE AMISH SPINSTER'S COURTSHIP

Emma Miller

For my best friend, Judith.
Thank you for your confidence in me. For your love.
You made me who I am.

Whoso findeth a wife findeth a good thing,
and obtaineth favour of the Lord.
—*Proverbs* 18:22

Chapter One

Hickory Grove
Kent County, Delaware

Marshall Byler stepped into the shade of the concrete block dairy barn that housed the new Miller harness shop and breathed a sigh of relief. The July sun was hot and the day was muggy, just what one would expect for midsummer in Kent County and sure to make the corn grow. He'd been cultivating his corn in his east field when a groundhog had startled Toby, the younger of his two horses, and he'd spooked.

Marshall had gotten the horses calmed down before they tore up more than a small portion of his crop. However, somewhere in the frantic shying of the team, Toby's *britchen* strap, a section of harness that kept the horse from getting tangled in the traces, snapped. Marshall didn't need the harness immediately, but he decided to go ahead and drop it off for repair right away, so it would be ready when he needed it again.

Miller's Harness Shop would save him time because

it was closer to his farm than the Troyer Harness Shop, which he usually frequented. And he also liked the idea of giving his business to the new place; there was enough leatherwork to be done in Hickory Grove to support both the Troyer and the Miller families. Besides, the shop was owned by his new friend Will's father and it seemed only right to go there.

Marshall waited a moment for his eyes to adjust to the shadowy shop with its massive overhead beams and concrete flooring. A section of the former milking stalls had been cordoned off from the rest of the barn, and the stanchions and feed trough was replaced with shelving, display space with an assortment of items for sale and a counter with a cash register.

"Hello! Anyone here?" he called. When he got no answer, he put two fingers to his lips and whistled.

Still no response.

When he and his brother had driven into the yard, they hadn't seen anyone around. Yet the wooden sign beside the half-open Dutch door read *Velcom* Friends. It was long past the midday meal, so where was the proprietor? Glasses and a pitcher of lemonade stood by the cash register with a sign that read Refresh Your Thirst. Ice cubes, mint and lemon slices floated in the clear pitcher, a sight that made Marshall realize just how thirsty he was. Noticing a brass bell beside the cash register, he rang it before pouring himself a glass of the lemonade and taking a deep swallow.

Marshall gasped as the strong taste of sour lemon filled his mouth and made his eyes water. He grimaced and began to choke just as the door swung open to reveal a young Amish woman in a green dress and white *kapp*. He tried to clear his throat and coughed.

"Atch," she said, and clapped a hand over her mouth to suppress a giggle. "You weren't supposed to drink that yet." She held up a pint jar of raw sugar in one hand and a wooden spoon in the other. "I still need to add the sugar."

"You're telling me," Marshall replied. Rather, he tried to reply, but his voice came out in a strangled croak and he began to cough again.

She pointed at him with her spoon and grimaced. "Sorry. Though my *mam* did teach me to make lemonade so you could taste the lemons."

"Did she?" He laughed, then choked again. When he found his voice, he spoke, captivated by the pretty young woman's eyes, her smile. "Your *mam* would approve of this batch for certain." Marshall wanted to ask her how he was supposed to know there was no sugar in the lemonade yet, but he was enjoying the back and forth too much. Instead, he wiped his eyes with his shirtsleeve. He spotted a smudge of topsoil and wished he'd taken the time to go to the house to change his shirt before coming to the shop. He also wished he'd worn his better straw hat; this one had a bite out of it, thanks to his brother's pet goat.

The woman hurried past him, putting the service counter between them before depositing the jar of sugar beside the pitcher. "I *am* sorry," she repeated. Then she giggled again.

Marshall watched her. "I can see I'll have to be more careful about reading signs literally when I come in here."

"Maybe you should." She smiled to herself as she added the sugar to the pitcher and stirred with the spoon.

He couldn't take his eyes off her. He was sure they'd never met before because he would have remembered her, but there was something so familiar about her. It was like the taste of his favorite pie. All pies were different, but blueberry had its own special flavor. This girl wore the Amish clothing of every other local girl he knew, but there was something remarkably different, yet familiar, about her...as though he'd known her all his life. And suddenly he wanted to know her for the rest of his life.

Just this morning he and his grandmother, who lived with him and his little brother, were discussing his marriage prospects. Or lack of, in her eyes. For months she'd been talking about how it was time for him to start thinking about settling down and having a family of his own. He wondered what she would think if he walked back into the house this afternoon and told her he might have found the girl for him.

The woman regarded Marshall with shining almond-shaped eyes as green as spring grass. "What can I do for you?" She eyed the leather strap in his hand.

"I'm Marshall, Marshall Byler," he told her, deliberately stalling in explaining his reason for coming. "I live just down the road. The farm with the old pear trees by the mailbox?"

She didn't respond.

Marshall wasn't in the least bit discouraged. He liked a bit of chase with a girl. "And you must be a Miller?"

She shook her head and continued to stir. *"Ne."*

He took a step forward and inspected her closer. She was tall for a woman, perhaps taller than he was. And slender as a willow. She wasn't a beauty in the usual sense, not tiny and softly rounded like his neighbor Faith King. But when this newcomer turned those intense green eyes on him, he found himself almost stunned. Not to mention slightly tongue-tied. She was sharp as a straight razor, this one, and direct in her speech, more outspoken than most of the girls around here. Deliciously tart...like her lemonade.

Marshall smiled at her, a practiced expression that had caused more than a few feminine hearts to flutter. Surely, this *maedle* behind the counter could see his charm and recognize him for the superior fellow he was? He held up the broken strap.

She seemed not to notice his smile. Instead, all business, she left the spoon in the pitcher of lemonade and put out her hand. "Let me see what we're dealing with."

"You're not a Miller?" he ventured, determined to have her name.

She accepted the piece of leather from him and scrutinized it. "This damage looks fresh."

"Ya," he admitted. "My gelding's young, still green in the harness. He shied at a groundhog and caused a bit of a panic with his teammate."

"Neither animal harmed, I hope?" she asked.

Marshall warmed to the concern in her eyes and shook his head. *"Ne,* both fine." He hesitated. "You asked about the horses, but not the man?"

She lifted her head and inspected him with a new

interest, or so he hoped. "You look to be in one piece, Marshall Byler."

Then she returned her attention to the harness. "This strap has given a lot of service and the leather is near worn through here and here." She indicated two places on the leather. "It could be fixed, but you might be better off with a new one."

"Let's see, if you aren't a Miller, you must be one of Rosemary's daughters. I've met two of your sisters." He eyed her. "You don't favor any of them, which is why I didn't make the connection. Why haven't I seen you at any of the singings?"

"Mended or made new?" she asked. "What will it be?"

Marshall drew himself up to his full height, bringing his eyes level with those intriguing green ones. "What's your name?"

Her lips tightened again, and flecks of gold tumbled in the green irises. "Lovage. Lovage Stutzman."

He rapped his knuckles on the counter. "Ah, I knew you were one of Rosemary's daughters. She was a Stutzman before she married Benjamin, right? My grandmother is distantly related to some New York Stutzmans. What kind of name is Lovage? I never knew an Amish girl called *Lovage*."

She tied a yellow paper tag to one end of his harness strap. "My mother likes herbs," she explained. "I'm Hannah Lovage, but I've never used Hannah."

He removed his straw hat and used his handkerchief to wipe his forehead. It had seemed so much cooler in the harness shop than outside, but it was definitely heating up inside. "Rosemary's eldest daughter, then. I know your stepbrother Will. You're the one who stayed behind to see to the sale of your mother's property."

She nodded, inspecting him through dark, thick lashes.

What was it about those eyes? And now that he studied her close up, something was striking about her high cheekbones, the curve of her jawline, the way her soft brown hair framed her face. *Ne*, perhaps she wasn't pretty by conventional standards, but she was handsome. She was what his grandmother would call a timeless beauty. A woman who would keep her looks over the years.

"And you live here now, right?" he asked. "Your stepbrother Will said everything was settled for your mother in upstate New York. He called you Lovey."

"Just moved in. Have you made a decision about the strap?" She held it in the flat of her palm.

"What?" He'd been concentrating so much on her appearance that he hadn't really heard what she'd said.

"Mended or replaced with new? Your *britchen* strap." She raised her eyebrows. "The reason you came to my stepfather's harness shop?"

"Um…whatever you think." He pressed his hands on the counter, leaning closer to her, and on impulse asked, "Lovey, would you let me drive you home from the singing this Friday night? It's going to be at Asa King's."

"It's Lovage and I would not." She wrote his name on the tag in small, perfect print. "Come back in five business days and this will be ready." She wrote on a receipt pad on the counter and ripped off the page.

"Why won't you let me take you home from the singing? Have you got a steady beau?"

"*Ne*, I don't have a beau. I won't go home with you from the singing because there is no singing at the Kings. It was canceled."

He grinned. "Fair enough." He thought fast, unwilling to walk away without some commitment from her. "Wait, there's a softball game Saturday night. At the bishop's farm. How about that? Men against the women. You do play, don't you? You look like a pitcher."

"Catcher," she replied. She handed him the receipt.

"So…is that a maybe you'll let me take you home Saturday night?"

She smiled sweetly. "*Ne*. It is not. Thank you for your business, Marshall Byler. Now if you'll excuse me, I'll take this back to the workroom."

"Will you at least think about riding home with me?" he called after her as she walked away.

She didn't respond, but Marshall wasn't in the least bit discouraged. She'd come around. He knew she would. The girls always did. "Nice meeting you, Lovey Stutzman. See you Saturday." He rapped his knuckles on the wooden counter a final time.

"Lovage," she called over her shoulder.

Marshall was still grinning when he walked out of the harness shop and back to the wagon, where Sam waited for him.

"What are you so happy about?" Sam asked, looking up at his big brother.

"I'm more than happy. I'm ecstatic, blissful, elated."

Marshall climbed up into the wagon and took the reins. "Because I've just met the woman I'm going to marry."

In the workroom in the rear of Benjamin's harness shop, Lovage stopped beside the worktable where one of her sisters was using an oversize treadle sewing machine to stitch a strap on a new halter. Ginger, twenty-three, was two years younger than Lovage and twin to Bay Laurel.

Ginger paused, glanced up at her and offered a teasing smile. "I see you met Marshall Byler."

Lovage dropped the *britchen* strap on the long plank table. "It can be fixed, but you might be better off just making him a new one. Look at it and see what you think."

Preferring harness-making to housework and minding children, Ginger had worked in Benjamin's shop for the past three years, first in New York where they used to live and now in Hickory Grove. Her small hands were deft at fashioning leather into everything from bridles to belts to dog leashes. Ginger may have been a woman, but she'd quickly become Benjamin's most skilled leather worker, surpassing even his sons.

"He's cute, isn't he?" Ginger's green eyes twinkled mischievously. "If I'd known that was him ringing the bell, I'd have waited on him myself."

"You know him?"

"Every Amish girl of marrying age in the county knows Marshall Byler. Wishes he'd ask her out."

"You, too?" Lovage asked, looking down at Ginger, who was seated on a wooden stool.

Ginger lowered her gaze to her work at hand. She

lifted the foot of the sewing machine, adjusted the leather and dropped the foot again. "Are you going to let him take you home after the softball game?"

Lovage gazed at her sister.

Ginger was the prettiest of the Stutzman girls, blonde and green-eyed. And she was a flirt if there ever was such a thing among Old Order Amish. Back in New York, several mothers and a matchmaker had contacted their mother inquiring as to Ginger's availability as a possible match for their sons. Apparently, half the young men in Cattaraugus County, New York, were smitten with her. Rosemary had declared her second daughter too young to marry yet and had then whisked her off to Delaware.

"You were eavesdropping on my conversation with Marshall Byler?" Lovage asked, not even a little bit surprised.

"Maybe." Ginger nibbled on her lower lip. "From this stool, I hear all sorts of things in the front shop. Last week I heard that Mary Aaron Troyer is trying to match her twin boys with twin sisters from Kentucky." She shrugged. "Not sure they're keen on the idea. Are you going to the softball game?"

"You're certainly interested in my comings and goings." Lovage crossed her arms over her chest, pretending to be put out with the whole discussion. The truth was she was flattered by Marshall's attention. Though she didn't quite understand it. Not many boys expressed interest in her. She wasn't pretty enough or flirty enough. If a boy wanted to walk out with a Stutzman girl, Ginger was his choice every time. "And no one invited me."

Ginger ran the length of stitch and when the sewing machine was quiet again, she said, "It sounded to me as if Marshall Byler just invited you. Everyone's invited, anyway. It's a neighborhood game. We've gone before. Sometimes boys from Rose Valley even come." She snipped off a bit of loose thread from the halter with a pair of homemade scissors. "We play at Bishop Simon's house. He has a good field, even a backstop. He's nice. Jolly. And not too long-winded on Sundays. You'll love his wife, Annie. She'll make chocolate whoopie pies with peanut butter filling for the snack table. Wait until you taste them." Ginger took a breath and went on without waiting for Lovage to respond. "You should accept Marshall's offer."

"I certainly should not." Now Lovage was slightly peeved with her favorite sister for listening to what should have been a private conversation. Or maybe embarrassed. "I don't even know him—don't care to."

"Then you wouldn't mind if I ride home with him." Ginger tilted her head and giggled. "Will you?"

"You're impossible." Lovage tried to sound vexed, but it was all she could do not to laugh at her sister's boldness. She knew she should admonish Ginger for eavesdropping, but with four sisters, and now a houseful of brothers, who could expect privacy? It was impossible. And she could never be cross with one of her sisters for long. Certainly not over a boy. "You like all the single young men," she reminded her.

"Most, but not all," Ginger agreed. "Nothing wrong with liking the boys, so long as I remember everything Mam taught me about protecting my reputation." Her sister's amusement brought out her dimples. "I think

Marshall is fun. Bay does, too. I know *she'd* ride home with him if he asked."

"He thinks he's so good-looking. Charming." Lovage frowned, secretly wondering if she dared be so bold as to accept Marshall's invitation. Then she asked herself, what would be the point? She wasn't the kind of girl a boy like him would be interested in. She couldn't fathom why he'd asked to take her home from the softball game. Was it a way to get in good with Ginger? But that made no sense, because Ginger already said she was interested in him. Marshall Byler probably knew he could get any girl in the country into his buggy.

"Marshall *is* good-looking. But also faithful." Ginger carefully studied the halter she'd finished, found no flaws and set it aside. She looked up at her sister. "And you really *aren't* interested in him?"

"*Ne*, I am not." Lovage said it with more conviction than she felt. "I just arrived in Hickory Grove. I'm certainly not going to get involved with some fast-talking farmer my first week here. Especially not now when Mam needs my help more than ever."

Ginger rolled the remaining thread onto the spool and tucked it into the drawer under the tabletop. "Probably just as well." She wrinkled her nose. "Marshall's not your type."

"And who is my type?" Lovage rested on hand on her hip. "Ishmael Slabaugh?" she asked, referring to the young man she'd come close to becoming betrothed to.

Her sister shook her head so hard that her scarf slipped off the back of her head. "*Ne*, I didn't care for him. Too serious. I'm glad you didn't marry him. You can do better." She removed the navy scarf and tied it over her hair again. Unruly tendrils of curly yellow hair framed her heart-shaped face, a face with a complexion like fresh cream, an unusually pretty face with practically no freckles and soft, dark brows that arched over thick lashes and large, intelligent eyes.

Envy was a sin, and only a wicked girl would be envious of a much-loved sister. But not resenting Ginger's golden hair, rosebud lips and pert nose wasn't easy when you were a brown-haired string bean with a too-full mouth and a firm German chin. Lovage had to remind herself to put it all into proper perspective. She, Ginger, Bay, Tara and Nettie had always been close, and having sisters that everyone called the catch of the county was her burden to bear. Aunt Jane, her *dat*'s older sister, hadn't made it any easier, always pointing out that Lovage took after her plain, sensible father and not her mother with her pretty face and quirky ways.

"It's probably just as well you don't ride home with Marshall. You're not suited for someone like him," Ginger continued. "He's looking for a fun girlfriend."

"What? And I'm not fun?" Lovage frowned, opening her arms wide. "How can you say that? I'm *fun*. I like to do fun things."

Ginger giggled. "You are a lot of things, but fun isn't the first thing that comes to mind when I think of you. You're strong and brave and caring. And you're dependable. You've always been there for your family and anyone in need. But *fun*?" She wrinkled her nose. "Not so much."

Lovage rolled her eyes.

"If anything," Ginger went on, "you can be the op-

posite of fun. You never do anything that's not comfortable for you. You never... What's the Englisher phrase?
Step out of your box? Bay and I are sure you'd have a
better chance of finding a beau if you didn't take yourself and life so seriously."

"You're wrong," Lovage insisted. "I don't have a
beau because I don't want one. And I certainly don't
want a husband. Not right now, at least."

"Me, neither," Ginger confided. She rose from her
seat and carried the newly finished halter to a peg on
the wall. "I want to go to frolics and enjoy myself for
a few years. When I marry, it will be for life. Plenty
of time to be serious then."

"Mam thinks I should be looking for a husband,"
Lovage mused. "Just last night when we were getting
ready for bed, she reminded me that I have a birthday
coming up."

"You've got time. Twenty-five isn't old age." Ginger
stood and perched on the edge of the worktable, crossing her legs at the knee and swinging a slim, bare foot.
"And the sooner you marry, the sooner Mam will start
thinking it's time for Bay and me to make a match.
And, like I told you, neither of us is in a hurry."

"*Goot*. We agree on something."

"But..." Ginger chuckled and shook her head.
"Since you brought up the subject, I may as well have
my say as chew on it like an old cow's cud."

"Say it then," Lovage replied. "You know you will,
anyway."

"Okay, so maybe..." Ginger leaned forward and
looked her straight in the eye. "Maybe you shouldn't
be so stubborn, and listen to someone once in a while.

You know I love you more than gingerbread, and I only want what's best for you."

Lovage grimaced. "All right, all right. Say it and get it over with."

"I've been talking to Bay and we agree. Our advice to you as the new girl is to make friends and go to the singings and the ball games and the frolics. Enjoy yourself before you settle down with a husband and babies. I'm going to the softball game. I think we all are. You should come with us. You're a mean catcher, and we need one. Most of the girls are afraid of the ball."

Lovage suddenly felt nervous. "What if this Marshall pesters me to ride home with him?"

Ginger shrugged. "I doubt he will." She broke into a sassy grin. "Not when I give him my best smile."

Lovage sighed and glanced away. A part of her wanted to go to the softball game, but this thing with Marshall suddenly seemed like so much pressure. "But what if he does?"

"Then you should go ride home with him. Like I said, you're not his type, but it might be a good way to meet other boys. To be friendly with Marshall. He knows everyone in the county."

Lovage crossed her arms over her chest. A part of her wanted to tell Marshall she'd ride home with him, just to prove to Ginger that she could be fun.

"Come on. I dare you to do it." Still grinning, Ginger poked Lovage in the arm with her finger. "Tell you what, sister. If you ride home from the softball game with Marshall Byler Saturday night, I'll take your turn at washing dishes for a whole week."

Chapter Two

Lovage knelt on a carpet of thick moss and pulled up a few dandelions that were sprouting up beside the fish pond. "Your herb beds are coming along beautifully, Mam. I didn't think you'd be this far along with them." She dropped the dandelions into a bucket with the few weeds she'd already pulled. "And the waterfall is perfect for this spot. I love the sound of the water. It's so relaxing."

Her mother placed freshly cut sprigs of lavender in a basket and rested her large, dirt-streaked hands on her hips. "I'm so glad you're finally here, Lovey. I've missed you so much. No one appreciates my garden like you do." She studied the twenty-foot, oblong pond with its bubbling cascade, miniature lily pads, cattails and decorative rock border, and smiled. "I wish I could take credit for this, but I can't. The pond, the Irish moss and the wrought-iron bench were already here when Benjamin brought me to look at the farm. When I walked through that gate and saw this herb garden and the flowing water, I fell in love with the place. I told him that this was the one before I even set foot in the house."

Lovage stood up and brushed the soil off her apron. She was barefoot, as was her mother, and both wore midcalf-length dresses, oversize aprons with large pockets and wide-brimmed straw bonnets over their prayer *kapps*.

Lovage was pleased that she and her mother had found a few minutes to be alone, even if it was to work in the garden. As the firstborn, she and her *mam* had always been close, and had become more so after her mother had been widowed three years ago. Lovage had missed her mother dearly in the time they'd been apart. She'd always considered her mother her best friend, so this morning was doubly precious.

When her mother married their late father's best friend the previous year, Lovage had remained behind in New York when her *mam* and her new husband, Benjamin, and all their children, had made the move to Delaware. Lovage had four sisters and a brother, and Benjamin had five sons still at home, so it had been quite an effort to move them all. While the family got settled in Delaware, their mother had entrusted her with the responsibility of selling the livestock and the farm equipment, as well as disposing of the household goods.

Blending two large families and two homes into one wasn't done easily or quickly, and the couple had decided that a new start, a new home and a new community would give them the greatest opportunity for success. Lovage was glad to remain behind to help her mother in whatever way she could, but she'd missed the bustle of her large family and was glad when the last of the decisions were made, the final shipment of household goods was on its way to Delaware, and she was free to come.

"Smell this lavender," her mother said, bringing her back into the present. "And see how the thyme is growing. I was afraid that it wouldn't. But there's more rainfall here than back home, and the pond helps. There's a good market for dried lavender, for sachets and hanging arrangements."

"The soil seems free of rocks," Lovage observed.

Her mother laughed. "No rocks in Delaware. At least not down here. Benjamin says it gets a little rocky upstate near the Pennsylvania state line. This whole garden used to be fenced in for the dairy cows. I wouldn't be surprised if my hoe took root and blossomed."

"The cows had a pond and wrought-iron bench? I'm confused."

"For years it was a cow pasture and then, when the English farmer retired, his wife wanted a pretty pond and an herb and flower garden. You can see someone loved and tended it. Either that or the cows wanted somewhere nice to sit."

Lovage laughed, picturing a cow sitting on the iron bench with a gardening trowel between her hooves. "I can see that this is a wonderful spot for you. But you inherited Grossmama's green thumb. Any plant will grow for you."

"And you have the gift, too," her *mam* replied. "It's a true blessing."

Lovage clasped both of her mother's strong hands and led her to the wide iron bench with the high back and the grapevine pattern. A grape arbor arched overhead with spreading leaves and tiny green concord grapes, providing relief from the hot July sun, something they both could relish. "Sit with me," she urged. "You've been on your feet since before six this morning."

Her mother's smile lit her green eyes. "And that's different from every other morning in what way, *dochtah*?"

"It isn't. That's the thing. You shouldn't have to get up so early. You have Ginger and Bay and the younger girls to help you with breakfast and the chores. And now me. I want you to take better care of yourself."

"It's a wonder how I managed before you got here, my love."

"Be serious." She caught her mother's hand again and clasped it with affection, taking in the broken fingernails and calluses. *The apple doesn't fall far from the tree*, Lovage thought with a glance at her own hands. Too bad she didn't inherit Mam's sunny disposition and lovely features instead of taking after her father.

She looked into her mother's smiling face and tried to reason with her. "You have to let us help you, especially now with all these extra boys in the house. Boys needing clothes washed, eating everything that isn't tacked down, tracking in mud and wood shavings. And now that I'm here, I'll be able to take over a lot of your chores, just like at home in New York."

"This is our home now." Her mother pulled her hand free and hugged her. "And those *boys* are Benjamin's sons and now my sons and your stepbrothers."

"I know that."

Her *mam* patted her cheek fondly. "Of course, I know how much you did for me both before my marriage to Benjamin and after. But…now that you're here, things have to be different. It's time you started thinking about yourself. About the life you'll have separate from me—marriage, your own home, babies, God willing."

"I told you I don't want to talk about that." Lovage gazed out over the garden. "My place right now is with you, helping you."

"Oh, Lovage." Her mother sighed. "You being my eldest, it's natural that you feel the most responsible. But it's time you flew the coop, my chick. Find yourself a good man and let him court you the way you deserve."

Against her will, Lovage thought of Marshall Byler and how he had flirted with her the previous day at the harness shop. "And what if that's not what I want?"

Her mother drew back, looking at her with true concern. "You don't want to marry and have your own home? You don't want a husband and children? I don't believe that. Children are God's greatest blessings. And His grace, of course. If any woman was born to be a mother, it's you, Lovage."

Lovage removed her straw hat and dropped it onto the brick walkway, letting the breeze ruffle her hair. Carefully thinking over her words before they spilled out all higgledy-piggledy, she straightened her starched white *kapp* and repinned the back of her hair securely. "I do want those things. It's every girl's dream… Her own kitchen…red-cheeked babies with sticky hands and butterfly kisses. But—"

"But nothing. If you want those things, you need a husband. And you need a partner to share the burdens of life," her mother said softly. "A godly man who shares your faith, and will laugh with you and lend you his strength when you most need it. Don't you want that?"

"I do want all those things someday," Lovage assured her. "But not now. Now, I want only to be here with you, to help you through this."

"Help me *through this*?" Her mother's eyes widened in puzzlement and then she sighed. "Lovey—"

"There you are, my Rosebud," boomed a deep male voice. Benjamin was a sturdy, fiftyish man of medium height, with rusty brown hair streaked with gray and a pleasant, weathered face with a high forehead and a broad nose under his straw hat. His full beard had a reddish cast and that, too, had begun to gray. At the moment, he was carrying a tray of assorted herb seedlings and had a twenty-pound bag of bonemeal tucked under one arm.

"I should have known to look here first." He swung the white picket gate wide and strode into the garden. "And you with her, *dochtah*. What do you think of the place? I warn you, your mother had the final say. So if it doesn't please you…" He chuckled. "You must blame her."

Lovage's mother laughed with him.

"Speak up, wife," he implored. "Where do you want the bonemeal?"

She got up and went to him. "Anywhere at all, Benjamin," she answered, taking the tray of seedlings from him.

"That's no answer. Shall I drop it in the pond or balance it on a fence post?"

"Anywhere will do, but preferably not in the water," Rosemary said, setting the plants on the ground. "Here."

"She's full of honey-do's, this wife of mine." Benjamin winked at Lovage conspiratorially and lowered the bag of bonemeal to the ground beside a section of newly worked, bare dirt. "You see how she treats me?" He straightened and slipped an arm around her mother's waist.

"Go on with you." Her *mam* blushed like a schoolgirl. "You're embarrassing Lovage. What will she think of us?"

"That we suit each other like bread and honey," he teased, wrapping his other arm around his wife.

Giggling, Rosemary tried to push her husband's hands away, but with no great effort.

Uncomfortable, Lovage glanced away. She truly liked her stepfather, but their outrageous behavior was going to take some getting used to. She could never remember her father acting so, and she knew their marriage had been a happy one. Physical affection wasn't something one saw often with an Amish couple. And certainly not one of their age. Both were old enough to be grandparents and Benjamin soon would be. His married daughter, Mary, was expecting twins.

"See, what did I tell you? Behave yourself in front of the children." Still chuckling, her mother stepped out of her husband's embrace. "Go see to your harnesses and buggy wheels and leave us in peace."

"There now, wife, I meant no harm," Benjamin said. "And no disrespect to either of you," he added, looking to Lovage.

"I know that." Lovage nodded, but avoided his gaze.

It was true. In spite of the current situation, she was pleased that her mother had found someone who obviously adored her and could provide for her. It was only natural that mixing two large families into one would require adjustment. Her aunt Paula thought her sister Rosemary had lost her mind to accept the offer of a man with six children, five under his roof.

"You must have chores of your own to do," her mother told Benjamin.

"If you say so, Rosebud," he agreed. "Unless you need me here."

She smiled at him. "I do not. Now off with you, before you embarrass poor Lovage even more." She watched him trudge away with a feigned sad expression. When the gate shut behind him, she turned to her daughter. "You mustn't pay his silliness any mind. Benjamin is so pleased to have you with us. And you're going to like it here," she added.

Lovage nodded.

Leaving the home where she'd been born and grown up hadn't been as difficult as Lovage had thought it might be. She could see that the move to a new place and a new, larger home that neither her mother nor Benjamin had shared with another spouse seemed the wisest course. It was too soon to know if she would like Delaware, but her mother clearly did. And Lovage was happy to be reunited with her sisters and mother, and her little brother.

"It seems like a good house and community," she said. "Of course, I haven't met the new bishop and preachers yet. Or the other families."

"You will like them very well," her mother said. "The sermons are short and pithy and our church members welcoming. Everyone has embraced us and they're eager to meet you.

"Now, to get back to what we were talking about before we were interrupted," her mother continued. "Why is it that you have set your mind against being courted by a suitable young man now? A sweet and capable girl like you. You could have your pick if you'd just—"

"Mam, please. Don't talk like that." She felt her cheeks grow warm. She knew what she was. Too tall, too lanky…too opinionated. But that wasn't the point. "It's not about me. It's about you. A woman your age… in your *condition*," she intoned.

"In my *condition*?" The amusement seeped from her mother's face and her chin firmed. "I am neither sick nor so decrepit that I can't run my own household. I'm forty-five and carrying a child. It is not an illness. It's a natural condition for a married woman and it's a blessing. God has given Benjamin and me another life to cherish."

Lovage knew she blushed. To have such a conversation with her mother made her uncomfortable, but if she was determined to have it, have it they would. "A pregnancy at your age is considered high risk. I'm worried about you and it's my duty to help you through this."

"Goose feathers! I'm as strong as a horse." Chuckling, she picked up the basket she'd been using to gather herbs. "You're the one who needs help, Lovage. And I would be neglecting my duty as your mother if I didn't see you happily wed to a good man. I think you should take that young man's offer and ride home with him from the softball game."

Lovage whipped around to look at her mother. "Ginger should not have told you. He wasn't—" She knew her cheeks were burning bright. "He didn't— Ginger should mind her own business."

Her mother headed for the garden gate. "It wasn't Ginger. It was Bay who—"

"How did Bay know Marshall asked me to ride home with him?" She crossed her arms obstinately. "I'm not going to, of course."

Her mother raised her brows under her broad-brimmed hat. "Marshall, is it? Your stepbrother Will's friend? Nice-looking young man." She made a clicking sound between her teeth. "And from a good family. I've met his grandmother, Lynita. Faithful woman. Knows how to work hard and live with joy." She opened the gate. "A good choice for a suitor, Lovey."

"He's *not* my suitor," Lovage called as the gate swung shut, leaving her alone in the garden.

The following morning, Lovage made her way back to the garden, hoping to beat the full heat of the day. Her mother was letting out the seams on one of her dresses, and the younger girls had taken over the task of cleaning up the kitchen and starting the chicken and dumplings for the midday meal. Lovage had offered to plant the new seedlings Benjamin had bought, and to finish weeding around the fish pond.

Family breakfast had been as noisy and satisfying as Lovage remembered. She approved of her mother's new house, especially the large kitchen with its attached, open dining room. Benjamin's twenty-two-year-old twins, Jacob and Joshua, who were apprenticed to a cabinetmaker, had built a fourteen-foot oak trestle table. The table provided enough room for all of them to eat together and this morning her brother, Jesse, who was ten, had declared it the finest dining table he'd ever eaten at.

How she'd missed Jesse's mischievous face in the months they'd been apart. He was brown-haired like her and her father, with green eyes, and his own special lopsided grin. That morning, Benjamin had promised to take Jesse to look at a pony for sale and the boy was so excited he could hardly sit still for grace, let alone eat his bacon and eggs. It was clear to Lovage that Jesse was very fond of his stepfather, and soon would begin to think of him as simply his *dat*. It made Lovage sad to think that eventually her little brother would barely remember their own father. She knew it was best for Jesse; it was just hard, no matter how much she liked Benjamin. But as her aunt Jane said, "Life moves on for the living. My brother is in heaven and beyond those earthly cares. You can't stop change. You may as well embrace it."

Lovage gazed out over the garden. It had rained sometime in the night, and the soil was wet. The garden smelled deliciously of mint, sage and rosemary. Finding her rhythm in planting, Lovage soon discarded the digging trowel and used her fingers. She hiked up her skirt to keep the worst of the mud off it and knelt on a folded-up burlap bag as she carefully transplanted each basil and tarragon seedling.

Herbs preferred cool weather, so July wasn't the best time to put them in the ground, but Benjamin probably hadn't realized that when he'd bought up the remainder of the neighbor's greenhouse herb stock. Her mother wouldn't have wanted to discourage him by rejecting his gift, so Lovage was determined to do her best to save the seedlings.

On her hands and knees, with her skirt hiked up, she planted most of the tray. Then, when she had to stretch to reach the last of the open area in the bed, she reached too far and slipped on the wet topsoil. She went down on both elbows, throwing dirt onto the bodice and sleeves of her dress, as well as liberally covering both arms, elbow to wrist, with wet soil. *"Atch!"* she exclaimed, and spat the dirt from between her lips.

"You okay?" came a male voice from behind her.

Lovage froze, not knowing who the voice belonged to, though it seemed familiar. Then, realizing what she must look like, sprawled in the herb bed, covered in mud, she scrambled to rise. *"Ya,"* she called, "I'm fine. I…" In her effort to get up, she succeeded only in slipping again and falling forward into the dirt again. "Oh!" As she went down, her right hand flattened a small seedling, while her elbow took out two more. That was when a pair of strong male hands closed around her shoulders and lifted her to her feet.

"You sure you're all right?" he asked.

She whirled around. Mortified, cheeks scalding, she

raised her gaze to look directly into Marshall Byler's amused eyes. "Oh," she breathed.

"Oh," he said, managing, somehow, to make it sound flirty.

"What…what are you doing here?" she sputtered, taking a step back from him. Out of his arms. She glanced down at her dress and bare feet covered in dirt, and then back at him as she shoved her skirt down where it had gotten tangled in her apron. Which was now also muddy.

He grinned and offered her a big blue handkerchief from his pocket. "You've got mud on your forehead," he informed her. "Right here." He tapped his own forehead in the center. "I can get it for you if you—"

"You'll do no such thing." She snatched the handkerchief from him and dabbed at her forehead.

"And…and your nose," he said helpfully, pointing.

Lovage rubbed her nose furiously with the blue fabric.

He tipped the broad brim of his straw hat as if to get a better look at her. "To answer your question, I came to check on my harness. One of your sisters sent me out here to ask you. Bay, I think?"

Lovage huffed. "I told you it would be five business days. Bay could have—" She suddenly realized that Bay had sent him out to the garden on purpose. Ginger was probably in on it. And their mother, as well, for all she knew. She blushed even harder and went back to scrubbing her nose with his handkerchief. "Bay shouldn't have sent you out here. She could have looked up the work order. You only dropped it off two days ago."

"A good thing for you she did send me, because I don't think you would have managed to get up anytime today." He grinned, indicating the wet spot in the garden. "Not the way you were slipping and sliding in that mud." Then he laughed, the sound deep and infectious.

Lovage didn't want to laugh. She knew that if she did, he'd take it as encouragement and continue his flirty talk. But she couldn't help it. She looked down at her arms and dress again and began to laugh, sounding not like herself, but oddly enough, more like Ginger. "I think I would have managed," she said, when she could talk again. "I'd have made it to my feet by noon."

His blue eyes danced. "Suppertime at the latest."

Still chuckling, she walked over to the pond, knelt and washed the worst of the mud off her arms. Next, she dipped her feet in, one at a time. Marshall watched as she wiped her wet hands on a relatively clean place on her apron. "Better?" she asked.

"Somewhat," he conceded.

"Goot." She met his gaze and it took her a moment to break free of it. "But you've made the trip for nothing." She shrugged. "I told you the harness wouldn't be done for at least five business days."

"Ne." He held up one finger. "I remember exactly what your words were. You told me to come back in five days. You didn't say the harness wouldn't be done today."

"But it isn't."

He made a show of appearing sad, thrusting his lower lip out in a pout. "A pity. I need it."

"If I could have fixed it for you, I would have, but it isn't what I do. Ginger and my stepbrothers, they're the harness workers. Benjamin has other work orders, people who came before you. They need their harnesses and halters and bridles, too. It wouldn't be fair to fix yours out of turn."

Lovage glanced back at the muddy mess of an herb bed. She'd have to salvage as many of the plants as she could. But she wasn't about to attempt it with Marshall as a witness. She turned away and walked down the path toward the gate, hoping he would follow. Hoping he would leave.

"So…what you're telling me is that *you* can't fix my *britchen* strap?" he asked, following her. "Only your sister can."

"I can't use the sewing machine. It takes a knack. Otherwise, you just break the thread. And sometimes the needle."

"Pity," he said, walking two steps behind her. "You'll be in over your head when we marry if you can't sew."

She stopped short, whirled around and looked at him. "What did you just say?"

"I said, if you can't sew, it could be a problem. I've never known an Amish woman who couldn't sew." He knitted his brows. "How will you make shirts for me or baby clouts?"

"*Baby clouts?* Who's making *baby clouts*?" She looked up at him wide-eyed, wondering if the summer heat had gotten to his head. Except that it was still morning and not all that hot out. "I was talking about harness-making. My sister is apprenticing as a harness maker. I can *sew*. I don't sew *leather*." She caught her breath, flustered again. "And that's not what I meant.

You're putting words in my mouth." She dropped her hands to her hips. "What did you say about me being in over my head?"

His smile widened. "I said you'd be in over your head when we marry if—"

"What are you talking about, marry?" she interrupted. "I don't know you. We're not even—" She blushed again. "We're not even walking out together."

"You're absolutely right," he said, interrupting her. "And that's a problem. We're not walking out yet." He sidestepped around her and opened the gate, standing back and holding it for her. "And I think that's important to our relationship. We should get to know each other before we take our vows. It's the custom here in Kent County. We walk out together, court, marry. In that order." He winked at her. "Is it different where you come from?"

"Enough." She raised her hands, palms out. "I'm not amused by you. We aren't walking out together. We aren't courting. And we certainly aren't getting married. You came to get a harness mended. I waited on you. That's it. That's the only connection we have."

"Not exactly." In an exaggerated motion with his hand, he indicated the garden behind them. "We've had this time together."

"What are you talking about now?" she asked, still flustered, wishing desperately that she wasn't. She also wished he wasn't so handsome. That his forearms weren't so tanned and muscular. That his smile wasn't so…beautiful.

"And we're neighbors," he told her. "We have that connection."

"We are *not* neighbors. You live two miles away."

His grin widened to crinkle his entire face. Marshall had a high forehead and a dimple in the center of his square chin. With his broad shoulders and self-assured manner, he was one of the most attractive young men she'd ever met. Which made her nervous. She wasn't used to attention from such a cute guy and she half suspected that he was poking fun at her. Because surely he wasn't *really* interested in her.

Once, at a frolic when she was fifteen, a cute boy had caught her eye and she'd wanted him to notice her. She'd even broken her own rule and smiled at him, trying to flirt casually like Ginger did. It worked. The boy had noticed her, all right, but he'd only turned to a friend and whispered something she couldn't quite make out. She had heard the word *broomstick*, then they'd both laughed, obviously at her. She'd cried into her pillow half the night, and she still remembered the slight painfully. Not for all the apples in an orchard would she make the same mistake a second time.

"Ah," Marshall continued, holding up his finger to her again. "You asked someone about me. You wanted to know where I lived, which means you *are* interested in me." He pointed at her. "Admit it. You like me."

"I do not *like* you," she protested.

"You don't like me?" He opened his arms. "What have I done to deserve that? I'm a nice fellow. Ask anyone. They'll tell you. Your brother Will likes me. He and I have become good friends."

"Will is my stepbrother," she corrected.

Marshall removed his straw hat and pushed back his dark hair. It was nice hair, neatly trimmed and thick. "That's what he said when I asked him about you last night."

He smiled at her and she felt her pulse quicken. He *did* have a sweet smile, a dangerous smile that made her stumble over her words and confuse her thinking.

Marshall met her gaze. "I wanted to see you again," he said softly. "That's why I came to check on my harness. I was hoping to see you, Lovey."

Suddenly, the oxygen was sucked out of the air. The sound of her pet name on his lips made her throat tighten. But she liked it. She did. Marshall was teasing her again, wasn't he? A boy like him couldn't like a girl like her.

Could he?

"I wanted to see you and ask if you're coming to the softball game tomorrow night," he went on.

"Maybe," she said quickly, still flustered. He just kept *looking* at her. "I… I haven't decided yet."

"I see." Marshall nodded. "Well, I hope you do. And if you do, will you let me drive you home in my buggy? It's a nice buggy…"

It had been a long time since anyone had asked Lovage to ride home in a buggy with him. So long that she didn't know how to respond. Lovage bit down on her lower lip.

Then she heard the sound of feminine giggling. She and Marshall both glanced in the direction of a hedge of blueberry bushes and she spotted her sisters Bay, Tara and Nettie all peeking around the hedge, watching them.

Lovage quickly looked back at Marshall. He was

waiting, smiling. He didn't give a lick that they had an audience.

"Come on, Lovey." He reached out and touched her elbow. "It'll be fun. Say you'll ride home with me Saturday night."

She swallowed hard and grasped at the first answer that came to mind. "I might," she told him. "If you're on your best behavior."

"I'll take that as a yes." Marshall walked past her, his stride long and powerful. "It's a date," he said, loudly enough not only for her sisters behind the blueberry bushes to hear, but possibly everyone up at the house.

"But, Marshall," she called after him. "I didn't say—"

"See you tomorrow, Lovey."

All Lovage heard then was a burst of giggles from the blueberry hedge.

Chapter Three

"You want to go ahead and get Toby unharnessed?" Marshall asked his brother. The wagon had barely come to a halt in the barnyard and he pressed the reins into Sam's hands and leaped to the ground. "Rub him down before you let him into the pasture. It's a hot day."

"Ya." Twelve-year-old Sam, a carbon copy of a younger Marshall, gripped the wide leather reins with both hands, seeming to puff up with pride at being given the task. "I'll give 'im a good rub and a scoop of grain."

"Mind you, the harness needs to be wiped down, as well." Marshall backed away from the wagon, clamping his hand down over his straw hat. Sounds coming from the henhouse distracted him for a moment. He could hear chickens squawking and flapping their wings. He looked back to Sam. "Give me a holler if you need any help."

Sam eyed his big brother from under the brim of his hat, which was identical to Marshall's. Small for his age, he sometimes struggled with the chores requiring brute strength or simply height, but he more than made up for it with heart. And smarts. If he wasn't strong enough to do something, like lift a hundred-pound bag of feed, he'd throw together a contraption of one sort or the other to accomplish the task. He had pulleys and levers all over the barn, mechanisms he'd built himself from scraps he found around the farm or scavenged at the county dump or friends' trash cans.

"I got it," Sam said. He wasn't a talker. But he was a hard worker. He was the first one up in the morning, the last to go to bed, and that was only when Marshall or their *grossmammi* sent him up to his room—with the warning there would be no reading. Otherwise, Sam would be up half the night scouring books and magazines on Plain ways to make work go easier on their farm.

Marshall watched Sam ease the wagon toward the drive-through shed his little brother had designed himself. It was a clever lean-to attached to the main barn, just wide enough for a horse and buggy to pull in to get out of the rain or sun. There, the vehicle, the horse and the man could stay out of the elements while hitching or unhitching. And when it was time to go somewhere, the horse could be hitched to the front of the buggy or wagon and then walk right out without having to back up. Their bishop had liked the design so much he'd built one himself at his own property, saying it would come in handy because a man with his responsibilities had to travel day or night, snow or rain.

The chickens continued to kick up a ruckus and Marshall strode across the barnyard, wondering if a fox had gotten in the henhouse. It had happened the previous year and they had lost half their layers in one night. But it was midday, nearly dinner, and not the time of day a fox was usually up and about.

As he crossed the barnyard, Marshall took in the big barn and multiple outbuildings. Every structure looked neat and tidy, all painted a traditional red with white trim: the old dairy barn, the henhouse, the smokehouse and carriage shed, the granary and other assorted structures. The dirt driveway was raked, the grass mowed and the beds of flowers weeded. And off behind the neat, white clapboard farmhouse, his garden of raised beds, rather than the rows his father had always planted, were neatly weeded. The raised beds were new this year. It had taken Sam two planting seasons to convince Marshall to make the change, but Marshall had to admit it was a good one. They were yielding more crops in a smaller space with less effort.

The sight of his little Eden made Marshall smile. He and Sam had grown up here, Marshall with both his parents, Sam with only their *dat*, after their *mam* died giving birth to him. Then four years ago, their *dat* died of cancer, and at the age of twenty-six Marshall had become the head of the family, responsible for his grandmother and his little brother. The transition from being the eldest son to the man of the house had been difficult at first for Marshall, especially with the transition from big brother to parent to Sam. It had put an end to his *rumspringa* days and nights of courting the prettiest girls in the county. But the three of them, Marshall, Sam and Grossmammi, had worked through their sorrow and come out the other side, seeing the good in the life God had given them.

The volume of the disturbance in the henhouse became louder and Marshall ran the last couple steps and flung open the door, half expecting to meet a fox with one of his chickens it its mouth. Instead, he came face-to-face with his petite grandmother, holding a basket of eggs in one hand and a flapping chicken by the feet in the other.

"Got her," Grossmammi exclaimed, holding the chicken high in the air.

The chicken squawked and beat its wings, trying desperately to escape her grip. "Thought she'd get away with it, she did."

She thrust the chicken upward and Marshall took a step back, raising his hands to keep the chicken from flapping its wings in his face.

He laughed. "Grossmammi, what are you doing?"

She lowered the chicken to her side, letting its head brush the dirt floor of the henhouse, but still held tightly to it. "Collecting eggs."

He grinned at his grandmother, who stood five feet tall only when she wore her heavy-soled black shoes. Despite her short stature, she was a hearty-sized woman, round with chubby cheeks and a smile that was infectious. Several wisps of gray hair had come free from her elder's black prayer *kapp*, evidence of the struggle that had apparently taken place between her and the black-and-white-potted Dominique chicken.

"I mean, what are you doing with the chicken?" He pointed.

She held it up as if she was surprised to find it in her hand. "I warned Emily, if she pecked me again, into the stew pot she went. I should have known not to buy any more Dominicker chicks. Small brains." She lowered the chicken and looked at him. "She'll make us a nice supper tomorrow night."

He removed his hat and wiped his brow before returning it to his head. "And how does Emily feel about that?"

"She should have thought of that before she pecked my hand again." She held up the hand that held the basket of eggs. "Look, she drew blood."

He glanced at her hand, which was, indeed, bloody. "She peck you before or after you hung her upside down by her feet?" He suppressed a smile. It made his grandmother angry when she thought he was making fun of her. And an angry Lynita Byler he did not want to deal with today. He was in too good a mood.

"She drew blood, *sohn*," she said, shaking the chicken. It began to flap its wings again, but with less effort. "I can't have my own chickens pecking me!"

He smiled. Even though he was her *kins-kind*, her grandchild, and not her son, it had been her habit for several years now to call him her own and that somehow eased his pain of being an orphan. Even being a grown man of thirty, he found it hard sometimes to be without parents. "I see your point." He studied the chicken for a moment. "But I'm afraid she's going to be awfully tough. How old is Emily? Three years old? Four?"

"Old enough to know not to peck the hand that feeds her grain," Grossmammi said indignantly.

He reached out and took the basket of eggs from her. "The other thing to take into consideration is that tomorrow is the softball game. Will says there's talk of cooking hamburgers and hot dogs. In that case, we won't be having supper at home. I know you don't want to miss a softball game and potluck to eat a tough old chicken."

She harrumphed, raised the bird high again and said, "Last time, Emily. I promise you that." Then she lowered the old hen to the ground and Emily had the good sense to hit the ground running.

Marshall stepped aside to let his grandmother pass and closed the henhouse door behind her.

"You go to Troyer's and get your *britchen* strap repaired?" she asked, watching him latch the door securely.

They crossed the sunny barnyard side by side, Marshall shortening his stride so his grandmother could keep up. She was wearing a rose-colored dress today, her bare feet dirty from work in the garden that morning.

"I went to Miller's," he told her. "Will's stepfather's harness shop. Thought it would be neighborly to go there rather than Troyer's. Give them the business. Which is a good thing because I met the woman I'm going to marry," he told her.

She stopped and cocked her head. She wore tiny, wire-frame glasses with lenses that darkened in the sunlight. Marshall couldn't see her eyes now, but her tone of voice was enough of a reprimand.

"Your wife!" she exclaimed. "You've already courted and become betrothed? Banns going to be read on Sunday?" She started walking again and he was the one who had to keep up.

"Not moving quite that quickly, Mammi," he said,

using her nickname. "What's the matter? I thought you'd be pleased."

"That you're ready to bring a wife into this house." She nodded. "I am. A man going to be thirty-one come Christmas Eve, you should have a wife and a house full of children. God willing," she added quickly. "Who are you talking about? One of Rosemary's girls, I suppose? That Ginger is a flirt. You've always been drawn to a pretty face."

"Not Ginger. Lovage. Rosemary's oldest. She's just come to Hickory Grove this week." They cut across the grass toward the back porch. "She's been in New York settling her mother's affairs this last year."

Lynita made a clicking sound between her teeth. "Lovage? What kind of a name is that?"

"Lovage is an herb," he explained to her as they rounded one of the hickory trees his grandfather, Lynita's husband, had planted two generations ago. They hadn't grown naturally on the property, but there were so many in the area, Marshall's father had told him, that Moses had dug up soldiers in the woods, planted them all around the house he built for his new wife. And now, though Grossdaddi had been dead two decades, they shaded the home where his sons and grandsons had been born and, God willing, his great-grandchildren would be born.

It was interesting to Marshall that in all his running-around years when he was in his early twenties, children had been the last thing on his mind. All he had wanted was a fast horse to pull his courting buggy and a pretty girl beside him. Marriage hadn't been a consideration and being a father had fallen even behind that.

But the last few months, he'd begun to feel a need to settle down and have a family of his own. Maybe it was his grandmother nagging him, or maybe it was God directing, Marshall didn't know. What he *did* know was that Lovey Stutzman was the woman for him.

"I like Rosemary, but a bit of an odd duck, isn't she? And marrying at her age, to a man with all those boys? Brave she is, too." Lynita studied him through her dark glasses. "I'm glad you're thinking about finding a good woman, but I think you'd best stay closer to home. A girl born and raised here." She went up the porch steps.

He followed her. "Not this again, Mammi. Faith is a perfectly nice girl, but—"

"She can cook," his grandmother interrupted. "She can sew as fine a stitch on a quilt as I've ever seen, and you won't have to worry about her bringing any fancy ideas from New York. She grew up here in Hickory Grove just like you. She knows how things are done." At the top of the steps, she took the basket from him, an egg basket she'd woven herself. "I like her name better, too."

Marshall glanced away, grinning. His grandmother was persistent, if nothing else. She'd been touting their neighbor Faith King's qualities since Easter Sunday, when she and Faith's mother had talked after services and she had learned that Faith was ready to start looking for a serious suitor. Faith was young and pretty and she cooked as fine a stuffed pig's maw as he had ever eaten. He'd give her that, but she didn't light a spark in him. Not the way Lovey had.

He looked at his grandmother, who, standing on the porch with him still on the stairs, was nearly his height.

"Grossmammi, you know I respect your opinion, but—"

"And her father's land meets ours to the north. Couldn't be more convenient. Eldest girl and no sons to inherit." She lifted her snowy-white brows. "The two farms together would make a fine piece of land someday."

"As I was saying before you interrupted—"

"*Ne*, I didn't interrupt. I'm older than you are, and wiser." She pointed a tiny finger at him. "It's not an interruption coming from an elder. It's a fact."

He chuckled, shaking his head. "You're not marrying me off to Faith King, Mammi." He turned and went down the steps. First, he was going to check on Sam's progress unhitching Toby, and then he intended to work on replacing a rotting post in the grape arbor until his grandmother called them for dinner. "I appreciate your concern, but I'll find my own wife." At the bottom of the steps, he turned to her, opening his arms wide. "I already have."

Lovage walked off the softball field, carrying a catcher's mask under her arm. The community softball games were so popular in Hickory Grove that Bishop Simon not only had a ballfield on his property, but equipment: bats, balls, extra gloves and an old catcher's mask he'd found at Spence's Bazaar. Lovage hadn't been to the market in nearby Dover, where Amish and Englishers sold wares and foodstuffs and shopped, but she'd heard it mentioned multiple times since her arrival in Delaware. It was a place one could find not just treasures like a used catcher's mask, but also handmade items like quilts and wooden crafts, deli sandwiches, homemade cakes and doughnuts and pickles and preserves.

"Nice game," one of the young men, John Mary Byler, who had played third base on her team, said as he walked by. He was with Lovage's stepbrothers Jacob and Joshua, who were identical twins. With matching haircuts, even knowing them her whole life, Lovage had to listen to their speech patterns to identify which was Jacob and which was Joshua. Their eldest brother, Ethan, said they purposely tried to do things exactly the same way, copying each other's gestures and such to confuse people purposely for fun.

Lovage nodded and looked down at the ground, feeling self-conscious. John Mary hadn't wanted her on his team; it had been obvious from the look on his face when Bishop Simon had divvied them up. She supposed this was his way of apologizing, now that he knew she could play softball pretty well, but he still made her feel uncomfortable. Or maybe it was his cousin Marshall Byler who was making her nervous. Marshall had played for the other team, but had kept up a running dialogue with her the whole afternoon, complimenting her on every good throw she made from behind the plate and assuring her she'd get the next one if she missed a strike thrown to her. He was the pitcher for the other team. And now the game was over and families were packing up to go home to tuck little ones into bed. Young men and women of courting age were beginning to break into groups or even pairs to spend an hour together—chaperoned, of course— before they went home.

"Thirsty?" Marshall seemed to come out of nowhere to walk beside her across the grass toward the area where families were packing up the leftovers from the cookout potluck. In the distance, she could see her mother filling one of their three picnic baskets while speaking to Jesse. Benjamin was shamelessly putting covers on food dishes and handing them to her as if every fifty-year-old Amish man cleaned up after supper.

"I'm sorry. What?" Lovage glanced at Marshall. They were the same height, something she hadn't noticed at the harness shop the other day. She was a tall woman and he wasn't a tall man. Not that that mattered to her. In fact, she liked being able to walk beside him and look him eye-to-eye. Or she would if he wasn't making her so nervous, meeting her gaze, holding it every time she looked his way.

"Would you like something to drink? There's some of my *grossmammi*'s lemonade left. I'm partial to it. She adds a little fresh squeezed orange juice to it. And plenty of sugar, unlike someone else I know," he joked.

She kept walking, trying not to laugh, because it would only encourage him. In the last couple hours, she'd gone back and forth half a dozen times trying to decide if she was brave enough to ride home with Marshall or not. A part of her wanted to because, against her will, she found she liked him. Not only was he fun to be around, always laughing and joking, but he was also such a kind man. Not self-centered like so many single men. He gave out compliments freely and seemed endlessly supportive, even to those members of his team who obviously couldn't play softball.

And he was the most handsome man on the field. Or at least she thought he was. He wore the same clothing all of the other eligible young men wore: homemade dungaree pants, a short-sleeved shirt and a straw hat. But there was something about him that made her a little light-headed when she was able to steal a glance at him when he wasn't looking. Maybe it was how tightly his sleeves fitted around his biceps, or the way his hair met his neckline, plain to see when he'd thrown aside his hat early in the game to make a play at home plate.

The other reason she was seriously considering riding home with Marshall was because of Ginger's dare. Not having to do dishes for a week was very tempting. But it was more than that. Ginger didn't think she'd ride home with Marshall alone in his buggy. She didn't think Lovage was brave enough. Or fun enough. Ginger said Lovage wasn't the kind of girl Marshall would ever be interested in.

What if she proved her wrong?

"Would you like to stay a little while?" Marshall asked. "Before we head home? Sometimes there are games for the singles after families head out. Singing and such."

She glanced at him. "At home that was more for the younger couples." The minute the word *couples* came out of her mouth, she blushed profusely and looked away. She couldn't believe she'd just said that, suggesting they were in any way a couple. "I… I didn't mean—"

"That I don't like to have fun because I've reached the ancient age of thirty?" he asked. His tone was teasing.

"That we're a couple," she blurted, knowing her face must be bright red.

He slid his hands into the front pockets of his pants thoughtfully. "I don't mind if you tell people we're courting, Lovey."

Her eyes widened. "We are *not* courting, Marshall Byler. I... I don't even know if I'm riding home with you."

"Sure you are. I already spoke with your mother and Benjamin about what time they'd like to see you home. She makes a mean strawberry-rhubarb tart, your *mam*." He smacked his lips together. "I think it would put my grandmother's to the test."

"You asked my mother for permission to drive me home?" Lovage asked indignantly.

"Not really. I think you and I are both old enough that we don't need permission from our elders. We know our own minds. I was just chatting with them, letting them know they'll be seeing more of me, now that you and I are courting."

"We are not courting!" she told him. "I don't even know you."

He stopped and tilted his head, looking at her. "Are we going to do this again, Lovey?" He gave an exaggerated sigh. "This is how we're going to get to know each other. Learn each other's likes and dislikes and such." He frowned. "I don't even know what your favorite color is."

"Blue," she said, before she caught herself.

He grinned. "Blue, of course. I would have guessed that. Blue because of my eyes."

"Blue is not my favorite color because—" She groaned in frustration. She would have liked to have said he was conceited, but he came off not as conceited but as the most confident young man she'd ever met. Which made him the total opposite of her. Lovage was definitely not confident, particularly around men.

He started walking and she walked with him, mostly because she didn't know what else to do. Her gaze strayed to her family gathered at the picnic tables under the hickory trees. Her mother and Benjamin had passed the baskets to her brothers. They'd be in their two buggies soon, headed home. If Lovage was going with them, she needed to say so.

"So that's a no on staying for the games?" Marshall went on. "In that case, we can take the long way home. I have a courting buggy, you know. A cozy two-seater." He winked at her. "I like your way of thinking, Lovey."

"Marshall," Lovage said, so rattled she couldn't even speak.

Just then, two young women in pretty rose-colored dressed walked past them. They were Ginger's age and pretty, with freckled noses and blond hair. Sisters, Lovage guessed.

"Nice game, Marshall," the taller of the two cooed.

The other giggled. "We got here late, otherwise we could have played on your team, Marshall," she said.

Marshall grinned. "Thanks. You should definitely join us next time."

Lovage cut her eyes at him. These girls were openly flirting with him! And he was flirting back. And— and it made her angry because *she* was walking with him. He had asked *her* to ride home with him. And she could be fun. She could flirt.

Maybe.

Gripping the catcher's mask in one hand, Lovage

turned to Marshall. "Yes," she blurted, so nervous that it came out too loud. Too forward.

"Ya?" He looked at her, his blue eyes twinkling in a way that made Lovage feel a little woozy.

"Yes, I'll ride home with you. I just…" She walked away from him. "I have to talk to my parents."

"Sounds like a plan." He was smiling now. Smiling at her. "I need to make sure my little brother and grandmother are set to go, anyway."

Lovage had learned from Ginger that Marshall's grandmother lived with him and that he had been caring for her and his little brother since their father passed away a few years ago. Lovage had to admit, at least to herself, that the idea that he was being a father to his twelve-year-old brother was evidence of what a truly good man he was.

"Meet you at the picnic tables in a few minutes?" Marshall asked. "We'll say goodbye to everyone, thank the bishop and his wife for having us and then go."

Lovage nodded as she hurried away.

"See you in a few minutes, Lovey!" he called after her.

Chapter Four

"**B**eautiful night." Marshall strode beside Lovage toward the buggies lined up on the far side of Bishop Simon's barn. He'd already hitched up Toby when he had walked his grandmother to her buggy and checked to be sure Sam had hitched old Jake properly. Sam had seemed proud that Marshall had given him the responsibility of seeing Grossmammi home safely, though he was disappointed he wouldn't be the one driving. Their grandmother would take the reins. Sam was turning out to be an excellent driver, but it would be nearly dark by the time they arrived home, and dusk was the most dangerous time of day to be driving a horse and buggy on the roads. Englisher drivers were too unpredictable. Marshall knew it was his duty to teach Sam how to navigate the busy roadway, but his first responsibility was to his family's safety.

Marshall smiled to himself as he glanced at Lovey, walking beside him. He felt like he didn't have a care in the world tonight. His team had won the softball game, he'd had an excellent chat with Lovey's parents, and now he was taking his sweetheart home alone in his buggy. The fact that she hadn't agreed to be his sweetheart yet was a minor detail. Marshall knew, in his heart of hearts, Lovey was the woman for him. He'd recognized it the moment he saw her at the harness shop. Spending time near her this afternoon had only given him more confidence in his choice.

Watching Lovey interact with her siblings and stepbrothers while she'd shared the cookout feast with her family had given him the opportunity to see what a fine sister and daughter she was. She was attentive not just to her siblings, but to her mother, as well. More than once, Marshall, who'd been watching her from his family's picnic blanket across the yard, saw Lovey jump up to do a task, allowing her mother to relax and enjoy getting to know her new neighbors. Then, watching Lovey play softball had shown him yet another side of her. She was competitive, but not in a sour way, and she tried her best, even when she knew chances were she wouldn't be successful. And while definitely on the shy side, she was willing to offer her opinion when asked. She was a smart player, kind and fair to the others on her own team as well as his. The fact that she was a good softball player was just a bonus.

He glanced at Lovey, who was walking with her head down. "Beautiful night for a *long* ride," he told her, slipping his thumbs behind his suspenders, stretching them and releasing them.

"It's not all that far to our farm," she responded. "Less than two miles, I'd say."

"Benjamin told me he turned in around ten. Said he and Rosemary liked all of his chicks in the house by then." Marshall pulled out a pocket watch that had been his father's and *his* father's before that, and checked the time. "We've got more than an hour before your parents will be expecting you. Which means we can take the long way home."

"Why would we go the long way?" she asked, sounding perplexed.

Just the sound of her voice made Marshall want to take her hand in his. She looked so pretty this evening in a blue, calf-length dress, the color of the cornflowers that grew in his grandmother's flower beds. Wisps of soft brown hair peeked from beneath her white prayer kapp pinned securely to her head. And she had a little smudge of dirt on her chin, which, in his eyes, made her even prettier. He could tell that Lovey wasn't one of those single women who spent their days sitting on their father's porches waiting for men to court them. Lovey wasn't afraid to get dirty on the softball field, which meant she wouldn't mind getting dirty in their garden, weeding beside him. In his mind's eye, he could just imagine the two of them in the early morning, tidying the beds, talking and laughing, enjoying the sunshine and each other's company.

That was the kind of wife Marshall wanted. A woman who could be his partner. When he lay in bed alone at night, he imagined having the kind of marriage his parents had shared. The kind where husband and wife tried to lighten each other's load. He didn't necessarily believe that opposites attracted; it was important for a man and his wife to have the same religious convictions, the same morals. But he *did* think that a man's weaknesses should be shored up by his wife's strengths, and vice versa. While he was outgoing, Lovey was more reserved. She was cautious, while he had been known to make snap decisions. In his eyes, the combination of those traits would only make them a better team to experience the joys and the trials they would face in their life together. He truly believed that was God's intention when he had created man and wife.

"Why would I want to take the long way?" Marshall asked her. "So I can spend as much time as possible with you," he explained.

She finally glanced at him. The look on her face was quizzical. "But why would you want to do that?"

He smiled, not entirely sure if she was serious or not. Did she really not know how beautiful she was? How smart and capable? "Because I want to get to know you. Because I enjoy being with you," he told her. "Is that so hard to believe?"

She narrowed her green eyes. "*Ya*, a little."

He tilted his head back and laughed hard, and when he looked at her again, she was smiling at him. It was a smile that warmed his heart. One look at the smile that was for him alone, and he made his mind up that once they were in his cozy, two-seater buggy and away from prying eyes, he was definitely going to hold her hand. Or at least give it his best shot.

"Tomorrow is visiting Sunday for our church," he told her as they rounded the corner of the barn to where the buggies were parked. "I was wondering what you would think about me bringing my grandmother and brother by your place. Benjamin made the invitation. To stop by and say hello if we were in the neighborhood." He chuckled. "Of course, obviously we're in the neighborhood. It's an easy walk between my place and yours. In fact, if it's nice—"

Marshall halted midsentence, staring in disbelief at what he was seeing.

Just beyond his cousin John Mary Byler's buggy was his own. It was a handsome two-seater that he had purchased when he was in his early twenties. It was a perfect buggy for courting, because it was light and fast and open, so no young woman's parents need be concerned for their daughter's reputation. It was perfect to take Lovey on what might be considered their first date. Perfect, except that sitting in the middle of the bench seat was a boy of about ten. A boy he was pretty sure he recognized from Benjamin's harness shop. And from Lovey's family's picnic blanket earlier in the evening.

He turned to look at Lovey, confident she knew better than he did what was going. She was grinning, and he found her smile infectious, even though he was pretty sure she'd gotten the best of him here.

"And who might this young man be?" he asked Lovage.

The boy had a shaggy head of brown hair, a cute grin and green eyes that were familiar to Marshall. "I'm Jesse. Lovey's brother." He pointed at her.

"I hope you don't mind, Marshall." Lovey's mouth twitched into a playful smile as she rounded the buggy, giving his horse a rub on the nose as she went by. "You asked me if I wanted to ride home with you. You didn't say I couldn't bring my little brother."

He glanced away and then back at her, not angry, but amused that his Lovey would play such a trick on him.

"Are you asking me if he can ride squeezed in between us?" Marshall asked, meeting her gaze.

Her green eyes twinkled with amusement. "That's not a problem, is it, Marshall?"

"Not at all, Lovey." He chuckled and walked over to unhitch Toby from the hitching post. "Not a bit."

Against Lovage's will, she found herself relaxing on the buggy ride home. With Jesse seated between them, actually squeezed in between them, as Marshall had observed, she felt more comfortable with Marshall, and with herself. With Jesse there to act as a buffer, she didn't feel so self-conscious. Usually, when she was alone with a man, she was uncomfortable, worrying so much about what she said or did that she never had a good time. Not that she'd had that many dates in her life.

Tonight was different and she didn't know why. Was it Marshall that made it different? Instead of worrying about where she put her hands or how often she looked at him, she found herself laughing at his jokes and enjoying his stories, which seemed endless. She'd laughed so hard when he told her about his grandmother catching one of their old hens and insisting she was going to put it in the stew pot. And she couldn't help smiling when he related a story about the neighbor's baby goat he had saved from a dog, nursed back to health and given to his little brother as a companion.

"I'm not exaggerating when I tell you the kid follows him around like a dog," Marshall told her. He glanced down at Jesse, seated between them. "You're welcome to come over and meet Petunia yourself, if you like."

Jesse giggled. "Who names a goat *Petunia*?"

Marshall, the leather reins gripped in his broad hands, leaned over as if letting him in on a secret. "Our grandmother named her because the first go-round with a name…" He raised his eyebrows. "Sam was calling him Peter. You see the fault in that, don't you?"

Jesse broke into another peal of giggles. "It was a girl goat, not a boy goat."

"I like your brother," Marshall told Lovage, talking over Jesse's head. "He's smart, this one. Catches on fast."

Jesse giggled again and Lovage couldn't help smiling. When she'd decided to have Jesse ride home with them to serve as a chaperone, as she'd explained to her mother, she'd half expected Marshall to change his mind. A single man as good-looking, as charming, as Marshall could have had his pick of any single girl there that night. Her sister Ginger indeed would have ridden with him. Lovage bet those two girls who were flirting with him would have let him drive them home, too. And none of them would have brought their little brother along.

But Marshall hadn't changed his mind. In fact, he'd had a good sense of humor about the whole thing. Not only had he agreed Jesse could ride with them, but he'd been kind to him, talking as much to him as to her. Marshall had taken the long way to Benjamin's farm, but it seemed to Lovey as if the hour had gone by in minutes. One minute she and Marshall were pulling onto the road from Bishop Simon's and the next, they were turning at the Miller's Harness Shop sign that her sister Nettie had painted. It was a beautiful handmade wood sign with a buggy in the background, indicating Benjamin and his son Levi also dabbled in buggy-making.

Lovage almost felt disappointed when their big white, rambling two-story farmhouse came into view. She couldn't recall the last time she'd so enjoyed a buggy ride. Or the company of a man.

Marshall eased his horse in the side yard near the house and jumped down.

As he walked up to tie Toby to the hitching post, Lovage turned to her brother and said quietly, "Mind your manners. Be sure to thank Marshall for giving you a ride home from the game."

"Ya," Jesse responded, beaming.

Lovage stood to get out of the buggy before Marshall reached her side, but she wasn't quick enough. And there he was, looking up at her, his hand out to help her down.

Lovage seriously considered not taking his hand, and climbing down herself. But before she could make up her mind, he caught her fingers with his and she felt a warmth that brought a rush of heat to her cheeks.

"Thank you for the ride home," Jesse said from behind Marshall. "You think it would be okay if I came tomorrow morning, after chores, to see Petunia?"

"Jesse, you shouldn't invite yourself," Lovage admonished. Her sneakers touched the ground and she found herself almost disappointed when Marshall took his hand away from hers.

"You're *velcom* for the ride. Anytime. Of course you can come tomorrow morning. As long as you have your mother's permission," Marshall told Jesse. He looked back at Lovage, shrugging his shoulders, which seemed even broader to her today than they had the first day they'd met. "He wasn't inviting himself. I already invited you, right, Jesse?"

Jesse beamed again.

Lovage bunched the fabric of her skirt in her hands. "Thank you for the ride home," she said, trying to think of a way to sidestep Marshall and make her escape to the house.

"You're welcome," he answered. But he didn't move, effectively keeping her pinned, her back to the buggy. "But I'm not done with you." He glanced over his shoulder at her little brother. "Off with you, now, Jesse. I want to talk to your sister alone."

Jesse yanked off his straw hat and took off toward the side porch. "Thanks again, Marshall. See you tomorrow."

When he was gone, Marshall turned back to Lovage. "That was pretty clever of you, agreeing to ride home with me and *then* inviting your little brother." He was smiling slyly.

A mosquito buzzed around her head, but she didn't want to swat at it and look foolish to him. "*Ya*, it was, wasn't it?" She crossed her arms over her chest, feeling awkward. He was standing so close to her that even though it was dark, she could see his blue eyes watching her.

He smirked, narrowing his eyes. "You don't really think you're the first girl I've ever dated who brought along a chaperone, do you? I walked out with a girl from Rose Valley who took her elderly aunt with her everywhere we went."

Lovage covered her mouth with her hand to keep from giggling. "We're not dating," she told him.

He rolled his eyes. "Of course we are. You rode home with me in my buggy. Half the county saw you. By the end of tomorrow, the rest of the county will know by way of the Amish telegraph." He stepped back. "Come on. Let me walk you to the door. I think someone is watching us from the front window." He nodded in the direction of the house.

Lovage looked over his shoulder just in time to see the curtain fall over one of the parlor windows.

"Which leads me to a question I've wanted to ask you since you threw Will out at third base."

"Marshall, we're not dating." She shook her head. "You asked the new girl in town to ride home with you. I did. Your curiosity is satisfied, and now we can both let this go."

"Oh, no. My curiosity is in no way satisfied." They followed a brick walk around the corner of the house, toward the side porch that opened into the big country kitchen that Benjamin had remodeled with all new cabinets when they moved in. "In fact," Marshall told her, "I'm all the more intrigued by you. Would you like to go for ice cream Thursday? Maybe we'll have supper first, then ice cream. Or the other way around, if you like. You can bring Jesse. I'll bring my grandmother. That way we'll have two chaperones." He cut his eyes at her. "I have to tell you, Lovey. That was smart of you to bring Jesse with us on our first date. Because had he not been sitting between us, I would have tried to hold your hand."

She looked at him, not sure if she was flattered or

shocked that he would say such a thing. Where she came from, couples were encouraged not to hold hands or to hug. Kissing was most definitely frowned upon. Courting was intended to be a way for couples to get to know each other, to find out how compatible they were. But unlike in the English world, in the Amish community, physical contact between a man and a woman was meant for a husband and wife only.

He stepped in so close to her that she could feel his warm breath on her face. "Oh, Lovey, don't tell me you were thinking the same thing? Is that why you brought Jesse along, so you wouldn't be tempted to hold my hand on our first date?"

She gave a little laugh. She'd never met anyone who said such ridiculous things. At least not to her. "I certainly was not going to hold your hand," she told him indignantly.

"Good, because I think we should wait a few dates. No need to rush things. Well…not in that way." He started walking again, then stopped. "Which, in a roundabout way, brings me to what I wanted to ask you."

The propane light beside the door on the side porch flared and Lovage caught a glimpse of Ginger slipping back into the house.

"I should go in," Lovage said, suddenly feeling nervous. "We have family prayer at ten before Benjamin and Mam say goodnight." She pressed her lips together. She didn't really want to say good-night, but that was girlish folly. She'd had a good time, but it was best she and Marshall parted now. For whatever reason he'd asked to take her home, surely he was content now. She'd be kidding herself to think he really wanted to take her for ice cream, even if it was with his grandmother.

"Marshall, my family—"

"Lovey." He caught her hand. His grip was firm and warm. "Will you marry me?"

"What?" She shook her head. "*Ne*—what—" She was so flabbergasted she didn't even know what to say.

It wasn't until he squeezed her hand that she realized he was still holding it. She pulled her hand from his. "No, I won't m—" She stopped and started again. "Marshall Byler, what would possess you to ask me to marry you?" she demanded, feeling embarrassed, angry and a little giddy at the same time. What kind of game was he playing that he would say such a thing?

"What would possess me?" He looked at her earnestly. "I asked because I want to marry. I'm in love with you, Lovey."

"How can you be in love with me?" She opened her arms wide. "You don't even know me."

"Which is why you should go get ice cream with me Thursday." He said it with such sincerity that she half believed he meant what he was saying.

Motion in a different parlor window than before caught her eyes. She grabbed the hem of his sleeve and tugged, moving them out of the line of vision of whoever was spying on her. "I have to go inside," she whispered loudly.

"So Thursday is good for you?" he asked.

"*Ya...*" She pressed her hand to her forehead. He had her so flustered. "*Ne*, Marshall. You don't want to— I don't want to—"

"You don't like ice cream?" He took a step back,

clutching both hands to his heart, looking as if he was heartbroken.

She closed her eyes, shaking her head, then opened them again. "Of course I like ice cream."

"Good." They reached the steps that led up to the kitchen porch. "When I see you tomorrow afternoon, we can make plans. I know you said hello to my grandmother when everyone was making introductions before we ate tonight, but it's important to me that you two get to know each other before you and I are married."

Lovage felt as if she was on a merry-go-round at the state fair. She threw her hands up in the air. "Now we're talking about marriage again?" she asked incredulously.

"Ne." He held his hand up, palm out. "We're not. It's okay. No need to answer me tonight. You're right. No need to be in any hurry." He took a step back. "Thank you for such a wonderful evening, Lovey. I'll see you tomorrow when we make the rounds in the neighborhood. My grandmother loves visiting Sundays."

Lovage watched him walk away, trying to think of something to holler to him. But she didn't know *what* to say. Except maybe to ask him if he'd lost his mind, asking a woman he didn't know to marry him.

Just as he reached his buggy, he turned back. "Tell your *mam* three o'clock is fine for us. And we'll bring the lemonade," he added.

"Not funny," she called after him, trying not to laugh.

Lovage stood on the steps watching Marshall until he turned his buggy around in the barnyard and headed back down the driveway. He waved as he went by and she felt a strange sense of light-headedness.

When she couldn't hear hoofbeats any longer, she reached for the kitchen door, only to have it pulled out of her hand.

"I can't believe you actually did it!" Ginger said, filling the doorway.

Lovage walked past her. "Close the door or you'll let the bugs in. One week of dishes. You owe one week."

"How was it? How was *he*?" Ginger followed her into the big country kitchen, which was dominated by two tables that could seat all thirteen members of their new family, as well as three or four guests, without even putting the leaves in them. The room smelled fresh and clean, no doubt thanks to her mother's little bundle of freshly cut mint on the windowsill. "I couldn't believe it when *mam* told me you took Jesse with you."

"He was my chaperone. A girl is better off to take a chaperone with her. Then no tongues can wag." Lovage reached the sink and turned to her sister, holding up her finger. "You're not getting out of doing my dishes. You didn't say I had to ride home alone with him." She reached for a pint-size Ball jar and filled it with water.

Ginger stood with one hand on her hip, staring at Lovage, making her feel uncomfortable.

Her younger sister crossed her arms. "Don't feel bad if he doesn't offer to take you home again. I heard from *mam*, who heard from old Grace Swartzentruber, that Lynita was just saying last week that Marshall wants to start dating again. Since his father's passing. It will probably be a different girl every week."

Lovage tipped the jar, taking a long drink of the cool, sweet well water. Benjamin had told her that he'd had a new well put in when he purchased the property. It was a deep well, which he was told would bring up the best water in the county, and she had to agree he may have been right. The water certainly was good, not like the water they'd had back in New York that sometimes tasted brackish.

"There's a singing Thursday night." Ginger swayed her hips, deep in thought. "I wonder if he'll ask me to go."

"Doubt it," Lovage said.

Ginger frowned. "What? You don't think he'll ask me because you didn't suit him? You think he thinks all the Stutzman girls are alike, do you?"

"I don't think he'll ask you to the singing because he's busy Thursday." Lovage took another sip of water, not knowing what had gotten into her.

Ginger pouted. "I don't understand."

"He won't be asking you to the singing because he asked to take me to get ice cream."

Ginger stood there in the kitchen, her mouth agape, as Lovage rinsed the glass, put it in the drain and then headed into the parlor to join the family for evening prayers.

Chapter Five

"I can't believe I'm making baby clouts and gowns again," Rosemary remarked, the straight pins in her mouth muddling her words.

Head down, Lovage pumped the treadle on her mother's sewing machine with both feet, easing the seam of a baby gown through the foot. It had turned out to be a rainy day, and while her sisters were busy giving the kitchen and mudroom a good scrub top to bottom, their mother had asked Lovage to join her in her sewing room to help with some baby clothing she had cut out but hadn't had time to stitch.

Most of the rooms in the new house looked very different than the ones in their old farmhouse in New York. And Lovage understood why her mother would do that, because this was Benjamin's and her house; a new house, a new husband, a new life. There was even a new baby on the way. But her *mam*'s sewing room was almost identical to the one she'd left behind. Lovage wondered if it was an acknowledgment to her father? Maybe to the life Mam once had?

A battered antique pine table under the window held a pile of fabric meant for baby clothing, as well as cut and pinned lengths of cloth that, once stitched together, looked like it would be a pink everyday dress for someone. Lovage guessed it might be for her sister Tarragon. About to turn eighteen, Tara had had a sudden growth spurt in the spring and had been making do with her sisters' dresses, according to a letter she had sent to Lovage while she was still in New York. Lovage knew her sister, the youngest of the five girls, would be pleased to have a brand-new dress of her own, especially since she often wore hand-me-downs.

Lovage lifted the foot on the old Singer sewing machine to cut the thread, and gazed around the room, feeling nostalgic for the old farmhouse where she and her siblings had been born. Nearly square, with two large windows, this sewing room, like the old one, was painted a pale blue, with a blue-white-and-yellow rag rug in the middle of the floor. There were two rocking chairs placed side by side where sisters, or mother and daughter, could sit and knit. One wall boasted an oversize walnut cabinet rescued from a twentieth-century millinery shop, and open drawers revealed an assortment of various sizes of thread, needles, scissors and paper patterns. A small knotty-pine table with turned legs stood between the windows, a big terra-cotta planter filled with fresh herbs and flowers in its center.

"The Lord works in mysterious ways," her mother went on. "That's what Benjamin says. That we should accept His gifts without question, but I have to admit there are times…"

Rosemary went on with her musings, but Lovage

was lost in her own thoughts. And all she could think about was Marshall. True to his word, he had brought his grandmother and brother on Sunday to visit with her family. Just as in her community in New York, the Old Order Amish churches in Kent County held church in someone's home every other Sunday. On the other Sundays, visiting Sundays, they spent time with family and friends. Like church Sundays, visiting Sunday was a day of rest and prayer. No work was done, except what was required to care for the animals in the barns. There was no gardening, no cleaning of stalls, no repairs made. Most families didn't even cook, but instead, particularly in the summer months, relied for sustenance on salads and sliced meats prepared on Saturday.

It had been a picture-perfect day for visiting, and Lovage's family had spent hours at picnic tables under the giant hickory trees in their side yard. There, they'd chatted with neighbors and spent time reconnecting with each other after a busy week. When Marshall and his family arrived, Rosemary was just serving an afternoon snack. Marshall had brought not only lemonade, but also fresh chicken salad, made with pimento and cheddar cheese of all things, and tiny croissant rolls that Lynita had baked herself. The snack turned into an early supper, and they had eaten the chicken sandwiches with an assortment of cold salads, including German potato, Waldorf and macaroni. There were also bowls of pickled cucumbers, a five-bean succotash-and-pepper slaw. And then, when the two families thought they could eat no more. Benjamin produced trays of huge slices of watermelon he'd chilled in the well house.

After the meal, Marshall had asked Lovage if she wanted to go for a walk with him in the garden. He had teased that he wanted to see if the herbs she had planted the previous week had survived. She had hesitated, but then Ginger had piped up, "I'll go," and popped off the bench she'd been sitting on under the trees.

So Lovage, Marshall and Ginger had taken a walk through the fenced-in garden and then around the farm, and Marshall and Ginger had chatted. Mostly, Ginger had talked. At first, Lovage was annoyed that her sister was monopolizing the conversation, but then she'd realized it was probably just as well, because her sister was so good at conversation and she wasn't. Marshall would certainly enjoy Ginger's banter more than any awkward exchange she and he would have. So Lovage had stayed mostly quiet, only speaking when Marshall had asked her something directly. And then, when they'd joined the others under the hickory trees again, Lynita had been ready to leave, as they were expected at her great-niece's house. Marshall had said goodbye without mentioning going for ice cream with him Thursday, and Lovage decided she was okay with that. Whatever reason he had asked her out in the first place had run its course. For all she knew, when Ginger was talking to him alone just before he left, they could have decided to go to the singing at the schoolhouse on Thursday instead. And she couldn't blame Marshall. He and Ginger had gotten along well. They had seemed so at ease together that she wouldn't be surprised if they were soon walking out.

"Lovey, are you listening to me? You're a million miles away."

Lovage blinked, glanced down at the unfinished seam of the baby gown, and then back at her mother. "I'm sorry, Mam. Gathering wool again, I suppose." She chuckled and began to pump the treadle that would turn the needle.

"I was saying that Benjamin and I were impressed Sunday with your young man. He's a little older than you are, but your father was ten years older than I was and it was never a problem. Lynita said he's thirty. Thirty-one on Christmas Eve. Not too old for you at all."

"He's not *my* young man," Lovage said over the rhythmic sound of the sewing machine.

Her mother set down the baby cap she'd pinned together and planted her hands on her broad hips. "Hannah Lovage Stutzman. A week ago, you were telling me you didn't want to talk about marriage because no man would ever be interested in you." She gestured with one hand. "Now a possible suitor—a handsome one, I have to say—pays you some mind and you're going to turn your nose up at him?"

"I think he likes Ginger." Lovage tried not to pout.

"Everyone likes Ginger. That doesn't mean everyone wants to marry her. And Marshall Byler didn't come to see Ginger on Sunday. He came to see you. And he took *you* home from the softball game. I think he's smitten with you."

Lovage felt her cheeks grow warm. "He is most definitely not—" She stopped peddling, realizing she was sewing the seam crooked. "He's not smitten with me."

She kept her head down as she pulled the baby gown out from the foot of the sewing machine and reached for her seam ripper. "Why would he be?"

"Atch, kuche." Rosemary sighed. "I was afraid of this."

"Afraid of what?" Still Lovage didn't look at her mother. She didn't look at her for fear she'd tear up. Because as much as she wanted to say she wasn't interested in Marshall Byler, it would be a lie—to her *mam* and herself. Because the truth was, the more time she spent with Marshall, the more she liked him. He was smart and funny and kind, and he seemed to enjoy each moment of the day to its fullest. The hours she'd spent with him were the best she could remember in a very long time. Maybe even ever.

"You know, *dochtah*, you did the right thing, not agreeing to marry Ishmael Slabaugh."

Lovage set her jaw and tugged at the errant stitches with the sharp seam ripper with a force that wasn't necessary. "I know that, Mam."

"He wasn't the right man for you." She made a sound between her teeth. "To tell you he was asking for your hand because Betsy Miller turned him down? Shame on him. Shame—"

"Mam, please," Lovage interrupted. "I don't want to talk about this. The past is the past. Forget what is behind and strain toward what is ahead. Isn't that what Preacher Clyde said in his sermon last time you visited me in New York? I think it's from Philippians."

"It was wrong of Ishmael to ask that way, to tell you about Betsy Miller turning him down, but, daughter, it was wrong of you to think it meant you weren't good enough for him. That you aren't good enough for—"

"Ouch!" Lovage cried, dropping the seam ripper. She watched blood bubble up from her index finger and then put her injured finger into her mouth with a groan. She'd slipped and poked herself, and now there was a tiny spot of blood on the new baby gown. "I'm sorry," she said, surprisingly close to tears. "I've gotten blood on the fabric."

Rosemary slipped the tiny piece of clothing out from under her fingers and studied it. "*Ach*, nothing that a drop of peroxide won't fix. Now listen to me, daughter." She took Lovage's chin with her free hand and tilted it upward, forcing Lovey to look at her.

"Ishmael wasn't the husband for you. He never was. And him asking you that way, you telling him no, doesn't make you less worthy a bride to another man. In fact, it makes you worthier." She met her daughter's gaze with steady green eyes.

Lovage lowered her own. She wanted to believe what her mother said was true, and logically, she knew it was so. But that didn't keep her from sometimes wondering if it wouldn't have been smarter to accept Ishmael's proposal. "Mam, please."

Rosemary released Lovage's chin and picked up the dropped seam ripper. "It makes you worthier because you have respect for yourself. Because you refuse to be second best to a man."

Lovey looked down at her lap, nursing her stinging finger. "Can we please not talk about Ishmael?"

"What did I do?" Rosemary exclaimed, setting down the things in her hands. "Where did I go wrong,

Lovey, that you never think you're good enough? That you think you don't deserve a kind, loving husband, the same as the rest of us?"

Lovage shook her head, feeling guilty that her mother felt that her struggles with self-esteem had anything to do with the way she had raised her. "You did nothing wrong," she said softly, trying to get control of her emotions. She was on the verge of tears and she didn't even know why.

That wasn't true. She *did* know why she was distressed and this wasn't about Ishmael; it was about Marshall. Maybe she was upset because she'd never expected to feel this way about a man and it scared her. It scared her because she was having a hard time believing Marshall liked her, wanted to be with her, even though he'd come right out and said it. Even though he'd proposed marriage their very first date. At the thought of it, she almost giggled out loud. And then suddenly she felt her heart buoyed. Two men had asked her to marry them in the last year. How many women her age could say that?

"Lovage, look at me," her mother pressed.

Lovage slowly lifted her gaze until she met her mother's.

Rosemary reached out and gently tugged on one of Lovage's prayer *kapp* strings, which fell just below her chin. "You are worthy of a good husband, of love. And I truly believe that God has a man in mind for you. So don't be foolish. Don't push Marshall away. Because what if he's the one God means for you to marry? I think God leads us to the answers to our prayers, but

He doesn't force us to accept His gifts. We all have the free will to accept love or not."

Rosemary seemed lost in her thoughts for a moment and then she went on. "I've not said this to anyone else, but you know, when Benjamin asked me to be his wife, I argued with him. I argued with myself. I argued with God. Benjamin was my beloved Ethan's best friend. It seemed wrong to marry him. To love him," she said softly. "But that was God's intention. It took a lot of praying and Benjamin's kindness and patience for me to come to accept that."

Lovage stared at the foot of the sewing machine. "But what if God means for me to be single? To stay here and care for you. With the new baby coming—"

"God means for my husband to care for me," Rosemary interrupted, now sounding exasperated. "You need to accept Benjamin as my husband."

Lovage looked up, surprised by her mother's words. "Of course I accept him as your husband. I love Benjamin. What would make you think I don't? Because never once did I disagree with your choice, Mam," she said passionately. "I do believe God intended you to be together."

Rosemary crossed her arms over her round belly. "I'd like to think that's true."

"It is true." Lovage rose. "I love Benjamin," she said firmly. "And I love him more because he loves you."

"Then you have to accept that this child and I—" she rubbed her swollen abdomen "—are Benjamin's responsibilities. As my husband and the babe's father." Rosemary sighed. "*Ach*, daughter." She put her arms out to Lovage. "I know as my firstborn you feel a responsibility to me, but your responsibility is to yourself. You—"

A knock on the door frame of the sewing room made them both look up. It was Jesse. "Got a customer at the shop, Lovey," he said. "Wants to see you."

Lovage frowned. "Isn't Ginger in the shop? And Jacob and Joshua? I'm not supposed to be working today."

"Said he won't see anyone but you." Jesse pressed his lips together. "Sent me to fetch you."

"I'm sewing for Mam. Is there a problem with something he had repaired?"

Jesse had a strange look on his face. "Said he'd only see you," he repeated.

Lovage glanced at her mother.

"Go," Rosemary said with a wave. "And put a Band-Aid on that finger before you come back." She picked up a section of the pink dress on the table and slipped onto the stool at the sewing machine. "I promised to get that dress stitched for Tara before the singing tomorrow night, but she'll have a fit if you bleed on it."

Annoyed to be pulled away from the conversation with her mother, but also curious as to what customer wanted to see her, Lovage grabbed a black umbrella at the back door and followed Jesse to the harness shop. The moment she walked into the store, she turned around and looked down at Jesse. It was Marshall Byler. And he was talking to Ginger. Who was giggling and leaning across the counter toward him.

"Marshall wanted me?" she whispered harshly to her brother. Without realizing she was doing it, she reached up to make sure her *kapp* was on properly, then down to smooth her dress. "Why didn't you say it was him?"

Jesse sheepishly held up a dollar bill.

Glancing over her shoulder at her little brother, Lovage strode toward the customer counter where Marshall waited. "You should probably go before you're in trouble," she told Jesse.

He took off.

When she reached the counter, Lovage looked at her little sister. "I didn't know you were working out front. You could have saved me the trouble of walking all the way from the house."

Ginger took a step back. "I should get back to work," she told Marshall.

He nodded, offering a quick smile. "Good to see you."

Lovage waited until her sister went through the door into the workroom before she turned back to Marshall. "Ginger couldn't have helped you?"

"Didn't want Ginger," he said, his tone playful. "I wanted you."

A warmth washed over as she thought about what her mother had said to her. *He came to see you, not Ginger.* "You sent my little brother to get me without telling me it was you?"

"Not his fault," Marshall said to her. "If you want to be angry with someone, be angry with me."

She exhaled, trying not to smile. "I'm not angry with him. When I was his age, I'd have done the same for a dollar."

He grinned.

"Still, you could have just sent him for me, saying

you wanted me." She crossed her arms over her chest, glad she'd changed her dress midmorning after spilling maple syrup on herself. "It wouldn't have cost you your hard-earned money."

"I was afraid you might not come." He rapped his knuckles on the counter and then pressed both palms to the smooth surface and leaned forward. "Would you have come out if you'd known it was me, Lovey?"

He'd shaved and had on a lavender short-sleeved shirt that looked as if his grandmother had pressed it for him. And he was wearing his good straw hat, not the one with the piece out of the brim that he'd worn the first time they met.

She glanced at the finger she'd injured, wanting to make sure she wasn't bleeding on her dress. "Maybe," she confessed. "Maybe not." She looked up at him. "What do you need? I'm busy. My mother needs my help."

"I like that blue dress on you," he said, holding her gaze. "You look pretty in blue, even though your eyes are green. A nice green. Not muddy like some."

Against her will, Lovage felt her cheeks flush. Marshall was flirting with her. Again. Maybe he really did like her. "I have things to do." She fought a smile. "You asked to speak to me, and here I am."

He sighed and stood to his full height again. "I came to see if my *britchen* strap was ready."

"It's not."

He laughed, gesturing with one hand in the direction of the workshop. "You didn't even check yet."

"I don't have to. I told you when it would be done. Five business days." She moved a stapler on the counter from one side of the cash register to the other. "Probably be next week."

He grinned again, his blue eyes twinkling with mischief. "I knew it wouldn't be ready."

She raised one eyebrow. "Then why did you come?"

He shrugged. "Not all that busy at home today, not with the rain. I'm working on building a tack room in our barn. I'll show it to you when you come for supper."

"I didn't know I was coming to supper."

"Sure you are. For Sam's birthday, next weekend. Your whole family is coming." He leaned on the counter again. "Anyway, the strap was just an excuse to see you. I know we're going for ice cream tomorrow, but I couldn't wait to see you."

His words surprised her. "Wait, we're still going for ice cream?"

"Of course," he said, seemingly genuinely taken aback. "Well, supper and ice cream. My grandmother likes fancy fast-food chicken." He frowned. "Why did you think we weren't going?"

Lovage pressed her lips together. She wanted to tell him that she didn't think they were going because she knew he couldn't really be interested in her. Not someone like her who took her responsibilities to her family seriously, someone who *wasn't fun.*

Marshall held her gaze again; he had the bluest eyes, like the color of the sky on a hot summer day. A long moment passed before he tapped the countertop with his knuckles. "Also, church is at Barnabas Gruber's on Sunday. I'd like to drive you home after."

"Drive me?" She gave a little laugh. "The Grubers

live on the road behind me. It's plenty close enough to walk."

He shrugged. "Good idea. I'll walk you home." He gave the stapler she'd moved a little push with his finger. "I'll pick you up about five on Thursday? I hired a van. Route 13 is too busy to take Toby out on. Any horse, really. Grossmammi and Sam are coming. You should bring Jesse."

"You really want me to have supper and ice cream with you?" she asked, still feeling like she should be suspicious. After all, who would choose her over Ginger? "There's a singing at the Fishers', you know. Because Asa King had to cancel hers last Friday night."

"*Ya*, I know there's a singing. Ginger just told me all about it." He flashed her another handsome smile. "But Grossmammi is looking forward to her chicken nuggets. So, five o'clock on Thursday?"

Lovage knew the smart thing was to end this flirtation, this…whatever it was, right now. She knew a man like Marshall couldn't really be interested romantically in her. Even if he did, how long would that last once he realized how dull she was? And then she would be crushed. But she liked him so much and he was so cute and he *seemed* sincere.

"Okay if Jesse brings his friend Adam, too?" she said in a rush of words. "Adam Raber from over at the next crossroad. I'll pay for us myself, of course," she added.

"It's definitely okay if Jesse brings a friend, and you will do no such thing. My treat." He hesitated and then said softly, "See you tomorrow, Lovey."

"It's Lovage," she called after him as he walked away.

"I know," he called back.

And then he laughed and she felt warm to the very tips of her toes inside her black canvas sneakers.

Chapter Six

After the final church service of the day, Marshall
stood in the Grubers' barnyard with a group of single men, discussing the weather and the state of their
wheat and soybean crops. As he listened to the conversation, he scanned the backyard for Lovey. They'd
barely spoken a dozen words all day, but that was just
because during services, the men sat separately from
the women. Then when it had been time for dinner at
the long tables set up under the trees, Lovey had been
busy helping to serve the meal. Marshall had wanted
to wait to eat until the second sitting, when most of
the women, including Lovey, would eat, but he'd gotten roped into a conversation with their new preacher
and had ended up sitting with a group of men at the
first sitting. The whole meal, Marshall had kept his
eye on Lovey, and though they'd made eye contact
several times and she'd smiled at him, she'd not come
to his table, not even to see if he needed more water
or iced tea.

They'd had a good week, he and Lovey. After a successful trip out for dinner with his grandmother, Sam, Jesse and his friend, he'd managed to see her again on Friday. He'd gone late in the day, just before supper, under the guise of checking on his *britchen* strap. It wasn't ready yet, of course, but she'd ended up standing in the barnyard talking to him until her stepfather had closed up shop and the dinner bell rang. Lovey was still definitely a little shy with him, but he could see her warming up. And the more time he spent with her, the more time he wanted to spend with her.

"What do you say?" Joshua, one of Lovey's stepbrothers, asked, poking Marshall in the ribs. "You have time for a little project?"

Marshall glanced at Josh, feeling guilty that he hadn't been paying attention. Last he'd heard, they were still talking about the rising cost of seeds and whether or not GMO seeds were a necessary evil of the modern world they often struggled to remain apart from. "Sorry?" he said.

"The greenhouse. Will was telling you about it at dinner. We've a mind to build Rosemary a greenhouse. Will's already drawn up the plans. We just need a couple of extra hands. We're thinking we can squeeze a few hours in here and there when we're not busy."

Marshall's gaze strayed to the house again as he plucked at his suspenders. Women were coming and going, with children trailing behind them. Everyone was putting away the last of the dishes and loading the benches on the church wagon, which moved from house to house, depending on who was hosting. "*Ya*, sure. I'm in. I can spare a few hours here and there." He glanced in the direction of the backyard again, hoping

Lovey hadn't already left. He thought he'd been clear that he wanted to walk her home.

Will, Lovey's stepbrother who he was good friends with, laughed and took off his black, wide-brimmed Sunday hat to wipe his forehead with a handkerchief. "If you're looking for my sister, she was in the kitchen last I saw. Your grandmother was questioning her pretty hard."

"Which one?" Jeb Fisher, Josh and Jacob's friend, joked. "That Ginger has a mighty cute smile." He slipped his thumbs behind his suspenders. "I've a mind to ask her to let me take her home, next time my parents have a singing."

Jacob gave Josh a playful push. "Aw, you been saying that for weeks. Just can't get up the nerve, can you?"

The other fellows joined in on the laughter and Josh looked over at Marshall again. "We're talking about our oldest sister, Lovey. Been seeing a lot of you around our place these last two weeks."

Marshall wasn't surprised his grandmother took the opportunity to talk with Lovey when she had her alone. He wasn't worried, though, because he had no doubt his girl could hold her own with Grossmammi. He looked to Josh. "You asking me if I'm sweet on your sister? Because I'll tell you the truth, I'm sweet on her, all right." He ground one boot into the loose gravel in the driveway. He'd polished them that morning, giving them a good shine because it was important that a man went to church looking neat and pressed.

Caleb Gruber, whose father had hosted church, slapped his hand on his leg. "Sounds like you've got it bad, Marshall. You best watch out, otherwise you're going to find yourself a married man."

The young men all laughed again.

"You're one to talk," Marshall teased, not in the least bit embarrassed. "It was your banns I heard read this morning. You and Mary Lewis marrying in the fall, according to the bishop." Mary, a girl from Kentucky with a sweet disposition, was living in Rose Valley with her cousins. Word was that her parents had sent her to Delaware to find a husband, and found one she had. She was a good match for Caleb, Marshall thought.

Caleb turned bright red and thrust his hands into his pants pockets, looking down.

Marshall grinned. "If you're asking my intention, Josh," he said, directing his gaze to Lovey's brother, "it's to marry Lovey, if she'll have me. This fall, same as Caleb."

"Marshall Byler!"

Marshall glanced up to see Lovey walking his way. From the look on her face beneath her big black Sunday bonnet, he could guess she'd heard what he'd said.

"If you're walking with me," she said, striding past him, her head held high, "you'd better come along."

Several of the guys snickered, but Marshall wasn't in the least bit self-conscious or annoyed. "Guess I'll see you fellows later." As he walked away, he called back, "Let me know when you want to start work, Josh. I'll be there."

Marshall and Lovey fell into step, side by side, walking across the barnyard toward the entrance to an old lane that led across the Grubers' back property, to the road he and Lovey both lived on, Persimmon Road.

It was probably only a fifteen-minute walk from the Gruber house to Benjamin's place, but Marshall figured if he walked slowly, he could stretch it out to twenty minutes of private time with her. Once there, he figured if he stalled, maybe helped Benjamin feed up, he might even get an invitation to supper. Rosemary hadn't invited him to eat with them yet, but he knew it was only a matter of time. She definitely liked him, and even though she hadn't come out and said so, he thought she liked Lovey with him.

"You shouldn't say those things," Lovey told him when they were out of hearing of the men he'd been chatting with.

He glanced at her, but couldn't see her face for the shadow cast by the black bonnet. "What's that?"

She turned her head so he could get a better look at her. Her cheeks were flushed, but he didn't think it was from the July heat. "You know very well what I'm talking about."

He could tell she was trying to sound annoyed with him, but he could also tell she wasn't really all that upset. Maybe she was even flattered that he would make such a public declaration.

"That you and I are to marry," she went on. "Shame on you. I've agreed to no such thing."

Feeling bold, he reached out and grabbed her hand. "*Yet.* You haven't agreed to marry me *yet.*"

They took a good five steps before she pulled her hand from his, and the minute she did, he missed it. He missed the warmth of her touch, the strength of her grip.

"Come on," he said in a playful voice. "You like me. You pretend you don't but you do."

She laughed and looked at him, then quickly looked away. Like her sisters and mother, she was dressed in black today, except for the crisp white apron she wore over her long-sleeved dress. While wearing all black to church wasn't a tradition in Kent County, apparently it had been where they'd come from. And though some women might have looked severe in the dark dress, his Lovey looked just as beautiful to him as she did in his favorite blue dress.

"Admit it," he cajoled, tapping her hand, but not being so bold again as to take it. "You're already half in love with me."

She pushed his hand away. "Behave yourself," she warned. "It's Sunday. You ought to know better."

He quickened his pace, then turned and began to walk backward in front of her along the path that was obviously well used by the Grubers and their neighbors. "I know you're coming Saturday for Sam's birthday supper, but what day can I see you before that?"

"I've got a busy week."

"Not too busy to see your beau, I hope?"

She pursed her lips but didn't correct his statement that he was her beau, which made his heart skip a beat.

"Your strap will be ready Tuesday," she told him. "If I'm working at the harness shop, I suppose you'll see me then."

"Okay, I'll be there right after morning chores on Tuesday." He continued to walk backward. "I'm taking Grossmammi to Byler's to shop on Wednesday. She wants to get a few things to make a cake for Sam.

He wants a blue cake with blue icing so I sure hope they have plenty of blue food coloring. You want to ride with us? We're going to get ice cream after. You wouldn't believe how big an ice cream cone you can get at Byler's for two dollars."

She cut her eyes at him. "Why are you always trying to bribe me with ice cream?"

He opened his arms wide, enjoying their banter. "Because everyone loves ice cream!"

She shook her head as if that was foolishness. "Sam will be thirteen. That's a big birthday," she mused.

"It is, but you didn't answer my question. Want to go with us Wednesday?"

Lovey stopped suddenly, her brow creased. "Marshall, why are you doing this?" she asked.

He stood in front of her. "What?"

"This." She motioned between them. "Because… because you could have any single girl we know." She gave a nervous laugh. "Any girl in the county, according to Ginger."

"But I don't want any girl," he told her, trying to control an urge to put his arm around her shoulders. It wasn't really fitting, especially unchaperoned and, as she had pointed out, on a Sunday. He squeezed her hand tightly. "I want *you*, Lovey."

She studied him. "But *why*?"

The look on her face told him she wasn't digging for compliments the way some young women did. She honestly wanted to know why he liked her. And honestly didn't see herself the way he saw her, which he found upsetting. In his eyes, any man in the county would be blessed to have her as his wife.

"Hmm." He slipped her hand through his arm and they fell into step side by side. "Let me see…because you're smart and—"

"I'm not smart," she interrupted.

He stopped. "*Ne*, you asked a question, now let me answer you," he chided gently.

She opened her mouth to speak, then closed it.

They were standing along the Grubers' fence line near a clump of wild Queen Anne's lace. Stepping off the path, he snapped off three white, lacy blooms and offered them to her. "For you."

She accepted them, but he could tell she was trying not to smile.

"Thank you," she whispered. Then she went on quickly, "You know these aren't native to North America. Colonists brought them here from their flower gardens in Europe and they grow like weeds now." She pressed her hand to one rosy cheek and then the other. "I don't know why I'm going on like this. You don't care about such things, flowers and such."

"Actually, I enjoy learning about anything I don't know about and I didn't know that they were once cultivated." He thought for a moment. "But they can't be weeds because I wouldn't pick weeds for you. Unless you wanted weeds," he teased.

Then Marshall tucked his hands behind his back, mostly so he wouldn't be tempted to take her hand again, and they started down the path that would lead them to her stepfather's farm. "Back to the one hundred reasons why I like you."

"There can't be a hundred," she argued.

He eyed her and she clamped her mouth shut. He

went on. "You're smart and clever and witty. But not mean in your teasing." He glanced at her. "And you're kind. You're a hard worker. A faithful woman, a woman of God who strives every day to please Him. You're completely devoted to your family." He met her gaze. "But not smothering. And pretty."

"Marshall—"

"*Ne*, remember, you asked me." He waggled his finger at her. "Now let me have my say."

She gave a huff but was silent.

"You're strong-minded. Some men don't like that in a woman, but I'm used to stubborn women who say what they think. My mother was like that. And so is my grandmother." He glanced at her. "I understand she had some questions for you today?"

Lovey smiled, and when she did, her whole face lit up. "Oh, she had questions for me, all right. Among other things, she wanted to know if I could make *hasenpfeffer*."

"*Hasenpfeffer?*" He laughed. "I don't even know what that is." He grimaced. "Something with *rabbit*?"

"*Ya*. It's a dish where you soak rabbit in vinegar for a day or so, add spices and onions and then fry it in butter." She wrinkled her nose. "I don't like it much, so I had to tell her that while I *could* cook it, it isn't something I prepare often."

"That's a good thing because I don't like rabbit."

He laughed and she laughed with him.

"I like chicken and dumplings, meat loaf, and I have to admit," he added, "I like a good *schnitz un knepp* once in a while."

"Pork and apple?" She pointed at him, using her

hand that held the flowers. "*That* I can make. How do you feel about beef-and-potato pie?"

He nodded. "I like it. I also like apple pie, peach pie and especially strawberry-rhubarb pie." At the end of the fence, they made their way around a small drainage pond. "But, Lovey, I don't care what Grossmammi says, I eat just about anything. I'd eat rabbit if you made it for me."

"Well, you've no fear of that," she declared.

There was more laughter, then they fell into a comfortable silence, walking side by side, enjoying the heat of the late day sun on their faces, the call of a grackle and the hum of bees. It wasn't until they reached a three-foot-high wooden stile that went over a hedgerow of poison ivy, thorns and wild roses between the Gruber and Miller properties that Lovey spoke again.

"How did you know?" She stepped away from him, lowering her arms to her sides, the flower he had given her still in her hand.

"How did I know what?"

"Those things. What makes you think they're true?" She scrutinized him. "That day you came into Benjamin's shop, why did you ask me to ride home with you from the softball game? You couldn't have known anything about me."

Marshall took his time to respond because he understood what she meant, and he also understood that he needed to choose his words wisely. She was just starting to relax with him. He wanted to take care he didn't do anything to make her shy away from him like an untamed colt. "I can't exactly explain it, Lovey, but the minute I saw you, I knew you were the woman who was meant to be my wife." He opened his arms and let them fall. "Maybe God led me to Benjamin's harness shop instead of Joe Troyer's that day. I don't know. I just know I was supposed to meet you. That we were supposed to walk out together. Those things about you?" He pointed at her. "I've learned those things, getting to know you." He offered a lopsided grin. "And I've asked around. Your stepbrother had nice things to say about you. He admires you."

"Who?" she demanded.

"Will. He and I have gotten to be good friends."

"Will Miller should mind his own mending." With her free hand, she grabbed a handful of the skirt of her black dress and started up the stile.

"Want some help getting over that? The rungs look wobbly," he called up to her.

"I can manage a stile just fine."

He stood back and waited his turn. "Will might have told me a few things about you, but I've been with you enough, Lovey. And I've watched you. I've seen what kind of woman you are. And you're the kind of woman I want to marry."

At the top of the stile, she turned to him and blurted, "Butter pecan." Then started down the other side.

Marshall took the first step of the stile, taking care not to touch any of the poison ivy growing on both sides of the wooden rails. "Butter pecan?" he asked. "Butter pecan what?"

"That's the kind of ice cream I want when we go to Byler's on Wednesday," she said from the other side of the hedgerow. "That's my favorite."

Marshall grinned because butter pecan was his favorite, too. "Would this be a good time to ask you again to marry me?" he called to her from the top as he watched the hem of her black dress sway as she walked away.

"No, it would not," she answered, not looking back.

But he smiled, because he could tell she was smiling, too.

"You should sit," Lovage said, taking a huge platter of fried chicken out of the basket her mother was holding. They had just arrived at Marshall's for his little brother's birthday supper, and the backyard where they would be eating was a confusion of guests arriving with baskets of food, squealing children, mothers settling babies and men unhitching their buggies.

"Put it next to the German potato salad and sourdough bread we brought," Rosemary instructed. The serving table had been set out on a screened-in back porch, which was smart, Lovage thought, because flies were bad at this time of year, especially at dusk.

"Mam, you've been tired all day. I can do this. Go sit in the chair under that nice apple tree." She pointed toward the orchard where Marshall, she presumed, had set up tables and chairs where everyone would eat. "Maybe put your feet up? One of the girls can fetch you a glass of water."

"Mind your own self, daughter," Rosemary said cheerfully, snitching a piece of crispy chicken skin that had fallen from the stoneware platter onto the table. She popped it in her mouth. "You should just get it over with and go say hello to your beau. Then you'll relax."

"I am relaxed and he's not my…" Lovage didn't finish her sentence because just talking about Marshall made her turn as red as a beet. "He's busy hosting. He has guests. A lot of guests," she said. The number of people there seemed overwhelming to Lovage. And not just from their church district, but others. There were to be sixty people coming.

"Look at all of this food," Rosemary observed, gazing over the table that was covered with a cheery gingham cloth. Besides the chicken and potato salad and bread they'd brought to share, there was roast beef, *schnitz un knepp*, corn bread, green beans, *kartoffle bolla*, mashed potato casserole, buttered beets, stewed tomatoes, gravy, English peas with dumplings, and enough gravy to swim in. And then there was the dessert table set off to the side, which featured a homemade three-layer cake frosted with bright blue, fluffy icing, and then assorted cupcakes, brownies, fruit fritters and what looked like fig pudding. It seemed as if every woman who had been invited to the birthday celebration brought her finest dish, not out of pride, but wanting to share her best with her neighbors and family. "Of course, with this many people, it takes a lot of food to feed them."

"How many people did he invite? Everyone in Kent County?" Lovage said under her breath, realizing she *was* nervous. When he had invited her and her family for Sam's birthday, she'd assumed there would be supper around his kitchen table and a slice of cake afterward. That was how her family celebrated birthdays. She had no idea it would be such a large gathering. And seeing so many people, most she didn't know, made her feel self-conscious. From the moment she got out of the buggy, she'd felt as if people were watching her. All because of Marshall's foolishness in the barnyard after church the previous weekend, she was certain. Because the Amish did like to talk, and a new couple, real or otherwise, was food for gossip among men and women. Of course, she and Marshall fell under the category of "otherwise" because they weren't even walking out.

Or were they?

"I think it's nice to have a midsummer party," Rosemary went on. "And I don't think it's *everyone* in Kent County or even Hickory Grove. Lettice and Noah from the end of our road have gone to Wisconsin to see their new granddaughters." Rosemary laughed, taking a baking powder biscuit off a plate and nibbling on it. "*Atch*, daughter, go find Marshall and say hello. You went to all that trouble finishing up your new dress." She indicated the pale blue dress Lovage had stayed up late the night before to finish. "Marshall will be pleased you wore it just for him."

Lovage wanted to protest, but her mother was right, she *had* worn it just for Marshall. Because he liked her in blue and because the blue made her feel pretty, despite her tall, thin frame and gangly arms. Because he said she was pretty.

"Let me at least get you in a chair out of the sun," Lovage fussed, slipping their handwoven basket under the table to fetch later. "And you should put your feet up. Your ankles were swollen last night. Benjamin told me."

"Another one who should keep his thoughts to himself," her mother responded good-naturedly.

"There you are!"

Lovage froze. She already knew that voice by heart.

"*Ya*, you, Lovey. I was looking for you."

She looked over to see Marshall standing in his grandmother's petunia bed, pressing his face to the screen. He was hatless, his dark hair wavy, and he was smiling a smile that warmed her to the tips of her toes and embarrassed her at the same time. He really had no shame, talking to her that way right in front of her mother.

"How are you at playing horseshoes?" he asked. "We're getting together a game."

"She's excellent," Rosemary said. "Better than Benjamin's boys, except for Will maybe." She made her way to the screen door. "Her father taught her. My Ethan was good at horseshoes. Once won a competition at a county fair when we were young."

Lovage walked over to stand in front of Marshall, looking at him through the screen, not quite sure what to do with her hands. Just seeing him made her nervous, but also excited.

"Come on, Lovey," he coaxed, pressing his fingertips to the screen. "Show me what you're made of."

Seeing his palm, she could almost feel it against hers. She flushed. "Where's your hat?" It was unusual to see an Amish man outside without a hat. As unusual as seeing a woman without her prayer *kapp*.

"I don't know." He opened his arms wide. "I put it down somewhere. On a tree branch by the horseshoe pits. The new game's about to start. Won't you come?"

Lovage hesitated. She really wanted to play. She liked playing, but to play in front of his friends, in front of all the other young women looking for beaus, felt intimidating.

"Come on, Lovey," Marshall cajoled softly.

Lovage took a deep breath. "*Ya*, I'll play. But let me get Mam settled first."

"I've got a perfect place for her to sit. Under my Asian pear tree." He hurried to the porch door and offered his hand to Rosemary as she started down the steps. "Have you ever tasted an Asian pear, Rosemary? They're like a cross between a pear and an apple. They don't soften like pears so they store well in the root cellar. They won't be ripe until September, but I'll bring you some when they are."

When Lovage reached the top step, he offered his hand to her, as well. She met his gaze, smiled and shook her head. Helping a middle-aged woman in the family make her way down steps was one thing. What was he thinking, trying to take her hand in front of everyone in Hickory Grove?

"Can't blame a man for trying to hold a pretty girl's hand every chance he gets," he whispered to her as she reached the grass.

She shot him a look that she hoped warned him to behave himself, and then hurried to catch up with her mother. As the three of them crossed the yard, Lovage saw her neighbors watching them with interest. She put her head down, looped her arm through her mother's and followed Marshall, embarrassed, but also strangely excited. Walking behind him, she couldn't help but notice his broad shoulders and muscled arms beneath his pale blue shirt.

"You can sit right over here," Marshall told Rose-

mary as they entered the orchard that ran directly off
his side yard. Easily covering a third of an acre, the
trees were well shaped and bursting with yet-unripe
fruit, the spongy grass beneath their feet freshly cut.
"Look, a chair just waiting for you," he said, indicating one of two old-style webbed folding lawn chairs.
"Plenty of shade here."

Lovage looked up into the tree, unable to resist her
curiosity. "What have you done to the branches?" she
asked, staring up at brown paper lunch sacks tied with
bailing twine all over them.

"This?" He tapped one of the bags over his head.
"It's how I protect the fruit. The bugs love these pears
and I'm trying not to spray with chemicals if I can
help it. I can't take credit, though. It was my brother's
idea. See?" He tugged on one end of the string, pulled
it free and then slipped the bag into his hand, reveal-
ing a green fruit about the size of a plum. "Keeps the
bees and flies off the growing pears."

Lovage laughed at Sam's cleverness. And she was
impressed that Marshall would let his brother convince
him to try such a thing, because it certainly did look
silly, three fruit trees in a diagonal line, with brown
paper bags hanging from the branches. Marshall's rec-
ognition of Sam's innovation made her like him all
the more.

"There he is! Come tell him what you brought. Applesauce cake is Marshall's favorite," called a com-
manding, feminine voice.

Lovage looked over her shoulder to see Marshall's
grandmother, the tiny Lynita Byler, practically drag-

ging a young woman across the yard and into the orchard.

"Marshall! She's here," Lynita called to her grandson. "Faith's here. She and her parents."

Faith King, a pretty, petite blonde who looked to be between Tara's and Ginger's age was flushing with embarrassment, Lovage suspected. And Lovage was immediately sympathetic. To be put on display in front of a single man at such a public gathering had to be mortifying. Mainly since it was clear that Lynita fancied the girl in the pale pink dress as a possible match for her grandson.

"Faith. Good to see you." Marshall reached over his head to replace the paper bag over the pear he'd just shown Lovage.

"Faith made your favorite, *sohn. Blitzkuchen*." Lynita pushed the girl ahead of her, surprisingly strong for such a petite woman. "Tell him, Faith." She beamed at her grandson. "I had her wrap a couple of pieces of the cake and put them inside the house. In case it's all eaten before you get a slice," she explained.

Lovage looked at Faith and smiled, her heart going out to the young girl, who had now broken out in a sweat. It was every mother's and grandmother's dream to see her children happily wed, but sometimes families pushed it too far. Lovage was instantly thankful that while Mam had expressed interested in Lovage at least considering Marshall's attention, she wasn't pushing her. "*Gudar daag*, Faith."

"*Goot* afternoon," Faith said, looking down at her small feet in pristine white canvas sneakers.

Lovage couldn't help but look down at her own feet.

Size ten in black sneakers so scuffed that she could see her big toe through the threads. She pulled her foot back so it was under her skirt. This was supposed to be a casual birthday dinner; she hadn't expected the entire church district to be here. No one wore their fancy shoes. She looked at the girl's Plain, pink dress with a starched white apron over it. Or their best dress.

Then Lovage felt guilty for being so critical. It was obvious the girl wasn't comfortable with the way Lynita was touting her lightning cake. And she herself had worn a new dress. She stepped forward. "Good to see you, Lynita." She looked at Faith. "I'm Lovage Stutzman. We said hello at church on Sunday, but we didn't get a chance to talk. I've just moved here. My mother is Rosemary Miller. Married to Benjamin, who has the new harness shop."

Faith offered a shy smile, seeming relieved to have someone to speak *to* her rather than *about* her.

"Faith's been helping her mother establish a new orchard. They lost most of their trees in that blight last year," Lynita told Marshall. "Why don't you take Faith through your orchard and show her what you're doing."

When Marshall looked down at his grandmother, he dropped the piece of string he'd been trying to use to fasten the paper bag onto the pear.

Lovage leaned over immediately and picked it up. When she held it out to him, he met her gaze. It was clear to her that Lynita wanted him to spend time alone with Faith. And it was clear Lynita favored Faith over her. Suddenly Lovage felt less confident in her budding relationship with Marshall. Faith was small and pretty and young, all the things Lovage wasn't.

"You should go," she said quietly to Marshall.

And she meant it because if he wanted to be with Faith, she didn't want him here with her. But at that moment, she hoped—no, prayed—he wouldn't go.

Chapter Seven

Marshall met Lovage's green-eyed gaze and held it a moment, wondering when he had fallen in love with her. He knew it didn't make sense. He'd known her such a short time and they barely knew each other. She hadn't even agreed to walk out with him, not officially. But sometime in the last two weeks, his feelings for her had changed, gotten stronger. This revelation and the distress he saw on her face made him realize that all he wanted was to protect her and care for her. It was all he could do not to throw his arms around her and whisper in her ear that she had nothing to fear from Faith King. That they had known each other since Faith was a toddler on lead strings and that even though his grandmother might think he and Faith would make a good match, the only woman he had eyes for was Lovey.

Marshall turned to his grandmother. "Grossmammi, is that Eunice Gruber going into the house?" He pointed in the direction of the house and grimaced. "I'm sure she's just looking for a serving spoon or something, but I know how you are about people in your kitchen. About Eunice in your kitchen."

Lynita spun around so quickly that her tiny round sunglasses slid down the bridge of her nose. She puckered her mouth. "Plenty of serving spoons out on the porch. That Eunice, she better not be checking to see if I've left crumbs in my pie safe. Just because she thinks she has the cleanest kitchen in Hickory Grove, she thinks it's her business to nose in ours. She needs to mind her own mending!" With that, she strode off toward the kitchen at a remarkable speed, head down, arms pumping, prayer *kapp* strings flying behind her.

Grinning, Marshall glanced down at Faith, who looked much like a startled calf as she watched Lynita race across the green lawn. "I really am glad to see you, Faith," he said gently. "I apologize for anything my grandmother may have said to you or *will* say to you the rest of her life." He looked to Lovey. "My grandmother has been trying to arrange a marriage between us since Faith was a schoolgirl," he explained. Then he hooked his thumb in Lovey's direction. "So, you've met Lovage. Have you met her mother, Rosemary? She's a gardener, too, like you. Not just vegetables, but herbs." He leaned over and whispered in Faith's ear, "She's Jacob Miller's stepmother, you know."

Faith turned crimson and looked Rosemary's way.

Marshall had heard through Will that Faith and Jacob had spent most of the last singing at the Fishers with their heads together and that he had given her a ride home. Although, apparently, she had Jacob let her off at the end of her driveway. So her parents wouldn't know she'd ridden home with him. At twenty-two, Faith had the right in their community to spend time with whomever she pleased, within reason. But that didn't keep parents of an only child from thinking they should have more control over their daughter and her future than they did.

"It's nice to meet you." Rosemary smiled up at Faith from her seat in the lawn chair under the pear tree. She was fanning herself with a little cardboard paddle on a stick that one of the other women sitting under the trees had given her. On one side of the old-fashioned church fan was a depiction of the Lord Jesus, and on the other side, the name of a local Mennonite church. "Come sit with me a minute and tell me everything about you that I should know, Faith King." She patted the chair beside her.

Marshall flashed Rosemary a grin, guessing she knew exactly what had just transpired. He didn't know her well, but suspected she would be kind to Faith and chat with her, putting her at ease, allowing her embarrassment to fade. If she knew the gossip on Faith and her stepson, Rosemary might even arrange things so the two could bump into each other.

With Faith occupied, Marshall turned to Lovage, who was moving away from the group of women under his pear trees. "So about that walk in my orchard. Now or after we play horseshoes?"

"I didn't know we were taking a walk in your orchard."

"Well, you know now, Lovey. I've been trying my hand at grafting, and I want you to see my trees with peaches and plums on the same tree."

The most beautiful, shy smile played on her lips.

"Horseshoes first. Then I imagine it will be time to eat. So if it's after dark when we take that walk, Jesse will have to go with us."

He headed toward the area on the far side of the farmhouse where he could hear horseshoes hitting a metal post and young men and women talking and laughing. Occasionally, one of the guys would give a hoot when he made a good throw. The whole gang of unmarried men in Hickory Grove would be there, trying to show off for their girls, or maybe hoping to impress a particular one he was sweet on.

"Need a chaperone, do we?" he asked Lovey.

"*Ya.* Where I come from, it's the way we do things. Unmarried men and women do things together in groups, or take a sibling with them. It protects everyone's reputation."

"We walked home alone together last Sunday," he pointed out.

"That was a *Sunday*," she exclaimed, as if there needed to be no further explanation.

Marshall was tempted to tease her about her naivete. Did she really think that young people who were inclined to kiss or get into worse trouble wouldn't do so on Sundays? But he decided against saying anything because she was in such a good mood, he didn't want to risk riling her. Besides, he liked her innocence. It was refreshing in a world where it was sometimes difficult to remain Plain and try to follow God's word each and every day by word and deed.

Instead, he asked, "What about once they're betrothed?" He swept off his straw hat, pushed back his hair and replaced it. "Once the banns are read, can we take a stroll through an orchard after dark?" He leaned closer, knowing he ought to behave himself and not tease her. The truth was, he would never risk her reputation or his own. He might tease, but his behavior would be nothing but acceptable to every parent in the county and their bishop, too. "How about if I promise I won't try to kiss you?"

Her face flushed. "Marshall Byler, we're not even walking out together. You keep talking like that and…"

"And what?" he said, nodding to two friends of his grandmother's who were standing in the shade of a hickory tree, their black *kapps* together, watching them, twittering like a pair of old birds on a branch.

Lovey exhaled in exasperation. "I… I…" She shook her head. "I don't know."

Then they both laughed and he wished they were alone, because then at least he could hold her hand. "Would this be a good time for me to ask you to marry me?"

"It would not." She sounded indignant. No, she sounded as if she was *trying* to sound indignant.

"Fine." He threw up his hands as he led her around the house.

"Fine what?" She looked at him suspiciously.

"Fine, when we go for our walk through my orchard, you can have your chaperone." He gestured with one hand. "Pick your chaperone. Jesse, Faith, you can even bring my grandmother if you like."

"How about Ginger?" Lovey said, her tone teasing. "She seems fond of you."

"*Ya.* Bring anyone you like. Everyone from our

church district and the next." He gestured in the direction of the orchard, which was now behind him.

She was giggling as they met each other's gazes, but something in the way she looked at him made him think she was finally beginning to take him seriously.

"Mam, how many times do we have to tell you, let us do the heavy lifting," Lovage said, setting down a pair of long-handled tongs to take a wooden case of empty Ball jars from her mother's arms.

"Ya," Tara said, from where she stood at the gas stove stirring a pot of boiling water.

For the second day in a row, they were canning tomatoes from their garden, which involved an all-day process of washing the tomatoes, blanching them, peeling them, cutting them up, putting them in jars and then running them through the pressure cooker. Rosemary and four of her daughters had been working since breakfast and they still had two bushel baskets of Big Boy and Roma tomatoes to process before it was time to put out dinner for the family. The good thing was that the women had been putting up tomatoes this way since they were little and had worked out a process over the years. Stations were set up for washing the jars and sterilizing them, cleaning and blanching the tomatoes, and pouring the hot tomatoes and juices into the jars. Each woman had a job and they moved gracefully in the kitchen, working together to preserve food for the coming year.

The only one missing that morning was Nettie, and that was because she was at the harness shop completing a special order for an Englisher. Nettie, who was an artist, was painting flowers and vines with acrylic paint on a dog leash, of all things. They had all chuckled over the idea of decorating a leather leash, but also agreed that if the buyer was willing to pay for the custom work, Nettie should do it.

"Didn't Benjamin tell you this morning, this was why the good Lord gave you daughters?" Tara asked. "So you wouldn't have to put up tomatoes by yourself."

Rosemary gave a huff, but she let Lovage take the wooden box from her. "I'll warn you. We're going to need at least two dozen more jars. They're stacked in the last room in the cellar."

"Sit," Lovage ordered, pulling a chair out from the end of the kitchen table with one bare foot. Then, realizing she sounded awfully bossy, she softened her tone. "Please, Mam. Sit and have a sip of iced tea. You've been on your feet since dawn."

"I worry about you girls," Rosemary said, lowering herself into the chair, her hand on her round belly. "If you think having a baby is an illness, your first will be hard."

Lovage decided not to bite on her mother's line of conversation. That morning, Benjamin had pulled her aside and told her he was worried that she was working too hard, not resting enough. With the August heat, he worried his Rosemary was wilting. He was also concerned for the welfare of their child, though he hadn't come out and said so directly. The Amish were funny about the way they dealt with pregnancy. It was all around them all the time. Most husbands and wives welcomed as many children as the Lord blessed them with, and families of twelve or even fifteen weren't uncommon. But it still wasn't a subject discussed between men and women, even a stepfather and his stepdaughter.

"I added ice to your tea. You should drink it. Benjamin went all the way to Byler's to get more ice this morning. His feelings will be hurt if you don't have a cold drink," Lovage said.

"I'll have a glass of tea with ice if you're pouring," Bay Laurel, Ginger's twin, volunteered as she walked out of the kitchen carrying a case of canned tomatoes, the lids still popping as they sealed. "Going down to the cellar."

"Get more jars," their mother called after her. Then she turned back to Lovage. "Fiddle," she remarked, reaching for the tall, sweaty glass in front of her. "Benjamin made the excuse of going for ice before it got too hot, but really he went for cookie dough ice cream. Those boys of his ate the last two half gallons after we went to bed last night."

"I think Jesse was eating it, too," Lovage admitted.

"This pot is ready for more tomatoes," Tara called.

"I'll get the next batch of clean ones from the sink," Rosemary said, starting to rise from her chair.

Lovage set the jars down on the counter next to the big double farm sink and reached over to rest her hand on her mother's shoulder. "You're getting ahead of us, Mam." She chuckled, trying to make a joke of it. "And wearing us all out in this heat. Will said the thermometer down at the barn was reading ninety degrees at eleven in this morning."

Rosemary eased back into her chair and reached for a copy of *The Budget*, a national newspaper written for and by Amish and Mennonite men and women. Benjamin had been reading the current news of friends and family back in New York that morning at breakfast. The family had laughed together about the story of one of their elderly neighbors, Emma Petersheim, in the yard without her glasses, mistaking a deer on her lawn for one of her pet goats and trying to herd it back into the barn. The funniest part, they unanimously agreed, was that she had written into the paper to tell on herself.

Rosemary fanned the paper in front of her face. "Do you think someone should run more iced tea out for the men? I hate to see them working so hard in the sun on a day like this. I'm thrilled Benjamin and his boys are building me a greenhouse, but I told him it could wait until fall when this heat lets up."

Lovage tucked a lock of damp hair beneath the scarf she wore over her hair and tied at the back of her neck. They were all dressed for working in hot weather in their oldest dresses, bare feet and kerchiefs instead of prayer *kapps*. While women were expected to cover their hair with prayer *kapps* in public, at home among family and friends the rules were less strict. The same went for their state of dress. Lovage was wearing an old dress of Ginger's that was baggy and so short on her that it barely fell to her calves.

"Ginger went out to refill their glasses," Lovage told her mother. Then suddenly suspicious, she glanced at the battery-operated wall clock that looked like a shiny red apple. "But she's been gone at least twenty minutes." She picked up the considerable colander of fresh tomatoes from the food side of the sink and carried it to Tara.

Tara grabbed a big, juicy tomato from the top of the colander and eased it into the boiling water. "I know where she is," she said, glancing over Lovage's shoulder. She dropped another tomato into the pot and pointed with the long metal tongs toward the window over the kitchen sink. "Out there chatting up Marshall Byler again."

Lovage whipped around to look out the kitchen window. Sure enough, there stood Ginger, barefoot, the hem of her skirt tucked into her apron, flirting with Marshall. "I'll be right back," she said, setting the colander down on the counter beside the stove.

Tara giggled as Lovage whipped off her filthy, tomato splattered apron and tossed it over the chair beside their mother. "I was wondering how long it would take for her to upset your applecart, sister."

"No one is upsetting my applecart," Lovage said defensively. "She's supposed to be in here working with the rest of us. I know she doesn't care much for kitchen work, but fair is fair." She tucked her damp hair behind her ears and into her scarf as best she could. "I'll be right back, Mam."

Lovage passed Bay in the mudroom on her way out.

"Where are you going?" her little sister asked, a case of empty Ball jars in her arms. She spun around as Lovage whisked by.

"Ginger's flirting with Lovey's beau again!" Tara hollered from the kitchen.

"I'll be right back," Lovage told her little sister as she tried to temper her anger. This wasn't the first time she'd caught Ginger flirting with Marshall. Only the day before, the first day he'd come to help their step-brothers with the new greenhouse, she had realized Ginger was missing from the kitchen, only to find her down in the barnyard, watching Marshall, shirtless, wash at the pump after a day of hot work.

Lovage stepped out on the back lawn and the hot, humid August heat hit her like one of the waves she'd seen down at Rehoboth Beach the previous weekend when she and Marshall and several other single folks, along with Edna and John Fisher as chaperones, had hired a van for the day to take them to the boardwalk. Lovage had been in awe of the beautiful strength of the waves, and just a little frightened by them.

She strode around the side of the house to where thirty feet of multicolored dresses and shirts flapped on the clothesline in the hot wind. "Ginger!" she called. Then, through the ripples of fabric, she caught sight of her pretty blonde sister. Sure enough, there she was with Lovage's beau. Well…he wasn't officially her beau because she still hadn't agreed to walk out with him, but her sister certainly was aware that they were *almost* a couple. "Ginger!" she called again.

Ginger, standing in front of Marshall, giggling, turned. The look on her face said she knew she'd been caught.

"Could you get Mam another case of quart jars from the cellar?" Lovage asked, ducking under the clothes-line and making a beeline for the two of them.

Marshall looked at Lovage, smiled lazily and lifted a frosty glass of iced tea to his mouth. "There you are," he said.

Lovage strode up to them. More of Ginger's blond hair was out of her scarf than in it and the front of her pale green dress looked like it was wet, making it almost inappropriately see-through. Lovage could practically see her slip! "Mam's waiting," she said tersely.

"You came out of the house to tell me you needed a case of jars from *inside* the house?" she asked with a chuckle. Shaking her head, she looked back at Marshall. "I guess I should go inside. Let me know if you boys need more tea or anything else. We have watermelon if you're hungry." She began to walk backward from him. "Just to tide you over until dinner."

Lovage rested her hands on her hips, watching her sister go. When Ginger disappeared through the door, she turned back to Marshall.

He smiled and wiped his mouth with the back of his hand. "You shouldn't be so hard on her. She's young."

"She was flirting with you, Marshall." She tried to sound annoyed, but now that he was in her presence, she wasn't really. He did that to her. He calmed her. And made her feel more confident of his feelings for her and hers for him. Feelings she could feel growing daily. *"Again."*

He shrugged his broad shoulders. "I was wondering when you were going to come out. I thought if you didn't come soon, I was going to have to make some excuse to come up to the house."

"You would have seen me for dinner. I made tuna salad." She fussed with her hair, wishing now she'd taken a moment to run to the mirror in the bathroom and adjust her scarf. "You told me you liked tuna salad."

"I like anything you make, Lovey." He turned, dragging his boot in the bright green summer grass. "Come on, walk back with me. I don't want the guys to think I abandoned them the second day on the job."

They walked around the clothesline. "How's it going?" she asked.

"Good. Footing for the foundation is in and we're starting on the rear wall. Will made a good blueprint. He's good at planning. He already knows exactly how much lumber we're going to need and has taken into account the square footage of the old windows we're going to use." He shook his head. "It's all I can do to plan out a plot of peas in the garden. I'm fine once I get my hands into it, but I'm not one for paperwork. Or building, really." He glanced at her. "Sam's the one who's handy around our place with a hammer."

"I was wondering why you volunteered to help out with the greenhouse." She walked closer to him, the skirt of her dress brushing against his pant leg. She was amazed by how comfortable she was becoming with him. How at ease. "I can't tell you how thrilled Mam is that the boys are building it for her. She had one back in New York, and even though she would never say so, I think she misses it."

"I'm just trying to make your mother like me." He winked at her.

She laughed and gave him a little push. "She already likes you."

"Enough to tell you to marry me?"

She made a face at him. "I thought you promised not to bring up marriage for at least a week."

He pretended to be thinking, then pointed to her. He was wearing dark denim trousers, a blue shirt, suspenders and his old straw hat with the piece missing from the brim. He looked like all the other men pitching in to build the greenhouse. Yet he didn't, not to Lovage. Because she thought he was the most handsome one among them.

"I thought I agreed to a day." He held up his finger as if thinking. "Okay, how about this. At least agree that we're walking out together."

"And why should I do that?" she teased, feeling a little giddy. Because she *was* ready to admit that she wanted to be his girl. That she practically already was, whether she would admit it or not.

"Because I'm irresistible," he explained. "And because everyone already thinks we are."

"Only because you keep telling people we are." She poked at his arm playfully.

"So that's settled." He flashed her a grin. "As far as building the greenhouse, I'm not great with a hammer, but I can do what I'm told. And I'm glad to help out." He glanced at her. "Plus, it's a chance to see you more often."

His smile was infectious. "I guess you could have broken another *britchen* strap. You used that excuse for two weeks."

He laughed and they stopped as a speckled black-and-white Guinea hen ran in front of them. "Well, you told me it would be done in a week and then it wasn't ready. I had to come every day to check on it."

She cut her eyes at him, feeling lighthearted. Mischievous. "What makes you think it wasn't ready on time? Maybe *I* was using your *britchen* strap as a way to see *you*."

"Ah, clever." He waggled his finger at her. "My grandmother warned me you might be one of those kinds of women. One to try to manipulate a bachelor."

"Oh." She sighed. They continued to walk side by side, past the fenced-in garden toward the sound of saws and hammers. "Is she still trying to convince you I'm not good for you?"

"*Ne*, she's coming around. *Will* come around."

Lovage caught sight of another one of her mother's Guinea hens racing across the lawn. The first she assumed was just a stray that had somehow escaped their coop, but now the second made her suspicious. "She is not," she teased. "You're just saying that to make me feel better."

"We just need to give her time." Marshall moved the glass to the other hand, glanced around and then caught Lovage's hand with his own. "Sam's already smitten with you. I think if you don't agree to marry me soon, my own brother will be moving in on my sweetheart. That was smart of you, bringing him that mechanics magazine you found at Spence's Bazaar. The way to some men's hearts is their stomach, but Sam can always be bribed with a gadget magazine or a ball of copper wire."

Lovage savored the feel of Marshall's hand in hers and felt her heart skip a beat. When she'd moved to Hickory Grove more than a month ago, she thought she knew what life had in store for her. She'd practically convinced herself she wanted to be an old maid. That it was her duty to remain at her mother's side and help her with the new ready-made family she and Benjamin had created together. But suddenly Lovage was dreaming of her own home, her own children, God willing. And of a life with Marshall.

"I didn't buy him the magazine to try to get him to like me," she argued good-heartedly. "I just saw it in a pile of old magazines for sale and thought it might be something he could get some ideas from, and it was only fifty cents. Two for—"

A third Guinea hen crossed their path, followed by a fourth and then a fifth.

"Oh, no," Lovage said, pulling her hand from Marshall's. "I bet Mam's Guineas are out again." She shook her head. "I should go."

They both stopped and stood there for a moment face-to-face, eye-to-eye. "So it's official," he said softly. "I'm your beau and you're my girl."

Lovage was just about to answer him when suddenly they were interrupted.

"Lovey!" Ginger hollered, running across the grass toward them. "Lovey, you have to come!"

The sound of her sister's voice sent a chill down Lovage's spine and she lifted her skirt and raced toward her. "What's wrong?"

"It's Mam!" Ginger shouted breathlessly. "Come quick! She's fainted!"

Chapter Eight

"I don't need to go to the hospital," Rosemary insisted, lifting the wet washcloth from her head.

From the stool beside the couch in the parlor where her mother was lying, Lovage gently replaced the cloth she'd soaked in cool water and a little eucalyptus oil. The room was relatively cool and semidark with the curtains closed, and it was quiet. Like their parlor back in New York, they rarely used the room except when they hosted church. Evenings with their new blended family, because there were thirteen of them living at the house, were usually spent in the kitchen or the larger family room, a phrase Rosemary had heard one of their English neighbors use, and now insisted that's what they call the large living room.

"Maybe just to check your blood pressure, Mam?" Lovage leaned closer, lowering her voice so that Ginger, Tara, Nettie, Bay and Jesse, who were out in the hallway where their mother couldn't see them, wouldn't hear her. "Benjamin said you told him that the midwife was concerned with your blood pressure last visit." She glanced over her shoulder at her stepfather, who was pacing the parlor liked a caged wildcat she'd once seen in a zoo. That had been her one and only trip to a zoo; she hadn't been able to bear it, seeing God's wild creatures locked up in cages, because no matter how large and airy they were, they were still cages.

"Benjamin." Rosemary made a tsking sound and turned on the couch to look at her husband. "That isn't what I said she said at all. What she *said* is that women my age can have problems with their blood pressure, and that I should get one of those fancy home blood pressure cuffs from the drugstore."

"And did you?" Lovage asked.

"*Ne*, but that has nothing to do with anything," Rosemary quipped. Then, patting her hair pinned in a bun, she cried, suddenly flustered, "Oh, my, my *kapp*! Did I—"

"Don't worry. I took it off so it wouldn't get mussed." Lovage had unpinned the starched white prayer *kapp* from her mother's barely graying red hair before they half walked, half carried her into the parlor. Once the girls had settled their mother on the couch, Lovage had placed it on a little rosewood table that had once been her maternal grandmother's. Like most women, Rosemary was very protective of her prayer *kapp*, a precious symbol of her faith. Each night, before getting into bed, Rosemary carefully removed all the straight pins that kept her *kapp* in place, removed it, stuffed it with tissue paper to keep its shape and placed it on her dresser.

"Did I wrinkle it when I fell?" she asked with concern.

Lovage smiled down at her mother. "*Ne*, not a bit, Mammi."

Rosemary sighed with relief and then glanced in Benjamin's direction. "I suppose you thought you needed to tell him," she said, not sounding all that upset about it.

"You would have wanted me to do the same if it had been Benjamin lying on the kitchen floor with tomatoes rolling all over," she teased.

Rosemary closed her eyes for a moment, resting her hands on her rounded belly. "My own fault. I should have let one of the girls move the basket of tomatoes. I just got light-headed, is all."

Smiling, Lovage glanced over her shoulder at her stepfather pacing back and forth across the room. He was hatless, his rusty brown hair plastered to his head with perspiration, except where one piece stuck up in the back like a rooster's comb. His broad, sunburned face was etched with lines of worry, his lips pressed flat together as he struggled to stay calm. Seeing him in such a state of worry brought a tenderness to Lovage's heart. He loved her mother so much that it seemed to physically pain him to see her in distress.

"Should I move the fan, Rosebud?" he asked, hurrying to adjust the direction of the big, old-fashioned metal-blade fan he'd run an extension cord to from the gas generator one of the boys had brought from the harness shop. "This better? A good thing I didn't let you talk me out of this contraption. I told you it would come in handy when I picked it up at Spence's a couple of weeks ago." He looked to Lovage. "Your mother thought it was a waste of money, an Englisher electric fan, but it moves the air around, doesn't it? Cools off the room." He stopped to stroke his gray-streaked beard thoughtfully. "Maybe I ought to get a second one, to circulate the air better in a big house like this."

"*Atch*, Benjamin, stop your fretting." Rosemary waved him away. "You're worse than a *die aldi*."

Lovage had to press her lips together and look away so as not to laugh out loud at the fact that her mother was calling her husband an old woman. Immensely relieved that it seemed her *mam* was all right, Lovage felt like she needed a good laugh.

Rosemary lifted the washcloth from her forehead again. "What are you doing in here, anyway, Benjamin?" she fussed. "A man doesn't belong in a woman's house midday. Don't you have something to do on this great big farm? Peas to hoe? A buggy to make?" She looked up at Lovage. "How long was I out?"

Lovage smiled tenderly at her mother and patiently replaced the cloth. "Just a minute, I think. You were already coming around by the time I got back to the kitchen. The girls did a good job when they realized you were going to faint. Everyone stayed calm. Tara caught you so you didn't fall and hit your head, or injure the baby." She whispered the last words in her mother's ear so as not to worry Benjamin any further. He was already distraught enough.

Rosemary closed her eyes for a moment, again exhaling. "What can I say? For the wisdom of this world is foolishness before God. Benjamin wanted to put that fan in the kitchen. He told me it was an awfully hot day for canning tomatoes. But they came ripe all at once. We certainly weren't going to let them rot on the vine. Stutzman women don't waste good food provided in abundance by the Lord."

"I told her to let me put the fan in the kitchen," Benjamin said, returning to his pacing. "I said, Rosebud, let me set that Englisher fan in the kitchen for you."

"But I hate the noise of that generator," Rosemary told him. "A person can't think with that monster rumbling!"

Lovage sat back on the stool, thinking this was the closest her mother and Benjamin had come to an argument in her presence since they'd married eighteen months ago.

"Rosebud, please let me do something for you. What can I do?" Benjamin approached the couch, wringing his beefy hands. "Could I call a driver? I can use the phone in the shop. It won't take me but a minute to run down there. I really think you *should* go to the hospital."

"Really, Benjamin, you're going to *run* to the shop. Then you'll fall, too, and what will our children do with us? We've only one couch in the parlor."

Benjamin stood over her, not seeing the humor in his wife's words. "Rosebud, please."

"I don't need to go to the hospital and that's final. What does a man know about such things? I have an appointment tomorrow with the midwife. That will be soon enough to see someone." Rosemary started to sit up. "I got overheated and closed my eyes for a moment, nothing more. I've always been a fainter, especially in the summer."

"Mam, please, lie down," Lovage insisted, "or you'll be dizzy again."

Rosemary lay back with a huff of exasperation. "Tell

him, Lovey. Tell Benjamin I faint when I get hot. It has nothing to do with my *condition*."

What her mother said was true. She *did* faint in the heat sometimes when she overdid it. But when she'd been carrying Jesse, Lovage remembered, it had happened several times late in the pregnancy. And she'd been ten years younger then. "I don't disagree with him, Mam," Lovage said softly. "Let him call a driver. Just get checked out."

"And go to an Englisher hospital with all of that sickness and disease? Certainly not," she insisted, her tone becoming terse.

"Rosebud, listen to your daughter," Benjamin pleaded quietly.

Rosemary looked up at Lovage. "Could you leave us a minute, daughter. Check on the girls in the kitchen. I don't want Tara overcooking the tomatoes. She always wants to leave them in the hot water too long. It only takes a minute or two to split the skins if the water is the proper temperature."

Lovage rose from the stool. "*Ya*, Mam. I'll see to it."

"And it's time to get dinner on the table. Past time," Rosemary fretted. "All those young men out there building my greenhouse. How ungrateful do I look, half past one and no dinner on the table?"

Lovage gently pushed Benjamin in the direction of the stool, indicating he should sit.

"Mam, I don't think the boys will mind if—"

"It's all in the icebox on the back porch. Half a ham, macaroni salad, tuna salad, sour cucumbers and watermelon pickles. Oh, and I think there's some corn salad left from yesterday. There's honey wheat bread in the bread box that Tara made yesterday. Just a simple meal."

"I'll see to it," Lovage promised.

"Three gallons of iced tea and raspberry lemonade in the icebox, too! And don't forget the blueberry pies in the pie safe. And the *ebbelkuche*! Benjamin's boys like my apple tart."

Benjamin slid onto the stool and took his wife's hand in his. "Enough now, *fraw*. Our Lovey knows how to lay out a dinner." He gazed down at her, his dark eyes filled with love. "She had the best of teachers, that one."

Lovage smiled as she backed out of the cool semidarkness of the parlor, leaving the couple to have a moment alone. Her mother was definitely feeling better, she thought as she stepped into the hall. She was giving orders again.

Lovage found Nettie, Tara and Jesse all in the hallway, standing in a cluster, whispering.

"How is she?" Tara asked, clasping her hands together anxiously. Tara was their worrier. She'd been that way since she was a toddler. She worried equally about the things that needed to be worried over and the things that didn't. Their *dat* used to say that every family needed a worrier, to take some of the burden of worrying from others.

"She's not going to the doctor?" Twenty-year-old Nettie rested her hands on her slender hips. She was still wearing her paint apron with streaks of every color of the rainbow on it. "Jacob said his father said he might be getting a driver to take her to the emergency room."

"Can I go?" Jesse asked. "Can I ride in the Eng-lisher ambulance?"

"There will be no ambulance. Mam's fine. She's not going to the hospital." Lovage opened her arms to shoo her siblings down the hall toward the kitchen, thinking that the best thing she could do for her mother right now was get dinner on the table and then finish up the canning. "She just got overheated." She looked to her two sisters. "Where's Ginger and Bay? We need to get dinner on the table for the men working on Mam's greenhouse."

"We'll find them." Tara grabbed Nettie's hand and the girls hurried toward the kitchen, seeming thankful to have been given a task.

Lovage rested her hand on her little brother's shoul-der. "Run down to the greenhouse and let the men know that dinner will be served on the back porch in fifteen minutes."

Jesse bobbed his head. "They're done working for the day. Marshall said he was going home, but said to tell him if you needed anything, if Mam needed any-thing, I should go fetch him."

Lovage smiled at Marshall's thoughtfulness, and a warmth washed over her as she recalled their stroll across the backyard earlier. He really was her beau!

"Oh, and he said to give you this." He slipped his hand in his pocket and pulled out a little bird nest. "He said he thought you might like it." He tilted his hand and slid it onto Lovage's open palm. "He found it in the grass in his orchard this morning."

"It's so tiny," she said, looking at the nest in her hand, truly touched by his gift. It was so small and perfect. She couldn't wait to see him again to say thank-you. Maybe she'd even walk over to his house after supper. Take Jesse with her. Pleasure curled in the pit of her stomach as she thought about how happy Marshall would be to see her for a surprise visit. Maybe they'd be able to take a walk together in his orchard. They hadn't gotten a chance the day of Sam's birthday. And maybe she'd even let him hold her hand.

A sense of guilt suddenly washed over her. Here her mother was, lying on her back on the couch midday, after a fainting spell. Her forty-five-year-old mother was in the family way and Lovey was thinking of flirting with a boy. Thinking of going to his house with the *intention* of flirting. It seemed wrong. And selfish.

"He said he knew you would like it." Jesse started down the hall and then turned back. "Oh, and he said not to forget about supper at his house Friday night. He said he hoped Mam would be feeling well enough to go, that Lynita was expecting us. We're going, right? Because I told Sam we were. He's going to show me this thing he's building so Petunia can pour herself her own grain." He laughed. "A goat feeder. Imagine that!" Her little brother turned and ran down the hallway.

"No running in the house," she called after him, wondering if maybe their family having supper with Marshall's family *wasn't* such a good idea. Maybe this wasn't a good time for the families to be getting to know each other. It wasn't uncommon for a courting couple's family to spend time together if they weren't already friends. It gave everyone a chance to get to know each other, because when a girl and a boy were courting, it was intended as a trial period before marriage. The intention of courting was to move forward to an official betrothal and then a wedding, often falling in quick succession. The Amish weren't like Englishers. They didn't date for years. They got to know each other within the confines of the rules of dating and then they made the decision as to whether or not to marry or break up.

Marshall was still asking her to marry him almost every time they were together. But what if this really wasn't the time for her to be thinking of marrying? Was her mother's fainting spell an indication that her eldest daughter needed to be here at home? Would it be selfish of her to marry and leave her mother with this huge household and a new baby?

By the time Lovage reached the kitchen, Jesse was gone. As were Tara and Nettie. There was no one else there but Benjamin's eldest son, Ethan, who would be taking over as the schoolteacher at the Hickory Grove school come September. She found him with a mop, cleaning the floor where the tomatoes had fallen when Rosemary fainted with the basket in her arms.

"Ethan, you don't have to do that."

He looked up, mop in his hand. He was a handsome man of thirty-one, tall and slender with yellow-blond hair and dark eyes. He looked like his mother, Alma, rather than his father. "I know I don't have to, but I needed something to do to feel like I was being useful to Rosemary." He shrugged. "Tara and Nettie went out to get the other girls to set the table for dinner. I told them I would finish here for them."

Lovage liked Ethan. She always had. He was soft-spoken, sincere and a man of great compassion. Three years ago, he had married and buried his wife in the same year. His Mary had been stricken with breast cancer and died on her twenty-fifth birthday. When Benjamin and Rosemary made the decision to move to Delaware, Ethan sold his own small farm and came with them, thinking he needed a new start. He didn't talk about his wife, but Lovage had a feeling he missed her deeply, so deeply that even though his father had encouraged him to start dating again, he hadn't been able to find his way there yet.

Lovage went to the cupboard and pulled out a stack of plates. "Jesse said Marshall went home?" She dared trying to sound casual.

"*Ya*, the other guys, too. They thought it best they leave us to ourselves. Let Rosemary rest. She's going to be okay, right? Tara said she'd be fine. Just got overheated. Not hard to do on a day like this."

"She'll be fine." She took down a second stack of plates. Even without the three men who had come to help with the greenhouse, Marshall, Jeb Fisher and Caleb Gruber, there would still be thirteen for the midday meal. "Probably just as well he went home," she said. "I have to see to Mam. I don't have time for Marshall's—"

"Don't do that, Lovey."

The tone of Ethan's voice made her turn to him, the stack of ironware plates in her arms. "Do what?"

"Chase him off."

"I'm not *chasing him off*," she said, prickling.

He stood to his full height of six feet, the mop looking small in his large hands. "He's a good man, Marshall Byler is."

"I know that."

"And he'd make a good husband to you, Lovey."

She felt her cheeks burn and she looked down at her bare feet. "I'm not sure this is a time for me to be courting *anyone*. Mam needs me. Today is proof of that. I should be here with her, helping her with the girls and…the work. It's a lot of work to run this house."

"What happened with Ishmael wasn't your fault, Lovey."

"I didn't say…" She frowned. "Who was talking about Ishmael? Water under the bridge."

"Don't let your chance at a good marriage with a good man—who is pretty smitten with you, I have to tell you—go because you're afraid you're not good enough for him. Because you are, Lovage. You—" His voice cracked with emotion. "You have to take the happiness you find when you find it, and enjoy every moment. Because you don't know when it will be gone."

Lovage pressed her lips together, her heart aching for her stepbrother.

"I miss her so much, Lovey. I miss her every day. And I just thank God that I was smart enough to accept the gift He gave me when He made her my wife. Even if it was for a very short time."

Lovage exhaled, her eyes tearing up. "I don't know what to say, Ethan." She hugged the plates to her. "I don't know how to ease the pain of your loss."

"You can't," he said simply. "But what you can do is accept God's gift of Marshall in your life. I'm not saying you should wed him tomorrow, but I think you need to give him a chance. Give yourself a chance."

Ethan stood there a moment longer in silence and then walked out of the kitchen, leaving Lovage to her thoughts.

Marshall met Lovage at the back of her family's wagon. The Stutzman women had arrived in their buggy a few minutes after Benjamin and his sons and Jesse in the open wagon. The men had been given the task of transporting six pies in the back, but Lovage had taken on the task of carrying them safely into the house.

"Here, I can take two," Marshall said, holding out both hands, trying not to stare at her.

Tonight, she was in purple. Her *kapp* was neatly in place, hiding every strand of brown hair; her apron was blindingly white, and her canvas sneakers were navy blue and looked to be brand-new. Lovey's face under the white *kapp* was so full of life, so beautiful, it made his breath catch in his throat.

"We're here at last," she said, sounding a little flustered. "We had to drop Ginger off at her friend Liz's. Helping babysit while Liz's parents visit a friend in the hospital. There must have been a mix-up." She fluttered her hand. "I was sure she knew we were all coming here tonight for supper as a family."

"That's too bad Ginger couldn't make it," he said, although he was a little relieved. Ginger was a sweet enough kid, but she was making him a little uncomfortable. She seemed to go out of her way to talk to him, while she never came out and said so. What Amish girl would? He got the impression that she was hoping he would ask her out. Which made no sense to him because she knew he was walking out with her sister.

Maybe it wasn't official—Lovey was just being stubborn about that. But everyone in Hickory Grove knew Lovey was his girl. She was his girl and he only had eyes for her.

"What have you got there?" He peered into the wooden boxes that had been built to carry casseroles and other various types of food. He had one himself that he and Sam had built, only they had added a slot between the chambers for hot bricks or bags of ice, depending on the type of dishes being carried to a friend or neighbor's home.

"Let's see…" She glanced at a pie that must have had three inches of meringue whipped into peaks and toasted perfectly. "Two lemon meringue…"

He groaned, gazing at the enormous pie in his hands. "I love lemon meringue pie."

"Two blueberry," she said pointing into the wooden box. "And two apple custard."

"All my favorite," he told her. "I think I'd better skip supper so I can just have pie. Which did you make?" he asked, as she handed him one of the blueberry pies, which was made with a shiny lattice top crust.

"All of them." She picked up the other blueberry pie. "I don't know where everyone's gotten to. I'll have to come back for these."

"You'll do no such thing," he said, making no effort to start for the house, because the moment they got in there, he knew they wouldn't have a minute to talk alone the remainder of the evening. They were standing face-to-face behind the wagon, only the two pies they were holding separating them. He gazed into her twinkling green eyes. "I'm really glad you and your family came tonight. You especially. I've missed you."

"Since yesterday?" she teased. Then she hesitated, as if she wanted to say something. She bit down on her lower lip. "Marshall…"

"Ya," he said quietly, the sound of her soft voice seeming louder in his ears than Jesse's and Sam's laughter coming from the barn, and the sound of Ethan and Will talking with their father on the steps of the back porch.

"The other day when you came to work on the greenhouse. The day Mam fainted…we were joking about me being your girl and you—"

The sound of a horse and wagon coming into the barnyard made them both turn to see who it was. To Marshall's surprise he spotted Ephraim and Lois King rolling toward him, their daughter on the seat between them.

"Sorry we're late. Hope you didn't hold supper," Ephraim said, as he reined in his black Thoroughbred he'd bought at an auction close to twenty years ago. "Trying to get a wife and a daughter ready to go…" He shook his head, rolling his eyes as if Marshall knew exactly what he meant.

"Faith made two lemon meringue pies," Lois declared, barely waiting for the wagon to roll to a stop before she was over the side.

The two of them were quite a pair, with Lois near six foot tall and skinny as a beanpole and Ephraim short and wide.

"Get your pies," Lois directed her daughter, pointing at her. Her voice seemed as sharp and bony as her finger. "Lynita said they were your favorite, Marshall, and to be sure to bring two."

Lois beamed at Marshall as if she might pounce on him. It was pretty obvious that his grandmother hadn't taken his hint the day of Sam's birthday. She still had it in her mind that he and Faith were going to walk out together. If she had her way, they'd be married by Thanksgiving. And from the look on Lois's face, he had a feeling she was of the same mind.

Marshall shifted his gaze to Lovey. She was as surprised as he was to see the Kings. And she looked uncertain, as if she still didn't quite believe he would choose her over sweet, cute little Faith. He wanted to apologize, to say he had no idea his grandmother had invited the Kings, but there was no way to say it without them hearing him. And while he would have preferred to spend the evening alone with the Miller family, getting to know them better, anyone was welcome to his table.

Lovage set her pies down and took the lemon meringue from him. "So good to see you all," she said, deftly sliding her lemon meringue pies back into the pie box in the back of her family's wagon as she greeted the Kings. "We've just arrived." She turned back to them with a big smile, handing Marshall a second blueberry pie. "So you're not late at all."

Chapter Nine

"I brought two of my rosemary roasted chickens," Lois chattered on. "Faith did most of the work, of course. She's an excellent cook, that one." She handed her daughter, who was already holding a lemon meringue pie in one hand, an enormous picnic basket with a solid wooden lid.

Even from across the driveway, Marshall could smell the chicken, which must have just come out of the oven.

"And macaroni and cheese," Lois went on. "Lynita said you love a good macaroni and cheese casserole. Faith…" She gave her daughter a nudge. "Show Marshall your pie. She makes an excellent merengue. Mile-high peaks. Better than mine, I should say."

"I didn't know they were coming," Marshall mouthed to Lovey.

Lovey pressed her lips together, looking away from him.

"We'll talk later," he whispered. *"Ya?"*

Her smile seemed forced when she made eye contact with him. *"Ya,"* she said, and then she started for the house, the apple custard pies in her hands. "Jesse!" she called to her little brother. "You and Sam see to Peaches." She indicated their white mare hitched to the wagon. "Give her a nibble of grain. There's a nose bag in the back."

"We've got grain," Marshall told her.

She didn't respond. She just kept walking, hips swaying in the lavender dress. Marshall was so mesmerized by her tall, slender form that all he could do was stand there gaping at her, the pies she had passed to him still in each hand.

"I know Lynita made a ham, but the Millers have such a big family. So many boys, I knew the chicken would be welcome." Lois was still talking as she loaded up her husband's arms with food, as well. "And grape conserve and…"

Lois was like a fly buzzing in Marshall's ear—annoying, yet harmless. "I'm sorry, what did you say, Lois?"

"I said, you like grape conserve, don't you? Who doesn't love a hearty grape conserve, that's what I always say, don't I, Ephraim?"

"Ya," Marshall mumbled. "I like it well enough. Let me run these inside, and I'll be back out to help you carry everything else in."

"No need," Lois clucked. "We can carry it in. Faith's small, but she's strong. Got good arms on her, that one."

"There you are, Lois!" Lynita called from the screened-in back porch, waving to her neighbor. She must have just passed Lovey.

Marshall strode toward the house, eyeing his grandmother. This was no slipup, her inviting the Kings to supper on the same night he'd invited Lovey and her family, and he was more than a little exasperated with her. "Grossmammi, where do you want me to put these pies the Millers brought?"

"In the pantry." Lynita opened the screen door for him.

"Where in the pantry?" He looked down at his grandmother. "You'd best show me."

"*Atch*, what's gotten into you, *sohn*? You know full well—"

"Show me where you want them, Grossmammi," he repeated, holding her gaze. His tone wasn't unkind, but the look on her face told him she knew he wasn't happy with her.

His grandmother's eyes behind her wire-frame spectacles darted in the direction of the Kings, now coming up the walk in a row like ducklings. All three had their arms laden with food, with Faith bringing up the rear, her little legs pumping to keep up with her parents.

"But the Kings have just arrived—" Lynita began.

"They will find the kitchen easily enough," he told her. "They've been here before."

His grandmother puckered up her mouth until she looked like she wasn't wearing her teeth. "Fine," she declared.

Marshall walked through the large country kitchen, past the Stutzman women, who were setting out food, and directly into the pantry. The moment Marshall and his grandmother were inside the eight-by-ten room that had floor-to-ceiling wooden shelves on three sides, he set down the blueberry pies he was carrying and slid the paneled pocket door shut behind him. She took a step back from him, fussing with a row of jars of freshly canned tomato sauce on the counter.

"You invited the Kings to supper," he said. Realizing he was still wearing his straw hat, he swept it off. "Without telling me, Grossmammi. What do you have to say for yourself?"

She looked up at him, fiddling with her fingers now.

"You knew I specifically invited Lovey and her family for supper because I wanted us all to get to know each other better. Because Lovage Stutzman is the woman I intend to marry. Don't think I don't know what you're doing. Faith King is a sweet girl, but she's not for me."

Lynita tucked her hands behind her back. "Eunice Gruber said she heard that Lovage Stutzman hasn't even agreed to walk out with you. She says you're making a fool of yourself, telling everyone you're going to marry her when she's not all that interested in you." She drew herself up to her full five feet. "Eunice said she heard from her cousin that Lovage was betrothed to be married back in New York and the boy broke it off. Eunice didn't know why, and it's not our business, but you do have to wonder—"

"Let me stop you right there," Marshall said, holding up a finger. "What did our preacher say only a few weeks ago about gossip? You and Sam and I discussed the matter that Sabbath after services. Something from Ephesians, I think." He stroked his chin.

"*Sohn*—"

"I remember," he interrupted her. He felt bad that he was practically chastising his grandmother, but as the only adult male of the household, the faith of everyone under his roof was his responsibility. And his grandmother would certainly never hesitate to call him on such a misstep. She was the one who had taught him when he was barely off lead strings and into long pants that one of the cornerstones of their faith was their intention to strive every day to live the life God wanted them to live, not just to talk about it come each *Sunndaag.* "'Do not let any unwholesome talk come out of your mouths, but only what is helpful for building others up according to their needs, that it may benefit those who listen,'" he quoted.

Lynita looked as if she had swallowed a sour, unripe grape from the vine in the yard. "Was she?"

"Was who what?" he asked.

"Lovage." She lowered her voice. "Was she betrothed in New York?"

He looked down at the blueberry pies Lovey had brought him. And thought of the lemon meringue pies she'd left in the wagon so as not to make Faith feel bad about bringing the same pie, or, he suspected, the fact that Lovey's pie was much nicer-looking. Faith's meringue wasn't as stiff or high and looked weepy, not to mention she'd burned it just a tad. But Lovey hadn't said a word; she'd just put her pies away. No one would accuse Lovey of *hochmut,* improper pride. She was a woman who lived her faith without making a show of it like some did.

"I don't know if she was betrothed, Grossmammi," he said carefully. He could hear Lovey and her mother and her sisters talking out in the kitchen. They were discussing a quilting project the women in Hickory Grove were planning to benefit the schoolhouse. "I don't care if she was previously betrothed."

"You don't care?" Lynita questioned. "But what if she did something improper? What if she's not…suitable to be your wife, a man as upstanding in our community as you. A man who has the care of his young brother and old, feeble grandmother."

He looked down at her and scowled. And then he had to smile, because there was nothing *feeble* about Lynita Byler. "You shouldn't have invited the Kings without talking to me first about it. You and Lois's scheming, it's doing nothing but making Faith uncomfortable." He leaned over her. "Because she doesn't like me."

"*Atch!* She likes you. What young unmarried girl in Hickory Grove doesn't like you?" She threw up her tiny hands. "Any girl in the county would have you for her husband."

"But, Mammi, I don't want any girl," he said, returning his wide-brimmed hat to his head. "I want Lovage, and if you can't be happy for me, I'd ask that you at least not interfere."

"But I haven't—" His grandmother pressed her lips together.

And Marshall knew that was as close to an apology as he was going to get from her. Hearing Lois King's high-pitched voice as she touted her daughter's stitching abilities, he moved to the pantry door. "Let's plan on making our plates in the kitchen and then eating out back under the trees at the picnic tables. I need to talk to Lovey. We'll be back in ten minutes and then we can eat."

"*Sohn.* I don't think you should—"

Marshall slid open the pantry door and everyone in the kitchen went silent…as well as his grandmother. They were all looking at him, the women and Benjamin and Ephraim, when he stepped out. He strode across the big room, the heels of his boots sounding loud on the wide-plank floorboards. "Come outside with me." He walked past Lovey, grabbing her hand as he went by.

She gave a huff but allowed him to lead her out of the kitchen and across the back porch. He heard the sound of Will and his brothers in the barnyard as he led their stepsister around to the side yard, where they could have a bit of privacy. He halted in front of a purple flowering butterfly bush. He looked into her pretty green eyes. "I'm sorry." He couldn't tell now if she was amused or upset. "My grandmother. The Kings." He still clasped her hand, and surprisingly, she was letting him hold it.

"It's fine," she said. "I was just surprised to see them."

"Me, too. You probably guessed, but my grandmother invited them."

"Because she and Lois are hoping you and Faith will get together."

"*Ya.*" He took a step closer to her. "But Grossmammi and I have had a talk."

"Ah." She smiled at him, a smile so beautiful that it

made his heart swell. "We wondered what was going on in the pantry."

"I reminded her that *you* were my choice, not Faith. I don't think we'll have any more trouble with her." He took Lovey's other hand. He could hear Sam laughing. He and Jesse had gotten out a red rubber kick ball and were playing with it in the grass near the barn. "The Kings are good people. They're good neighbors. I enjoy sharing supper with them. I'm just disappointed they're here because I wanted to spend time with you and your family." He took a deep breath and let it go, letting his annoyance over the change of plans go with it. "Before the Kings came up the driveway, I think you wanted to tell me something?" He cocked his head. "About… us maybe?"

Lovey blushed and looked down, but then up at him again. *"Ya."* She said it in an exhalation. "Just that… that I'll be your girl."

He pulled his head back. "Not that you'll marry me?" he teased, pretending not to understand. "I thought you were going to tell me you want to be wed as quickly as I can make the arrangements with the bishop."

She laughed. "That's putting the cart in front of the horse, don't you think? Since you've only been my beau less than a minute." Her green eyes twinkled.

He squeezed both her hands, smiling so hard that it hurt his face. He wanted to ask her what had changed her mind, but didn't want to push her. He could be impulsive at times, but his Lovey took time to consider words before speaking them, deeds before acting on them. And he liked that in her.

She tugged on his hands, but not hard enough to break his clasp. "I'd best get back to the house, and you should probably be a good host and go talk to my brothers while we lay out supper."

"Why can't we stand here a minute longer?" he said quietly. "So I can look into your beautiful eyes." He winked at her. "I might even try to steal a kiss."

She bit down on her lower lip, suppressing a giggle. "We can't stay any longer like this because we have an audience," she whispered. Then she pulled one hand from his and pointed over his shoulder.

He turned around to see his little brother and hers standing side by side, not twenty feet from them, the red ball idle between them. Both were gawking, their eyes wide, as if they'd never seen a courting couple standing so close, holding hands.

Marshall turned back to her and they laughed together, and the sound of her laughter in his ears made him wish time would move swiftly forward, because he couldn't wait to make Lovey his wife.

It was just after breakfast, the dishes were drying in the rack, and Lovage and her sister Tara were washing eggs Tara had collected in the henhouse that morning. It was the first week of September already, but the summer heat hadn't yet broken. Benjamin's Englisher fan rattled in the far side of the kitchen. For once the house seemed quiet, though. Rosemary had gone upstairs to strip the sheets on her bed and had taken Nettie with her. Ginger and Bay were working at the harness shop. Lovage had no idea where Jesse was, but she could guess he wasn't far from Benjamin's side; the two were

becoming inseparable. Their stepbrothers were all occupied in the north field cutting the summer wheat before the real heat of the day was upon them.

With the kitchen empty for once, Lovage was enjoying spending a few minutes alone with her sister.
Being seven years older, Lovage never felt she was as
close to Tara as their other sisters. Since she'd arrived
in Hickory Grove from New York, she'd been making
an effort to do household chores with her because it was
a great way to better get to know her little sister, who
seemed to have grown into a young woman overnight.

"My friend Sarah says you and Marshall are going
to get married," Tara said to Lovage as she handed her
two fresh eggs.

"I am walking out with Marshall, but I've not agreed
to marry him yet," Lovage explained, feeling a flush in
her cheeks. She glanced at her sister. Tara was skinny
like her but shorter, so she didn't look gangly. Her eyes
were green, too, but her hair was the prettiest shade of
light red under her the scarf she wore. Their *mam* called
it strawberry blonde. "How about you? Any boy caught
your eye? You've been going to the Fishers' singings
pretty regularly."

Tara shook her head, seeming emphatic. "I just go
so Sarah can go. My friend Sarah Gruber. Her parents
won't let her go without me. They say I'll keep her out
of trouble."

Lovage set the eggs on the wet dish towel in the sink
and took two more from her sister. "Is Sarah the kind
of girl to get herself into trouble at a church singing?"

Tara shrugged, hesitated and then went on. "Ginger
doesn't think you really like him."

"Thinks I don't like who?" Lovage picked up one of the eggs and rubbed a dirty spot with the dishrag. They never soaked eggs to clean them because the shell was semipermeable. Instead, they rinsed them off and gave them a good rub with a dishrag. If the egg was really dirty, she might spray a little watered-down vinegar on it.

It had been Bay's idea to sell extra eggs in the harness shop from their mother's hens. At first, Rosemary had thought it a silly idea. Their Amish customers all had their own eggs. But it turned out that Benjamin had enough Englisher customers that they were selling out what eggs they had every day. They were doing so well that Bay was talking about buying her own chicks come spring and raising them just to have eggs to sell.

"She says you don't really like Marshall." Tara kept her gaze fixed on the basket of eggs. "She says you're just walking out with him because he, you know... asked. And there hasn't been anyone since Ishmael," she added quickly, and then stole a peek at Lovage. "But I think she's just saying that because she's jealous. Because she liked him first."

Lovage sighed. Living with so many sisters, there was always some sort of mild drama, and she had learned a long time ago not to get worked up over things that were said. Especially when she was told something secondhand rather than receiving it directly. "I'm sure that's not it," she said, wanting to give Ginger the benefit of the doubt. "Hasn't Ginger been spending time with Sarah's big brother Thomas? They were sitting together at the school picnic Friday night."

Tara giggled. "Sarah says Thomas is definitely smitten with her. But all the boys are."

Lovage set the clean eggs on a towel on the counter to dry. "Your time will come. You'll see."

Tara shook her head. "Not me. I'm not walking out with anyone for years. How would I decide who to let court me?" she said, sounding worried. "Who to marry? It's such a big decision."

"Tara!" Nettie called. "Tara, we need help!" She sounded as if she was shouting from the top of the back staircase.

"Coming!" Tara shouted at the ceiling.

Lovage handed her a dish towel to dry her hands. "Go, I'll finish here. Don't let Mam lift those heavy baskets of laundry," she warned, as her sister hurried out of the kitchen. "You girls carry them."

Lovage started transferring more dirty eggs from the basket into the sink, gazing out the window as she went about the familiar task. She found it interesting that Ginger was telling Tara that she didn't really like Marshall. Lovage wondered if maybe Ginger *was* a little jealous, although maybe *jealous* was too strong a word. Envious perhaps. She'd always been that way. As children, if Ginger picked a butter cookie and Lovage a molasses one, halfway through her snack, Ginger would always wish she'd chosen the molasses cookie and would then spend five minutes trying to convince her big sister to give up the remainder of hers.

It had to be something akin to jealousy, because nothing had passed between Lovage and Marshall in the last three weeks that could have been interpreted as Lovage not really liking him. The truth was, the more time they spent together, the more she liked him. There was something about Marshall's easygoing attitude that gave her a confidence she'd never felt before. Not that she never questioned herself anymore, but he was making it easier for her to believe that she really *was* the things he said she was. Maybe even pretty. She smiled to herself. Pretty in a gangly kind of way.

A part of Lovage still wondered why a man like Marshall would be interested in someone like her. And sometimes at night, she lay in bed thinking of all the things that could go wrong between them. She worried he might become bored with her, because while she was trying to be more spontaneous, she was never going to be a girl like Ginger. Also, she was sticking to the guidelines of proper chaperoning. She rarely spent time completely alone with him; they almost always had other couples, Jesse, Sam or even Lynita. But what if he was looking for a fast girl? He was always teasing her about trying to kiss her, even though he hadn't actually tried. Would he be upset with her if he tried and she said no? Almost worse, what if she was so daring as to let him kiss her, and she was terrible at it?

Moving the clean eggs into a square cardboard egg carton, Lovage almost laughed aloud. Mam often teased Tara that she would go out of her way to find something to worry about. Was Lovage being just like her? Because she didn't want to be a worrywart. She wanted to enjoy her courting time with Marshall and let their relationship unfold as it may over the next few months. The fact that he was still asking her to marry him every time they were together had to be a good thing, didn't it? So maybe she needed to just relax and enjoy getting to know each other. And maybe she could even let herself start dreaming of being his wife, because suddenly it seemed that her life was full of possibilities. And all because she'd been slow to put sugar in lemonade!

Chapter Ten

Lovage lifted the skirt of her green dress and got down on her knees to restock the shelf of horse salves and ointments. Initially, when the family moved to Delaware, Benjamin had intended only to repair items likes harnesses and bridles, and sell a few goods like halters and bridles. But the old dairy barn was so spacious, and Tara so enterprising, that over the last few months more shelving was going up in the front of the shop and they were selling more and more items like the topical agents she was restocking now.

As she opened each box, she checked the packing slip to be sure they'd received what was ordered wholesale, just the way Tara had shown her. Marking each item as accepted, she then lined up the bottles and boxes on the right shelf. Today she was restocking wound dusting powder, antibacterial spray and a betadine solution for horses and other livestock. All the items were treatments most Amish kept in the barn. Not that they wouldn't call a veterinarian when they needed one. Most families in Hickory Grove used Albert Hartman over at Seven Poplars. Once Mennonite, he was now Amish. Will had explained to her the other day, when Albert came out to have a look at their mares, that Albert's bishop had permitted him to continue his veterinary work and even to drive a truck, but only during working hours. The rest of the time, he used a horse and buggy like all the other Old Order Amish.

"Lovey?"

She turned around to see Benjamin standing behind her, his wire-frame reading glasses perched on the end of his nose. "Could I… I need to speak to you about something," he said, seeming anxious.

"Ya." She got to her feet, hoping she hadn't made a mistake in the restocking she'd been doing all morning.

He held a small piece of paper in his hand. "A little bit of an awkward situation," he told her, waving it. "I wasn't sure how to handle it. I went up to the house and…"

Benjamin was breaking into a sweat and Lovage couldn't help but wonder what on earth he was trying to tell her.

"Rosemary was the one who suggested I come to you," he continued.

At that moment Lovage realized that the piece of paper he was holding was a bank check.

"This came back today." He fluttered the check again. "From the bank. Insufficient funds."

"You mean it's a bad check?"

"Ya." He kept looking at her.

"So…" She frowned, feeling bad for him. "You want me to, what? Call the customer?" It seemed like an odd

request from him, since it was his business. But then
again, he'd just commented the previous day at the
supper table about how comfortable she was with his
Englisher customers and what a great addition she was
to his business. His praise had made her blush and get
up to refill the serving bowl of mashed potatoes even
though they didn't really need them. The fact that he
had such confidence in her made her feel good.

"Ne." Benjamin shifted his sturdy frame from one
worn boot to the other. Then he plucked at his reddish
beard that was shot through with gray. *"Ya,* I just…
I'm concerned about his reputation, Lovey. This isn't
something… Not a matter to be shared outside the family."

The family? Lovage had no idea where this conversation was going. She absently swatted at a curly roll of
flypaper that hung above her, precariously close to her
head. The flies had been terrible all week. Everyone
was hoping that the heat would soon break and cooling winds would bring more temperate days and fewer
flies. She found it was taking her a bit of time to adjust
to the sweltering heat of the summer here, which went
well beyond summer weather in upstate New York.

"Benjamin, I'm not following."

"Marshall Byler," he finally said, speaking Marshall's name as if it pained him.

She shook her head in confusion. "I don't understand. Marshall…" Then she realized what he meant.
Marshall had written him a bad check. She clamped
her palm over her mouth in disbelief. Then put her
hand out, and Benjamin passed it to her. Sure enough,

Marshall's name and his house number on Persimmon Road were printed on the pale blue security check.

Lovage looked up at Benjamin. "There must be a mistake. Marshall wouldn't write you a bad check." From the look of his property, of his livestock and the clothing he and his family wore on Sunday, he seemed to be comfortable financially. He didn't seem like a man who couldn't pay his bills.

"*Ya*, that's what I thought. So I called the bank. They said the same. Insufficient funds."

She stared at the check for a moment. The first thought that went through her mind was why would Marshall have written a check for sixty-two dollars if he didn't have it? But that thought was immediately followed by a second, which was that a mistake had been made. In the time she'd known Marshall, she'd found him to be honest to the core. He would never write a check for money he didn't have. And he would never risk his reputation in the community.

"I'll take care of this," she said, reaching down to scoop up the box of products she was supposed to be stocking.

"Now?" he asked.

"*Ya.*" She pushed the box into his arms. "Now." She walked away. "Is Mam still lying down?"

"She is," he told her, watching her go.

"That's good. I'm going to take her pony cart. I'll be back shortly and then I'll finish stocking the shelves. I'll make sure Tara is here to wait on customers."

Half an hour later, Lovage rode into Marshall's barnyard. Spotting her in the pony cart, which had a bench only wide enough for two, Sam came running out of the grain shed. "Lovey." He beamed. He was now calling her Lovey, too, and she'd given up telling him that only family called her by her pet name. Maybe, secretly, she was hoping they *would* become family.

"Your brother here?" she asked, noticing their buggy wasn't in its usual spot in the carriage lean-to.

"*Ya*, in the house, I think." Sam caught the dapple-gray pony's harness and held the little gelding still while she climbed down from the cart.

"Your grandmother?"

"Gone down the road. To the Grubers. They've got relatives in from Ohio. Someone Grossmammi knew when she was a little girl. We might have to get our own supper, but Marshall said it's a good idea for a man to know how to fry up a pork chop."

Lovage couldn't help but smile at Sam. When she had first met Marshall, Sam had been so shy around her that he'd barely spoken in front her, but now he was becoming a regular chatterbox. "And how's the conveyor belt invention going?"

Sam was trying to build a conveyor belt for a friend of Lynita's. Joe Crub from over near Marydel had recently lost a leg to diabetes and was struggling to get his chores done around his farm. One of his issues was trying to carry things like corn and grain into the barn while on crutches.

"I think I've almost got it," he told her, beaming. "Of course, it's got to be hand cranked. Joe doesn't even use propane on his farm. Says it's too fancy."

"You have to respect a man's convictions," she agreed. "Do you mind getting Taffy some water?" She pointed at the little dapple-gray pony, which was older than she was. Rosemary had brought Taffy to her marriage to her first husband, Lovage's father. "No need to unhitch her. I just need to talk to your brother for a minute."

"I'll pull her into the shed," Sam said. "Get her out of the sun." He indicated the lean-to he and Marshall had built against the barn that allowed them to pull a horse and buggy through. It was a clever design that she'd never seen before on an Amish farm.

"I won't be long." With her hand in her apron pocket, touching the check, Lovage crossed the barnyard. The barn, the outbuildings, the house and the *dawdi* house in the back were all in excellent repair, with freshly painted trim and windows that were sparkling clean. Lovage didn't think she'd ever seen a neater barnyard. Even the hard-packed dirt in front of the barn had been raked recently. The lawn was neatly mowed and someone had edged around all the buildings. Marshall had more energy than any man she'd ever met. And this was not the farm of a man who couldn't pay his bills.

She walked up the porch steps. At the kitchen door, she called through the screen. "Marshall? Hello?"

"Lovey?" he called from inside.

He appeared at the door bareheaded, grinning. "What are you doing here?" He shook his head. "That didn't come out right. I meant, what a surprise." He held the screen door open for her. "A good surprise. I wasn't expecting to see you until tonight at the softball game. You're still letting me take you and Jesse home, right?"

"*Ya*. But Jesse is going home with Adam, the boy

who went for chicken and ice cream with us, so it will just be the two of us."

He raised his eyebrows. "You're going to ride home *alone* with me? Without a chaperone?" he teased.

"We'll see," she told him, following him into the kitchen.

"Sorry about the mess," he said, pointing at the kitchen table, which was covered with papers. "Trying to put together some receipts so doing my taxes next year won't be so confusing." He brought the heel of his hand to his forehead. "I've been keeping it all in grocery bags, but…"

She looked at the heaping piles of paper: checks, printed receipts, handwritten receipts on bits of paper. Her mother had always done their taxes for her father. She kept a plastic box with properly labeled files for such record keeping. It was funny that many Englishers were under the impression, for some reason, that Amish didn't pay taxes. They did. What they didn't have, which she thought sometimes was what confused Englishers, was health insurance.

He ran his hand through his hair, seeming overwhelmed, which she found interesting because she'd never seen this side of him before.

"Trying to pay some bills," he explained.

She rested her hands on her hips. "Funny you should say that, because that's why I'm here."

His forehead wrinkled. "To pay my bills?"

She shook head, staring at the mess. On the far corner of the table, she spotted a pile of checks with what appeared to be a deposit slip on top. She glanced at him as she drew the check he had written to the harness shop out of her apron pocket. "Your check wasn't good."

"What?"

She handed it to him. "You wrote this out to Benjamin's shop last week to pay for that bridle you had shortened and… I don't remember. Whatever else you had repaired."

He stared at the check. "I don't understand." He looked at her, even more flustered now. "Lovey, I have money. I'm…comfortable."

She immediately understood that he was trying to say he wasn't poor. It wasn't considered polite among her people to talk about how much money one had, not the way she sometimes heard English*ers* do. Of course, the excellent state of Marshall's house and outbuildings showed that he had adequate…probably *more* than sufficient income from his farming.

"Benjamin said that the bank told him you didn't have money in your bank account."

He was still staring at the check. "Didn't have money?" He groaned. "This is embarrassing." He looked at her. "Here I am trying to convince you to marry me. Trying to convince you that I can care for you. For a family and…" He didn't finish his sentence. "Can…can I just give you cash? *Ne*, I should probably take it to Benjamin myself and apologize personally to him." He was still shaking his head. "But why isn't there any money in my account? There should be."

"What about those checks?" she asked, pointing at the pile on the corner of the table.

"What?"

"Those checks." She pointed again. "On the end of

the table. That looks like a deposit slip. I used to deposit my father's paycheck for him when we would go to market on Friday. That's a deposit slip, right?"

Marshall walked over to the far side of the table and picked up the stack. "Oh, no," he groaned.

"The money you thought was in your account?" she asked.

"*Ya.*" He looked up at her. "I wrote out the deposit slip." He rifled through the pile. "Actually three. Never went to the bank, I guess," he said sheepishly.

"Well, it's no wonder, looking at this mess. How do you keep anything straight?" She pointed at the table. "Is it okay if I have a look?"

He opened his arms. "Of course, Lovey. I don't want any secrets between us. When I marry you, what's mine will be yours."

She ignored that comment, focusing on the subject at hand. "You need a system," she told him, picking up a couple pieces of paper. She started to make piles. "And something better than a grocery bag. Whatever you spend on the farm to produce your crops is deductible, but you need the receipts. Put all those together. It helps if you have a receipts book. A way to log everything. But you still need to keep the pieces of paper." She found several bank statements, from two different banks, that didn't even look as if they'd been opened. "And you need to balance your checkbook. That way, if you think you've made a deposit and you haven't—" she continued sorting papers, going faster now "—you'll know right away. My *dat* always balanced his checkbook every Saturday morning. He showed me how it was done. I did it for him when he got sick. I can show you."

She looked up at Marshall, to find him watching her. "I'm sorry," she said, suddenly feeling self-conscious. She set down the stack of bank statements and stepped back from the table. She felt her face flush. "I over-stepped." She looked down at her canvas sneakers, wishing she hadn't agreed to come today. Wishing she had just told Marshall about the check and not said anything more. "I should go," she mumbled.

"Ne." Marshall came around the table. "You didn't overstep, Lovey. I need your help." He motioned to the table and chuckled. *"Obviously* I need your help. I need you."

She looked up, meeting his gaze. "You do?"

"This is just one more example of why we're meant to be together. A marriage should be a team—that's what my *dat* always told me. That he and my *mam* were two, but they were also one. A man's and a woman's abilities should complement each other. That's what he said. My weaknesses, such as my organization—my *lack* of organization—is one of your strengths. You lack confidence in yourself sometimes." He spread his arms wide. "But I probably have too much."

He took a step closer to her and he was so near that she could feel his breath on her lips. She could feel herself falling in love with him.

"Oh, Lovey, say you'll marry me," he said softly, his voice husky.

When he said the words, it was on the tip of her tongue to say yes. Because something in her heart told her that if she didn't say yes, she would regret it the rest of her days. Something told her that for all his joking and lightheartedness, he still spoke sincerely. That he really did want to marry her.

"Let's get your finances in order," she said softly, barely trusting her own voice. "Then we'll talk about marriage. Because if you went to speak to my mother and Benjamin right now about taking my hand in marriage—" she grimaced "—I'm not so sure they would be agreeable."

"Are you saying you'll marry me, Lovey?" He took her hand and leaned close, so close that their lips were almost touching. "Because if you don't agree to marry me, I don't know what I'll do. Because…because I've fallen in love with you."

"Just give me a little time," she whispered, mesmerized by his closeness.

Then their lips *did* touch, ever so lightly, and Lovage felt a tingling warmth pass from his mouth to hers. And she wanted to kiss him again. And again.

Then she came back to her senses. "No more of this," she whispered shakily, taking a step back, out of his arms.

Which was just in time, because Sam walked into the house. "What are you doing?" he asked.

Marshall met Lovage's gaze again and then they laughed. They laughed so hard that Sam, who had no idea what was going on, began to laugh with them.

Chapter Eleven

The first Saturday of October was bright and crisp, and the scents of autumn leaves and fresh-cut hay filled the air. Marshall and several of his friends had gathered at a farm near Rose Valley to cut hay for Caleb Gruber's grandparents. The field was a relatively small one, but Huldah and Jethro Gruber kept to the traditional ways of their childhood and wanted no automation of any sort. The hay had been cut and raked using horse-power the day before, and now the men were piling the drying hay into fragrant stacks and transferring some of it by wagon for storage in the barn.

Most men in Hickory Grove with larger farms baled their hay, or even had their English neighbors come in with tractors. They then packed the timothy and clover into huge circular bales that could be covered with weatherproof wrap so that it could be left in the field until needed. But with such a small field, the old way worked, and Marshall thought that harvesting the loose hay was a reminder of the rich past and all the wisdom that had been passed down from generation to generation.

As Jethro drove his team of gray Percherons, the men followed behind the wagon, pitching hay in and talking. Marshall had brought Sam along and his little brother was busy standing in the back of the wagon, forking hay into the center, and talking to Jethro, who seemed happy to have a companion.

As the men worked, the conversation eventually turned toward women, because that was what unmarried young Amish men liked to talk about. All unmarried young men, Amish or Englisher, Marshall suspected, liked to talk about girls. Along with Marshall and the Gruber boys, John and Caleb, Gabe and Asher Schrock, who were Caleb's grandparents' next-door neighbors, were also helping out.

"Heard the announcement was made in church a few weeks ago for your marriage to Mary Lewis," Gabe said to Caleb, lifting a forkful of hay into the wagon ahead of them. He was a short man in his twenties with a broad back and beefy hands. "You pick a day?"

Caleb grinned, lowered his head and swung his pitchfork. "First Thursday in November."

"Whoowee," Asher said, shaking his head. "Coming up awful fast. You sure you're ready to settle down?"

Caleb just kept grinning. "It is and I am. It can't happen sooner. Mary's everything I wanted in a wife— smart, pretty and she cooks a great hot *mummix*."

"I love a good hash. She have a sister?" Asher asked.

Unlike his brother, Gabe, Asher was tall and slender, taller than Marshall by half a head. Of the two brothers, Marshall liked him better. Gabe tended to be a bit mouthy, which was not a becoming trait in an Amish man. He also did this annoying thing, clicking his thumb and middle finger all the time when he talked. It was as if he always needed to be the center of attention. And he chewed tobacco. But he was only twenty-two, so Marshall was trying to cut him a little slack. Marshall suspected he'd had some bad habits as a young man of that age. Gabe would mature.

The men chuckled at the sister comment.

"Hold up!" Jethro called from the hay wagon, and he eased his Percherons to a stop. "Got a twist workin' in the harness."

"Sam," Marshall called up. "Jump down and give Jethro a hand."

As they waited to get the operation under way again, the men gathered behind the wagon. Someone had brought an insulated gallon jug of water and they passed it around.

"I don't know why you're asking about Mary's sisters, Gabe," Caleb said. "I heard you've been walking with a girl from Seven Poplars. Elsie somebody from Wisconsin. Staying with the matchmaker?"

"Elsie? *Ne.*" Gabe laughed and spat a stream of tobacco on the ground. "We're not walking out together. I've taken her home from singings a few times, but I like keeping my options open. My parents say there's no *rumspringa* here in Delaware, but I like to think I can keep my options open with that, too."

The men laughed again, but Marshall didn't join in. It wasn't that they were saying anything inappropriate. The conversation was harmless enough, and a year or two back, he probably would have laughed, as well, maybe even had something to add. But now that he had Lovey, now that he was certain she was weeks, maybe days, from agreeing to marry him, any pretty girl other than her didn't interest him. Recently, his mind had turned to more domestic thoughts, like when they would marry and if Lovey would like to travel out west for a honeymoon. Couples often did that. After marrying, they would hire drivers and spend a few weeks visiting relatives on both sides, staying in their homes. It was a way to get to know each other better without the day-to-day stresses of housework and fences that needed to be repaired. In their case, it would also be a good opportunity to spend some time alone before they joined Sam and Lynita on the farm.

"What about you, Marshall?" Asher asked, leaning on his pitchfork. "Any plans for a wedding? I heard you were walking out with that girl who just moved here from Vermont."

"New York," Marshall corrected, accepting the water jug from Caleb.

Asher frowned. "Sorry. Gabe told me she was from Vermont."

"She's Benjamin Miller's stepdaughter," Marshall said. "Benjamin has the new harness shop in Hickory Grove."

"Wait a minute!" Gabe passed his pitchfork to his brother and snapped his fingers as if trying to recall something. "She's the girl who made a bet with her sister?"

Marshall had the water jug halfway to his mouth when he stopped. He was quickly becoming annoyed with Gabe. He just wanted to finish the work here and

get home. He and Sam had plans that afternoon to repair a blade on their windmill. "I don't know what
you're talking about."

"Sure you do." Gabe was doing that clicking thing
with his fingers again. He laughed, but it came out as
more of a cackle. "The girl from Vermont or New York
or wherever, she's the one who accepted the dare. Girls
are like that, you know. You want to think they're not,
but they are."

"Gabe." Caleb shook his head. "No gossip."

"*Ne*, this isn't gossip." Gabe stepped into the center of the circle of men, coming to stand in front of
Marshall. "The sister dared her." He started the finger
clicking again. "Cute thing. Ah," he groaned. "What
is her name?"

Marshall took a drink from the water jug and wiped
his mouth with the back of his hand. Out of the corner
of his eye, he saw Sam and Jethro getting back into the
wagon. "Looks like we're ready to go again."

"Ginger! That's it! I met her at Spence's one day.
Pretty little thing," Gabe declared. "Her name was definitely Ginger. Ginger Stutzman. And Elsie heard directly from Ginger, so it's not gossip, that she'd dared
her sister to walk out with some guy." He shrugged.
"You know. As a joke. And she did it." He cackled
again and pointed. "And that was you. You're the one
she went out with. Are you still dating her?"

Marshall stood there with the water jug dangling
on its handle from his hand, trying to decide how to
respond. A part of him felt like he needed to correct
him. He didn't like the idea of anyone making up stories about the Stutzman girls. Or any young women,

for that matter. But a part of him thought maybe he should just let it go, that arguing with Gabe would only egg him on.

"Gabe, don't." His brother Asher shook his head. "It's not funny."

"*Ne*, you're the one." Gabe was pointing at Marshall again. He was like an old dog that had gotten ahold of a bone. He wasn't going to let the subject drop. "What's the sister's name. Not Ginger. The other one. The one you're going out with, I guess. Got an unusual name." Yet again, he clicked his fingers.

Marshall just stood there and stared at Gabe for a minute. His annoyance was turning to anger. "You don't know what you're talking about."

"Marshall, come on. Let's get back to work." John Gruber took the water jug from him. "Gabe's like this. He likes to talk."

"Her name is Lovage," Marshall told Gabe stiffly. "I'm walking out with Lovage Stutzman."

"Well, good for you." Gabe looked at his brother and laughed, but his brother didn't laugh with him.

Marshall hesitated, debating whether or not to ask his next question. He didn't want to, but now he had to. "What dare?"

"I just told you." Gabe spat tobacco juice on the ground between them. "Ginger dared her sister to walk out with some guy from Hickory Grove."

Marshall made a show of pulling his boot back. "What do you mean, *dared*?"

"I don't know." He threw up his hands. "He…*you*, I guess…asked her out and she said no, and then her sister, the blonde, dared her to go out with you. The blonde ended up doing the sister's chores for, like, a month or something."

"Jethro's ready to go," John told the group. "Let's get the rest of this hay in before dinner. We've all got things to do at home."

"Good idea." Caleb walked past Marshall, patting him on the back as he went by. "Don't pay Gabe any mind," he said. "He's one who likes to stir up trouble. And he never gets his facts right. He probably made the whole thing up."

Marshall nodded, and took a minute to take off his hat, wipe his brow and put it square on his head again. He wanted to tell himself that Gabe had fabricated the whole story to get attention, but the fact that he knew Ginger's name and that she was a blonde and that Lovey had just come to Hickory Grove? He suddenly felt like he was falling. He saw all of his dreams tumble away. He was heartbroken and he felt like a fool. He'd told Lovey he loved her. He'd asked her to marry him. Not once, but over and over again. And all this time, she'd been silently laughing, making him the butt of her and her sister's joke. And now, thanks to Gabe, everyone in the community would know that she'd just been playing with his feelings.

"Ohh…can we have snack cakes?" Tara pointed to a display of snowball-looking cakes covered in coconut and sold in individual packaging in boxes. She turned down the next aisle of Byler's store, but was still looking back. She was pushing one cart, Nettie was pushing the other, and Lovage and her mother were loading the carts and checking items off their lists.

"We don't need snack cakes," Rosemary said absently as she scanned a section of shelves featuring spices. "I need anise, but I want the whole stars. I like to grind it myself." She rubbed her protruding abdomen as she searched. She'd been quiet all day and seemed preoccupied, but Lovage wondered if that was just normal. With only six weeks to go before the baby was born, she had to be tired, getting up at dawn every day and working until evening prayer.

Lovage grabbed a large shaker jar of cinnamon, eyeing her mother, and contemplated asking her if she was feeling all right. But she'd asked earlier in the morning and her mother's rely had been a curt "I'm *goot.*" Lovage had later suggested that maybe she could take the buggy into Dover with the girls and leave her mother home to rest, but Rosemary would have none of it.

"I've been buying our groceries once a week since I married your father!" she'd declared when Lovage had tried to convince her to stay home. "An eight-pound *bobli* is not going to slow me down!"

Lovage checked the cinnamon off her list and looked for the next item. They also needed baking powder and baking soda. As she searched the next shelf, she spotted a little Englisher boy peeking at her from around the corner. He had big almond-shaped eyes and a round, flat face with a small mouth and nose. She recognized the features at once. The little boy, who looked to be about four, had Down syndrome. Back in New York, there had been a family in their church district with twins, a boy and a girl, who had it.

Lovage smiled and waved at him and his eyes grew

round with surprise. Then he shyly wiggled his fingers at her. She wiggled her fingers at him.

The little boy crept around the display and stood at the end of the aisle staring at her. He had on a blue coat and a long, colorful knit stocking cap with a big pom-pom on the end that looked like something Lovage had once seen in a children's book set in Switzerland.

The little boy slowly raised his hand to his cap and then pointed at her head.

"What?" She touched her hand to her black dress bonnet. It had been chilly in the morning when they left the house. First, they'd gone to Spence's, because it was Tuesday and their *mam* had had a hankering for some pickled fish she bought at a stall there. Then they came here to Byler's, making it their last stop because ice cream was on the grocery list. They were all wearing their black cloaks and black Sunday bonnets over their prayer *kapps*. "My bonnet? You like it?"

He nodded, a little smile playing on his lips. Then he pulled off his hat and offered it to her with one hand, while pointing at her bonnet with his other hand.

Lovage laughed and her heart swelled for the little boy. She knew that some societies sometimes looked at people with a disability like this child's negatively, but among the Amish, all children were a gift from God and a blessing. Seeing the little boy made her imagine what it would be like to have a child of her own. Marshall's child. And the thought brought a mist to her eyes.

Did she love Marshall? She'd been denying it for weeks. Afraid of her feelings for him. But why should she be afraid? He'd already told her he loved her, that day at his house when they'd talked about organizing his finances.

After that day, she'd gone to his house several times, with Lynita always there, to help him put it all in order. She'd specially arranged her visits around Lynita's presence because after the kiss she and Marshall had shared, Lovage understood why parents preferred their unmarried, courting children to always have a chaperone. The feeling she had experienced when his lips had touched hers were nothing like any she'd ever had. Now she knew why Amish couples weren't encouraged to court long term. Especially at the ages she and Marshall were at. Marshall was right to push marriage at this point, because if they were committed to each other, to a Godly life, it was better that they not struggle long, fighting temptation.

"Duncan? Duncan?" a woman called from the next aisle over, sounding distraught.

Lovey walked closer to the little boy and leaned down so she was at eye level. "Is your name Duncan? Is that you?"

The little boy nodded slowly.

Lovage took his hand. "I'll be right back," she called to her sisters over her shoulder.

Tara was leaning against the cart, reading the ingredients on a box of the snowball cakes she'd somehow gotten ahold of, and their *mam* had two jars of spice in her hands, comparing the two. Lovage didn't know where Nettie had gotten to. Maybe she'd backtracked to get something their mother had forgotten. Rosemary was tiring more easily now than in the first two trimesters of her pregnancy, and even though she wouldn't admit it aloud, she was making concessions for the health of herself and the baby.

Lovage led the little English boy named Duncan to the next aisle. "Here he is," she said to a distraught-looking woman standing in the pasta section. She was wearing a baby in one of those pouches Englisher mothers liked to use and there was a toddler in the front of her grocery cart, which was so full of stuff that Lovage didn't know how she pushed it.

"Oh, Duncan, sweetie. Mama was looking every-where for you." She leaned down to brush her son's chubby cheek with one hand, then stood. "I'm so sorry," she told Lovage. "He was here one minute and then, poof. Gone. He knows he's supposed to stay with me." She glanced at him. "Otherwise he'll have to stay home with Mom-mom, isn't that right, Duncan?"

"It's fine. It's my fault," Lovage said. "He was look-ing at my bonnet. I think he was trying to trade me his hat for my bonnet."

"Oh, I'm so sorry." She took the knit cap from her son's hand and pulled it down over his hair. "We don't trade hats with strangers in stores, remember, Dun-can?" She smiled at Lovage. "He has this thing for hats. He *loves* hats. He has an entire storage bin at home full of them."

Often Englishers stared at the Amish. Sometimes they even pointed. Or worse, came up and asked silly questions, like the woman in a market back in New York who had asked Lovage if she watched the reality TV show about the Amish people who'd been shunned from their communities and were living in the English world. Duncan's mother either wasn't as curious about

the Amish as most Englishers, or had enough sense not
to behave rudely.

"You like hats, do you, Duncan?" Lovey asked him.
He nodded.

"I'm sorry. I can't give you mine, but I *can* show
you another one I'm wearing. Would you like that?"
she asked.

"He doesn't talk much," his mother explained softly.
"But he understands everything we say."

"This is my outside bonnet. I wear it when I go to
town or to church," Lovage explained. "But under-
neath, I wear my inside hat." She lifted her black bonnet off her head. "See?" She gently touched her prayer
kapp. "This is what we call a *kapp*," she said, using a
Pennsylvania Dutch accent.

"Isn't it pretty, Duncan?" the woman asked.

He stared wide-eyed and nodded, obviously fas-
cinated.

"Lovey," Tara called from the next aisle. "Mam's
ready to move on. I don't know where Nettie's gotten to. You'll have to push the cart. I can't push both
of them."

"Coming," Lovage called. "I have to go," she told
the mother. "My sister." Then she looked down at the
little boy. "It was very nice to meet you, Duncan. My
name's Lovey."

"Thank you," the mother said. She looked down at
her son. "Tell Lovey goodbye, Duncan."

The little boy didn't speak, but he waved, and
Lovage was still smiling when she went back around
the corner to the next aisle. Tara was standing there
alone, with both carts nearly full. It took a lot of food

to feed thirteen people, especially when half of them were men.

"Mam said never mind, and for me to just stay with the carts. She's almost ready to check out but she wants you to stand in line at the deli. She says get three pounds of sliced honey ham, two pounds of sliced smoked turkey and four pounds of American cheese. Be sure to get the white kind, not the yellow."

Lovage nodded and, as she put her black bonnet carefully back over her white *kapp*, repeated the order to her little sister.

"That's it," Tara said. "Mam said we're almost done here, so meet us at the registers."

Lovage eyed the grocery carts and spotted a box of the snowball cakes on top of one. She tapped it.

"Mam said get two boxes," her sister said defensively. "That way everyone can try one after supper tonight."

Lovage rolled her eyes and headed for the deli section. She took a paper slip with a number from the little dispenser and stepped back to get out of other customers' way. As she waited, arms crossed, she nodded at two Amish women about her age, maybe a little older, also waiting their turn at the deli counter. She didn't know them, but there were a lot of Amish families in the Dover area, and even though she'd traveled a couple times to the homes of folks outside her church district, her circle of friends and acquaintances was still small. Both Amish women had red hair and one was holding a newborn. The woman with the baby smiled and Lovage got a warm feeling as she imagined what it would be like to hold her own baby.

With nothing to do but wait her turn, she glanced at other customers waiting for service. There was so much to see that she felt like her head was spinning. Two middle-aged, blonde women were bickering loudly over someone they knew named RuPaul. One liked him and one didn't. There was a woman on her cell phone in very tight pants, wearing high-heeled boots and a green sweater that had big holes in each arm so that her shoulders were bare. Lovage felt sorry for the woman; she couldn't imagine what it would be like to stand there in line perched on those shoes and feeling cold. Standing beside Lovage, an old Englisher with big hearing aids in his ears smiled at her and she smiled back. A clerk called out another number to serve the next customer.

Turning to look behind her, to see if she could spot either of her sisters or her mother, Lovage caught sight of a man holding a gallon of milk. He was leaning over a display of bread, with his back to her, but even from the rear she knew the broad shoulders and the dark hair that stuck out from beneath the black beanie.

"Marshall!" she called, trying not to be too loud or obnoxious. She hurried over to him, a big smile on her face. She hadn't seen him since Friday. There had been talk of going visiting together on Sunday, but the plan must have fallen through because he never came by. Then she'd heard, through Will, that on Monday Marshall had hired a van and taken both Lynita and Sam to the dentist. "Marshall," she repeated, and when he didn't seem to hear her, she brazenly put her hand on his back. Right in front of everyone in the store.

Marshall whipped around. He seemed startled to see her there. "Lovage."

She smiled at him and saw at once that he looked tired. There were tiny lines around his mouth, which seemed strained. "I haven't seen you since Friday." She chuckled. "I thought we were going visiting Sunday. I guess you decided not to go?"

"I, um… Grossmammi wanted me to stop for bread. I had to go to the, um…hardware store next to Redner's grocery." He pointed in the general direction with his free hand.

She nodded, thinking that was a strange response to her asking him what happened to their Sunday plans, but maybe she'd been confused about the whole thing.

"Rye bread," he said, not sounding anything like himself. "With seeds."

"Right there." She pointed to one of the loaves. She recognized the brand because Benjamin liked rye bread with seeds. While they made a lot of bread at home, rye was time-consuming and it took different flours, so her *mam* often picked it up at the store for him.

"She's out in the buggy. Waiting," he added. "Grossmammi."

"Oh, *ya*, well, Mam and Tara and Nettie are here. I'm getting lunch meat." She pointed to the deli counter, feeling as if their conversation was rather awkward and unsure why. Was it just because they'd been seeing each other every day, and a couple days had passed without them spending time together?

He just stood there and didn't say anything.

Lovage glanced away and then back at him, feeling uneasy and not sure why, because in the last couple weeks she'd become so comfortable with him. "I guess you should go."

He started to turn away from her and she said, "Oh, are you still going to the Fishers' with me tomorrow night? Not for the actual singing. Just to help out and ride along in the hay wagons. I think we're sort of chaperones. A few weeks ago, some of the boys got into some trouble. Painted the bishop's goats with pink chalk or something." She laughed, but it was a tense laugh because his awkwardness was making her feel awkward, too. "So…we're still going?"

"Can't."

She looked at him, but he wouldn't make eye contact with her.

"Okay…" She drew out the word.

At that moment, the deli clerk called her number. She needed to go or she would lose her place in line.

"Something…came up," Marshall mumbled.

"Okay, that's fine. So…you want to come over Thursday night for supper? Some of our pumpkins are already ripe. We were thinking about carving a few before we eat. Not faces or anything, but Benjamin saw somewhere where people were carving ears of corn and such into them." She smiled. "He thought maybe we could decorate the harness shop with a few. You could bring Sam and your grandmother, too."

"I don't know." He looked away. "We'll have to see. I need to go." And with that, he walked away.

"Marshall," she called after him. "You forgot your grandmother's bread!" She picked up a loaf to take to him, but then the clerk called her number again, sounding impatient this time, and she reluctantly returned the bread to the display and hurried up to the counter.

A short time later, with pounds of lunch meat and cheese in her arms, Lovage walked to the registers at the front of the store. When she got there, she didn't see her mother or sisters, but the lines were short so she wondered if they had already paid and gone out to load the buggy. But that didn't make sense. Lovage had a little money with her, but not enough to pay for everything she'd gotten at the deli.

"There you are!" Nettie called, bursting in through the automatic doors that were marked Exit Only. "Mam says come outside right now."

"But all this lunch meat—"

"Those are our carts. Tara already spoke to a lady at customer service." She grabbed her and pulled her toward two carts that Lovage hadn't noticed when she walked up to the registers. "Just put it all in there."

"Nettie, what's going on?" Lovage opened her arms, dropping the wrapped lunch meat into one of the full carts.

Nettie grabbed her hand and pulled her toward the door. "Mam says she has to go to the hospital. She's in labor."

Chapter Twelve

There was a soft tap at the door and Lovage sat up in her chair. For a moment, she wasn't positive she had heard a knock. All she heard now was the rhythmic pulse of the heartbeat on the fetal monitor. A streetlamp outside threw a yellow glow of light through the window and across the floor and onto the hospital bed. Lovage glanced at her mother. She lay asleep, a white sheet to her chin, the blue scarf that covered her hair neatly framing her beautiful face. Benjamin, who had nodded off to sleep, too, sat upright in a chair beside Rosemary's bed. Their hands were clasped.

The knock came again.

"Come in," Lovage said softly, not wanting to wake her mother or Benjamin. He had been at her side since shortly after the ambulance had brought her to the emergency department at the local hospital. Lovage still didn't know how he'd gotten here so quickly after she called the harness shop. It was determined that her mother was in preterm labor, and she'd been admitted to the labor and delivery floor, where she had been given medication to try to stop her contractions. At thirty-four weeks, with another six to go, it was too soon for her to go into labor.

"Just wanted to see if anyone needed anything." It was Julie, Rosemary's nurse for the night. She was a short, round woman in her midfifties with white-blond hair pulled back in a ponytail. She had a voice that put everyone in her path at ease. "Some coffee? A snack? For us to leave you alone and stop asking?" She chuckled.

Lovage stood up from her chair, feeling guilty that she had dozed off for a few minutes. Her gaze flickered to the clock on the wall. It was two fifteen in the morning. "*Ne*, we don't need a thing," she answered, keeping her voice low. "Thank you. She's been asleep for nearly two hours."

"Good. That's what she needs now." The nurse walked over to look at one of the monitors Rosemary was hooked up to. One brightly lit display showed the mother's contractions, a nurse had explained to Lovage earlier in the day. The second display showed the mother's heart rate and the baby's. In this case, the *babies'*. A surprise to Lovage, but not to Rosemary and Benjamin. Apparently, they had been aware that they were having twins because she had been seeing a midwife for her care, but they had decided not to share the information with anyone.

"We keep an eye on things from the nurses' station," Julia went on. "But there have been no contractions in six hours, and Baby A and Baby B are both looking great."

"That's good, right?" Lovage asked. "If the contractions have stopped? That means the babies won't come too early?"

Julie hit a button on one of the monitors and it beeped and began to spit out a strip of paper. "Well, I can't promise you she won't go into preterm labor, but she's not going into labor tonight. The doctor will be here in the morning to talk to her and explain everything again. It's a lot to take in when it's all actually happening."

"You think she'll be able to go home tomorrow?" Lovage asked, clasping her hands. The moment the contractions had stopped, Rosemary had started fussing about wanting to go home and sleep in her own bed.

"It's not my decision, but I suspect the obstetrician on call will send her home with instructions to take it easy." Julie spoke quietly, but with an air of confidence that put Lovage at ease. "Just giving these babies another three or four weeks will make a huge difference in birth weight and lung maturity."

"I knew she was doing too much." Lovage worried aloud, glancing in her mother's direction. "There are plenty of others at home to cook and clean, but my mother likes things just so. She likes to be in control."

Julie chuckled. "Who doesn't?" She tore the strip of paper from the monitor and smoothed it between her hands. "Truthfully, it might be nothing she's done. Her age, the number of children she's had and the fact that she's carrying twins are all factors in preterm labor." She walked away from the monitor and shrugged. "No one likes to hear this, but sometimes it just happens."

She reached out and patted Lovage's arm. "Try to get some sleep. Your mother has a blood draw at five thirty, but I'll try to keep everyone out of here until then."

"Thank you so much," Lovage said, surprised by the emotion welling up in her. When they had arrived at the ED, not only had Rosemary been having contractions, but there had been some irregularity in her heartbeat. For a short time Lovage had been petrified they might lose her and the baby. Babies. But then everything had "righted itself" as her mother liked to say. Her heartbeat went back to normal and the contractions stopped. There was talk by doctors and nurses that stress had elevated her heart rate, or that there may have been a glitch in the equipment. But Lovage believed it was the prayers of her family and friends that had brought her heart back to a safe rhythm.

"You're welcome, Lovage. Please let me know if there's anything I can do for your mom or you or your family." Julie smiled. "You have a nice family. Reminds me of my own, growing up. Your stepfather was so attentive to your mother when they came in. And your brothers and sisters? I think the last of them didn't go home until midnight."

"We do have a nice family," Lovage said proudly.

Julie held her gaze for a moment in the dim light from the outside lights seeping through the window. Then she said, "Get some sleep. She's going to be fine." She took Lovage's hand, squeezed it and then walked out of the room, closing the door quietly behind her.

Lovage walked to the window and looked out at the grass a story below. She closed her eyes and murmured a silent prayer of thanksgiving for her mother's improved health and for the little babies who would soon be born into their family. Rosemary had specifically told the staff when they had done ultrasounds that she didn't want to know the sexes, but whatever the babies were, whatever their mental or physical states, Lovage knew they would be loved.

Lovage opened her eyes and looked out into the darkness again. She had never been more afraid in her life than she had been today. While she'd been waiting for the doctors to examine her mother and to do their tests and then to treat her, Lovage had been torn between wanting to be with her mother and wanting to be with Marshall. She had been so scared and so sad, but the comfort she had longed for wasn't from her sisters or even her mother. It was Marshall she had wanted. It had been the strangest feeling. To wish she could have called him, asked him to come wait in the waiting room with her. Because once Benjamin had arrived, she'd been sent to be with her sisters and brothers. Waiting there for hours, she had secretly hoped that word would get to Marshall and that he would come to the hospital. Not for Rosemary, but for her. The need to be with him had almost been overwhelming.

And that was when Lovage realized she had fallen in love with Marshall.

She didn't know when it had happened or how. She had never been in love, but in her heart, she knew that the feelings rushing through her right now were not the physical desire she had felt for him that day they had kissed, but a genuine love. A love that would be the makings of a solid, happy marriage. Not that she didn't think there would be bumps along the road, but if Marshall possessed half the love for her that she felt for him, she knew they could have a faithful, honorable, loving life together. And he had told her he loved her. He'd told her the day they had kissed and had told her every time they'd said goodbye since then.

Just thinking about it sent a shiver down her spine, as if she were cold, but also as if she were warm. She smiled and saw her reflection in the window glass: angular face, wide-set eyes, high cheekbones, a small nose, small chin and wisps of brown hair that had fallen from her *kapp*. She had never thought she was beautiful. How could she have when she was so tall and skinny and browned-haired like a wren, and surrounded by the red-haired, oval-faced loveliness of her mother and sisters? But looking at her own reflection tonight, she smiled. Because Marshall had said she was beautiful. And that made her feel beautiful.

"Lovey..." Rosemary called, sleepily.

Lovage spun around and then rushed to her mother's bedside. "Mam? How are you feeling?"

"Shh," Rosemary whispered. She pointed to Benjamin. "He needs his sleep."

"Ya," she murmured, pulling her chair closer to the side of the bed. "But you should be asleep, too."

"Nonsense." Mam glanced at the clock on the wall. "I've slept most of the day and all of the night away." She reached for her daughter's hand. "Where are the other girls? Not still in the waiting room, I pray."

"Ne. Ethan sent them all home around eight. Jesse, too. And the boys. Only he and Will stayed. To be sure you or their father didn't need anything. I think they left around midnight."

"They're good boys," she mused. "I'm glad everyone went home." She squeezed Lovage's hand. "You should have gone, too, *dochtah*."

"I thought maybe Benjamin—" Thinking better of her words, Lovage didn't finish her sentence.

What she had intended to say was that she had stayed thinking Benjamin would go home. But she realized she'd been foolish to ever believe that. Because she had been blind to the relationship her mother and Benjamin had. And now, suddenly, she understood it. Her feelings for Marshall made her realize that the bond between Benjamin and her *mam*, the love between them, was about togetherness, not separation during times of trial. The thought made her sad that she hadn't seen it sooner, that she hadn't listened to her mother when Rosemary had tried to tell her. But she also felt hopeful that she and Marshall could share that same kind of love.

Lovage looked down at her mother and smiled. "*Ya*, I probably should have gone home, but it's too late now. Ethan said he would be back in the morning."

"I'm sorry I caused such a fuss." She shook her head. "Really, an ambulance. And *atch*!" Her hands flew to her head. "All those groceries, so much for those girls at Byler's to put back on the shelves."

"Not to worry," Lovage told her. "Will went by Byler's, paid for it all with cash from the household money jar, and Eunice and Barnabas took their wagon and fetched it. Eunice came to the waiting room later. She said to tell you it was all put away properly." She chuckled, remembering the conversation that had taken place while they stood in front of a big machine full of snacks in a cubby in the waiting room. Lovage had been so hungry at that point that she had seriously thought about getting herself a bag of pretzels and a candy bar. "And she also said to tell you that you buy too much ice cream and that will make you fat." She looked quizzically down at her mother. "She said you would know what she meant?"

Rosemary laughed. "It's a joke we have." She rested her hand on her big belly. "That we're fat because of what we've been eating and not for the real reason."

Lovage looked away, feeling the heat of embarrassment on her cheeks. But also, deep down, she was pleased her mother would share such an intimate little joke with her. As if they were friends and not mother and daughter. And she couldn't help wondering if the change had something to do with her feelings for Marshall. Did her *mam* know?

Lovage looked at her and said softly, "I'm glad you and the babies are all right. I didn't tell anyone, not even Ginger, that there are two babies."

"I hope you don't mind that I didn't say. The midwife heard the two heartbeats months ago, but Benjamin and I talked and—" she hesitated "—we decided not to say anything, not because we were afraid something might happen, but because we wanted to just have a little secret between ourselves. That may be hard for you to understand, but sometimes a couple—"

"*Ne*, I do understand." Lovage smiled, thinking about the revelation she had experienced tonight in regards to her feelings for Marshall. And now she just wanted to see him, to be with him so she could tell him. And so that the next time he asked her to marry him, which seemed to happen nearly every time they were together, she could say yes. She could agree to be his wife. "I think I understand now that…" She looked away, feeling a little shy. "Since Marshall and I have…"

"Fallen in love?" Rosemary asked, with a mixture of amusement and happiness in her voice.

Lovage made herself look at her mother. "*Ya*, I think… I *know* I love him." And then for the first time all day, she remembered her exchange with him in Byler's. She frowned. "I didn't get to tell you. I saw him at Byler's when I was getting the meat from the deli." She shook her head slowly, thinking it felt like such a long time ago. "We just spoke for a minute but…he said he couldn't go to the singing tonight with me. We were supposed to chaperone."

"Something came up?" Rosemary reached for a plastic cup of water on a table beside the bed.

"*Ya*… I suppose." Thinking back, Lovage met her mother's gaze. She was a little concerned now. Because his behavior had been so odd. "I'm not sure. He was in a hurry. Lynita was waiting in the parking lot, but… He didn't really say why he couldn't go tonight or why he hadn't come for me Sunday. Remember? I thought we were going visiting?"

"It's probably nothing," Rosemary assured her, taking a sip of her water. "It's harvest time. There's a lot of work to be done to get the house and farm and livestock ready for winter. Benjamin has been preoccupied, as well."

"*Ya*, I'm sure he'll come by the house tomorrow. When he hears I've been here all night with you." Lovage sat back in her chair. "I'm sure it's nothing," she agreed, despite a sudden niggling feeling that maybe something *was* amiss.

"Toby," Marshall said impatiently. "Hold still, boy!" Standing in his barnyard, he lifted the horse's hoof again and rested it against his knee. The young gelding had seemed a little lame this morning when he and Sam had gone to the feed store with the wagon. They had gone to get a couple hundred pounds of horse, cow and goat chow that he would use in the coming winter to supplement the corn and hay he was harvesting from his fields now.

Marshall suspected that Toby had picked up a stone along the way, but now, looking at the horse's hoof, he thought otherwise. He was immediately annoyed. "Sam, did you clean Toby's hooves this morning before harnessing him?"

Sam was playing with his brown-and-white goat, Petunia. He'd fashioned a blanket with pockets on each side from two burlap feed bags and was trying to tie it on the less-than-cooperative animal. "*Ya*, I cleaned his hooves."

"Not well enough. Look at this." He tapped Toby's horseshoe and then used the hoof pick in his hand to point out a tiny pebble wedged between the frog—the V-shaped inner part—and the wall of the hoof. The soft flesh around the pebble was slightly swollen, indicating it had been there longer than an hour or so. "This could have seriously injured the horse, Sam," he said sharply.

His brother stared at the hoof. "I... I'm sorry. I must have missed it."

"When you tell me you've done something, I expect you to be truthful with me."

"I *am* being truthful." Sam's voice quavered. "I cleaned his hooves, but I guess I missed that little rock. I'm sorry."

"Do it correctly next time." Marshall popped out the rock and then exchanged the pick for a hoof brush from his back pocket. "Pigs watered?"

"*Ne*, but I'll do it now," Sam said, backing away from him.

"And put that goat up," Marshall called. "We have work to be done today. If you want to do a man's work, you shouldn't be wasting daylight playing with a pet."

The moment the words came out of his mouth, Marshall regretted them. Maybe not the words. It was his job to teach Sam how to care for animals, how to run a farm. But he regretted the tone he had used with his little brother. But he didn't stop Sam to apologize then; he let him go. He would do it later.

Marshall had been in a foul mood all morning. Actually, for days. Long enough for both his grandmother and brother to notice. And she was so perceptive that she had figured out almost immediately who he was upset with, and had been asking questions.

"Haven't seen Lovage in a few days," she had commented that morning at breakfast. She'd made French toast, link sausages with maple syrup and freshly baked buttermilk biscuits with hot apple butter to slather them with.

"Bloom off the rose?" his *grossmammi* had pressed.

"I don't want to talk about," he'd responded.

"I hear Rosemary's home from the hospital. I was

thinking I would pay a visit this afternoon. I made an apple cake. You want to go with me?"

Marshall had shaken his head and forked a large square of French toast into his mouth. "*Ne*, too much to do around here today. We need grain and I need to disk up part of the garden, but I've got a bent blade that needs to be repaired. I don't know how a disk blade gets bent," he grumbled. "We've got no rocks in our soil."

His grandmother had opened her mouth as if wanting to speak again, then closed it and refreshed his coffee.

Finishing Toby's last hoof, Marshall grabbed the halter and led the horse back around to the pasture gate. He slipped off the nylon halter and gave the gelding a pat on its haunch as he set it free. He closed the gate, but then just stood there, gazing out at the pasture.

The sun was shining and there was a light breeze coming out of the west, carrying the scent of the last of his ripe apples. Only he could barely feel the warmth on his face. He couldn't appreciate the sweet, sharp scents of fall.

Because he was miserable.

How could everything have gone so wrong with Lovey? How could he have been such a fool? He had known in the beginning, when he'd first met her at the harness shop, that she'd not really be interested in him. But then she had seemed to take a liking to him. And she'd continued to agree to go out with him. She'd let him ask her to marry him again and again. She'd stood there and let him tell her he was in love with her. And now he knew that it had all been a game to her. Fun between two sisters.

Marshall groaned and rested his back against the gate. He didn't know what to do. He'd been so upset Tuesday when he'd seen her at Byler's that he'd barely been able to speak to her. He knew he should confront her and make her confess that the only reason she'd been going out with him was because of some silly dare Ginger had made. But would she even admit it? And what would be the point? She didn't love him. She was never going to love him.

He closed his eyes, wishing he had someone to talk about this with. Someone who could give him advice. But who could he talk to? His grandmother had been set against Lovey from the beginning. And his best friend, Will, was Lovey's stepbrother.

With a sigh, Marshall headed for the barn. Right now, the best thing he could think to do was work. Hard work tired a man's muscles and made him sleep at night. It kept him from thinking too long on the love that had almost been.

Chapter Thirteen

Lovage stood near the Fishers' farmhouse, listening to the neighborhood women speak softly in Pennsylvania *Deutsch* as they loaded children into their buggies to go home. It had been a long day of church services. They'd had a guest preacher, Bishop Simon from Ohio, and he had been so long-winded that parishioners had to be gently poked to wake them during the second service. Both the morning and afternoon sermons had been related to mercy, but Lovage had to admit, though she refrained from falling asleep, she'd not been in a good frame of mind to hear and digest God's word.

A fierce wind coming out of the north tugged at the hem of her heavy wool cloak and pulled at the strings of her black bonnet. It was a cold, late afternoon with black skies, but she had decided to walk home rather than ride with her family, to give herself some time to think.

About Marshall. About what she should do about him.

For a day or two following her mother's release

from the hospital, Lovage had told herself that Marshall hadn't come around because he didn't want to bother the family. It made sense he might think that, considering the circumstances, Rosemary's household needed as little commotion as possible. Maybe he'd even been embarrassed, because his grandmother must have told him why Rosemary had been hospitalized, and pregnancy was not something discussed among Amish men. But when Lynita had stopped by to visit Rosemary, she had sounded as if she was making excuses as to why her grandson hadn't come with her. Something about a plow blade being broken. Fall chores to be done. A sagging shutter. But then another day had passed. Then another. And today, while Marshall had been present for the district church services, he had openly avoided Lovage. Not only had he kept away from her during the services and the midday meal, but he'd refused to make eye contact with her, even from across a room.

Lovage was heartbroken. She couldn't possibly imagine how he could have seemed so in love with her less than two weeks ago, how he could have asked her to marry him yet again, and now he couldn't even look at her. Had she done something, *said* something, to upset him? Or worse, had he realized how dull she was? Had he decided he really did want someone fun to be his wife?

A buggy rolled by and three-year-old Elsa Gruber waved excitedly from the open rear window. Lovage waved back with one cold hand, wishing she'd worn her wool knit gloves. In this wind, her hands would be near frozen by the time she got home. The sight of little Elsa's face as the buggy went down the driveway brought a lump up in Lovage's throat. What if Marshall didn't love her anymore? Didn't want to marry her? If this was over, could she ever find love again? Because seeing Benjamin and her mother together in the hospital had made her realize that she really had done the right thing when she had refused Ishmael's marriage proposal. Because she knew what a marriage of love looked like. And she wasn't going to settle for less. Amish couples didn't always marry for love. There were various alternative reasons, such as arranged matches or security for a widow. But Lovage wanted what Benjamin and her mother had. What her parents had had.

Tugging on the brim of her bonnet to shield her face from the wind, she started across the barnyard. There was a gathering of older men near the smokehouse, their heads bowed, the brims of their black hats almost touching as they engaged in conversation with the visiting preacher. Bishop Simon saw her and nodded, then returned his attention to the group. That was when she spotted Marshall hitching Toby to his grandmother's buggy.

She halted, the wind in her face, watching him. His head was down, and a knit watch cap had replaced his black Sunday church hat. His shoulders were hunched inside a black wool coat and he seemed to be moving in slow motion. She stood there for a moment in indecision. If he'd changed his mind and didn't love her anymore, did the reason matter? Should she just let it go and not subject either of them to the awkwardness of him having to say why he didn't want to marry her anymore? Or should she confront him?

After another moment of uncertainty, she strode across the barnyard. She waited until she was right behind him to speak his name. He didn't hear her approach, maybe because of the howling wind.

"Marshall?" she said to his back a second time.

He hesitated before he turned around, almost as if debating whether or not to acknowledge her.

Lovage's heart fell further.

"Marshall, I have to talk to you." Tears burned behind her eyelids and a part of her wanted to turn and run. But Rosemary hadn't raised her to be a coward. And wouldn't it be better to know why he didn't love her anymore than to never know? "I need you to tell me what's happened," she managed to say when she found her voice again. "Between us. Last I knew, all was well. You asked me to marry you two weeks ago at Chupps' barn raising and then…then you didn't come for me last Sunday and I saw you at Byler's and you acted strange." She lifted her arms and let them fall to her sides. She was shivering, but she wasn't sure if it was because she was cold or because she was so upset. "What changed?"

He didn't make eye contact with her and her resolve wavered. Maybe it would be best if she turned around and walked away. But she deserved better. If he didn't love her anymore, he needed to say so. And he needed to tell her why. If he was going to break her heart, she deserved an explanation.

She waited, but he was silent.

"Marshall, say something," she said finally. "Anything."

He ran his hand along one of the thick straps of his horse's harness. "You know very well why I'm upset." His voice was harsh and angry, a tone she'd never heard from him in the three months she had known him.

"*Ne*, I don't," she said softly. "At the barn raising everything was fine." She gave a strangled little laugh. "You told me—" Her voice caught in her throat. "That you loved me," she finished in a great exhalation.

Marshall slowly lifted his gaze until he was eye-to-eye with her. "You know why," he repeated, harsh accusation in his voice. Pain. "Everyone knows."

"Knows *what*?" she demanded, raising her voice to him. "Marshall, how can I explain myself to you, defend myself, if you don't tell me why you're upset with me?"

"I felt like a fool when I heard, Lovage. Everyone in Hickory Grove and Rose Valley knew and I didn't. The joke was on me, wasn't it?"

"Marshall, you have to believe me when I say I don't know what you're talking about." She hesitated, racking her brain, but still could think of nothing she had done. "What did you hear? I have a right to know."

"I'm not a playing piece in a game of checkers, you know. My intentions were honest and honorable from the first day I met you. From that first day, I meant every word I said. Lovey, I—" His voice cracked and he went silent.

"Marshall," she begged, making fists of her hands. "Please tell me what we're talking about."

"The dare," he told her.

She held his gaze for an instant, truly having no idea what he was talking about.

And then she knew. And she was crestfallen.

It seemed as if it had been so long ago and so...*trivial* to her. Silliness between sisters. Ginger had genuinely wanted Lovage to get out and make new friends, perhaps even find a beau. "The dare," she murmured. Wind tugged at the skirt of her black dress. "Ginger's dare."

Marshall turned and stroked Toby's flank. "Ginger's dare."

"So Ginger told you," she said. It was a statement, not a question.

"*Ne*, worse than that." His voiced sounded flat now, which seemed worse than his anger. "She told others. Everyone is talking about it. Guys in Rose Valley knew. Everyone is laughing about it. Laughing at *me*."

She closed her eyes for a moment. The sun was setting fast. Soon it wouldn't be safe for her to walk home along the road because she'd brought no flashlight with her. And her family had already left in their buggies.

"Marshall," she said. "It's true that Ginger *did* dare me to ride home from the softball game with you, but..." She exhaled and started again. "I accepted her dare, but it was all in good fun. And you have to believe me when I tell you that after that, I walked out with you because I wanted to. Because I *wanted* to be with you."

"She did your chores for a month, so was that the deal? That you would walk out with me for a month?" he asked. "What did she offer you for the next month?"

She almost laughed, his accusation seemed so ridiculous, but she knew from the look on his face, from the tone of his voice, that he didn't think it was ridiculous. "It was dishes and it was only for a week. One ride home with you and Ginger said she'd take on my dishwashing chore for a week. I'm sorry. I should have told you after that first date." She clasped her hands together, almost as if begging him. "It was wrong of me not to tell you, Marshall. But I have to be honest with you, I didn't take you entirely seriously at first. When you started asking me to go places with you. Who asks a woman to marry her on their first date?"

"I'm sorry. I have to go. My grandmother and brother are waiting out front for me to pick them up." He stepped between her and the buggy and swung up into the seat.

"Marshall, what are you doing? That's it?" She opened her arms to him, looking up at him on the buggy seat. "You're not going to talk with me about this?"

"Nothing to talk about." He slid the door shut, lifted the reins and urged Toby forward.

Lovage stood there in the cold, fighting tears until he was gone. Then she walked home alone in the dark.

When Lovage walked into her mother's kitchen, Rosemary was sitting at the table with Benjamin, both with cups of tea. He was reading aloud to her from the Book of Ruth, Rosemary's favorite. He glanced over the top of the newspaper at his stepdaughter, his wire-frame reading glasses perched on the end of his large nose. "Have a good walk home, Lovey?"

"Ya," she answered. "It was cold, but the exercise

felt good after sitting so long today." She'd removed her cloak in the laundry room and left it there. She now took off her bonnet and added it to the row of her sisters' and Mam's on a shelf inside the kitchen door.

Rosemary was sewing a button on one of the boys' shirts. Technically, there was supposed to be no work done on the Sabbath, but Benjamin was lax in some regards. In a household so large, there was so much to do. Mending seemed a minor infraction, especially while listening to a reading from the Bible.

"Did you speak with him?" her *mam* asked. If she could tell that Lovage had been crying on the walk home, she didn't say.

Lovage pressed her lips together. Her mother was aware that something was going on between her and Marshall, but she didn't understand how serious it was because Lovage didn't want her to know. Her mother didn't need the worry. "*Ya.* Do you know where Ginger is?"

"Gone upstairs, I think. Looking for her favorite shampoo. She seems to believe that Nettie borrowed it, but they disagree." Rosemary held her gaze a moment longer, seeming to debate whether to press her any further on the subject of Marshall, but then let it go and returned her attention to the errant button. "We'll begin putting supper on in a half hour. The boys are out milking and feeding."

"*Ya*, I'll be right back down. The stew left on the woodstove all day will be easy to serve," Lovage said, crossing the kitchen, which smelled deliciously of roasting beef and hearty vegetables. "And there's still plenty of corn bread and cinnamon applesauce and two huge dishes of blueberry crisp that Nettie made yesterday."

Benjamin waited until Lovage left the kitchen and began reading aloud again.

Lovage took the stairs two at time. "Ginger?" she called from the landing at the top.

"In the bathroom!" her sister called back. "I can't find my shampoo in the gold bottle. The one that smells like almonds," she went on. "Do you know where it is? Nettie says she put it back, but I can't find it anywhere."

Lovage stepped into the large family bathroom to find Ginger, still in her black *karrichdaag* dress, on her hands and knees on the floor, her head thrust under the sink. The airy room was painted a buttercup yellow with white trim and smelled of dried herbs and fresh linens hung to dry in the outdoors.

"*Ne*, I've not seen it." Lovage closed the door, because she didn't want anyone else to hear them.

"I know Nettie used it. I hope it's not all gone. I bought that shampoo with my own money..." Ginger chattered on.

Lovage crossed her arms over her chest, still feeling chilled from her walk, though the house was warm. "I don't think I'll be seeing Marshall anymore," she said, her voice sounding strained.

"Oh, Lovey." Ginger came out from under the sink and looked up at her. "I'm so sorry. But it's better that you decide you're not like-minded now, than after you're married, *ya*?"

Lovage shook her head slowly, trying to fight the anger that was abruptly bubbling up inside her. She tamped it down. "I hadn't even agreed to marry him.

But I was going to, because I've fallen in love with him," she said evenly, when she had found her voice again. "But now it's too late, because he found out about the dare. About you daring me to ride home with him that first night. And he's furious. He thinks the only reason I've been seeing him is because of the dare. And…" Tears unexpectedly filled her eyes. "And I think he's broken my heart."

"Oh, Lovey." Ginger stared up at her for a long moment, and then got to her feet, tears springing into her own eyes. "I didn't know… I didn't realize you cared for him that way."

Lovage wiped her eyes with the back of her hand. "It doesn't matter now, because I don't think he loves me anymore. He feels betrayed by me, I think. He thinks I've been toying with his emotions."

Ginger just stood there, tears running slowly down her cheeks.

"Is that why you told people?" Lovage asked softly. "So it would get back to him? So it would cause trouble between us?"

"Ne!" Ginger's pretty little chin quivered. *"Ya…"* She hung her head. "I told some girls at Spence's. We were just talking and—" she took a breath "—it just came out." She rushed forward to take Lovage's hand. "I was so jealous that Marshall picked you, when I'd been trying to get him to ask me out for weeks and… and he was so handsome and the girls were talking about their beaus and…and I was jealous. Jealous of you, of them." She hung her head again. "I knew it might get back to him and I don't think I cared. Oh, Lovey, I'm so sorry. Please forgive me."

Lovage didn't know what to say. She was hurt that her sister had purposefully done something that could have potentially ruined her relationship with her beau, which it probably had. Lovage was upset that Ginger would cave in to the wickedness of gossip; their mother had taught them better. But she was also proud of Ginger for admitting her mistake. For asking for forgiveness, because God forgave His people for their sins. And didn't He teach that His people had to forgive each other, as well?

Ginger squeezed her hand. "And that happened weeks ago, and I didn't think you were serious about him, and I didn't—"

She began to cry in earnest then and Lovage put her arms around her.

"I'm so sorry," Ginger kept repeating. "It was a terrible thing I did. I can't believe I would do such a thing."

"Shh. It's all right," Lovage soothed, hugging her sister. "I forgive you."

"But it's not all right," Ginger wailed. "You said that Marshall doesn't want to see you anymore."

Lovage held tightly to Ginger, resting her head on her sister's shoulder. "Maybe it's for the best," she admitted, her voice quivering.

"*Ne, ne,* it's not. Not if you love him." She drew back and looked up. "If you love him, you should fight for him. You should tell him that he mustn't let this come between you. Not if he loves you."

Lovage shook her head. She was crying again. "But maybe he doesn't," she whispered.

"Don't say that." Ginger set her jaw stubbornly. "Lovey, I know you have never thought any man would fall in love with and want to marry you, but I never believed that. You're the kindest, strongest woman I've ever known and I believe that any man who got to know you would want to marry you. And that goes for Marshall, too. He'd be a fool not to have fallen in love with you."

Lovage pushed hair that had fallen from her prayer *kapp* behind her ear. "It might be too late, Ginger," she said, the fight gone out of her. Now she just felt sad.

"It's not too late." Ginger grabbed her sister's hand. "I'll go to Marshall. I'll tell him exactly what I did and why I did it. I'll tell him how sorry I am and not to blame you." She wiped at her teary eyes. "I'll go right now." She started for the bathroom door.

"*Ne*, you won't." Lovage caught her elbow, stopping her. "You're going to go downstairs with me to set the table for supper and you're not going to speak a word of this to Mam. She doesn't need to worry herself over it."

"But I have to make it right," Ginger said fervently. "I have to go to him!"

"*Ne*, you won't go." Lovage slipped her arm around her sister's shoulders. "I don't want you involved. You've caused enough trouble."

"Oh, Lovey," she breathed, hugging her close. "He'll come to his senses. Marshall is a good man. He'll realize he made a mistake. And mark my words, I'll soon stand at your side on your wedding day."

Chapter Fourteen

Marshall walked into the small room off the tack room in the largest of his barns, where he kept his tools, and halted in the doorway. He gazed at the wall where an assortment of tools hung: hammers, screwdrivers, pliers, wrenches and saws, all sorted and displayed neatly on pegboards.

He pushed his straw hat back a bit and stared at the wall absently. He had no idea why he'd come into the tool room or what he needed.

With a sigh, he walked back out into the main area of the barn. The double doors that led out into the barnyard were open, allowing the crisp autumn air and sunshine to reach the darkest corners of the two-story structure. A couple of his grandmother's Guinea hens, which she gave full run of the farm, scratched in the clean straw outside the feed room. Lu, one of his milk cows, bellowed contentedly and he glanced in her direction. She'd had a run-in with a gatepost the previous week and had sustained a pretty big gash in her shoulder, so he was penning her up inside to keep her quiet. The wound was healing nicely, though, and he figured that in another day or two, he could let her back out with the other cows.

He walked over to the makeshift table he'd made with a piece of plywood and two wooden sawhorses he and Sam had built the previous year. He had removed the screen door from the back porch and laid it out on the table so he could repair or replace the screen. The day before, Petunia had broken through, trying to get to a bucket of scraps Grossmammi had left on the porch for Sam to add to the compost pile. Once Marshall had had a chance to survey the damage more closely, he had decided that the whole screen would have to be replaced. He'd retrieved a roll of galvanized screening from the shed, but that was far as he'd gotten. Now he needed rip out the old and put in the new.

That was the plan, at least, except that Marshall was feeling so scattered he couldn't concentrate on the project. He'd been like this for days. He kept starting tasks only to lose interest or energy. He continually misplaced objects; last night he'd spent ten minutes looking for his favorite pitchfork. The day before it had been his wool beanie. And sometimes he found himself standing somewhere with no idea why he was there or how he'd gotten there.

Petunia bleated and he looked up to see her standing in the open doorway, a leash dangling from the collar around her neck. He shook his head. The goat spent more time running loose than penned up. "Where's Sam?" he asked.

The goat didn't answer. Which made perfect sense. Marshall had been so grumpy for the last week that not even the pet goat wanted to be near him. Sam and Grossmammi had been steering clear of him, too.

Marshall was so miserable without Lovey. He didn't want to admit it at first, but it was true. He'd always been a positive type of person and she'd made him so happy. And now he wasn't. He missed her so much. Missed her smile. Missed talking to her. Missed just sitting beside her on the porch swing, so much that he didn't know which way was up. And he didn't know what to do about it.

Lovey had come to him Sunday after services to talk to him. She'd even admitted she'd gone out with him as a dare, but only that first time. What was he supposed to do with that information? He was so hurt. As he'd told her, he felt foolish. He could only imagine how many people—people he respected—were talking behind his back.

"Come on, girl," Marshall said to the goat. "You shouldn't be running around loose. That fox will eat you."

The goat took a step back and bleated at him again. With a sigh, Marshall moved quickly and grabbed the end of the leash just before Petunia could back out of his reach.

"Gotcha. Come on." He tugged on the leash and led her to her stall, which he and Sam had had to reinforce twice because she kept climbing over it. "Inside you go." He unclipped the leash and gave her a nudge. Then he dropped a soft, mealy apple from a bucket on the floor into a small trough on the other side, through a lit-tle hole in the door. It was another of Sam's inventions.

Petunia bleated one last protest and then began to munch on her apple.

Marshall walked back to the screen door, studied it for a minute and then remembered what he'd gone into the tool room for: shears. He walked to the room, grabbed the shears he used to cut metal and went back out to finish his task. To his surprise, he found his grandmother standing beside the table, studying the door.

"Can't fix the hole?" she asked.

"Ne." He pointed at the door with the shears. "That goat chewed it here. A patch won't hold. Especially not if she tries to get onto the porch again."

Lynita nodded and fingered Toby's leather halter, which was hanging on a post. Petunia had somehow managed to get ahold of it and he'd barely gotten it out of her mouth before she chewed it through. His *grossmammi* lifted it off the post and studied the chew marks.

"Also Petunia," he said irritably.

"It's in a goat's nature to chew things." She peered up at him. She was wearing a dark blue dress, a black prayer *kapp* and a pair of rubber shoes that made her look like she had duck feet. "Just like it's in the nature of a man to sulk."

It was obvious she was referring to him. "I'm not sulking." He set the shears down and started pulling away the rubber spline that held the screen in place in the groove.

She looked up at him. The October sun was bright enough that her transition sunglasses were dark. "Sam and I and the goat have had about enough of it." She hooked her thumb in the direction of Petunia's stall.

He frowned and tugged at the spline, thinking that if he didn't say anything, his grandmother would go away.

"You told me what happened with Lovage. The whole thing with her sister." She gave a wave of dismissal. "Silly girlish nonsense. You've taken it all too seriously."

He went on ripping out the spline; the screen came away with it.

Lynita rubbed the oiled leather of the halter between her fingers. "What you didn't say is what you were going to do about it."

"*Do* about it?" He kept his head down, avoiding her gaze. "Nothing to be done. It's over. She made a fool of me."

"Maybe, but now you're making a worse fool of yourself. First little problem that comes along and you give up?" she tsked. "And you think you're ready for marriage? I've got news for you, *sohn*. You marry any girl and you're going to come up on bigger logjams than this one."

Marshall grabbed the spline with his pliers, pulled too hard and it snapped, leaving a piece still partially embedded in the door. He groaned impatiently. "I thought you'd be happy. You didn't want me to marry Lovage. Faith's the girl you picked for me."

"True enough." Lynita gave a humorless laugh. "But you think I'm no better than that?"

"What do you mean?"

"Look at me," she said.

Slowly he lifted his gaze, until he looked down at her tiny face.

"What kind of grandmother do you think I am, that I'd be so set on a woman for my grandson I'd see him unhappy?" she demanded.

He stared at her, not quite comprehending what she was saying.

"*Sohn*, all I want is for you to live a Godly life and to be happy. For Sam to be happy. Would I have liked it if you had settled on Faith King? *Ya*, but you didn't." She shrugged. "You love that girl from New York? Then you better make this right. Because you won't be happy. You'll never be happy without her. And if *you're* not happy, *I'm* not happy."

His grandmother's words surprised him. He had just assumed she didn't like Lovage. That she was against him marrying her, plain and simple. "Make it right how?" he asked. "She played me."

"*Ya*, maybe. But then she apologized. She cares for you, Marshall, and I think you care for her. You think you looked like a fool when those two girls played a little joke on you?" She waggled her finger at him. "You're going to look a bigger fool if you don't go to that girl, accept her apology and ask her to forgive you for not doing it days ago. Because let me tell you, a girl who can apologize for a mistake, those are few and far between. You better beg her for forgiveness and snatch her up fast."

Marshall set down his pliers. "You really think I should forgive her?"

"I think you better be asking her to forgive *you*." She frowned. And then she reached for the shears on the table and, to Marshall's astonishment, cut the nose-band of Toby's halter right in half.

"What are you doing?" he asked, staring at the piece of tack in her hand.

She handed him the leather halter. "Needs fixing. You know a good harness shop?"

When Marshall pulled his wagon up in front of Benjamin Miller's place, he almost headed right back down the driveway. He was so nervous that his legs were wobbly as he walked through the shop door and the little bell jingled overhead. He was nervous and he was scared. Nervous because he wasn't sure what he was going to say to Lovey. Scared because what if he didn't say the right things? What if he had ruined everything, being so petty?

Over the top of a shelf, he spotted an Amish prayer *kapp*. A young woman was bent over the register, pushing buttons. When he came around the shelf, he saw that it was Lovey and he almost hightailed it for home. Instead, he strode toward her.

"How can I help—" When she saw who it was, she went quiet.

"Lovey," he murmured, sounding much calmer than he felt.

"Marshall," she breathed.

He couldn't look away from her. She was so beautiful in the midmorning light coming from a skylight overhead. Her blue dress was neatly pressed, her white apron and prayer *kapp* pristine. And she was watching him with the green eyes that had captivated him the first time they had met in this very same place.

"What— How can I help you?" she said, awkwardly setting her hands together on the counter.

"I, um…um…" He'd almost forgotten the halter his grandmother had purposely damaged to get him here. He held it up, dangling it from one finger.

She slowly moved her gaze to the piece of tack. "You came because you needed a halter repaired?" She sounded disappointed.

"*Ya*, I…" He closed his eyes. If he didn't find his nerve now, he never would. And as much as he dreaded this conversation, the possibility of living without Lovey was far worse. *"Ne,"* he said firmly, opening his eyes. "This was an excuse. To see you." He dropped it on the counter. "Is Ginger here?"

"*Ya*. Working." She pointed to the door behind the counter. "In the back."

Without asking permission, Marshall pushed through the swinging half door beside the counter. And without permission, he grabbed Lovey's hand and led her to the back, flinging open the door and stepping into the workshop area. Spotting the little sister who had started this whole mess to begin with, seated at a sewing machine, he hollered, "Ginger!"

She looked up, startled, and lifted her foot off the treadle, bringing the needle to a standstill. "Marshall!" She looked scared.

"Go watch the cash register out front," he ordered, already starting to weave his way across the large workroom toward a door in the rear. "I need to talk to your sister privately."

Wide-eyed, Ginger flew off her stool. "Sure." She

hurried toward the door to the shop. "Take as long as you want."

Still holding tightly to Lovey's hand, Marshall flung open the back door. Luckily, it actually led outside.

"Where are we going?" Lovey wasn't exactly protesting, but she was pulling back a little. Maybe trying to take her hand from his.

"Somewhere private," he told her. It had been his first thought to take her to the greenhouse he had built with her brothers. There, they could be alone, unseen, out of earshot. But a secluded place like that wasn't exactly the appropriate place for an unmarried couple to talk. They'd taken care to protect their reputations for three months; that wouldn't change now. Besides, it was too far away. Instead, he led her to the woodshed beside the old dairy barn that Benjamin had converted to his shop. He pulled her inside. The shed had three sides and was stacked to the ceiling with cords of wood for the woodstoves not just in the farmhouse, but the shop, as well. He stepped behind a neatly stacked pile of walnut.

"You should let go of my hand," she said, when they were facing each other.

"I'm not going to do that. Not until I've had my say."

She stood in front of him, her head bowed. But she hadn't taken her hand from his, not since they had stood at the cash register. And that gave him hope.

"Lovey, I came to apologize to you."

She lifted her head suddenly. "You did?" Her eyebrows knitted. They were the same color as her hair and neatly arched so that they framed her gorgeous green eyes. "For what?"

"For the mess I've made of things. For getting so upset about Ginger's dare. For caring what other men thought about me when I should have cared what *you* thought of me. For being embarrassed in front of the guys because of some silliness you had with your sister. Why do I care why you rode home with me from the softball game that night? All that matters is that you did." He looked down at the packed dirt floor of the woodshed; the shed smelled of sweet apple and pungent walnut. "It was foolish and prideful of me not to accept your apology on Sunday, Lovey. On Sunday of all days," he added.

She smiled at him, her gaze seeming to search his. "I'm sorry I didn't tell you about the dare. Once I got to know you, I should have told you." She shrugged. "I guess I forgot about it. It just didn't seem all that important. Not once we started walking out together. Once I began to…care for you."

"You're right, it wasn't," he agreed.

She nibbled on her lower lip. "But I still should have told you."

He took her other hand so that he was clasping both of them. He had so much to say, words he hoped he would have a lifetime to share with her, but for now, he just wanted her to know how he felt. How much he cared for her. "Lovey, from that first day I walked into Benjamin's shop and saw you, I've been in love in you. I know I may seem lighthearted at times, but you have to believe me when I tell you I was never playing games with you. From that first ride home in my buggy when I asked you to marry me, I meant it, then and each and every time. I mean it now."

Tears filled Lovey's eyes and he squeezed her hands.

"I was never playing with your heart, either," she said, taking a step closer to him. Standing so close now that he could feel the warmth of her body and smell her honeysuckle shampoo. "Because I love you, too, Marshall. So, *ya*, I'll marry you. But only if we can marry soon, because I don't think I can wait much longer to be your wife."

And then she shocked him by pressing her mouth to his as she held his gaze. Her kiss was so sweet, so tender, that Marshall's knees felt weak. And just when he feared he wouldn't ever be able to stop kissing her, he heard a peal of giggles. The two of them parted and turned to see Ginger, Nettie, Bay, Tara and Jesse all standing on the far side of the woodpile watching them, and he and Lovey laughed, too.

Epilogue

Four Years Later

"Marshall! Elijah! Dinnertime," Lovage called from the steps of the screened-in porch.

"Coming," Marshall called, striding across the grass toward her. "We were in the orchard." He opened his arms wide to her. "Wait until you see how many Asian pears we have on the trees this year!"

She smiled and felt a little flutter in her chest that had been there since the first day she met him. "Where's Elijah?" she called. "He needs to wash up."

"Coming, Mam!" Their son, almost three years old now, burst out of the orchard and raced past his father.

Marshall scooped up the little boy, who looked just like him but had her green eyes, and plopped him on his shoulders.

"Look at me!" Elijah called. He was dressed just like his father in dungaree jeans, a blue shirt, suspenders and a battered straw hat. He held his little hands high. "Look how big I am, Mam!"

"Just don't fall and crack your head like an egg," she warned. Then she looked to Marshall, who was grinning at her. She felt her cheeks grow warm. The Thursday in November almost four years ago when they had married, she thought she had loved him. But what she felt in her heart now was so much more. Her love for him had grown and matured beyond what she could possibly have imagined.

"Grossmammi and Sam have gone to the Grubers'," Lovage told Marshall. "I think he's sweet on May. He jumps at every invitation he can get out of the family." She held open the screen door for them.

"Where's Elsa?" Marshall asked, flashing her one of his handsome smiles.

"Napping." She sighed. "Thank goodness. I have a pile of ironing to do that's a mile high and she'd have no part of that this morning." She pointed to the table they kept on the porch most of the year round. It was their favorite place to eat. Here they were protected from the bugs and the sun and the wind, but in full view of their orchard, which was flowering now. "I'll be right back with the food." She looked up at their son on his father's shoulders.

Marshall lowered him to the porch floor and Elijah scooted past his mother and into the house.

"Sit down," Lovage told her husband, pointing to his chair at the table on the porch. "I've got everything on a tray to bring out. I just need to grab sugar."

"You want any help?"

"*Ne.* How are *your* hands?" she teased from the kitchen door.

He held them up, palms to her. "I washed at the

barn because I knew better than to come to your table with dirty hands."

Lovage laughed and walked into the kitchen. First, she checked the baby, who, thankfully, was sound asleep in her little cradle Marshall had made with his own hands. Then she picked up a tray with ham sandwiches, broccoli slaw, potato salad and a measuring cup with sugar in it. "Hurry up, Elijah," she called in the direction of the downstairs bathroom. She could hear the water still running. "We'll wait for you."

Using her foot to open the door, Lovage stepped out onto the porch, just in time to see Marshall lift a glass of lemonade to his mouth. He must have poured it for himself from the big glass pitcher in the center of the table.

"*Atch!* Don't—"

But it was too late. He took a big gulp of the fresh lemonade she'd just made, and his eyes got wide as he struggled to swallow.

"You've done it again," she said, trying not to laugh as she set down the tray and raised the measuring cup of sugar. She looked at the pitcher of lemonade and then at her husband. She couldn't help but laugh because his eyes were watering and his mouth puckered.

"I've done it again," he choked. And then he grabbed her by her hand and pulled her against him.

Lovage gave a little squeal. "Marshall, Elijah will—"

"Elijah will what?" Marshall asked, taking the cup of sugar from her and setting it back on the tray. "See that his parents love each other? Or that his mother's trying to poison his father?"

She sighed with happiness as he pulled her close,

and she pressed her hand to his chest to look into his eyes. "I'll have you know, husband, that no one has ever died of unsweetened lemonade."

"*Ne?* Are you sure of that, wife?"

Marshall kissed Lovey on the mouth and she laughed as she tasted the sourness of the lemonade, and the sweetness of her life.

* * * * *

HER NEW AMISH FAMILY

Carrie Lighte

For mothers and mother figures everywhere,
with special thanks to L.D. and S.D. for their help.

And be ye kind one to another, tenderhearted,
forgiving one another, even as God
for Christ's sake hath forgiven you.
—*Ephesians* 4:32

Chapter One

Trina Smith expected to find a gas stove in the little Amish house, but the refrigerator surprised her. She hadn't considered a fridge could be powered by gas, too. Not that she had much use for either appliance; Trina lost her appetite when her mother, Patience, died six months ago of leukemia. When Trina did eat, it was only to nibble a piece of toast or an apple, and even then she had to force herself to swallow. Just like she had to force herself to go to bed at night and then to rise in the morning. She was going through the motions because nothing seemed to come naturally anymore.

She set her suitcase down on the floor of the tiny kitchen. Although no one else was in the house, she tiptoed into the parlor. From- the dark braided rug to the gas lamp to the sparse furniture, the room was exactly as her mother had described, right down to the ticktock of the clock on the wall.

"As loudly as that clock marked off the seconds, I felt like time was standing still," her mother once said.

"I think it was the clock that made me realize nothing would ever change unless I changed it for myself."

And so, when she'd turned eighteen, Patience had left the little house. She left the Amish community in Willow Creek, Pennsylvania. And, most significantly, she left her family, which by that time consisted only of her austere, indifferent, drunkard father, Abe Kauffman. Now Patience's daughter was returning in her place.

Trina walked down the hallway with its bare wooden floor and opened the door to a back room. This would have been where Abe slept. Trina quickly closed the door again. She peeked into the other bedroom, her mother's girlhood room. It was furnished with a wooden chair, a plain dresser and a bed covered with a quilt that reminded Trina of those her mother had stitched for both of them to use in their own house. Trina remembered how, toward the end of her mother's illness, no amount of blankets could keep Patience warm.

Trina shivered and walked back to the kitchen, hoping to find a canister of coffee or tea. The first cupboard she opened contained neatly stacked rows of white dishes. The second held glasses and mugs. The third was empty except for a small gray mouse that scurried to the back corner where it squeezed through a crack.

"Ack!" Trina yelped and slammed the cupboard door.

"What's wrong?" someone asked from behind.

Trina shouted, "Ack!" a second time. Whirling

around, she saw a short, plump, white-haired woman wearing glasses and traditional Amish attire.

Squinting, the woman repeated, "What's the matter?"

"I-I saw a mouse," Trina stuttered. "It startled me."

"I dare say you startled it, too," the woman said with a chuckle and set the basket she was carrying on the table. "I'm Martha Helmuth. I live next door. You must be Trina?"

Martha Helmuth—of course! Trina's mother had often said she would have run away long before she turned eighteen if it weren't for Martha Helmuth, whose door and arms were always open whenever Patience needed a place to escape to or someone to embrace her.

"Yes, I'm Trina. Trina Smith," she confirmed, wondering how Martha knew her name, as her mother hadn't been in contact with anyone from Willow Creek since Trina was born twenty-five years ago.

"*Wilkom* to your home, Trina," the woman said warmly. "The *Englisch* attorney told us you wouldn't arrive until the first of March on Tuesday. I would have stocked the cupboards with staples yesterday if I had known you'd be here today. I hope you don't mind I held on to Abe's spare key. I've been trying to clean up the place for you."

"*Denki,*" Trina said, automatically using one of the many *Pennslyfaanisch Deitsch* words her mother had taught her. "That's very thoughtful of you."

"My, don't you sound just like your *mamm*," Martha replied. "*Kumme* closer, so I can get a better look at you. My eyesight isn't what it used to be."

Trina obediently took a step toward Martha, who reached out and clasped Trina's hands in her own, squinting upward. Ordinarily Trina would have felt too self-conscious to allow a stranger to scrutinize her like this, but knowing how loving Martha had been to her mother, Trina was completely at ease in her presence.

"You're tall, *jah*? And you're a brunette, too. That means your eyes must be blue like your *mamm*'s, as well?"

"*Neh*, they're green like my *daed*'s." Trina immediately regretted mentioning her *Englisch* father, Richard Smith, who'd divorced her mother while she was pregnant with Trina. He'd promised to see Trina, but aside from visiting briefly one Christmas or sending an occasional belated birthday card, he rarely kept in touch. And although he became a successful property developer, he'd never contributed financially to Trina's care; she and her mother had lived in near poverty for most of Trina's childhood. She hadn't even known how to contact him when her mother died. Not that he would have come to the funeral, but Trina thought he should at least have been informed his ex-wife had passed away. She hoped Martha wouldn't ask questions about him.

But the woman just clucked her tongue and said, "I can't get over how much you sound like Patience. Can you sing as beautifully as she did, too?"

Trina was surprised by Martha's praise. The Amish rarely complimented someone's singing voice lest she become proud about her abilities, which were a gift from the Lord. Yet she was pleased the older woman remembered this trait about her mother. Patience had taught Trina several songs from the Amish hymnal, the *Ausbund*. They were sung in German, a language her mother also made sure Trina knew as part of her homeschooling.

"*Neh*, no one has a voice like hers," Trina answered more wistfully than boastfully.

Martha's sunny countenance clouded when she murmured, "I was so sorry to hear of your *mamm*'s passing."

Moved by the sincerity in Martha's voice, Trina blinked back tears. *"Denki."*

Then Martha said, "We heard you were a schoolteacher."

"A preschool teacher, yes," Trina replied, figuring the *Englisch* attorney managing her grandfather's estate must have told Martha she was a teacher. Rather, she *used* to teach preschool until her mother became ill. Then Trina took a semester off to be with her mother as she went through chemotherapy. After Patience died, Trina was so devastated she could hardly take care of herself, much less manage a classroom of rambunctious preschoolers, and she lost her job.

Trina had depleted her savings account helping cover her mother's medical expenses, and she'd racked up a substantial amount of debt, too. For the past four months, she had been living off her credit card. If she hadn't been so impoverished, she never would have come to Willow Creek to claim the inheritance her grandfather bequeathed her. She figured the money she'd receive from selling his house would repay the debt Trina incurred from her mother's hospital bills. It wasn't for her own sake she wanted the restitution, but for her mother's. *Patience's father owed her at least that much.*

For some reason the attorney couldn't explain, Abe Kauffman had attached an odd condition to Trina's inheritance: she had to live in the house for two full months before it would be hers to sell. Otherwise, ownership would go to the Amish *leit* in Willow Creek. Trina suspected the stipulation was her grandfather's way of making a point, but she could only guess what that point might be. Was he trying to punish her somehow because her mother left the Amish? Did he think Trina would be so intimidated by the prospect of living there she'd automatically forfeit the house? If so, he underestimated her determination as well as how desperate her situation had become.

She had no idea how she was going to pay for groceries and other necessities, but at least for now she had a place to live. Her mother had told her Main Street was within walking distance. Maybe there was an *Englisch* business owner in need of temporary help. Trina was certain she'd find a way to earn an income. As challenging as her financial and life circumstances had often been, she relied on the Lord to sustain her. Even during her mother's illness and subsequent death, God had faithfully carried—was *still* faithfully carrying—Trina through her grief. Surely if He could help her survive that kind of loss, He would provide a way for her to earn enough money to cover her living expenses.

"It must have been difficult for you to leave your friends and job to *kumme* here," Martha said. To Trina's delight, the older woman pulled tea and honey from the basket.

"Mmm." Trina's boyfriend had broken up with her around the time her mother got sick, and Trina had spent so much time at the hospital with her mother she'd lost touch with the other teachers from school and acquaintances from church.

"Well, we're glad to have you as our neighbor now," Martha said. "As for that mouse, I'll ask my *groosskin*, Seth, to see what he can do. Seth and his *kinner*, Timothy and Tanner, moved to Willow Creek from Ohio when Seth's wife died. Now they live next door with me."

"Oh, no need to bother him," Trina said. While she was grateful for the offer, she didn't want anyone else visiting her. She and her mother had managed without a man in the house for Trina's entire life. She didn't need one helping her now, especially not an Amish man.

When Seth and his sons returned from hiking along the creek that ran behind their yard and found their house empty, Seth's first impulse was to panic. *What's happened to* Groossmammi? Then he remembered she said she was taking a few items to Abe Kauffman's old house for his granddaughter. Martha had already put fresh sheets on the beds and linens in the washroom, but she wanted to make sure everything else was clean and in place.

Personally, Seth thought Martha was getting too involved, acting as if she were preparing a homecoming for one of her own relatives, of which there were few still surviving. Yes, Martha had gotten to know Abe well in the past few years since he quit drinking. And, yes, she'd told Seth she had loved the young Patience Kauffman like a daughter. But it bothered him she was going to all this trouble for an *Englischer* she'd never met.

It's as if she's completely forgotten what happened with Freeman. Freeman was Seth's older brother who'd left the Amish ten years earlier to marry an *Englisch* nurse, Kristine, who'd tended to him when he was in the hospital after injuring his back during a barn raising. What made the situation doubly painful was that Kristine initially insisted she wanted to join the Amish and had even quit her job in order to work and live in Willow Creek and learn *Deitsch.* But in the end, she'd decided she couldn't leave her career and lifestyle behind, so Freeman had "gone *Englisch.*"

By that time, Seth and Freeman's father—Martha's son—had already died, but their mother was devastated by Freeman's decision. She passed away less than two years later from what the doctor called congestive heart failure, which Seth translated to mean a broken heart. On some level, he blamed his brother's leaving for his mother's death. So, in light of the devastating influence an *Englisch* woman had had on their family, Seth was perplexed that Martha was eager to become involved with another one. But when he voiced his concern, she reminded him what the Bible said about loving one's neighbors. Since he couldn't argue with that, Seth kept his mouth shut, but it troubled him that Martha had wandered off to the little house next door. Her vision was too poor for her to navigate the bumpy yard, even if she did use a cane.

"*Kumme*, Timothy and Tanner. Let's go next door

to see if *Groossmammi* is there. On your feet, not on your bellies."

The four-year-old twins were as imaginative as they were energetic, and they reveled in pretending to be various animals. Today they were acting like snakes, and they'd spent the afternoon trying to slither on their stomachs on the banks by the creek.

"Your boots are too dirty to go indoors, so you may play in the front yard. Stay where I can see you," Seth instructed after they crossed their yard to the only house located within half a mile of them. He bounded up the porch stairs, pulled the door open and, before his eyes adjusted to the light, questioned the figure in the kitchen, *"Groossmammi?"*

But it was a young woman who turned from the stove with a teakettle in her hand. Her long dark hair was drawn up in a ponytail, accentuating the sharp angles of her face. Seth knew the *Englisch* considered thinness attractive, but this young woman was so spindly she appeared fragile. Dark eyebrows framed her big, upturned green eyes and her lips were parted as if she were about to speak, but she didn't say a word.

"I'm sorry if I scared you," he said, feeling self-conscious for entering her home uninvited. "My name is Seth Helmuth and I wondered if my *groossmammi*— my grandmother—is here?"

Before the woman had a chance to answer, Martha stepped into the kitchen. "Ah, Seth, there you are. This is Patience Kauffman's *dochder*, Trina Smith."

When Trina held out her hand, Seth reluctantly took it; shaking hands was an *Englisch* practice, not an Amish one. Her fingers were slender and icy but her grip was firm.

"Hello," she said. Closer up, she appeared more mature and taller than she'd seemed at first glance, and her voice had a melodic quality when she gestured toward the kettle, explaining, "Mrs. Helmuth and I were about to have tea."

"Mrs. Helmuth?" Seth repeated with a chuckle because he wasn't used to hearing his grandmother referred to by that title. The Amish didn't use Mr. or Mrs. to address each other; they simply used first names.

"Dear, you can call me Martha," his grandmother said to Trina before giving Seth the eye. No matter that she could hardly see or that he was twenty-eight-years-old, when Martha gave Seth a certain look, he knew he had better watch his step. She told him, "Trina found a mouse in that cupboard over there. I'd like you to take a look."

Seth obediently crossed the room. In his peripheral vision he saw Trina inch even farther away from the cupboard than she already was. Did she think the mouse was going to fly out and nip her nose? He tugged the door open.

"It's empty, but there's a crack in the wood. Since you saw the mouse in daytime, it was probably really hungry and searching for something to eat," he said. Anticipating Martha's request and eager to get out of the house, he added, "I've got a spare trap. I'll go get it. *Groossmammi*, will you watch the *buwe* in the yard until I get back?"

"I'll keep an eye on them, for what good that will do," Martha joked. "You know what my vision is like.

When we're inside or they're close by, it's not difficult watching the *buwe*, but when they're running around outdoors…"

"I'll go watch them if you'll stay here and listen for the teakettle," Trina offered, following Seth to the door. "Just give me a call when it whistles."

Seth hesitated to leave his sons in Trina's charge, but since he'd only be gone for a few minutes, he said in *Englisch* to the boys, "Timothy, Tanner, this is, er, this is Miss Smith. She's going to stay with you while I go get something from our house."

"Miss Smith?" she repeated, pointedly imitating the tone Seth had taken when she referred to Martha as Mrs. Helmuth. "My name is Trina. It starts with the letter T, just like Timothy and Tanner."

The boys raced to her side. "Do you want to see something?" they asked in *Englisch*.

Seth hurried home, grabbed the trap, a jar of peanut butter and a spoon, and then raced back to Trina's house. As he crossed the yard, he spotted the boys and Trina taking turns jumping over a partially frozen mud puddle. Recently the deacon's sons had returned from a family trip to a popular Amish vacation destination in Pinecraft, Florida, and they'd filled Timothy's and Tanner's heads with visions of alligators. Ever since then, the boys pretended puddles were swamps where the toothy creatures hid. They'd created a game in which they had to leap over these so-called swamps without falling in and being bitten. So far, they'd been successful, and it looked as if Trina was holding her own, too. Satisfied they'd all be fine, Seth went inside.

"The tea will be ready soon. Have a cup with us,"

Martha coaxed him as he smeared peanut butter on the trap. "Trina is a lovely *maedel*. She's a preschool teacher, you know."

"*Jah*, I know," Seth replied. "You've told me almost every day since the attorney told you, *Groossmammi*."

"You ought to consider hiring her to watch the *buwe*, then. She'd be perfect."

Seth glanced out the window. He had to admit, he would have expected someone as thin as Trina to be lethargic but she was matching Timothy and Tanner's energy levels.

"*Neh*, I don't think that would be right. She's *Englisch*."

Martha snickered. "What difference does that make? She seems to know plenty of *Deitsch* words and the *buwe* are almost fluent in *Englisch*. Besides, they'll formally learn *Englisch* as soon as they enter school. This will help them along."

"It's not that," Seth hedged. Even if he wasn't already wary of *Englisch* women because of Freeman's wife, he would have been reluctant to hire one to watch the boys. Seth owned a leather shop in town and he'd seen how *Englisch* customers behaved. In his opinion, the parents were too permissive with their children, allowing them to do and say whatever they wanted.

"Then what is it? Being *Englisch* isn't contagious, you know!"

Martha was so shrewd about his bias that Seth had to try a different approach. "You told me the attorney said she only has to stay here for two months. After that, she'll move on."

"Which is exactly why you should hire her." Martha

was really digging her heels in about this. "It's only a little over two months until school lets out and then there will be three or four *meed* vying for the opportunity to earn money taking care of the *buwe*."

"That's right. It's only a couple more months. We can manage until then," Seth insisted. He supposed if worse came to worst and Martha really couldn't handle the boys at home, he could take them to work with him.

"The sooner you get someone to watch the *kinner,* the sooner you'll have an opportunity to visit the matchmaker and begin courting. You won't have to stay home every night in order to give me a break from minding the *buwe*."

Clearly Martha was appealing to Seth's expressed desire to remarry. It had been four years since Eleanor died in childbirth and he was ready to consider courting again.

"I've waited this long. A couple more months isn't going to make a big difference," Seth replied, but his resolve was wavering.

Martha pointed to the window. "Listen to how much fun they're having out there."

Seth glanced out at them. Just then Trina attempted to hurdle the puddle, but Timothy stepped into her path. Trying to avoid him, she veered and lost her footing upon landing. She fell backward, splintering the puddle's thin layer of ice and landing on Tanner, who hadn't given her enough time to clear it before he jumped over it, too. Seth charged out of the house and down the steps. By then the boys had untangled their legs and arms from Trina's and they were pulling on her hands. Instead of helping her up they were stretching her forward and she struggled to rise.

"Stop that!" he yelled as he noticed Trina's leg was bent awkwardly beneath her. The boys immediately released Trina's hands and she dropped backward into the puddle again.

Thudding onto her backside in the mud a second time, Trina got the wind knocked out of her. Before she had a chance to catch her breath or unfold her leg, Seth slid one arm under her knees, wrapped the other around her waist and swooped her up. As he carried her to the porch, Trina's cheek brushed against his woolen overcoat and she closed her eyes. Never had she felt so cared for by a man and she was overwhelmed by his chivalrous gesture.

"Are you alright?" he asked after gingerly placing her on the porch steps. He leaned forward and looked into her eyes. His own eyes were gunmetal gray, a few shades paler than his sons' baby blues but just as big and round. They'd also inherited Seth's curly blond locks, although his hair was more waves than curls. *Wholesome* was the clichéd word people used to describe anyone who lived in the countryside, but in Seth's case, Trina found the adjective to be accurate. Not merely because of his looks, but because of the honest quality of his concern.

"I'm fine, just a little wet," she replied, embarrassed. She could feel her skirt clinging to her skin.

"I'm sorry," Timothy said mournfully. "I shouldn't have stepped in front of you."

"And I shouldn't have stepped in back of you," Tanner chimed in.

The boys looked so pitifully sad Trina forgot about her own discomposure. "It's nobody's fault but my own. I'm such a klutz," she said, rolling her eyes. When the boys didn't smile, she assured them, "I didn't break any bones. My skirt got a little dirty, but I'll wash it and it will be as good as new."

Seth looked dubious. "It will get clean, but I doubt it will be as *gut* as new. Abe's house doesn't have an *Englisch* washing machine, you know."

Now Trina couldn't tell if he was speaking matter-of-factly or tongue in cheek. "I'm familiar with Amish wringers," she replied. She was familiar with them in the sense that her mother had described how they worked—Trina hadn't actually used one herself.

"Even so—" Seth started to say, but he was interrupted by a muted cry from inside the house.

"Fire! Help! Help!" It was Martha.

"*Buwe,* stay here!" Seth commanded. He vaulted past Trina and was up the stairs in two strides.

Chasing close behind, Trina peered through the smoky room to see Martha doubled over, coughing, as something burned atop the stove. Seth clicked off the burner, grabbed the flaming item by an edge and tossed it into the sink. Then he turned the faucet on full force.

While he was dousing the flame, Trina led Martha out of the house.

"*Groossmammi,* are you okay?" Tanner asked. The crease between his eyebrows made him appear like a wizened old man.

Martha nodded but she was still coughing and couldn't answer. Trina and the boys eased her into a sitting position on the stairs and then Trina darted back into the house to fetch a glass of water.

Seth moved away from the sink. "Looks like my *groossmammi* started a towel on fire, but I don't see any other damage. Is she alright?"

"Yes, I think so. She just needs to catch her breath." Trina filled the glass and they both stepped outside, leaving the door open behind them.

By then, Martha was no longer gasping. "I spilled water on the stovetop when I was pouring tea, so I tried to dab it up with the towel," she explained. "I was certain I had turned off the burner first."

"*Neh,* you had turned it *up,*" Seth said.

"Ach! Well, that explains how the tea towel caught fire." Martha's eyes were watering and Trina didn't know if she was crying or recovering from the sting of the smoky air. Suddenly Martha seemed tiny and frail as she prayed aloud, "*Denki,* Lord, for keeping us safe."

"It's cold out here and you're trembling," Trina noticed. "Please come back inside and we'll have that tea now."

"Alright," Martha agreed. "Seth, *kumme* get the woodstove started, please."

Trina took Martha by the arm and assisted her up the stairs and into the parlor. She expected the others to come in, too, but when she returned to the kitchen to retrieve the tea, she heard Seth on the porch warning the boys not to leave the front yard or go near the puddle.

"They're probably cold, too. They should come in," she said from the doorway.

"*Neh*, their boots are muddy." Seth waved his hand. "They're fine outside. Here in Willow Creek, we believe fresh air is *gut* for *kinner*."

Once again Trina wasn't sure what he meant by his remark. She replied, "We believe fresh air is good for children in Philadelphia, too."

"*Jah*, but there's less of it in Philadelphia than there is here, so our *kinner* can stay outside longer." Seth grinned widely at her before he began filling his arms with logs from the woodpile stacked next to the porch stairs, and since she didn't disagree, Trina chuckled, too.

As she and Martha were sipping tea and Seth was lighting the fire, the older woman said, "Imagine what would have happened if you weren't here!"

Seth stood up from where he'd been kneeling in front of the woodstove and brushed his hands against his pants. His grandmother had a valid point and he knew she was waiting for him to acknowledge defeat. "Okay, okay, you win," he said to Martha.

Trina glanced at Martha and then at him, curious.

"I, uh, well, we wanted to ask if you'd be available to watch the *buwe* while you're in Willow Creek," he stuttered. "As a job, I mean. You'd be paid."

"You could watch them at our house, so I could help and we'd get to know each other better," Martha added, beaming again.

Trina hesitated. Although the will stipulated she had to live in Willow Creek, she hadn't intended to become very involved with the Amish—or the *Englisch*, for that matter—during her residence. She'd planned to mostly keep to herself. But the boys were well behaved and fun, and after today's incident she hated to think of Martha trying to manage them on her own. Still, she had her misgivings about Seth. He wasn't as strict as she imagined an Amish father might be, based on her mother's depiction of Abe, yet there was something about his attitude toward her that gave her pause. She couldn't discern whether his comments were meant to be comical or condescending. But Martha had been so helpful to Trina's mother that it would almost be like honoring her mother's memory to show Timothy and Tanner the same kind of care. And she did need the money...

"I'm only going to be here for a couple of months," she warned. As soon as her two months were up and she sold the house, she was moving back to the city.

Seth replied, "That's all the time we'll need your help. After school lets out in late May, we'll hire one of the graduating *meed* to help. But right now, no one else is available to watch them."

"Okay, it's a deal," Trina said, but this time she didn't hold her hand out to shake on it. She was already catching on to Willow Creek's Amish traditions.

Martha leaned on Seth's arm, slowly shambling across the barren ground to their house while the boys galloped ahead. If he didn't know better, he'd have suspected his grandmother deliberately started the fire to scare him into asking Trina to mind the boys.

"Why are you moping?" Martha asked him.

"I'm not moping. I'm thinking."

"When you're thinking with a frown on your face, I call that moping."

Seth laughed. "I hope I made the right decision by asking Trina to watch after the *buwe*."

"Pah!" Martha sputtered dismissively. "It's not as if you've asked her to marry you, Seth. If things don't work out, you can tell her as much. But I think they will. If she's anything like her lovely *mamm* was as a *maedel*, you won't find a better woman to care for the *kinner*."

Seth bit his tongue so he wouldn't ask the obvious question: if Trina's *mamm* was so lovely, why did she go *Englisch*? Nor did he say that the best woman to care for the *kinner* was their *mamm*.

Eleanor's pregnancy had been an easy one, especially considering she was pregnant with twins, so when she'd passed away during childbirth, it had come as a shock to Seth. Eleanor, however, had seemed to have a sense of foreboding about her delivery.

Once, shortly before the boys were born, she'd whispered to Seth as they cuddled on the sofa, "If anything happens to me, please choose a wife who will take *gut* care of the *bobblin*."

"If anything happens to you, I'm going to look for a wife who doesn't burn the meatloaf. Or chide me when I track mud across the kitchen floor. Or say *lecherich* things," Seth joked, trying to make light of her sentiment.

Usually she played along with Seth's teasing, but this time Eleanor had scolded, "Seth, I'm serious." She'd rubbed her rotund stomach counterclockwise, repeating, "Marry someone who will take *gut* care of the *kinner*."

Although Seth knew it was irrational, he often wondered if he had taken Eleanor's sentiment seriously, could he have alerted the midwife to her concern and somehow prevented her death? He felt guilty for not paying closer attention to what Eleanor had said, especially since she'd ordinarily been such a calm and practical woman.

In fact, it was her practicality that had made Seth decide to court and marry her. The pair had been friends since they were children and Eleanor was sensible, forthright and humble. While the love they shared was more comfortable than ardent, it had been rich and deep. No, Seth couldn't claim he and Eleanor had ever "fallen in love," like Freeman had with Kristine, but look at all the hurt that kind of love had caused his family. Passionate emotional attachment wasn't important to Seth; compatibility, commitment and common sense were. He and Eleanor had found those qualities in each other and their marriage had been a strong and happy one.

With Martha caring for the boys after Eleanor's death, Seth felt little need to remarry at all, which was why he hadn't courted anyone in the over four years since Timothy and Tanner were born. But now, given his *groossmammi*'s declining vision, he understood the wisdom in Eleanor's request. The boys needed someone to care for them. Not just a teenage *maedel* and certainly not just an *Englischer* for a few months. They needed a permanent mother figure.

As Martha tottered along beside him, Seth figured maybe his grandmother was right; now that Trina would be watching the boys he'd have more time to work on finding a wife. Meanwhile, he hoped Trina's

Englisch ways wouldn't unduly influence his sons. Seth was going to have to keep a close eye on her.

The prospect should have troubled him more than it did. Maybe he'd let his guard down because Martha had taken an instant liking to Trina, but Seth was oddly amused by the skinny woman with mischievous eyes and a musical voice, and he rather enjoyed trying to get a rise out of her. How much influence could she have on his family in two months anyway?

Chapter Two

After Seth and Martha left, Trina washed the cups and began unpacking her suitcase. It didn't take long. By the time she moved out of her apartment, she'd either sold or given away nearly all of her belongings and she only had a few outfits that were suitable to wear in Amish country. It wouldn't be appropriate to dress like the Amish, but out of respect for the people she was living among she decided she'd wear dresses or skirts instead of slacks or jeans. Unfortunately, she only owned one dress and three skirts—one of which was now very dirty.

The only nonclothing items she'd brought were a framed photograph and her cell phone and solar battery charger. The photo was of her and her mother and it had been taken on a beach when they went to Cape Cod for a rare week of vacation the summer before Patience got sick. Trina had other photos saved digitally, but it was this printed one she cherished the most. In it, they were both smiling, healthy and tan, and their cheeks touched as they leaned together in a sideways embrace. One rainy afternoon as Trina and her mother strolled through the art galleries, admiring the paintings and sculptures they couldn't afford, they'd come across an ornate picture frame. Handmade from small pieces of aqua, green and blue sea glass the artist found on the bayside, the frame reminded Trina of the ocean itself. That Christmas, Trina's mother presented her with the frame as a gift. Trina never knew how she managed to pay for it or sneak away to buy it, but combined with the photo it held, it was Trina's one and only prized possession.

She considered keeping the photo on the dresser in her room, so it could be the first thing she saw when she awoke, but then she decided she wanted to put it in a more visible area, somewhere she could see it all the time and draw strength from the memory. She carried it into the parlor and placed it prominently on the end table next to the sofa.

Then she considered where to store her cell phone. It wasn't as if she'd be receiving any calls. Trina had moved to a new suburb shortly before her mother was diagnosed with cancer. She was acquainted with other teachers there but she hadn't begun to make friends. And the church she attended was so big no one there was likely to notice her absence. Yet, knowing she'd probably need to be in touch with a realtor as well as the estate attorney her grandfather hired, Trina had purchased a solar panel charger to power her phone. She decided to set it up on the windowsill in Abe's old bedroom, where it would get plenty of sunshine but be out of her way.

Exhausted from cleaning her apartment, packing

up and traveling, Trina changed into her nightgown. She slipped beneath the quilt, which smelled of fresh winter air—Martha must have hung it on the clothesline—and shut her eyes, thinking of how protected she felt when Seth carried her to the porch. Within minutes she drifted into a deep slumber for the first time in over a year.

She woke to a banging on the door. Disoriented, she blinked several times at her surroundings. It was morning. She was in Willow Creek. The fire must have died out because the floor made her feet ache with cold. She wrapped the quilt around her shoulders and shuffled to the door. Peeking out the window, she saw Seth pacing back and forth. *Oh no! I was supposed to be at his house by seven forty-five so he could review the rules for the children with me.*

"It's eight o'clock," Seth said in greeting. "Look at you, you're not even dressed yet."

Trina pulled her quilt tighter around her shoulders. She understood the Amish didn't place a high value on physical appearance, except for tidiness and modesty. She could only imagine how rumpled she appeared. "I'm so sorry. I must have overslept."

"I thought you *Englischers* relied on alarm clocks."

Rankled, she cracked, "I figured the Amish rooster would wake me."

Something resembling a grin crinkled the skin around Seth's eyes, but he didn't allow it to move to his lips. "Just *kumme* to my house as soon as you can."

She pulled on her clothes, brushed her hair into a ponytail and quickly scrubbed her teeth before running across the yard. When she arrived, she apologized again. "I really am sorry I'm late. I didn't mean to oversleep."

Seth seemed less cantankerous now. "It's alright. Fresh air can tucker a person out." There it was again; the kind of comment that made her wonder if he was joking or not.

"*Guder mariye*, Trina," Martha said as she entered the room, her hands extended in front of her so as not to bump into anything. It seemed she only used her cane outdoors. Timothy and Tanner scooted around their grandmother, calling out their greetings, as well. Their curls bounced as they hopped up and down, unable to contain their excitement.

"*Guder mariye,*" Trina replied to the three of them.

"We're going to show you the creek today," Tanner announced.

"*Neh*, I don't want you by the creek," Seth contradicted. "It's too dangerous. The current is too strong."

The boys looked crestfallen but they didn't argue. Didn't they tell Trina they'd been to the creek just yesterday? It hadn't rained, so the water couldn't be any deeper. Then she realized Seth must not trust her with the children yet. She understood. In time, he'd change his mind.

"I'm sure we'll do something else that's just as interesting," Trina said.

"*Jah*, so will you and I," Martha chimed in. "When they take a nap, you can look through my fabric to choose what you want to make a new skirt since yours became stained yesterday."

Trina appreciated the offer, but she had no idea how

to make a skirt. "Oh, that's alright. The stain will come out. My skirt is still wearable."

"With the way you'll be running after the *buwe,* it won't hurt to have an extra one," Martha said. "If it's the material you're worried about, don't be concerned. I have an assortment of colors. Blue, green, even burgundy. I haven't been able to see well enough to sew for ages. It will be *gut* to know the fabric isn't going to waste."

"I don't think it's the color of the fabric she's worried about, *Groossmammi*," Seth quietly pointed out. "The *Englisch* don't sew like we do."

Trina bristled. Why did Seth constantly call attention to how different the *Englisch* were from the Amish? "Don't be *lecherich*. Plenty of *Englischers* sew their own clothes." She used a couple of *Deitsch* words to emphasize she wasn't completely unaware of Amish culture.

"And you're one of them?" Seth pressed.

Trina felt her cheeks burning. Her mother had tried to teach her to sew, but Trina never had the inclination. "Yes, I can sew my own clothes. I can hem them, anyway."

Seth snorted. "It's not the same thing."

"Just how much do you know about sewing clothes?" Martha chastised him. "As fine as your leather stitching is, I have yet to see you make your own britches, my dear *bu*."

Trina's gratitude for the woman surged. It was obvious Seth wouldn't contend with Martha. He set his hat on his head and buttoned his wool coat.

"The *buwe*'s chore for the day is to rid the front yard

of sticks," he instructed Trina. "And they must lie down for an hour in the afternoon, whether they sleep or not."

"Don't worry," Martha said, answering for Trina. "I'll fill Trina in on everything she needs to know. Now, since you were so worried about being late, you'd better skedaddle."

After the door closed behind Seth, Trina released her breath. In her experience as a teacher, the parents were often more difficult to manage than the preschoolers were. *I should tell Seth that's* one *way the* Englisch *and the Amish are alike,* she thought, chuckling to herself.

Because Seth was in a hurry, he'd forgotten to put on his gloves so he blew on his fingers as he walked to town. He could have taken the buggy, but that would have meant leaving his shop several times a day to make sure the horse was watered, fed and dry—and it looked like rain. Or snow. It was difficult to tell at this time of year.

Besides, he liked the walk and the shop was only about a mile and a half away. He used the time to mentally prepare for work and ask the Lord to guide him in his interactions with the customers, especially the *Englisch* ones. When Seth moved from Ohio to Willow Creek, all the stores on Main Street were taken. He'd made it his goal to one day open a shop there, because that's where most of the *Englisch* customers and tourists came through town. While he had a healthy business selling harnesses and other horse leatherworks to the Amish, the *Englisch* had little need for such items.

Instead, they wanted custom-designed purses, belts and wallets, and they wanted them at their convenience.

Since the workshop at his home was slightly off the beaten path, Seth had recognized that, in order to increase business, he had to meet his customers' needs—or their preferences—and he watched and waited for one of the Amish business owners to relinquish their prime real estate on Main Street. When one of the bigger spaces recently opened up, Seth jumped at the chance to lease it. It was a stretch for him financially, but the space was so big it allowed him to have a workshop in the back in addition to the storefront where he could display and sell his wares. He figured in time the sales would be worth the initial investment.

Now that I'm paying Trina to watch the buwe, *I'll have an added expense I hadn't counted on until school lets out,* he thought.

As he contemplated his sons' care, Seth asked the Lord to watch over Trina as she cared for the boys. Once again he second-guessed his decision to hire her. Martha seemed to think highly of Trina, but then, his grandmother had an unusual gift for making people feel welcome and needed—that's how Seth felt when he moved in with the boys, who were only newborns at the time. What would he have done without Martha's help? He supposed the least he could do now was make more of an effort to show a modicum of hospitality toward Trina, since Martha had shown an abundance toward him.

He was so lost in thought that when he arrived at his shop, he was startled to find three *Englisch* women standing on the doorstep, peeking through the window into the store. In his experience, the *Englisch* customers tended to be more impatient than the Amish. It seemed to him *Englischers* were often in a rush and they expected others to be in a rush, too, whereas Seth felt if he couldn't do a job both quickly and well, he'd rather do it well than quickly.

"We were afraid you were closed for the day!" one of them said.

"*Neh*, just for the first ten minutes," Seth replied with a grin as he keyed into the shop. He found humor often kept him from becoming too stressed and his customers appreciated it, too. Especially the *Englisch* ones, who often seemed taken aback initially, as if they were under the impression the Amish were humorless dullards. But they usually ended up smiling back.

Sure enough, the women giggled as Seth held the door open for them. Soon after, a few more customers trickled in. Seth noticed one of them discreetly lifting a cell phone and he knew he was being photographed. He had half a mind to post a sign forbidding cell phones and cameras in the store, but he decided if people weren't going to voluntarily respect his beliefs and privacy, it was useless to try to *make* them do so.

By the end of the day he was relieved to walk home and when he went through the door, the boys bounded into the kitchen to greet him as they usually did.

"Guess what, *Daed*," Tanner said. "Trina taught us an *Englisch* song."

"And we had lots and lots of vegetation for dinner," Timothy claimed.

"You mean vegetables," Seth corrected him.

"*Neh*, it was vegetation."

Just then Trina entered the room and said above the boys' heads, "*Hungerich* bucks need a lot of vegetation to stay strong."

Ah, so that was it. Seth had to smile. He and Martha had a difficult time getting the boys to eat any vegetables except potatoes and corn. If Trina had been able to get the boys to eat more greens by appealing to their interest in animals, that was terrific. But he drew the line at teaching them *Englisch* songs.

"*Buwe,* please go into the other room while I talk to Trina," he said. After they scampered away, he asked Trina how her day went.

"It was *gut,*" she said. He noticed she was using *Deitsch* words more frequently already. "The *buwe* picked up the sticks in the front yard and half the sticks on the west side of the house, too. They sure have a lot of energy."

Seth nodded before getting to the point. "They said you taught them an *Englisch* song. May I hear it?"

He saw a look of confusion pass over Trina's face before her cheeks broke into a blush. He regretted embarrassing her, but he had to be sure the boys weren't being taught songs about superheroes or other ideas that were contrary to Amish beliefs.

"It's more like a poem than a song. At least it was the way I presented it," she said and her usually mellifluous voice was marked with defiance.

"All the same, I'd like to hear it."

Trina exhaled audibly and then began, "One, two, buckle my shoe…" She continued reciting the verse until she got to the number ten, at which point she said, "That's as high as we went. I was trying to teach them how to count while they were doing yard work."

"I see," Seth said. He'd been taught that same verse as a child and he felt as foolish as he'd obviously made Trina feel. Still, he wasn't sorry he asked her to tell him how the song went. "We didn't have time this morning to discuss what kinds of activities are appropriate for Amish *kinner*, so I just wanted to be sure—"

"There you are, Seth," Martha interrupted from the doorway. "It smells like supper is about ready, isn't it, Trina?"

Trina peeked inside the oven. "*Jah,* it's bubbling," she confirmed, removing the pan from the rack and setting the chicken-and-cheese casserole on a hot pad on the table. "You should let it cool a bit before you eat it. And don't forget the asparagus. It's steaming on the back burner."

"I thought you were going to stay for supper. You know we made plenty," Martha said.

So much for demonstrating hospitality; Seth knew he was the reason Trina changed her mind about supping with them. "*Jah,* you should stay," he echoed.

"*Denki,* but I need to be on my way. I'll arrive a few minutes early tomorrow, Seth, so we'll have plenty of time to review your list of restrictions about the *kinner* with me."

"There's no *list,*" he mumbled feebly, but Trina didn't seem to hear as she zipped her jacket. Unfortunately, Martha was listening intently, and from the look on her face, Seth was going to get an earful about his attitude tonight after the boys were in bed.

Completely humiliated, Trina slinked home. After spending most of the morning and afternoon outside with the boys, her appetite was raging in a way she hadn't experienced since before her mother took ill. But there'd been no way she was going to sit down at a table with that smug, controlling Seth Helmuth. She respected that Amish people abided by their church's *Ordnung*, and without knowing what it said herself, it was possible she might have accidentally violated one of its precepts. But she'd felt like a criminal when Seth demanded she recite the song like that. She hoped he felt utterly ridiculous when he heard how it went!

In the kitchen, she removed her jacket and hung it on the peg beside the door. Almost immediately she took it back down and put it on again. It was freezing in there. Now she was cold as well as hungry. How was she going to go grocery shopping? The stores within walking distance closed by the time Seth returned home and she didn't have a car. What was she going to subsist on? Water and Willow Creek's superior fresh air?

She went into the parlor and lit a fire in the woodstove. Then she looked around for her handbag, which contained half a packet of crackers with peanut butter she'd bought at the train station. When she found it, she gobbled a cracker and then brought the rest into the kitchen where she put the kettle on to fix a cup of the tea Martha had left for her. Once the water came to a boil, Trina filled a mug, put the crackers on a plate and sat down next to the woodstove.

Even with her jacket on and the warm cup in her hands, she was shivering, so she retrieved the quilt from her bed and wrapped herself in it before returning to her chair. The silence was punctuated only by the ticking clock and Trina understood why her mother had felt like time stood still in Willow Creek. Trina had only been there two days and it already seemed like a lifetime. It was enough to make her want to pack her bags right then.

Of course, Trina's mother had had a far more significant reason to leave Willow Creek behind: Abe Kauffman. But as miserable as her mother's life with Abe had been, she'd rarely spoken against him in detail. Patience had only described how, after her own mother died, her father changed.

"Mind you, he never lifted a hand against me," she told Trina. "But he wouldn't lift a hand toward me, either. Not to help me, not to embrace me. He hardly spoke a word to me. It was as if I didn't exist—as if I had died when my mother did. All that existed was his bottle of beer. So, in a way, I felt as if he'd died, too. At eight years of age, I felt orphaned."

No wonder her mother had never wanted to return to this house. When Trina was young and used to ask her mother if they could visit Willow Creek, Patience's face would cloud with sadness as she said no, it was better for everyone if they didn't. "We're happy right where we are, aren't we?" she'd ask Trina, and Trina always answered yes because it was true. As long as they were together, they were happy. Trina sniffed as she realized her mother would never be with her again. Did that mean Trina would never be happy again, either? She knew she couldn't allow herself to dwell on such thoughts or she'd never make it through her time in Willow Creek, so she prayed the Lord would give her peace and then she went to draw a bath.

But before she reached the washroom, there was

a knock at the door. In the kitchen, Trina peered through the door's glass pane to see Seth holding a plate wrapped in tin foil in one hand and Martha's basket from yesterday in the other.

"Yes?" she said coldly after opening the door.

"My *groossmammi* sent these for you," he replied, lifting the items in her direction.

Since they were from Martha, Trina couldn't refuse them. "Please tell her I said *denki*." She reached for the plate but Seth held on to the basket, stepping into the kitchen uninvited.

"How's the mouse situation?" he asked. "Did the trap do the trick?"

"I don't know. I haven't checked."

He set the basket on the table, crossed the room and pried the cupboard open. To Trina's relief, he announced, "*Neh*, nothing yet." Then he closed the cupboard and rubbed his arms. "Seems a little cold in here. I can show you how to get a *gut* fire roaring if you'd like."

Trina didn't know why he was suddenly being so congenial, but she wished he'd leave. Not just because she was still miffed, but because the aroma of the meal he brought was making her feel even more famished and she could hardly wait to eat. "Actually, I'm rather warm," she said, tossing her ponytail.

"I imagine you are," Seth replied, his lips twitching. "Wearing a quilt has that effect on people."

Trina rolled her eyes and shrugged the quilt from her shoulders. She folded it into a misshapen square, which she held in front of her stomach to muffle the growling sound it was making. "I suppose I could add another log to the fire."

"I'll grab a couple more from outside, since the bin in the parlor is probably low," Seth volunteered and exited the house before Trina could object.

As soon as he left, Trina lifted an edge of the tinfoil from the plate and dug into the casserole with a fork. When Seth returned, her mouth was full, but she mumbled, "*Denki* for bringing those in, but I've gone camping before, so I'm capable of stoking the fire myself."

"Is that what you think being Amish means? It's like going camping?"

Why was he suddenly defensive again? "No, that's what I think *lighting a fire* is like," Trina clarified after swallowing. "If you've built one outside, you can build one inside."

"Actually, that's not necessarily true. *Kumme*, let me show you."

She reluctantly put her supper down and went into the parlor with him.

"Ah," he said when he opened the door to the woodstove. "Look at this."

Trina crouched down beside him. She watched his hands gesturing as he spoke, oddly aware those were the same strong hands that had lifted her the day before.

"You've done alright with the kindling, but you've piled the logs too tightly together," he explained, not unkindly. "There needs to be a little room between them for the oxygen to get through. Otherwise, the logs won't take and the flame will burn out like it has now. It's better if you stack them like this."

As she listened to him, it occurred to Trina he would make a good teacher. She glanced sideways at his face, noticing the reddish undertone to his short beard. She wondered if it would feel like his wool coat had felt against her cheek. Suddenly her skin burned and she knew she couldn't attribute its warmth to the fire now crackling in the stove.

"Denki," she said, standing up.

Seth rose, too, saying, "I want to apologize if I embarrassed you when I asked you to tell me the song you taught the *buwe.*"

If Trina's face hadn't felt hot before, it would have now under Seth's earnest gaze. "It's alright," she conceded, and suddenly, it was.

She realized if a virtual stranger—especially one who had traditions that were different from her own—came to watch her children, she'd give them guidelines about what the kids could and couldn't do. In fact, when she used to babysit as a teenager, parents always told her what the house rules were. It wasn't personal, she'd just taken it that way because of Seth's comments about her being *Englisch.* But maybe she was the one who was being defensive because he was Amish, instead of vice versa. Or maybe it was a little of both.

"I respect the way you're raising your *kinner* and I want to instruct the *buwe* according to your guidelines," she said. "Do you have a few minutes to talk about that now?"

"Jah." Seth grinned, and his jawline visibly softened as he sank into the sofa.

First, Trina hoped she put Seth's mind at ease by telling him she shared his strong Christian faith. Then they briefly discussed his expectations of the boys as well as their interests and the activities they were forbidden to do. Nothing Seth mentioned seemed unduly prohibitive or out of the ordinary to Trina, but she was glad they'd had the discussion anyway.

"I'll see you tomorrow morning, then?" Seth confirmed as he was leaving.

Did Trina catch a note of uncertainty in his voice? "*Jah*, I'll be there bright and early at seven forty-five," she assured him.

"Then I'll be sure to set the rooster for six forty-five," he said over his shoulder before closing the door, and Trina laughed in spite of herself.

Her supper had cooled but she didn't care. The casserole was so delicious she couldn't believe she'd made it herself—well, with advice from Martha. Trina never had much interest in cooking, aside from a few traditional Amish desserts her mother taught her to make. Usually by the time she returned home from work she was so hungry and worn out she would just to throw a meal into the microwave.

She was pleased to see the basket contained eggs, milk and half a loaf of bread. Martha was as thoughtful and generous as Trina's mother had said she was. Her tummy full, Trina washed the dishes and before she got ready for bed, she retrieved her cell phone and set its alarm. She didn't want to be late again, especially now that she and Seth were on better terms with each other.

Once he'd cleared the air with Trina, Seth felt more comfortable having her mind the boys, who relished their time with her. Each evening when he came to the door, they regaled him with anecdotes about the adventures they'd had with her during the day. And although his grandmother had always been lively, she seemed even sprightlier now. Seth couldn't tell whether that was because Trina had taken over the boy's care, or because Martha enjoyed having the company of another woman, but he was pleased the arrangement was off to a good start.

On Saturday he woke to the racket of raindrops pummeling the rooftop and he eased out of bed. After milking the cow, he collected eggs from the henhouse. Usually this was Tanner and Timothy's responsibility, but it was raining too hard to allow them to go outside.

When Seth returned to the house, Tanner was standing in the kitchen, knuckling his eyes sleepily. "*Daed*, is it time for Trina to *kumme* yet?"

"She doesn't *kumme* until you and your brother have changed into your clothes, eaten your breakfast and brushed your teeth. I already collected the *oier* because it's raining and I don't want you to go outside today unless it stops."

"We're teaching Trina how to collect *oier*, too, but she's afraid to put her hand in the coop. She thinks the *hinkel* will peck her. *Groossmammi* told us it isn't kind to laugh at her so we never do," Tanner reported solemnly. Then he corrected himself, admitting, "We did laugh the first time, *Daed*. But we never do anymore. Not even when she's scared and she jumps like this."

Tanner's imitation of Trina's jitters reminded Seth of how she'd flinched when he opened the cupboard to check for the mouse, and he suppressed a chuckle. "*Groossmammi* is right. It isn't kind to laugh at Trina.

Most *Englischers* buy their eggs in a store, but in time she'll learn how to collect *oier* from the henhouse. Now go wake your brother."

Tanner obediently thumped back upstairs. Meanwhile, Martha shuffled into the room. Anticipating her question, Seth said, "*Guder mariye, Groossmammi.* I haven't made *kaffi* yet but I'll get it started as soon as I put these *oier* in the pot to boil."

"*Denki,* but I can fix breakfast for us." Martha removed a pot from the cupboard. With her back to him, she added, "Don't stand there watching me. I still know my way around a pot of *oier.* I only had an accident the other day because I wasn't used to Abe's stove."

Seth left the room to wash his hands, returning a few minutes later with Timothy and Tanner. After breakfast Martha served coffee while the boys went to brush their teeth.

Seth took a long pull from his mug and then said, "I probably won't be home until around suppertime tonight."

"Why not? You don't keep the shop open past two o'clock on Saturdays during winter."

Even though his grandmother knew he intended to eventually visit a matchmaker in the neighboring Elmsville district, Seth felt embarrassed to remind her about it now. "I, uh, I'm going to see Belinda Imhoff this afternoon."

Martha stopped sipping her coffee. "Ah, I see. Then I guess we'll have to do our shopping at the *Englisch* market tonight instead of the one on Main Street this afternoon."

"If you write out a list for me, I can pick up what

you need before I set off to Elmsville. It's chilly enough that the perishables will keep in the buggy until I get home."

"*Neh*, I'd rather go. It will get me out of the house. Besides, Trina will need to *kumme* shopping, too."

"Trina? With us?" Seth questioned.

"*Jah*. In case you haven't noticed, she doesn't have a car and it wouldn't do her any *gut* to walk to the market in town, since it's closed by the time you return in the evenings. I don't know how she has any stamina to keep up with the boys. I try to get her to eat more at dinnertime, but she refuses. I think she feels as if she should bring her own dinner, which is *lecherich*."

"*Neh*, I doubt that's it. She's probably just on a diet. You know how the *Englisch* are."

"I know how *people* are. *Englisch* or Amish, they need food in their houses."

Seth pulled on his beard. As grateful as he was for Trina's help, he worried about the boys becoming confused about her role in their lives. This was only a temporary employment situation. If Martha kept treating Trina like one of the family, it could lead to disappointment for Timothy and Tanner once she left.

"I don't think it's a *gut* idea for her to accompany us to the market," he said.

"*Jah*, you're right." Martha gave in so easily it surprised Seth—until she proposed, "She'd probably prefer going to the market alone anyway. So, instead of going to see Belinda Imhoff this afternoon, perhaps you could *kumme* home and teach Trina how to hitch the buggy and handle the horse. That way, she'll be all set to go to the market on her own during the day on Monday. I'll watch the *kinner* while she's gone. If they're napping, it shouldn't be a problem."

Seth shook his head incredulously. "*Neh.* She's not going to use my horse and buggy any more than I'd drive her car."

"*Gut.* Then you'll put off going to Elmsville this afternoon so we can all make it to the market in town before it closes," Martha stated as if it were a done deed.

Although frustrated, Seth knew he couldn't compete with his grandmother's cunning logic. "Alright. She can accompany us to the *Englisch* store in Highland Springs tonight."

His grandmother smiled in his direction. "The *buwe* will be delighted."

On that note, Timothy and Tanner scrambled into the room, dragged a chair to the window and climbed atop it together to watch for Trina.

"There she is," shouted Timothy. They got down and ran to open the door.

"Hurry, Trina. It's raining!" Tanner called, as if she wasn't aware.

"*Guder mariye,*" she sang out, shaking raindrops from her long hair after she hung up her jacket. "What a *wunderbaar* day."

"You're joking now but wait until you've been shut indoors all day," Seth said. "I don't want the *buwe* going outside. Do you hear me, Timothy and Tanner?"

"*Jah, Daed,*" they chorused.

"That's alright. We're going to play a rainy-day animal game inside. It's called Noah's Ark," Trina promised and the boys capered in circles around her. Turning to Seth she added, "If I remember correctly, Bible stories are permitted, *jah*?"

Seth's ears and forehead stung. She was being cheeky, but it didn't feel offensive like the brazen remarks some of his *Englisch* customers made. "Of course Bible stories are allowed, provided they're in German, since that's the language our Bibles are printed in and the language our preachers speak when they're delivering a sermon."

"Naturlich werde ich sprechen Deutsche." In German Trina said of course *she'd* speak in German. Seth had only meant to be facetious. He didn't realize she actually knew the language. Once again, he felt his face flush.

But his ultimate embarrassment came when his grandmother bid him goodbye. *"Mach's gut,* Seth. I hope your meeting with the matchmaker goes well. We'll have supper on the table and you can tell us all about it tonight!"

The youth in Willow Creek usually made a rigorous effort to keep their courtships private, even from their family members. Since Seth had already been married once, he didn't exercise the same level of discretion about courtship when speaking with his grandmother now as he would have when he was younger. Still, he was thoroughly abashed to have her announce his intention of going to a matchmaker in front of Trina. Realizing his humiliation wasn't so much because Trina was *Englisch* as it was because she was a woman, he couldn't get out of the house fast enough.

Chapter Three

Trina felt sorry for Seth. He clearly was embarrassed that Martha had said anything about him going to a matchmaker, especially in front of her. But the boys clamored for Trina's attention and she turned her focus to them.

"How do we play Noah's Ark?" Timothy asked.

"We start by reading Noah's story in the Bible," Trina told them. They sat on the braided rug in front of the woodstove while Trina read to them from the book of Genesis and Martha listened from her spot in the rocking chair. When Trina finished the passage, she instructed the boys to go into the hall and agree on an animal to imitate. When Trina called them into the room, which they were pretending was an ark, they were to enter as a pair, miming their chosen animal. If Trina guessed what they were, they'd go back into the hall and return as a different pair of animals. The boys loved the game and Trina and Martha were entertained by their imitations.

"You have such a way with *kinner*," Martha later

complimented her as she and Trina were preparing dinner together.

"Denki." Trina placed the bread Martha had coached her to make on the cutting board.

"You'll make a *wunderbaar mamm* someday soon, too," Martha said. "Is there a special man in your life in Philadelphia? Someone you're...how do the *Englisch* say it? Dating?"

"Jah," Trina responded absentmindedly. The bread hadn't risen as high as she anticipated it would and it seemed tough. "I mean, *jah,* we call it dating. But *neh,* I'm not dating anyone."

Martha clicked her tongue. "Those *Englisch* men can't be too smart to let such a kind, bright and becoming *maedel* like you pass them by."

Trina laughed. "I don't meet that many *Englisch* men. Most of my time is spent at school where there are only two male teachers and both are married. I've dated a couple of men I knew from church, but those relationships didn't last. Besides, I'm not really interested in getting married." She extended the loaf of bread in Martha's direction. "Does this feel hard to you?"

Martha took it from her. "Perhaps. The rainy weather probably affected the yeast."

"Oh, *neh.* I wanted it to turn out!"

"It's alright, dear. The *buwe* won't mind."

It wasn't the boys Trina was worried about; it was Seth. For some reason, she wanted to prove to him she wasn't the microwaving sort of cook he probably took her for. Even if she was.

After they'd eaten dinner, Martha had intended to tell

the boys a story while Trina cleaned up in the kitchen, but the older woman had a *koppweh*, a headache.

"It's the light," she explained. "If there's a white glare like there is today, it bothers my eyes. If I turn on a lamp at night, I see halos. If I'm out in the sun, my eyes hurt then, too."

"Would you like an aspirin?" Trina offered.

"I'm afraid we're out. That was one of the items on my grocery list."

"I might have some at my house. Let me run over and get them."

"Can we *kumme*?" the boys pleaded, but Trina reminded them their father said they couldn't go out in the rain, so she dashed home by herself.

She quickly searched her toiletry bag, but she hadn't any bottles of aspirin in it. There was, however, a pair of sunglasses. Maybe they would help. Trina slipped them into her pocket and bounded back to Seth and Martha's house.

"Oh, that does feel better, dear. *Denki*," Martha said after she'd put the lenses on over her own glasses.

"*Groossmammi,* you look *voll schpass*." Of course Tanner would think she looked very funny; he'd probably never seen mirrored lenses before.

"I can see me in your eyes," Timothy declared. He made a funny face in front of Martha and studied his reflection.

"*Buwe*, I'd like you to help me in the kitchen. Tanner, you may sweep while Timothy brings the dirty plates to the sink," Trina instructed. Then she asked Martha if she could get her anything else, but Martha said she was just going to sit there and take a quick catnap.

"*Katze* don't nap sitting up. They curl around like this." Timothy fell to the floor to demonstrate. Chuckling, Trina beckoned him to his feet again.

"*Daed* says we can't have *katze* in the house," Tanner explained as he followed Trina and Timothy. "*Groossmammi*'s 'lergic. That means she sneezes when she touches *katz* fur."

Trina suddenly understood their fascination with pretending to be animals. "Do you know what makes me sneeze? It starts with the letter S." She emphasized the S sound.

"Snakes?"

"Skunks?"

"*Neh*. Soap!" Trina exclaimed as she scooped a handful of dish soap bubbles over the boys' heads and pretended to sneeze, blowing the bubbles everywhere. Timothy and Tanner whooped and tried to catch them. Despite their exuberance, it was time for their nap, so when they finished cleaning the kitchen, Trina tucked them into their beds and returned to the parlor where Martha was rummaging through a bag of fabric.

"I thought you were going to rest," Trina commented.

"I did. Now let's get you started on making a new skirt."

Martha instructed Trina how to take her measurements and began guiding her through creating a pattern. Trina made so many erasures she figured that even though Martha's vision was impaired the older woman could do a better job of it.

"It's alright. Take your time," Martha said the fourth time Trina botched her penciling. As Trina erased the markings, Martha hummed, but it wasn't a hymn from the *Ausbund*.

"My *mamm* taught me that one," Trina said and sang a few lines. "She usually hummed or sang while she was sewing. Did she learn to do that from you?"

Martha smiled. "More likely, I learned to do that from her. Sometimes when Patience used to *kumme* over, we'd sit here sewing together. If we weren't talking, she was always humming or singing. At the time, my husband, Jacob, thought it was because she was so happy."

Trina stopped erasing. "But you knew that wasn't the reason," she said quietly, knowing the answer.

"*Jah*, I knew it wasn't the reason." Martha nodded. "I knew it was because she couldn't stand the silence in her house. Singing or humming was her way of keeping herself company."

A fat tear plopped onto the paper Trina was bending over. She was simultaneously relieved her mother had had someone like Martha in her life who understood her so well, yet saddened to be reminded of her mother's loneliness as a child. She might have started crying in earnest if Timothy and Tanner hadn't clomped into the room at just that moment.

Martha decided to lie down while Trina accompanied the boys to the basement. Largely empty, the room served as an ideal place for them to ride their bicycles—with training wheels attached—during inclement weather, but Trina liked to be present to make sure they didn't pedal too fast, since the floor was cement and she didn't want them getting hurt.

Much to Trina's relief, it was soon time to make supper. Seth had been right; after a full day of rain,

she did feel cooped up. Also, although she'd never especially liked the constant noise and bustle of the city,
she'd become accustomed to it, so it seemed strange
not to see any people other than the Helmuth family
for an entire week. Itching to get out and go shopping,
she was eager for Seth to return. Admittedly, she was
also curious about his trip to the matchmaker, but for
his sake Trina hoped Martha wouldn't ask him about
it during supper.

Seth's trip to see the matchmaker paid off quicker
than he expected. Belinda suggested he consider courting Fannie Jantzi, a widow who lived just over the Elmsville town line. The matchmaker said Fannie was
a pet project of hers and Seth didn't know if that was
a good sign or a bad one. But when Belinda told him
Fannie could be available the next day, Seth agreed to
pick her up at a nearby phone shanty after their separate church services ended. Feeling hopeful, he hurried
home to eat supper with Martha, Trina and the boys.

After taking a bite of bread, Seth set it aside on his
plate. He had made leather purses that were probably
easier to chew. Trina must have baked it. He tried to be
discreet, but Tanner noticed he wasn't eating his slice.

"*Daed*, you have to tear into the bread with your
teeth like this," he advised, showing what he meant.
"Pretend you're a lion and it's carrion."

"That's enough, Tanner," Seth scolded, discon-
certed. Trina appeared drained tonight as it was; he
hoped she wasn't offended by Tanner's remark but he
couldn't tell because she dipped her chin toward her
chest. Then he noticed her shoulders shaking a little.

Was she crying over such a small thing? But when she glanced up and swallowed a drink of water, he could see she was fighting laughter. He had to give it to her; she was awfully good-natured.

"Look, *Daed*, you can see two of yourselves in *Groossmammi*'s eyes," Timothy pointed out, waving to his reflection in Martha's glasses.

"Put your hand down and eat your vegetation." Seth had meant to say *vegetables* but he subconsciously adopted Trina's word choice. He'd been thinking about how he'd have to pick up a pair of less conspicuous sunglasses for Martha tonight. He was embarrassed he hadn't thought of buying her a pair earlier, but she'd never complained about the lighting before. Or was it that he'd never thought to ask? Once again, he was thankful for Trina's attentiveness to his family.

After they ate, Martha and Trina quickly cleared the table and washed the dishes while Seth and the boys hitched the horse and brought the buggy up the lane.

"I'll sit in the back with the *buwe* and Trina can sit up front with you," Martha said.

Inwardly Seth groaned. It would be difficult to conduct a conversation between the front and back seats, and he didn't know what to converse with Trina about on his own. He hoped the boys would call out their many questions, but instead, Martha engaged Timothy and Tanner in a spirited conversation about sheep shearing that Seth could barely hear from his seat in front.

"This is such fun!" Trina trilled, spreading the blanket Seth had given her over her lap.

Seth chuckled. "It's a mode of transportation, not a

carnival ride." *Uh-oh, did that sound rude?* He actually thought her delight was charming, so he quickly added, "It's probably a big change from driving a car around Philadelphia."

"I wouldn't know about that," Trina said breezily. "I don't own a car."

"Then how do you get around? Bus? Train?"

"Sometimes, but mostly I walk. Or ride a bike."

"In Philadelphia?"

"It's a city, not the moon," she said, imitating his tone when he remarked about the buggy not being a carnival ride. Then she teased, "*Englischers* have feet, too, you know."

Seth chortled. "*Jah,* but do *Englischers* eat carrion for supper?"

Trina giggled. "I promise I didn't teach them that. I don't know where they learned it."

"From me." When Trina twisted sideways and looked at him in surprise, Seth added, "We see a lot of things when we're out walking in the countryside. Not all of it is pleasant, but it's a fact of life."

"The same might be said for walking in the city," Trina mumbled. There was a hint of sadness to her dulcet voice.

"Staying in Willow Creek must be a big adjustment for you."

"In some ways, *jah*. But my *mamm* told me so much about it when I was growing up it almost seems like I've been here before."

Now there was no mistaking her melancholy tone. "I'm sorry about your *mamm*," he said. "You may know this already, but the first year is the most difficult. The grief never goes away completely, but after a year, it changes. And with more time, it will change again. At least, that's how it was for me after I lost my Eleanor."

Ordinarily Seth wouldn't share such an intimate sentiment with an *Englisch* woman—or an Amish woman, for that matter. But Trina's voice carried such a note of fragility, he found himself wanting to comfort her.

"I do take comfort in knowing my *mamm* is with the Lord, but sometimes I'm unbearably lonely without her."

That was exactly how Seth felt. "*Jah*, if there was any consolation for me about Timothy and Tanner, it was that they never knew their *mamm,* so they didn't miss her the way I did. Even so, it's been hard on them not to have a *mamm* in their life."

"Oh, I see," Trina spoke quietly, presumably so the boys and Martha wouldn't hear her. "So that's why you visited the matchmaker today—you're ready to court again?"

Seth didn't feel comfortable continuing this conversation, but when he didn't respond, Trina assured him, "There's no need to be embarrassed. I've had friends who've tried online dating services and—"

"Ha!" Seth sputtered. "A matchmaker is nothing like an online dating service."

"How do you know?" Trina challenged. "Have you ever tried an online dating service?"

"Have you ever tried an Amish matchmaker?"

"*Neh*, but my *mamm* told me enough about them for me to know they're not so different from online dating services, especially from dating services that screen people to find out what their values, interests and hopes are. How is that so different from going to a matchmaker?"

"The very fact you call it *dating* shows the difference," Seth argued. "Courtships among the Amish are primarily intended to see if a couple is compatible for marriage. *Englischers* date for social entertainment."

"That's true for some *Englischers*, but not everyone dates casually. Some are very selective and when they enter a romantic relationship, it's with the hope of eventually marrying."

Seth didn't know how the conversation had jumped from talking about buggy rides to courtships and marriage—topics he would have been reluctant to discuss with his closest Amish friends, much less with an *Englischer* he barely knew. But since she'd been so bold as to ask him about going to the matchmaker, he figured he could venture an inquiry, too. "Don't tell me, you're the kind of person who only dates with the intention of marrying?"

"Neh," Trina answered, the verve suddenly gone from her voice. "But I don't date for fun, either. I mean, there was someone I thought I'd marry, but…"

"But the dating service made a bad match?" Seth couldn't resist needling her a final time.

"I didn't meet him through a dating service." Trina seemed a million miles away when she said, "But you're right, he wasn't a *gut* match. He broke up with me when my *mamm* became ill. He said he couldn't compete with her for my time and affection."

Seth regretted bringing up such a painful subject. What kind of man wouldn't support the woman he loved when her mother had cancer? "What a self-centered *dummkopf,*" he said aloud, answering his own question.

"It's better I found out sooner rather than later." Trina sounded genuinely sincere when she added, "But I hope things turn out well for you."

Trina was quiet the rest of the way to Highland Springs and Seth felt terrible for spoiling what had started out as such a fun excursion for her. Once they arrived at the store, he and Martha took Timothy and Tanner with them, despite the boys' expressed preference for accompanying Trina. Seth figured she needed time to collect her items in peace, and besides, he didn't want to mar her evening further by making any more cloddish remarks.

Trina was relieved when Sunday came; it meant she'd made it through one week in Willow Creek. Only a little more than eight weeks to go until May first. She rose early to attend the nearest *Englisch* church, which, according to the map on her phone, was two and a half miles away. Since she didn't have a car and couldn't afford to hire a taxi to come from Lancaster, she had to walk. On the way, she hummed as she thought about Seth, Martha and the boys traveling to the worship services hosted this week by an Amish family, the Planks.

The sky was overcast with white clouds and Trina hoped the light wasn't bothering Martha's eyes. Seth had bought his grandmother a new pair of sunglasses the evening before, but they didn't fit over Martha's regular glasses as well as the pair she'd borrowed from Trina. When Trina told Martha she should consider going to an eye doctor and getting prescription sunglasses, Seth said he doubted that was necessary and

Martha seemed to agree. Trina was puzzled by this; they didn't seem excessively frugal, but she supposed they might have considered the expense to be a waste.

Because it was chillier than Trina expected and she hadn't worn a hat, halfway to church she stopped and let her hair down from its ponytail so it would provide a natural covering for her ears. Fortunately there was no wind as she trod up and down the hilly roads of Willow Creek, but by the time she arrived at the little church and ducked into the women's room, her nose and cheeks were bright pink, and she felt famished from hiking in the cold. She ran her hands under warm water and then joined the small but friendly congregation. The pastor's sermon on God's faithfulness was comforting to her and she especially loved worshipping through song. She hadn't realized until today how long it had been since she was able to sing in church; ever since her mother died, she was afraid to lift up her voice, in fear she'd begin crying in public. But today she sang as loudly and cheerfully as anyone.

After the service, the elderly couple sitting next to Trina turned to introduce themselves to her as Sherman and Mabel Brown. They were delighted to learn she was new in town and they quickly invited her to the potluck dinner being held in the basement of the building. Trina's stomach rumbled as she accepted their offer.

She was eating her second plate of spaghetti and meatballs when a young man approached the table where Sherman and Mabel had introduced her to another couple with two children. The man took a seat next to Trina. Dark-haired and soft-spoken, Ethan Gray told her he was the local pediatrician. Like Trina, he'd only arrived in Willow Creek recently. After dessert—Trina had both a cupcake *and* a brownie—Ethan offered to give her a ride home, but Trina declined. Warm and invigorated again, she wanted to see Wheeler's Bridge, which was located not too far from Main Street. Trina's mother had told her that when she went grocery shopping in town as a girl, instead of walking on the roads she always followed the creek behind their house all the way to the bridge. She said the route took her through the thick woods and beautiful Amish farmland, so Trina was eager to journey where her mother had once found beauty.

Following the directions on her phone's GPS, Trina had been walking for almost half an hour when it began drizzling. Within minutes, she felt the prickle of sleet against her scalp and she dashed to take cover beneath a willow tree in the middle of a field. Since the tree had no foliage yet, it provided little shelter and Trina's hair became ropy and wet as she consulted her phone to figure out a shortcut home. She concluded if she cut across the field she was standing in and took a short jaunt through a wooded area, she'd wind up on a street that ran parallel to Main Street. Since it was the Sabbath, the Amish shops were closed, but she hoped there would be a convenience store or a coffee shop she could stop in at to dry off and get a hot chocolate.

But she must have gotten confused in the woods because when she finally emerged some forty minutes later, she recognized the fence as being the same one that bordered the east end of the field where she first began. Or was it? There were so many fences and farms in Willow Creek it was difficult to distinguish one from another. And since the trees and hills hadn't yet begun to show signs of spring, it wasn't even as if the walk had been especially scenic. Worst of all, by now it was raining so hard it was soaking right through her jacket. Trina had no choice but to use her phone to navigate along the roads instead of taking a shortcut.

By that time, she'd been walking for over an hour, her toes were numb and she wished she'd accepted a ride from Ethan. She was half tempted to flag down a passing car, except that no cars passed her. She had just trudged up a long, steep hill when her phone rang. It had been so long since she'd received a phone call, she jerked when it vibrated in her pocket.

"Hello?" she answered, pushing a string of wet hair from her eyes. Droplets rolled off her eyebrows and she squinted against the rain.

The caller, Kurt Johnson, explained he was a realtor who'd heard she had a small house that might be for sale. *Who could have told him that?* she wondered. Kurt asked if they could meet soon. Just then, a car came over the hill at a high speed, its wheels spraying Trina with dirt and mud as it passed.

"Oh, no!" she wailed.

"I'm sorry?" Kurt asked.

"Nothing," Trina replied. "Listen, this isn't a *gut* time—a good time—for me to talk. Try again later, okay? I have to go. Bye." Hanging up before he could say anything else, Trina felt kind of rude but she didn't think it was very polite of him to call her on a Sunday, either.

Great, she thought, looking down. *Now this skirt is*

muddy and I haven't even washed the other one yet. Can this excursion possibly get any worse?

As Seth crested the hill, he saw a flash of lavender on the descending side. Only one person he knew wore a jacket that color: Trina. Her dark hair was plastered to her head as she stood on the roadside four miles from home, talking on a cell phone in the pouring rain.

"Narrish Englischer." Seated next to him, Fannie said aloud what Seth was thinking: Trina was a crazy *Englischer*. But she was also his boys' nanny. And she was extremely wet. So, despite the fact he was technically courting Fannie—really he was just taking her to his home for a Sunday afternoon visit—he knew he had to stop and offer Trina a ride. The very last thing he wanted to do.

"Why are you pulling over?" Fannie questioned after they passed Trina by several yards and he had time and room to halt the horse and buggy.

"That's my *buwe*'s nanny. She lives next door to me. I'm sorry but I have to see if she needs a ride."

Fannie's brown eyes bulged with surprise. "An *Englisch* nanny takes care of your *kinner*? No wonder you're eager to marry again!"

Seth's own eyes widened at her comment. It seemed a brash thing for her to say, considering they'd only just met, but he recognized there was truth to her remark. Like him, Fannie had two young children and was eager to wed.

"You're bringing a woman to our house?" Martha had asked the previous night after they returned from the market and Timothy and Tanner were in bed. "Do you think that's a *gut* idea?"

"Why not? I need to find out how she gets along with the *buwe*. And with you."

Martha shook her head. "I'm not the one courting her. Neither are the *buwe*. And I dare say you won't be for long, either, if your idea of courtship is to bring her home and test her compatibility with the *kinner* and me. Besides, I didn't even make a dessert."

Seth was stumped by Martha's remarks. He and Fannie weren't youth; they'd both been married before, and according to Belinda, their shared objective in courting again was to find a suitable parent for their children as well as a spouse. If things went well today, he fully intended to meet Fannie's daughters next Sunday. He hadn't, however, intended for Fannie to meet Trina. Certainly not today and possibly not at all.

Sighing, he hopped down from the buggy. "What are you doing out here?" he asked when Trina approached.

She put her hand to her forehead as if to shield her eyes from the sun, but clearly it was the rain she didn't want interfering with her vision. "Am I ever glad to see you!" she explained. "I'm lost. I was trying to—"

She looked so bedraggled and worn out that Seth cut her off. "Never mind. You can tell me in the buggy. You'll have to sit in the back."

After Trina was seated and Seth had made introductions, Trina apologized for interrupting their afternoon. Her teeth chattered as she spoke, but she projected her voice so they could hear her. "I was coming home from church when the skies opened up. I started out by using my GPS but then I thought I'd figured out a shortcut through the woods, but I must have gotten all turned around because I ended up back where I started."

"It must be so difficult when you have to rely on technology to get where you need to go," Fannie said over her shoulder and clicked her tongue against her teeth.

Seth couldn't tell whether her comment was meant as sympathy or criticism, but suddenly he found himself defending Trina. "She wasn't using technology to get where she wanted to go—she was using her feet. Which is more than you and I are doing."

Fannie cracked up, as if he'd intended to amuse her. "*Lappich!* I wasn't talking about her transportation. I was talking about using her cell phone to figure out where to go."

"Actually," Trina countered, "I rarely use GPS and I wouldn't have used it today but I didn't have a map, I'm new in town and I really didn't want to miss church. Besides, it's not the GPS that failed me. It was my own sense of direction I was following through the woods."

"What church did you go to?" Seth asked and when Trina replied, he whistled. "You must have walked a *gut* three miles to end up where you are now. It's another three miles home."

"Wow, I really did go out of my way. The church was only two and a half miles from my house when I started out this morning," she joked.

"Either that or the road grew longer while you were in church," Seth teased. "That must have been some lengthy sermon!"

Trina giggled but Fannie shook her head. "I don't think it's proper to joke about worship," she said under her breath and then was silent for the rest of the trip.

"*Denki* for the ride," Trina said to Seth when he dropped her off at her house. Then she told Fannie it was nice to meet her.

As Trina climbed the steps to her door, Fannie remarked, "The poor thing, her husband is going to think she looks like something the *katz* dragged in."

"She doesn't have a husband."

"Ah. I wondered about that."

Seth didn't know what she was getting at. "Why would you wonder about whether Trina has a husband or not?"

"Oh, just because she went to church alone," Fannie said. Then, before Seth could offer to drop her off at his front door, she asked, "Could you let me off here? I'll get wet walking from the stable and since your buggy doesn't have a heater, I'm already cold."

Once again, Seth couldn't tell if she was being critical. Their *Ordnung* allowed certain kinds of heaters in their buggies, but he felt blankets worked just fine for the short distances they usually traveled. Would Fannie expect him to get a heater while they were courting? His mind jumped to Trina's remarks about how much fun it was to ride in the buggy the previous night. Then he realized Trina hadn't complained at all about being cold on the way home today, even though Fannie had two blankets on her lap and Trina had had none. Seth shook his head and told himself he was probably the one being critical about Fannie. *I need to see how she interacts with the* buwe *and* Groossmammi *before I make any quick judgments,* he thought.

When Seth returned from the stable Fannie was already in the parlor with Martha and the boys, sitting next to the woodstove. "Have you met everyone, Fannie?" he asked.

"*Jah*. Your *groossmammi* and I thought we'd have tea as soon as my feet warm up, and then Timothy and Turner are going to show me how they play a game called Noah's Ark."

"You mean Tanner," Tanner told her.

"What?" Fannie asked.

"My name is Tanner. You called me Turner."

"Oh, did I?" Fannie asked. "That's probably because you've been spinning in so many circles since I arrived, I thought your name was Turner."

"I can spin, too!" Timothy announced, showing them.

"I'll say you can," Fannie agreed. "You can spin just like a tornado. I should call you Twister. Turner and Twister."

The boys' laughter allayed some of Seth's reservations and he offered to get the tea.

"Nonsense," Fannie objected. When Martha rose from her chair, Fannie said, "I'll make it. Martha, you just stay put. This will give me a chance to familiarize myself with your kitchen."

If there was one thing that nettled Seth's grandmother more than anything else, it was having another woman in her kitchen. It didn't matter that Martha was nearly blind; she was in charge of her kitchen and that was that. In fact, it had surprised Seth when his grandmother allowed Trina to make suppers, but he assumed it was because Martha was teaching her to become a better cook. In any case, Seth held his breath, waiting to see how his grandmother would react to Fannie saying she'd get the tea.

"Denki," Martha finally replied, lowering herself into the chair again. "That would be *wunderbaar."*

Seth exhaled and sat down at the end of the sofa.

"Seth," his grandmother whispered loudly and gestured toward his head. "Your *hut.* Take off your *hut."*

Seth chuckled. He'd forgotten to remove it. As he went to hang it on a peg, he smoothed his hair. It was damp near the back of his neck, but not nearly as wet as Trina's had been.

Poor maedel, *she must be chilled to the bone,* he thought. *I hope she remembers how I showed her to build a fire. Maybe I'll have time to check before I take Fannie back to her home.*

Then he thought better of it. Fannie seemed to disapprove of *Englischers* even more than Seth sometimes did and he sensed she didn't think it was appropriate for him to be so concerned about Trina. He supposed Fannie was right. Trina wasn't his responsibility. He had a courtship to pursue, if not with Fannie—he still wasn't sure what he thought about her—then with another Amish woman Belinda would introduce him to. So he returned to the parlor and joined Martha and Fannie as the boys showed them the game their *Englisch* nanny had taught them.

Chapter Four

After Seth left the house on Monday, Tanner and Timothy filled Trina in about Seth's afternoon with Fannie. Although Trina hadn't prompted them, she was curious about what kind of woman Fannie was. Trina's initial impression was that she was a little uptight, but that might have been because it was her first time out with Seth and she was nervous.

"Yesterday we showed *Daed* and Fannie how to play Noah's Ark," Timothy told Trina as they walked along the bank of the creek. Just as Trina expected, once Seth saw how closely she kept watch over his sons, he'd allowed the trio to trek along their favorite path.

"That must have been fun," Trina replied, pleased they liked the game enough to show it to their father.

"It wasn't as much fun as with you. Fannie couldn't guess we were being inchworms," Tanner complained.

"We did this," Timothy said. He imitated an inchworm alternately raising itself into an arch with its hind legs and advancing forward with its front legs until it was stretched flat again.

Trina clapped, laughing. "That was excellent, Timothy!" The child had really captured the essence of an inchworm's movements. The boys had probably studied the little critters on one of their countryside walks with Seth.

"Fannie didn't think so. She thought I was being a camel."

"Maybe she thought you were making your back into a hump, like a camel's." Even as she offered the diplomatic explanation, Trina wondered how Fannie could have mistaken Timothy's movements for anything other than an inchworm. The imitation was so accurate it didn't take much imagination to guess what he was doing. "Did your *daed* guess?"

"*Neh*, he said 'ladies first,' so Fannie kept guessing and guessing and she didn't ever give him a turn. Then Tanner told her we being were inchworms."

"She was taking too long and I wanted us to be bears, instead," Tanner said.

Trina tried not to giggle. That was exactly how Fannie had struck her, as someone who didn't easily admit defeat. Not that it mattered much to Trina. Seth was the one who'd have to figure out if she was a "*gut* match" for him or not. Trina said, "Well, I think it was kind of you to show Fannie the game. In time, she'll learn how to play."

"*Jah*, like you and the *oier*," Tanner said, stopping to toss a rock into the creek.

"What do you mean, like me and the *oier*?" Trina asked.

"*Daed* said *Englischers* collect their *oier* from a grocery store and it's not nice to laugh if you're scared of the *hinkel*. In time you'll collect *oier* from the henhouse, too."

Trina didn't know whether she felt indignant or grateful for Seth's instruction to the boys. Yes, he was teaching Timothy and Tanner to demonstrate kindness, but he was also emphasizing her difference. "Your *Daed* is right. I will learn to collect *oier* from the henhouse. In fact, I'm going to collect them from now on, without any help from you *buwe*."

"Aw, but we like to help you, Trina." Tanner stomped on a fallen pine cone.

"You can still help. You'll hold the basket for me."

Indeed, the next day, Trina retrieved the eggs on her own. One broody hen didn't want to relinquish her spot in the nesting box, but Trina successfully shoed her away on the second try. She placed the warm brown eggs in the basket Tanner held out for her and then Timothy carried it into the house.

Martha had planned to use a couple of the eggs to make custard pie for her friends, Pearl Hostetler, Ruth Graber and Ruth's daughter-in-law, Iris. They were coming to work on one of the quilts they donated to a charity for children in foster care. But after dinner Martha's eyes were bothering her so much she developed a headache and had to lie down.

"Ruth will probably bring a treat from her nephew's wife's bakery anyway," Martha said.

Trina had heard about the renowned treats Faith Schwartz made and she hoped she'd get a chance to visit the bakery. She was amazed by how voracious her appetite was lately; it was as if she was making up for all the months she'd subsisted on nothing but fruit and crackers or bread.

Once she put the boys down for a nap, Trina decided to bake something on Martha's behalf, in case Ruth showed up empty-handed. While she didn't know how to make custard pie without a recipe, her mother had taught her to bake funny cake—a popular Amish dessert that was a cross between a coffee cake and a chocolate pie. *I might be new to collecting* oier, *but I'm no stranger to rolling a pie crust,* she thought as she worked the dough.

Knowing the boys would want a piece, she doubled the recipe and she was pulling the second pie from the oven when Martha meandered into the room, sniffing.

"That smells *appenditlich.* Is it cake?"

"*Jah,* it's funny cake. You have a *gut* sense of smell."

"Not half as *gut* as Seth and his *seh.* They can smell dessert a mile away. I'm surprised Timothy and Tanner haven't *kumme* running."

"They're napping—"

Trina was interrupted by someone tapping the windowpane on the door.

"*Wilkom,*" Martha said as she ushered her guests inside. "*Kumme,* meet Trina Smith, Patience Kauffman's *dochder.*"

"Look at you! You're the image of your *mamm* at your age, isn't she, Ruth?" Pearl asked.

"*Jah*, she is. She is, indeed," the other elderly woman agreed. She pulled Trina close and kissed her cheek, whispering, "May *Gott* comfort you in your grief."

"*Denki.* He already is," Trina whispered back.

Moved by the warm reception she'd received, Trina offered to make tea for the three older women and Iris, who looked to be about Trina's mother's age.

"That's a *gut* idea. Let's have dessert while it's warm

before you take out your material and supplies. Go ahead into the parlor, we'll be there in a minute," Martha directed.

Trina accepted when Martha offered her assistance. She knew nothing bothered Martha as much as being treated as if she were incapable of helping, especially in her own kitchen.

"There are only four slices here," Martha said, holding the tray. "Where's yours?"

Trina didn't expect to be invited to join the group. "The *buwe* will be awake soon, so—"

"So you'd better cut yourself a slice and *kumme* sit down before they do."

Trina couldn't argue with Martha any more than Seth could, so she obediently cut herself a piece of the funny cake and went into the parlor, too.

"Mm-mmm!" Ruth murmured. "You outdid yourself this time, Martha. I intended to stop by the bakery to get sweets for us, but now I'm glad I didn't."

"I wish I could say it's mine but Trina made it with no help from me."

"This crust…" Iris began to say but finished chewing and swallowing before she continued "…is so flaky. What's your secret?"

"Denki," Trina answered demurely. "My *mamm* taught me how to make it."

"Ah, then, you're not going to tell us your secret, are you?" Ruth winked at her and turned to Pearl. "Remember how Patience would never tell us the secret, either?"

"Jah, all she ever said was her *mamm* taught *her*!" Pearl laughed. "No matter how often we pleaded, she

didn't give in. In the end, we decided we'd rather eat it than make it anyway, and we quit pestering her."

Trina giggled. Her mother had told her that the secret—which involved working the dough and using baking powder—was something that had been passed down for generations. It was such a comfort to hear the women share their recollections of her mother that Trina was sorry when the boys woke up.

She allowed each to eat a slender slice of cake in the kitchen before taking them outdoors. As she was lacing Tanner's boots for him, she overheard Pearl ask Martha about Seth's afternoon with Fannie. Trina's mother was right; she always said there were no secrets in Willow Creek—except for recipes, perhaps. Trina strained to hear Martha's reply.

"I can't tell if Seth thought she was a *gut* match or not, although who knows what that *bu* is looking for."

"What about you, what did you think?" Ruth asked.

"She took over my kitchen!" Martha replied frankly and Trina could hear the others gasp in exaggerated horror before bursting into laughter.

While she knew it was uncharitable of her, Trina would be lying if she said she wasn't a tiny bit glad neither Martha nor the boys took a liking to Fannie. And, although she couldn't say why for certain she felt this way, she was even happier Seth didn't seem crazy about her, either.

As Seth clomped up the porch stairs the smell of something delicious tickled his nostrils. He only had to open the door before he identified the aroma: funny cake. Martha hadn't made that in over a year.

"Martha? Trina? *Buwe?*" he called, but no one answered. The table was set and stew was simmering on the stovetop, so they couldn't have gone far. He lifted the plastic wrap off the pie plate. A little slice wouldn't ruin his appetite.

"*Daed,* no sweets before supper," Tanner scolded when he, Timothy and Trina came upstairs from the basement and caught Seth devouring his second piece over the sink without using a plate.

"I couldn't resist," Seth explained to Trina. "Martha hasn't made this in years. She sure hasn't lost her touch, though."

Timothy corrected him. "*Groossmammi* didn't make that cake. Trina did."

"*Jah*, with *oier* she collected all by herself."

"Please go wash your hands," Trina instructed the boys, who charged from the room.

Chagrinned, Seth clapped the crumbs from his hands. "It really is *gut.* So, did giving you baking lessons wear my *groossmammi* out? Or is she lying down because she has a *koppweh?*"

"*Neh*, she went with her friends to deliver the quilts to the charity. She'll be back soon." Trina moved toward him to wash her hands at the sink. "By the way, Martha didn't teach me how to make a funny cake—my *mamm* did."

"Oh, sorry about that," Seth apologized. In an attempt to make up for his blunder, he added, "I'm sorry the *buwe* didn't help you at the henhouse, too. I'll talk to them tonight."

Trina's tone was smug. "No need to apologize—I wanted to collect the *oier* myself."

Seth's voice cracked with disbelief when he asked, "You did?"

This time Trina laughed. "It's not all that much different than sticking my hand into a refrigerator at a grocery store and pulling out a carton of eggs like we *Englischers* all do, is it?"

"I admit, I'm impressed by your progress," Seth replied, leaning toward her and grinning. "Next thing you know, you won't need me to help you catch mice, either."

Trina's eyes were so sincerely fearful as she said, "Please don't make me do that myself," that Seth had the impulse to tousle her hair in consolation, the way he might do to the boys.

Instead he said, "On one condition. You make another funny cake again soon. This one is almost gone."

She ribbed him, saying, "Hmm, I wonder why. But okay, it's a deal." She thrust her hand out to shake his but then she suddenly dropped it to her side. "Sorry. That's an *Englisch* habit."

He lifted her hand in his anyway, peered into her dancing green eyes and said, "Deal."

True to her word, the following Saturday morning, Trina showed up bearing a pie plate covered in foil. "I think I heard the trap snap last night. Will you check it for me?"

Seth guffawed. "I wasn't serious about the cake but *jah*, I'll go check the trap."

When he returned a few minutes later, Timothy and Tanner were waiting for him on the porch. "*Daed*, Trina says we have to ask you if we can have a piece of your cake."

"*Jah*, but not until after your afternoon nap," he answered. Then he told Trina he'd emptied the trap. Now that the mouse was out of the wall, he could patch the crack, but he'd have to wait until he returned from work around two thirty or three o'clock before he could get to it.

"I wouldn't mind taking a piece of that cake with me, though," he said, and she cut him a generous slice.

Just the thought of it made his mouth water and he looked forward to eating it during his break, but at noon Joseph Schrock, the owner of Schrock's Shop a few doors down Main Street, stopped in to visit.

"Have you heard the news? It's *baremlich*, isn't it?" the bespectacled man asked.

"What news?"

"About Abe Kauffman's property."

Joseph proceeded to tell Seth a developer was interested in buying it once Trina met the requirements to sell. Apparently, after several failed attempts to reach Trina at home, the realtor stopped by Joseph's shop and inquired about her. He was excited to tell Joseph he had an investor who wanted to buy the property—not for the house, but for the land. The client's intention was to raze the house and build a beer, wine and spirits store there, since Willow Creek didn't have one on that side of town. He said with so many buses coming through Main Street, tourists would be thrilled to frequent a liquor store nearby. As a nod to local history, the shop would specialize in German beer and hard cider.

"A liquor store?" Seth echoed. He couldn't believe his ears. What could be worse than living next door to a liquor store? The traffic, the parking lot, the noise, the lighting…how was he going to raise two boys next to a business like that?

He was so discouraged he left his dinner uneaten and brooded for the afternoon, hardly able to concentrate on his customers' questions. To him the *Englischers* seemed unnecessarily preoccupied with the colors of the purses and wallets he made. As long as they securely held money, how much did the color matter? It was a frivolous concern, just like building a beer, wine and spirits store next door to him was an unnecessary pursuit.

It never occurred to him Trina wouldn't sell—she'd made it crystal clear she was leaving in two months. But Seth wondered if she could be persuaded not to sell to that particular developer. Perhaps she'd be willing to sell to an Amish family or at least to an *Englisch* family instead of a business. By the end of the day, he felt more hopeful and he polished off his lunch, funny cake and all, before walking home.

"*Buwe,* you stay here with *Groossmammi,*" he told Timothy and Tanner when he got there. He hoped to talk to Trina about the rumor he'd heard and he didn't want the boys listening.

"How was your day? Did you have a lot of customers?" she asked as they strolled across the yard to her house so he could take care of the crack in the wall.

"There was a steady stream, *jah.*"

"What kind of leatherwork do you sell in your shop?"

"My general inventory includes purses, harnesses, belts, tool pouches, that kind of thing. But often *Englisch* customers ask me to custom design something special. As long as it's made of leather, I can probably honor their request. Except for shoes or boots. I don't make those."

"Why not?"

She's certainly inquisitive today. Seth explained, "Usually the people who want me to custom design footwear for them want it because they can't find their size in a regular store. So if I make shoes for them and they change their minds, I'm stuck with a size fourteen boot. Or a double-wide size eight shoe. Those are hard to sell."

"Have you ever considered making them pay up front?" Trina asked as she opened her kitchen door.

"*Neh.* I believe people should be true to their word," Seth said, following her inside. "The problem is, the *Englisch* don't."

Trina twirled around so abruptly Seth didn't have time to stop walking and he almost bumped into her. She was nearly as tall as he was and they were so close he could see each individual lash on her lower eyelid. "I'm *Englisch* and I honor my word," she said, narrowing her eyes.

Seth didn't mean for another one of their conversations to become contentious, but with her standing so near, he couldn't think of what to say to fix it. Nor did he want to move away. "I—I…" he stammered.

Trina stepped backward and giggled. Oh, so she was only pretending to be angry. "Now it's your turn to honor *your* word." She gestured toward the kitchen cupboard.

Seth could feel his lips lift into a goofy smile but he didn't respond aloud. The tension between them was broken but it took him a moment to recover before he began patching the crack inside the cupboard. As he worked, Trina put on a pot for tea and he was almost ready to sit down and share a cup with her when someone knocked at the door.

"Yes?" Trina questioned after opening it.

"I'm Kurt Johnson," the short man with unusually bright teeth said. "You know, the realtor who called you last week. We talked about getting together, remember?"

So Trina had already been in touch with him. How could she have agreed to meet with someone who was going to sell to a developer? Didn't she understand what living next door to a liquor store would be like for Seth and his family—especially the boys?

"Sorry. I'd forgotten," Trina replied. "Um, this is my…my neighbor, Seth Helmuth."

Seth nodded and then turned his attention to collecting his tools.

"We were just about to sit down for tea. You're *wilkom* to join us," Trina said.

"Terrific!" Kurt seemed overly zealous to Seth.

"I'm actually heading home now," Seth told Trina. If she was going to make a deal with someone like Kurt, he didn't want to be there to bear witness to it.

Trina was disappointed when Seth left, but she didn't blame him; he probably thought Kurt was a pushy *Englischer*—and he was right. From the moment he sat down until the moment Trina ushered him out the door, the realtor tried to convince Trina it was in her best interest to sell the property to a developer who wanted to use the land for commercial purposes. Specifically, to build a liquor store. When Trina heard that, she nearly choked on her tea.

"You'd be doing the community a service," he said. "And you'd stand to profit so much more than if you sold this house to a family."

"This community is Amish. They wouldn't patronize a liquor store," Trina replied. "And you still haven't told me how you knew my house might be for sale."

Kurt shrugged. "We have our ways of finding out. Now listen, even if the Amish won't patronize the shop, the tourists and non-Amish locals will. Indirectly, you'll be helping the Amish businesses flourish because it's only a tiny detour from Main Street to here. Business for the liquor store means business for the Amish shops and vice versa."

Trina shook her head. "I'm not selling to a developer. They'd ruin the land. There's a beautiful creek out back. The two *buwe*—I mean boys—living next door love to play out there. They won't be able to if cars are constantly driving in and out."

"You're being sentimental. This lot could command almost half a mil," Kurt said. "If you sell the house and land as-is for someone to reside in, you won't even see six figures."

Even five figures would have felt like a windfall to Trina, but that was beside the point. Trina absolutely wouldn't do that to the people of Willow Creek—especially the Helmuths. Besides, it would dishonor her mother's memory to allow the location to be used for a liquor store when alcohol had played such a detrimental role in her childhood.

Standing, Trina said, "I appreciate your input, but I have things to do." She had really hoped to get into town, since she was itching to see Main Street, but now it was too late, so she'd probably just do her laundry and then read.

"Alright. Here's my card if you have any questions. When can I stop in and see that you've changed your mind?"

"Never," Trina blurted out. "I mean, I'd prefer you call instead of stopping in. I'll give you my cell phone number."

"Already have it, remember?" Kurt held up his phone to show her. "And before you ask how I got it—"

"I know, I know. You have your ways," Trina said and Kurt gave her a cheesy grin.

After realizing she still had one clean skirt to wear to church the next day, Trina decided to forego washing her clothes until Monday, when she could hang them on the line first thing in the morning. Instead she ate a bowl of chili and curled up with a book Martha had loaned her, followed by studying the Bible in preparation for church.

Stretching out in bed that night, she felt toasty warm and thought of her mother. Trina wished she had a photo of her when she was a girl, but of course, photos were prohibited among the Amish. She loved it whenever people said she looked like her mother, although Trina thought Patience had been far prettier than Trina would ever be. Then she found herself wondering what Seth's wife must have looked like, since the boys looked exactly like him.

More and more her thoughts turned to Seth lately.

Instead of being annoyed when he teased her about the *Englisch*, she enjoyed being the focus of his attention and she rather liked teasing him back. She thought of how close their faces had been this afternoon and she shivered. What was wrong with her? Did she have a crush on him, or was it simply that he was one of the only two adults she spoke to on a regular basis? As she rolled onto her side and adjusted her pillow beneath her neck, she anticipated going to church would help refocus her thoughts.

Indeed, the next day Trina's mind was wholly occupied with the pastor's sermon and with singing praises to the Lord. Once again, after the service ended Ethan offered her a ride home, and once again she declined. She was sure she could make it to Main Street today. Even though the stores were all closed, she could peek into the shop windows. The mercantile and Schrock's Shop were the only stores she remembered her mother mentioning; the bakery, seasonal ice cream parlor, and furniture restoration shop must have been new since her mother was a girl.

Also, there was Seth's leather shop. Or, as the plain sign said: Helmuth's Leatherworks. Trina peeked in the large glass window. The storefront wasn't as large as she expected, but she remembered Seth saying most of the space was dedicated to his workshop, which was located in the back of the store. Even from a distance she could see how beautiful his handiwork was and she felt a sense of admiration. You couldn't buy such finely crafted items in the most extravagant *Englisch* shop in Philadelphia.

From there, she walked to Wheeler's Bridge and

Wheeler's Pond, which had a few slushy ice chunks floating in it but otherwise wasn't frozen over. This was where her mother used to go skating with her friends. She remembered her mother telling her how, on her thirteenth birthday, she and her friend Katrina spent the afternoon skating there and then Katrina's mother had brought the girls home for hot chocolate and whoopie pies, Patience's favorite. Trina was filled with happiness at seeing these sights and she practically pranced home.

The creek meandered behind several houses and when she spotted a few Amish farmers or Amish children, she worried they'd forbid her to trespass, but they merely waved and she waved back. Finally, just as she was climbing the hill leading home, she saw Timothy and Tanner, and her heart skipped a beat as she imagined Seth was close by. But no, it was Martha sitting on a rock, her face turned toward the sun. They must have finished their family's worship services, since it was an *off Sunday*, meaning Amish families gathered separately in their own homes instead of as a community.

"*Guder nammidaag*, Martha!" Trina called.

Martha waved in her direction and the boys darted straight for her, each trying to outrun the other. Tanner won.

"I prayed we'd see you today," he said after he caught his breath.

"Me, too," Timothy echoed.

Trina's heart absolutely swelled with affection.

"Specially 'cause we asked *Daed* if you could *kumme* to our house for worship but he said *neh*."

"*Jah,* he said you're *Englisch* and you go to an *Englisch* church and you're like a puppy."

"A puppy?" Trina questioned as the threesome trod toward Martha.

"*Jah.* We found a lost puppy and we wanted to keep it but *Groossmammi* is 'lergic. *Daed* said not to get too close to you or we'll be sad, like we were about giving away the puppy."

"Am I too close to you now, Trina?" Timothy asked, taking a step away from her.

Now Trina was angry. It was one thing when Seth teased her about her *Englisch* ways; she enjoyed their banter. But it was another thing altogether to point out her differences to the boys and make them afraid to be near her. Didn't he know how children took language literally at this age?

"*Neh,* you're not close enough," she said, squatting down and holding her arms wide. "*Kumme* closer and give me a hug."

Both Tanner and Timothy squeezed closer, nearly knocking her over. She hugged them tightly and then let go. "Now, did that make you sad?" she asked.

"*Neh,*" they answered in unison.

"Then I guess I'm not like that stray puppy, after all, am I?"

"*Neh,* a puppy goes like this." Timothy scooted away, barking, and his brother pretended to wag his tail as he followed.

"Give me your arm, dear," Martha said when Trina reached her, and Trina steadied her as they walked home behind the boys. Trina's cheeks were stinging, but it wasn't from the cold. She was so distraught over

Seth's remarks she could barely manage one-word replies to Martha's questions about church.

Finally the old woman stopped and said, "Please don't mind the *buwe*'s comments. I heard what they told you and that's not exactly how Seth explained the differences to them."

"But it's the gist, I'm sure," Trina said sharply, not even censoring her anger for Martha.

"Perhaps, but you have to understand. He's actually trying to protect the *buwe*."

Trina dropped Martha's arm. "Protect them? From *me*? If I'm so dangerous, why is he allowing me to watch Timothy and Tanner at all?"

"Ach, I've said the wrong thing," Martha muttered and her eyes filled. "I didn't mean you were dangerous. I meant…you see, Seth's brother, Freeman, fell in love with an *Englischer*. She promised she intended to join the Amish and she lived with an Amish family not far from here for almost two years in preparation. But in the end, she couldn't give up her *Englisch* lifestyle, so Freeman gave up his Amish one."

Trina took Martha's arm again, feeling guilty, as Martha continued speaking.

"It broke Seth's *mamm*'s heart and she died shortly after. Seth's *daed* had died years before, so Seth was left alone. I don't know if he's ever forgiven Freeman or his wife. I think he carries a lot of fear and hurt, which manifest as intolerance. No matter what Freeman chose, I know Seth still loves and misses his brother. I think he wants to be sure the *buwe* don't miss you like that when you leave. That's what I meant by protecting them."

Trina felt the anxiety dissolve from her body. *"Denki*, Martha, for telling me that. It helps." Then she laughed. "I guess I am kind of a stray, aren't I?"

"Neh!" Martha vehemently denied it. "You're a gift from *Gott* to our family."

"So is your family to me," Trina said, patting Martha's arm. She was assisting the older woman up the stairs to her home as Seth exited the house. The bright blue collar of his good church shirt turned his eyes from steely gray to bright blue and his honeyed hair shone in the sunlight before he set his hat on his head.

"Guder nammidaag, Trina," he said tersely before turning to Martha. "I'll see you this evening. Don't keep supper for me."

When he was out of earshot, Martha whispered, "He's going courting again."

Even though Trina had expected as much, her heart sank as she led Martha inside for tea.

On his way to Fannie's house, Seth thought more about Trina than he did about Fannie. He kept wondering what she'd told the realtor. He could only hope she hadn't made any decisions, because he wanted to talk to her first. Maybe if he presented his case, or if he found a family who was looking for a new place to live, he could get her to change her mind.

With those thoughts preoccupying him, he arrived at Fannie's house. Her two girls, Greta and Hope, ages five and eight, respectively, greeted him in the yard as he was hitching his horse to the post. They led him inside, where Fannie was preparing a tray of dessert with coffee for the adults and hot chocolate for the children. Seth was a little taken aback when each of the girls helped themselves to two thimble cookies and a honey bar each before Fannie even set the tray on the coffee table in the parlor. A few minutes later the girls discarded the treats, half eaten.

When he and Fannie finished theirs, he suggested, "Why don't we go for a walk? It's unusually sunny and warm outside today."

But Hope whined about wanting to play a game of Go Fish. Apparently, Fannie had promised her they'd play together. Before the end of the game, Greta was in tears because she lost, and Hope and Fannie were arguing over whether Hope peeked at her mother's cards. Seth was glad when they'd eaten supper—or, in the girls' case, had eaten half their suppers—and he could head home. He'd already decided to ask Belinda to introduce him to someone else.

Martha had managed to put the boys to bed herself and she was waiting for him in the parlor. "So, how was your afternoon with Fannie and her *dechder*?"

When he finished telling her about the game and the desserts, Martha clicked her tongue. "I guess it's not just the *Englisch* who spoil their *kinner,* after all, is it?"

Seth realized she was referencing remarks he sometimes made about *Englisch* customers. "*Jah*, you're right. But the Amish would never build a liquor store next door to us." Then he told Martha what Joseph had told him, peppering the conversation with references to the realtor as "a little weasel."

"I'm sure Trina would never sell her *mamm*'s house to a developer for a wine and spirits shop," she said dismissively.

"How do you know that?"

"Because I knew her *mamm* and she didn't raise a *dochder* like that."

"How can you say that?" Seth asked incredulously. "Her *mamm* left the Amish! She became an *Englischer*. She abandoned her *daed*! You can't trust—"

"Listen here, young man," Martha interrupted. "You don't know what you're talking about. Trina's *mamm* didn't abandon her *daed*—her *daed* abandoned her. That *maedel* practically had to raise herself because her brute of a *daed* was too consumed with the bottle to care for his *dochder*. By the time she turned eighteen, Abe's drinking had gotten so bad sometimes he'd pass out on their front lawn. She was probably so tired of taking care of him she did the only thing she could think to do—she took care of herself by leaving."

Seth opened his mouth to say that's not how Abe seemed to him, but Martha continued lecturing him. "You didn't know him before he gave up the booze. But I did. And I know Trina wouldn't have any part in supporting a liquor store."

Seth felt terrible. He hadn't realized Trina's grandfather had been an alcoholic, or that he'd been negligent in caring for Trina's mother. He was wrong for judging Patience. And he hoped he was wrong in imagining Trina would sell out, too.

Chapter Five

In the week following Martha's confiding in her about Freeman, Trina tried to drop hints to Timothy and Tanner about the fact she wouldn't be with them very long. She agreed with Seth it might be painful for them when she left, so she wanted to prepare them for her eventual departure. On Wednesday afternoon, as she put them down for their naps, Timothy asked if she'd still be there when he woke up.

"Of course I will," she told him, realizing she may have overdone it in warning them she wasn't going to be with them permanently. "I'm not leaving until May. I'll show you how many days that is on the calendar when you're done napping."

"Will you *kumme* to visit us after you leave?" Timothy asked.

"Well, Philadelphia is pretty far away."

"That's okay. *Englischers* can drive a car or fly in an airplane." Tanner yawned before adding, "*Daed* said he doesn't want you to sell your house."

Trina's ear perked up. "When did he say that?"

"At night when I was getting a drink. He told *Groossmammi* a weasel came to your house to ask you to put a concrete jungle in your backyard. Will there be monkeys in the jungle?"

Trina was mortified. "*Neh*, your *daed* was only teasing. After all, weasels can't talk, can they?"

Tanner shook his head and Timothy asked, "Will there still be a jungle in our backyard?"

"I'm afraid not," she said. "Although that doesn't mean there won't be two of my favorite little monkeys swinging from the trees." She tickled each boy's stomach and they laughed before rolling over and falling asleep.

Later, when Seth returned home, he didn't even have time to remove his hat before Trina asked to speak with him on the porch. He looked surprised but he agreed. She was so insulted he thought she was the kind of person who'd allow her mother's property to be exploited for the sake of selling alcohol that she didn't waste time with any pleasantries.

"For your information, I'm not selling the property to anyone who wants to use it to build a liquor store!" she said, planting her hands on her hips.

Seth removed his hat and scratched his ear as if he hadn't quite heard right. "I suppose Martha told you about our conversation?"

"*Neh*, the *buwe* did. But that hardly matters. What matters is that I'm *not* selling the house to a developer and if you have a question about something like that, you should ask me instead of spreading rumors. Especially within earshot of the *kinner*."

Seth responded defensively, "Who are you to lecture me on what I should or shouldn't do in front of my own *buwe*?"

Scowling, Trina countered, "Who do *you* think *you* are to spread false rumors about me?"

"I didn't," he said and his shoulders drooped. "At least, I didn't intend to—I didn't know the *buwe* were still awake. But I wasn't spreading a rumor. Not exactly. I was discussing my concerns with Martha, who, by the way, adamantly informed me my fears were unfounded."

Trina's cheeks were still burning. "*Jah*, and I would have informed you of the same thing if you'd only asked me first."

"I know that now." Seth lowered his voice and compassionately explained, "My *groossmammi* also told me about…about your *groossdaadi*'s drinking problem and the effect that had on your *mamm*. I had no idea. That must have been so difficult for her."

"*Jah*, it was," Trina admitted, "which is why it's so important I honor her memory by selling her childhood home to a family who will be happy together in it."

Seth's relief was evident. "I'm really glad to hear that's your intention. And I'm sorry I didn't consult with you first instead of jumping to conclusions."

"It's alright." Trina hesitated before confessing, "Martha told me about your brother's decision, too. I can see how that would influence your perspective on *Englischers*."

"I try not to let it, but I'm afraid I'm not always successful." It was too dark to see Seth's eyes, but his voice was heavy. "So *denki* for bearing with me."

Glad their argument was over, Trina jested, "Speaking of *bears*, you're going to have two very disappointed boys on your hands. After hearing your comments about the realtor, they thought they were getting an actual jungle in their backyard."

When Seth laughed, his straight, bright teeth shone in the dark. "Serves me right, I guess."

Hesitantly, Trina said, "I wouldn't think of telling you what to do with your *buwe*, but could I offer an observation?"

"Of course."

"*Kinner* their age tend to take figurative language literally. Not only can it get their hopes up, but it can be scary for them, too. For example, the other morning I told Martha the *buwe* were so funny I almost laughed my head off. Timothy overheard and was terrified his antics were going to make my head roll off my shoulders."

"Ah, point taken," Seth said, again giving her a toothy smile.

Was he laughing at her or at the boys? "What's that smile about?" she asked.

"Oh, I was just thinking you must be a *wunderbaar* teacher. Not only because of the way you teach Timothy and Tanner, but because of the way you just made your point with me, too."

Trina's insides felt wiggly. She loved being a teacher and she was glad it showed. "*Denki.* And since you mentioned careers, I'd like to say I could see from the detail you put into your leatherwork that you care very much about their quality."

Seth adjusted his hat. "*Denki.* Did the *buwe* show you one of my harnesses in the stable?"

"*Neh.* I peeked into your shop window when I walked home from church the other day. I'd love to take a closer look when the shop is open, though."

"Whoa. You walked all the way to Main Street from church and then home again?"

"*Jah.* I'm heartier than I look."

Was she imagining it or did Seth just give her the once-over? "Some off Sunday when we're not at church, I could pick you up and take you to my shop," he suggested. "With the *buwe* and Martha, of course."

Of course—Trina understood the rules of propriety. "I'd like that. And I'd also like it if you'd check out the rest of my house for mice. The one in the cupboard is gone but I heard something scratching last night. It might have been a branch against the walls but just in case..."

"I thought you said you were hearty," Seth joked. "What harm is a little mouse going to do to you?"

Trina didn't know if she should confide in him, but since he'd been so understanding about her *mamm* and about Abe's alcoholism, she decided to risk it. "I know it's a ridiculous fear. But when you've lived in the city, or when you've been poor, it's not always mice you hear. Sometimes it's...rats." Even the word made her shudder, or maybe it was the fact she'd just confided to Seth that she and her mother had once been very poor. Suddenly self-conscious, she turned her head even though it was too dark for Seth to see her expression.

Seth cleared his throat. "I'd be happy to help rid your house of the little critters," he said warmly. "And if I'm not successful, I know two little *buwe* who act like very convincing *katze.*"

They both laughed. Trina was glad what started out as an uncomfortable, intense conversation had ended so well and even gladder Seth had complimented her abilities as a teacher.

On Thursday evening after putting the boys to bed early, Seth visited Belinda Imhoff to discuss potentially courting a different woman. He would have waited to see Belinda after work on Saturday, but he had reserved that afternoon to more thoroughly mouse-proof Trina's house. He was so relieved she didn't intend to sell the property to a land developer that he would have done almost anything to get the house into better shape for a family to move into.

Belinda suggested matching him with Emma Lamp, who was from Willow Creek. Seth had never considered courting her previously because she was so young—perhaps only eighteen or nineteen. It seemed she would have had plenty of opportunities for courtships through attending singings or other social events with youth her own age. But he wanted to keep an open mind, especially since Belinda seemed disappointed he had already decided against Fannie. Belinda suggested he try meeting her a few more times, but Seth had a sure sense that Fannie and her daughters weren't compatible with him and his family. More time wasn't going to change his mind, and he had to make the most of the next several weeks while Trina was still there to watch the boys. So, he asked Belinda to arrange for him to take Emma to his home after church that Sunday.

Because there was a torrential downpour on Saturday afternoon, he didn't allow the boys to accompany him to Trina's house while he repaired the woodwork. He didn't want them dirtying her floors as well as theirs, and Martha said she could handle them for an hour or so.

After pointing out where she'd heard the scratching sounds in the parlor, Trina retreated to the kitchen, and Seth examined the baseboards and flooring, which were definitely in need of repair. He wanted to fix them for her, as well as for any potential buyers. He was kneeling behind the sofa examining the baseboard when he heard Trina enter the room. Rising to face her, he knocked his shoulder against the end table and toppled its contents—a Bible and a framed photo—onto the floor. He managed to catch the Bible but the picture frame went crashing down and broke into several pieces that skittered across the floor.

Trina gasped. "Oh, *neh*!"

Seth clumsily stood up. "Ach, I'm sorry. I'll clean that up," he offered.

Trina dropped to her knees and picked up the broken frame, which appeared to be made out of fragments of glass. She rocked it in her arms and cried as if it were her baby that had fallen. He began collecting pieces of glass from the floor but she snapped, "Leave them alone—and leave me alone, too. I want you to go home."

"What?" Seth didn't understand why she was acting so devastated over a few pieces of glass. Even Timothy and Tanner wouldn't have cried like that over a broken object.

Her lip was quivering as she raised her tear streaked face and repeated, "Please leave."

"What about the cracks in the walls?"

"I don't care about the stupid walls or this stupid house," she wailed.

"That makes no sense," he pointed out. "You're bawling over something that's already broken instead of prioritizing something that can still be fixed."

Trina rose to her feet and held up the jagged frame. "This was important to me," she cried. "It was the most important possession I owned."

"But that's just it, it's only a possession. It's not as if it's a life that's lost." He didn't know why, but that really set Trina to sobbing. He didn't give in. "I don't understand why the *Englisch* are so preoccupied with photos anyway. It's *narrish*."

"I wouldn't expect you to understand," she wept. "Amish men don't have feelings. Or at least they don't show them if they do. They're heartless, absolutely heartless."

Heartless? That was the most preposterous thing he'd ever heard. "Oh, we have feelings, alright. But only for things that matter. We're not like the *Englisch* who care about their material possessions more than anything."

"You have no idea what we care about," Trina countered. "How could you? You're too busy judging us to understand us."

"And the *Englisch* are just plain too busy," Seth retorted. "Everything is hurry, hurry, hurry, now, now, now. You're pushy and impatient and overbearing."

"Oh, *denki* very much for that. Is there anything else you want to say about the *Englisch* before you leave?" Trina sniped.

Seth knew the argument had gotten out of hand, but he really resented being called heartless. "*Jah*, the *Englisch* are so concerned with being thin they don't care if they look sickly. I have healthier looking scarecrows in my garden."

He knew he'd gone too far even before Trina's expression wilted and she turned her back to him, but at that moment, he felt his remarks were justified. After all, she'd asked him what he thought of *Englischers*.

Hours later, he was still stoking the ashes of his anger, when Timothy asked, "Can we invite Trina to supper tomorrow night, *Daed*?"

"*Neh*," he barked and Martha popped her head up from where she was crocheting on the sofa. She always said when you crocheted for as many years as she did, you didn't need vision; you could do it in your sleep.

"Tomorrow Emma Lamp is visiting for supper," he explained, as if that were the only reason he didn't want Trina around.

"Emma Lamp?" Martha echoed. "Isn't she a little young?"

"It's not age that matters. It's maturity," Seth groused, thinking of Trina's tantrum over a broken picture frame. He didn't need a lecture from Martha but he knew one was coming when she sent the boys to the basement to ride their bikes.

"You've been moping all afternoon. Do you want to tell me what's wrong?"

"*Neh*," Seth replied curtly.

"Well, tell me anyway," Martha said, and as usual he gave in, explaining what had happened between him and Trina at her house.

"Can you believe it?" he asked. "I was there as a favor and she showed me no gratitude. It wasn't as if I broke her frame on purpose. And I said I was sorry!"

"What was in the picture frame?"

"A picture, of course," Seth sputtered in exasperation.

"A picture of what?"

"I don't know. I think it was of Trina and her *mamm*."

Martha nodded, but remained silent as the realization washed over Seth. He reluctantly conceded, "Alright, I suppose she valued the frame because of the photo."

"I think she valued both the photo and the frame because of the memory they contained."

Seth sighed heavily. He remembered, as irrational as it was, after Eleanor died he'd kept her prayer *kapp* hanging on the bedpost until the day he and the baby boys moved out of the house. It wasn't the *kapp* he cherished; it was that the *kapp* reminded him of all the times his wife faithfully prayed for their family.

"I'm not heartless," he muttered.

"*Neh*, you're definitely not. And Trina knows that. But in the moment, you probably seemed that way to her."

Seth went to bed that night feeling sadder than he'd felt in a long time. So much for loving his neighbor; he'd all but stomped on Trina's memories and then called her a scarecrow. He'd have to find a way to apologize.

Trina lay in bed and imagined calling a cab and running away from Willow Creek in the middle of the night without telling anyone she was going. Her mother had done it with even less education and resources than Trina had, so why couldn't she?

Her mother. The tears hadn't stopped flowing since her photo frame shattered across the floor. It was as if her mother herself was warning her about Amish men. Ha! What a joke it was for Seth to caution his sons not to get too close to her—the reverse was actually true. Trina should have been more cautious about getting too close to Seth. She had come dangerously close to trusting him, the way her mother must have trusted Trina's father at first.

"Your *daed* was the opposite of mine," Patience told Trina once she was old enough to begin dating. "He was physically and emotionally demonstrative and I was starving for affection. But that wasn't a good enough reason to marry him. When you date, Trina, don't do it out of a sense of loneliness."

Of course, Trina wasn't *dating* Seth. Not even close. But if she was honest, she had to admit she had feelings for him that were more than just neighborly congeniality. And it was largely because she was lonely. *How pathetic!* she scolded herself. She would have left Willow Creek right then, but out of spite and the sheer willfulness to prove she could make it in that community she decided she'd stay. She wasn't going to give up her inheritance—her mother's home—just because of a couple of coldhearted men like Abe and Seth.

Plus, no matter that the boys were related to Seth, she couldn't take off without at least saying goodbye to Timothy and Tanner. Nor could she leave Martha alone to care for them. Not yet. But the instant her sixty days were up, she was out of there. She wasn't going to stick around until the house sold, either. She was feeling stronger now. She could get a teaching job again. She'd take out a loan until the sale went through so she could afford rent, or else she'd sell the house dirt cheap to the first buyer. But she wasn't going to give up what was hers simply because a clumsy ox of a man thought she was materialistic and as scrawny as a scarecrow.

The next morning when she tried to button her skirt for church, she actually had to suck in her stomach to get it to close. It was true she'd lost a lot of weight and she supposed she did look scraggy to Seth, but she was making progress. She pulled on a dress, instead, and arranged her hair in a bun at the nape of her neck instead of her usual ponytail and set off for church.

The sermon was on God's forgiveness and the pastor had hardly uttered three sentences before she realized she couldn't carry her grudge against Seth. She had to forgive him but that didn't mean everything would be the same between them again. She couldn't risk letting her defenses down a second time.

"Hi, Trina," someone said after the closing song, tapping her on the shoulder.

She turned to find Ethan giving her an enormous grin. "Hi, Ethan. It's nice to see you."

"You, too. I almost didn't recognize you with your hair like that. Are you going somewhere special?"

"Neh," she said and then repeated, "No. I'm not going anywhere special."

"Good. Then you'll let me give you a ride home?"

After confirming she didn't have special plans,

Trina had no choice but to accept Ethan's offer. "Thank you. That would be nice," she agreed.

On the way they chatted about what brought them to Willow Creek. "My grandparents were Mennonites, so I've always had an interest in Mennonite and Amish culture and beliefs," Ethan explained. "I knew this is where I wanted to practice medicine. I mostly see patients in Willow Creek and one day a week I volunteer at the Highland Springs clinic for the Amish. How about you? Why did you relocate to Willow Creek?"

"I didn't," Trina said. "I mean, I'm only staying here for a couple of months because—oh, it's a long story, but I have to live here for sixty days before I can inherit the house my mother grew up in. She was Amish. Anyway, once my time is up, I'm selling the house and moving back to Philly."

"I just left Philly!" Ethan exclaimed. "That's where my fiancée lives. She'll be joining me after our wedding in June. It's a great city, but I prefer the country life here, don't you?"

"I'm becoming accustomed to it," Trina admitted, relieved to hear Ethan was engaged. So, his interest in her was merely because she was a new resident like he was, and nothing more. "I especially enjoy walking by the creek, knowing it's where my mother once walked."

"Can you believe I've been in Willow Creek for over two months and I still haven't seen the creek the town is named after?"

Trina impulsively suggested, "Oh, you'll have to take a look, then. It runs behind the property near my house."

As they were strolling by the banks of the creek a

few minutes later, Trina heard a sound. "I recognize those voices," she said.

"Voices? I only heard something growl."

Trina laughed. "It's the two boys I care for during the day. They like to pretend they're animals. If I'm not mistaken, they're being bears again."

Just then, Tanner and Timothy pounced out at Trina and Ethan from behind a rock. "Rrroar!" they thundered.

"Look, it's a pair of grizzlies!" Ethan declared good-naturedly.

"Guder nammidaag, buwe," Trina greeted them. "Stand up on your hind legs now. I want to introduce you to my friend, Ethan Gray. He's a doctor, so you might go to his office one day when you're sick and he'll make you feel better."

"Animals don't go to doctors. They go to vegetarians," Timothy said wisely, cracking Ethan up. After they told Ethan their names, Trina asked them if they were walking with Martha.

"Neh. We're with *Daed* and Emma," Timothy answered.

Trina's stomach did a flip and she suddenly felt dejected. But after what she'd learned yesterday about Seth's feelings—or lack of feelings—toward her, why should she care if she bumped into him and some new woman he was apparently courting?

"Timothy, Tanner!" Seth's voice cut through the crisp air. "Where are you?"

"We're here with Trina," Tanner bellowed back.

"What have I told you about staying within my sight near the creek?" Seth asked the boys before greeting

Trina or Ethan. "If you wander off again, we'll have to march right back to the house and you won't be able to return for an entire week."

"Sorry, *Daed*." The boys hung their heads.

"Oh, look, it's Dr. Gray," a young woman said when she caught up with Seth. She had light blond hair and a sturdy, feminine shape. Her skin was so pink and her face so full it looked like she literally had apples in her cheeks. No doubt she was just the kind of healthy, patient, sensible woman Seth was looking for.

"Emma… Lamp, isn't it?" Ethan asked.

"*Jah*. What a *gut* memory." Emma even had dimples when she smiled. She was the picture of Amish benevolence. "Seth Helmuth, have you met Dr. Gray? He took care of my brother when he came down with a nasty flu."

"Please, call me Ethan." The doctor smiled. Trina noticed Ethan didn't extend his hand to shake; apparently, he knew the customs already. To Emma he said, "How is Thomas doing?"

"He's better than ever before. Tormenting our sisters and chasing them around the barn."

"Glad to hear it. I assume you know Trina Smith?" Ethan asked, gesturing toward her.

"Only by reputation," Emma said, smiling. "The moment I walked through the door, the *buwe* showed me games you taught them. They're very fond of you."

Oh, no. Emma was nice as well as sweet and pretty. "I'm fond of them, too," Trina said. She could hardly look in Seth's direction, lest she see *his* fondness for Emma in his eyes. Or worse, his disdain for Trina.

"Looks like we're going in opposite directions, so

we'll keep walking," Seth said. "Now, where did those two scamper off to?"

"I believe they're in the den to our right, up ahead," Emma said, motioning toward a large rock the boys had covered with sticks and fern. Trina had to give it to her, she was playing along with their games well. As if reading Trina's thoughts, Emma winked at her and said, "I've got a brother and two little sisters around their age at home."

Wow, she must have been really young herself to have siblings that age! Trina felt glum all the way back to the house so she was happy when Ethan accepted her invitation for tea and dessert. At least he seemed to like her. Granted, he appeared to like her the way a big brother would, which made her feel embarrassed she'd ever suspected him of being interested in dating her.

"I don't know, Trina," he said slowly before leaving. "Willow Creek is awfully beautiful. Are you sure you want to leave it behind for Philly?"

"I'm sure," she said.

On the way home from dropping off Emma, Seth felt sick to his stomach and his palms were sweaty. It wasn't nervousness. Not about Emma, anyway. No, it was easy to be around her. She was pleasant, light-hearted and she got along well with the boys. But she was also young. Too young. It wasn't that she was immature, exactly, but in a way her youthful innocence made Seth feel as if he had another child in his care. Halfway through the afternoon he decided to tell Belinda Imhoff he'd made a mistake and he'd give a courtship with Fannie Jantzi one more try.

But for now, he had to apologize to Trina and it was unnerving him like nothing ever had before. Bumping into her in the woods had been uncomfortable and he wished he hadn't seen her with Ethan. An *Englisch* pediatrician. Who could be better for Trina? Together they'd make the perfect couple, with her teaching children and him healing them. Seth should have been happy that she'd found a friend in Willow Creek. A boyfriend, even—someone who might be a good match. But he wasn't happy. And the fact he wasn't happy was unsettling. Furthermore, he was doubly upset because he had to apologize to her and he didn't know if she'd accept his apology.

She'd hardly glanced his way in the woods, although for his part he'd noticed she wore her hair in a neat bun. With her face framed by its softness, her cheekbones looked less severe and her eyes stood out even more. Seth shook his head. How could he have been so boorish as to imply she looked like a scarecrow? He'd never found any *Englischer* so attractive before. Not simply because of her eyes and height and the way she carried herself, but because of the way her character manifested itself through her physical traits. It pained him to think she thought of him as heartless.

He took extra care stabling his horse, procrastinating before he crossed the yard to Trina's house. Instead of inviting him in when he asked to speak to her, she stepped onto the porch, closing the door behind her. She wasn't wearing a coat; he'd have to make this quick.

"I've *kumme* to apologize. I'm truly sorry for breaking your picture frame," he began. "But I'm even sorrier for hurting you. I shouldn't have implied you're overly concerned with possessions. Later, when I thought things over, I realized I just said that because I… I was trying to do something helpful for you and instead I broke your frame. I felt like such a klutz that I somehow turned things around and tried to pin the blame on you for valuing a possession instead of acknowledging I'd ruined something that was special to you."

Trina didn't say anything until she'd walked past him and stood by the railing of the porch, gazing at the sky. "I don't own many material things, but the picture frame was a gift from my *mamm*."

Seth was quiet, sensing he needed to give her time to say her piece before she forgave him.

"She gave it to me the Christmas before she became ill. She'd bought it at the Cape—Cape Cod, in Massachusetts. I don't know how she could have afforded it, but—" Trina choked and a sob escaped her lips.

Seth walked to her, removed his coat and draped it around her shoulders. "What is one of your favorite memories of being at Cape Cod with your mother?" he asked.

Trina sniffed and gestured out toward the lawn, as if remembering the ocean. "We loved to get up early in the morning and go to the beach before anyone else arrived. There were these little tiny birds called sandpipers that ran along the edge of the surf. They were so quick they made us laugh." Trina wiped her eyes with the back of her hand and added wryly, "You wouldn't like them, they looked like they were in a hurry."

Seth chortled. "I'm sorry for saying that, too. I know not all *Englischers* are in a hurry."

"Most of them are. I don't disagree with you on that," Trina said. "But I'm not."

"And I'm not heartless," Seth said, quietly but firmly. "But I understand that your *groossdaadi* acted that way to your *mamm*."

"Oh, Seth!" Trina exclaimed, angling sideways to look at him again. "I'm so sorry I said that. You have a bigger heart than any man I know. The amount of love and care you show for Timothy and Tanner—and for Martha, too—well, I've never seen a man demonstrate anything like it."

From the way his heart was battering his ribs, Seth was sure Trina could hear it. He replied, "And I'm sorry for implying you look like a scarecrow."

"Well, I have lost a lot of weight this past year and those *seh* of yours can make me look pretty disheveled by the end of the day."

Neh. You're the best sight I see at the end of my day, Seth thought. It was a bold sentiment and he was in a dangerous position to think such a thing, much less to say it. He didn't, of course, but neither did he stop looking at her. There was something about her lips that made them seem as irresistible as the taste of funny cake. Yet he had to resist. She was an *Englischer*, like Freeman's wife. In a throaty voice he said, "*Jah,* my sons can have that effect on a person. But you don't look disheveled now. I like your hair like that."

"*Denki.*" Trina lifted her hand to the nape of her neck and turned back toward the lawn in one graceful motion. She paused before playfully referencing her angry remark from the previous day, "Anyway, if you're willing, I'd still like you to fix my stupid walls."

"*Jah*, I'm still willing to fix the stupid walls in your stupid house," he said and they both laughed.

But he wasn't laughing later that night in bed. He was agonizing over how much he had longed to kiss an *Englischer*. It was forbidden by the *Ordnung*, but even if it weren't, it was forbidden by him, personally. His family had already paid dearly for allowing one *Englischer* into their lives, and Kristine had claimed she was going to become Amish. Trina made no such promise; on the contrary, she was leaving in a matter of weeks.

If only Seth had been ashamed and regretful that he wanted to kiss her, he could confess and be done with it. But the sorry truth was, he may have been ashamed of it, but he still wished to kiss Trina.

That's lecherich, he thought. *I'd never do such a thing. Never!*

Besides, for all he could guess, Trina was interested in Ethan. Seth knew the best way to rid his mind of fanciful thoughts about her was to keep squarely focused on courting an Amish woman, and before falling asleep he decided he'd definitely invite Fannie and her daughters to the house for supper at the first opportunity.

Chapter Six

As pleased as Trina was that she and Seth had cleared the air, she was unnerved by what had transpired—or nearly transpired—between them. It was one thing for him to give her his coat; that was a gallant gesture, but one he would have made to Martha, as well as to any woman who was cold. But the way he'd looked at her before he told her he liked her hair... She wasn't misinterpreting the ardor of his expression, was she? *Don't be silly,* she told herself. *I was wrong about Ethan's intentions and I'm probably wrong about Seth's, too.*

Not that it mattered much. She was *Englisch* and he was Amish, so there was no possibility of any romantic relationship between them. She didn't want one, either. Alright, perhaps she wanted one a little. Perhaps she wanted him to kiss her instead of just look like he wanted to kiss her. But that was inconceivable. It was permissible to be friends with him and to care for his children, but after all Patience had gone through to raise her daughter as an *Englischer*, Trina felt disloyal to her *mamm*'s memory for even entertaining thoughts of kissing an Amish man. Besides, Seth was courting Emma. That was serious; that was for the explicit purpose of pursuing a marriage relationship. It wasn't just some passing infatuation.

Trina knew what she needed to do was to call a few realtors and start preparing to sell the house. She couldn't officially put it on the market until May, but she decided she should probably get the ball rolling. The sooner it sold, the sooner she could go back to Philly. The summer months were always the best hiring times for new teachers, so she didn't want to miss those opportunities.

For the rest of the week, Trina wore her hair up in a ponytail again because she felt too self-conscious to be reminded of Seth's compliment. She went out of her way to focus their discussions on the boys whenever she was with Seth, and if she wasn't mistaken, he also seemed to limit their conversations to the weather or his sons. And on Saturday evening, when they all traveled to the *Englisch* store in Highland Springs, Trina sat in the back with the boys on the way there. On the way back, however, Martha insisted she take the front seat next to Seth.

Trina kept her arm tight to her side so she wouldn't inadvertently bump into him as the buggy wiggled toward home. They were quiet for a while as Martha and the boys chatted in the back until the silence between them felt unnatural.

"It's getting warmer. I hardly need this blanket any longer." Trina referenced the wool blanket on her lap, at a loss for what else to discuss.

"Oh, here, I can put it in the back for you if you're too hot," Seth replied.

His hand grazed Trina's knee as he reached for it. At the same time, Trina tried to grab it, saying, "*Neh*, that's okay. I just meant the weather is changing." Their hands collided on her lap and they both immediately pulled back. Trina's arm buzzed as if she'd touched an electric fence.

"*Jah*, spring will be here soon," Seth blandly remarked. "I mean, I know it's here on the calendar, but it will be here in the weather, too."

Trina giggled nervously. This conversation was becoming more ridiculous by the sentence. "I'm almost to the end of my fourth week here. Do you know anyone who wants to buy a house?" she joked nervously.

"I wish I did." Seth's comment disappointed Trina. Was she expecting him to say he was sorry to see her go—if not for his sake, then for the boys'? He continued, "That way I'd know who our neighbors were before they moved in."

"Isn't part of being neighborly taking time to get to know the people living next door?" Trina wondered aloud. As soon as she asked the question she worried if it sounded flirtatious, which wasn't her intention.

"*Jah,* I suppose you're right," Seth allowed. "I only meant I'd like to know in general if they're *Englisch* or Amish so I could put up a fence ahead of time if necessary."

Now Trina was annoyed. "Don't tell me, the fence would keep the *Englisch* out of your yard." *And out of your life,* she thought. "Has having me for a neighbor been that bad?"

Although he kept his eyes on the road, Seth emphatically shook his head. "*Neh*, I didn't mean it like that. I'd want to build a fence to keep the *kinner* in. If the neighbors are *Englisch* and they have cars, I don't want the *kinner* running over there."

Relaxing, Trina said, "The *buwe* are usually pretty *gut* about not going where they shouldn't—unless they're pretending to be wild creatures down by the creek."

"It's not Timothy and Tanner I'm worried about. It's Fannie's girls. They don't seem to mind too well."

Trina was too surprised to hold her tongue. "Fannie's girls? What about Emma?" she asked. "I thought you were courting Emma."

"Emma's too young. Barely twenty," Seth said.

So that was it, then? Emma didn't work out so he simply defaulted to the better of his two choices and now he was already considering marriage with Fannie? "Wow. And you think *Englischers* are impatient," she couldn't help saying snidely under her breath.

"What?"

Quietly so no one else would hear, and staring straight ahead, Trina said, "You've been on what, two dates with Fannie and you're already considering building a fence for her *kinner*? That must mean you plan to marry her. Even the *Englisch* don't rush into marriage that quickly."

Seth huffed so loudly Trina thought it was the horse at first. "I've told you, we don't call it *dating*. But when you've been married before you know what you're looking for in a spouse."

"It may be true that you know what qualities you're

looking for in a woman, but finding them doesn't necessarily mean you've found love, does it?" Trina understood she was crossing a line by talking about such things with an Amish man but she felt too argumentative to give in.

"The Amish tend to base our decisions on practical considerations, not emotional ones. Love is a choice. It's something you work at developing. It's not something that you either have or don't have."

"So you'd marry a woman you're not in love with?"

"Not that I think it's appropriate to be having this conversation, but *jah*, I'd marry a woman I wasn't necessarily 'in love with.' Because being 'in love' is just an emotion and emotions are fickle. They're dangerous," Seth explained. He added, "Over time and with work and mutual cooperation, a couple can *kumme* to love each other deeply."

Trina didn't know how to respond to that. She didn't necessarily disagree with Seth, but she certainly didn't agree fully, either. After all, her mother had fallen in love with her father based on her feelings, and look where that had gotten her. Conversely, her mother's father had shown a severe lack of emotion and that was damaging, too.

Trina swallowed and forced herself to say, "Well, then, I'm glad for you if you've found what you're looking for in a spouse. As soon as I know whether the people who buy the house are *Englisch* or Amish, I'll be sure to tell you."

Seth couldn't believe he'd just indicated to Trina he intended to marry Fannie. He felt as verbally awkward as he was physically, touching her knee, bumping her hand; it had thrown him off. Especially since all week he'd tried to restrict his contact and dull his conversations with her. Now she was sitting right next to him, talking about one of the most intimate subjects they could discuss. As much as he denied the power of emotions, his were wreaking havoc on him. He feared he'd come across as even more of a dope if he tried to explain.

The truth was, he wasn't actually *planning* to make a fence for Fannie's daughters—he'd just been thinking aloud. In his mind, it was more like a complaint, as in, *"If* I were to marry Fannie, I'd better put a fence up because her girls are ill behaved." The emphasis had been on the girls' behavior, not on marriage, but how would Trina have known that? He was relieved he wouldn't have to see her the following day. Maybe by Monday some of his embarrassment would have burned off and he wouldn't feel so oafish around her again.

After the next morning's worship, Timothy excitedly asked, "Can we *kumme* with you to get Fannie and her *dechder, Daed*?"

Seth didn't think it was a good idea to have the children's initial introduction to each other taking place within the confines of a crowded buggy. "*Neh*, but as soon as Hope and Greta arrive, we'll all take a walk along the creek together. For now I want you to stay here and help *Groossmammi* with whatever she needs."

"What I need is for Trina to *kumme* and help me put together a light supper," Martha grumbled.

"*Neh!*" Seth objected. He couldn't think of anything worse than having Trina around after their conversation yesterday. She'd no doubt scrutinize every interaction between him and Fannie and see there was no spark—no *emotional* connection—between them. "Trina is probably still at her church. Besides, Fannie will help you with whatever you need to do in the kitchen."

"That's what I'm afraid of," Martha muttered.

Her comment made Seth wonder why he was going through with introducing Fannie's children to his. He didn't want to make his household problems worse by bringing in disobedient children and a pushy woman who clashed with Martha. But as he was pulling out of their lane onto the main road, he saw a car turning onto Trina's lane: Ethan was giving Trina a ride home. Again. Seth could guess what this meant; they were falling in love. It served as a reminder to Seth to stay focused on following through with his own plans for matrimony.

The girls sang all the way back to his house and Fannie sang with them. While he appreciated their desire to praise the Lord with songs on the Sabbath, Seth felt like Fannie was so involved in amusing her children she had no time to speak with him, and his thoughts again wandered to Trina. Her speaking voice was so euphonious he wondered what she sounded like singing. Once, before entering the house, he'd heard her warbling through the door as she was washing dishes, but as soon as he turned the knob, she stopped... A dip in the road jarred the buggy and Seth realized he shouldn't be thinking of Trina, especially while he was courting Fannie, so he joined the others in song until they arrived at his house.

Martha must have told the boys they could wait

outside as long as they didn't leave the porch, because they were both hopping up and down on the stairs without venturing into the yard when the buggy pulled up.

"Do you want to see the dens we built by the creek?" Tanner asked as soon as he and Timothy had been introduced to Hope and Greta.

"How about if we go inside first?" Fannie suggested. "The girls want to meet your *groossmammi* and I'm sure she's prepared us something to eat. We don't want it to get cold."

Seth thought it was presumptuous of Fannie to think there was a hot meal waiting. Firstly, he hoped Martha hadn't used the oven or stove, no matter how competent she said she was around it. Secondly, on the Sabbath most of Willow Creek's Amish had cold cuts and fruit or molasses and peanut butter on bread, not a warm meal. But Seth had warned the boys they needed to be polite to their guests and he was pleased when they agreed with Fannie. They even allowed the girls to enter the house first.

"Wilkom," Martha said in their general direction. She was standing at the sink, drying her hands on a towel. She bent down toward Greta and said, "I'm Martha and you must be Greta." Standing a little straighter so her head was even with Hope's, she added, "Which means you're Hope, right?"

"How did she know that?" Hope asked her mother, as if Martha couldn't hear. "You said she was blind."

Seth cringed but his grandmother, who was being as polite as he'd warned the boys they had to be, just chuckled and said, "People sometimes say bats are blind, too, but have you ever seen one fly into a wall?"

Hope shook her head. *"Neh."*

Timothy told her, "That's because they have something called echo...um, echo..."

Seth helped him out. "Echolocation."

"Echolocation," Timothy repeated. "Trina read it to us in a book Ruth Graber brought from the library."

"You have echo—the thing he said?" Hope asked Martha incredulously.

Tanner answered before Martha could. *"Neh.* Only bats have that. But my *groossmammi* has eyes in the back of her head even if the eyes in front of her head are blurry. So if you do something disobedient behind her, she'll catch you."

Seth, Martha and Fannie all laughed heartily. Martha must have used that expression in front of the boys. Trina was right; they seemed to take everything literally. But once again, Seth had to banish thoughts of her.

The seven of them sat down for dinner and Seth was relieved to see that today the girls' table manners were about as good as his boys', even though Greta spilled a glass of milk in a way Seth suspected was deliberate.

"I'm sorry. This happens daily," Fannie said. "She's at that age, you know, where her fingers are still too small to grasp a glass in one hand, but she forgets to use both hands. It's probably like that with Timothy and Tanner, too."

Although his grandmother couldn't have seen the way Greta tipped her glass over, Seth suspected if it had been Timothy or Tanner, Martha would have told them an accident that happened every day wasn't an accident. Instead, she simply said, "No sense crying over spilled milk," and asked Seth to refill Greta's glass for her.

"But I don't want more milk," Greta whined when he set it in front of her.

"I'll drink it," Fannie quickly offered. "It will taste *gut* with dessert."

Now Seth was perturbed. Didn't Fannie ever wait until she was offered? "I'm not certain *Groossmammi* had an opportunity to make dessert yesterday, since we didn't get to the market until later last night—"

"You're right. I didn't. I know it's the Sabbath, but I don't think there's any harm in my whipping up a batch of cookies in the oven while you're taking a walk. It's a way to show hospitality and the Lord loves it when we reflect His character like that," Martha rationalized.

As the others were donning their coats and shawls, Seth whispered to Martha, "You don't have to make dessert, *Groossmammi.* Really. We've had plenty to eat."

"You just don't want me starting another fire."

She was right; her safety was part of Seth's concern. But he was also annoyed Fannie was putting Martha in a position of feeling she wasn't being hospitable. What did the woman expect from his eighty-three-year-old grandmother?

Martha continued, "I'll be fine. Just turn the oven on 375 for me before you go. By the time you return, I'll be done and you can check to make sure it's off. Nothing is on the stovetop so there's no chance of anything catching fire."

Seth wanted to protest but he knew that would be adding insult to injury. Especially if Fannie became worried, too, and offered to stay behind and help Martha bake.

"*Denki, Groossmammi,*" he whispered, kissing her on top of her prayer *kapp* before heading to the creek with the others.

Trina spread herself across a big rock alongside the creek. Her mother had referred to the boulder as Bed Rock, which was a play on words and also a descriptive phrase because the large rock's surface was as flat as a bed. The day was unseasonably warm and Trina positioned her face to the sun to absorb its warmth. But her head was thrumming so she sat up again and loosened her hair from its elastic band. Then she removed her jacket, rolled it into a pillow and lay back against it. That was better.

She was out of sorts and she didn't know why. That morning in church, she'd asked Sherman and Mabel if they knew a reputable realtor in the area and they recommended someone in the congregation. That person was out of town, but Mabel promised to introduce Trina to her as soon as the realtor returned.

This should have made Trina happy, but instead she was downcast. She didn't like to think about leaving Willow Creek. Her mother was in Heaven; of that she was sure. But there was something about being in the town where Patience had lived as a girl that made Trina feel closer to her. Not all of the memories of her mother's childhood there were pleasant, but many of them—especially those that didn't involve her father— were, and it brought Trina joy to see the places or meet the people her mother once knew.

Plus, Trina was growing terribly fond of the boys. Instead of reminding them she'd be leaving soon, she should have worked harder at reminding herself. *Maybe the house won't sell right away and I can watch them until school lets out in June*, she thought. But then what? Wasn't she postponing the inevitable? What did she hope to gain by staying longer in Willow Creek?

She knew the answer: she wanted more time with Seth. She felt like a traitor to her mother to even think the thought, but she couldn't help it. She liked him in a way she hadn't liked any man before. It was partly because he was so loving toward his family and partly because he'd been protective and understanding of her.

It was also because of his dependability and loyalty. With all of the other important males in her life, once times got tough, the men got lost. Her grandfather emotionally abandoned her mother when he lost his wife. Her father took off when he was confronted with the responsibilities of parenthood. Her boyfriend dumped Trina when her mother was ill. Seth had lost his wife and mother and brother, but he stayed true to his faith and to his boys and grandmother. In a way, he'd stayed true to Trina, too, by making up instead of firing her after they'd had an argument. No man had ever apologized like that for hurting her before.

Granted, theirs was a small argument. And she was his employee, so it was in his best interest to reconcile. So she feared she was kidding herself to believe he felt the same strong pull toward her that she felt toward him. And even if he did, there was no chance he'd ever act on those feelings. There was no chance he'd *date* her; the very term was too *Englisch* for his liking.

What if I were to become Amish? The thought whisked over her like a warm breeze rattling a few branches overhead. No, Trina could no sooner convert than Seth could become *Englisch.* If Patience Kauffman had wanted her daughter to be Amish, she would have returned to her community after Richard Smith divorced her. But Trina's mother wanted the exact opposite. She chose poverty and isolation instead of bringing Trina up in an Amish community, so there was no way Trina was going to convert just to capture the attention of an Amish man.

An Amish man, who, at that very moment, was courting someone he intended to wed. *Don't lose sight of that*, she told herself. Yet no matter how illogical it was, her emotions said otherwise. She actually felt sick with longing for Seth. Maybe he was right—maybe emotions were dangerous. She opened her eyes but the sun made her see blinking spots so she closed them again.

She must have dropped off to sleep because she was awakened by the voices of children. She sat up to find Timothy and Tanner clambering up the steep side of the rock.

"Hi, Trina," they chorused. "We're playing mountain lions. These are our new friends, Hope and Greta."

Trina greeted them and then as she pulled her jacket back on, she asked if they'd all wandered off by themselves.

"*Daed* said it was alright as long as we stopped at this rock," Timothy explained.

Standing below, Hope rolled her eyes and said, "I told Seth I'd keep an eye on them."

Trina didn't know whether to think the girl was funny or precocious. "I'll climb down and let you mountain lions have this rock, then," she said.

"Aww," whined Tanner. "Please don't leave. You can be the lioness of the pride."

"Jah," Timothy agreed, admiringly adding, "Your hair looks like a mane."

Trina touched her head. She'd forgotten she'd loosened her hair. Where had her elastic band gone? She thought she'd set it right beside her. She didn't care. She had to get down from the rock before Fannie and Seth arrived. Not only did she not want to see Seth, but she didn't want either Seth or Fannie to see her. There was no ladylike way to descend the rock and she didn't want to appear immodest in front of Fannie. But it was too late.

"Why, look, it's the *buwe's* nanny," Fannie said, and Trina bristled at being referred to by her occupation instead of her name.

"You may have forgotten, but her name is Trina," Seth said. Trina could have hugged him for that. "Sorry if the *kinner* interrupted your peace."

"Daed, we're not *kinner.* We're cubs," Tanner interjected. "And Trina's the lioness of our pride."

"Actually, I was just leaving, Tanner. I'll see you tomorrow," Trina said. She scooted on her bottom to the edge of the rock and peered over. If she jumped, she'd probably fall to her knees and hands upon landing. But if she used the same crevices to lower herself as she'd used to climb up, she'd appear unladylike. And now that she'd wiggled this far to the edge, the only way she could lower herself using the crevices was to roll onto her belly and squirm back to the other side of the rock. She dangled her legs over the side, wondering what to do.

"Here, let me give you a hand," Seth offered, stretching his arms upward.

Was he going to lift her down under her armpits like a child? She couldn't have been more embarrassed. He couldn't reach that high, so she'd have to jump into his arms. What if she knocked him over?

"You'll have to push yourself off a little to clear the edge," he said. "Don't worry, I'll catch you. It might be clumsy but I won't let you get hurt."

Trina hesitated. It might be better just to jump without his help and take her knocks.

"*Buwe*, I want you to *kumme* down, too. You don't want to get stuck like Trina did," Fannie instructed. Timothy and Tanner were the ones who'd shown Trina how to navigate the rock in the first place; they were expert climbers. Still, they obeyed Fannie without complaint.

After they scrambled down, Timothy said to the girls standing nearby, "*Kumme*, we'll show you where the elephants live in the grass by the water. They're prey for lions."

"I'll follow them while you help her," Fannie directed and the five of them disappeared into the woods.

"I really can get down by myself now," Trina told Seth. "I just didn't want everyone watching me. Please, go ahead and catch up with the others. I'll be fine."

Seth didn't seem to be in a hurry to leave. "Just jump, Trina. I'll catch you. You can trust me."

The words resonated in Trina's heart. What man

could she ever really trust? "Okay," she agreed reluctantly. "One, two, three!"

She lurched forward and her hair flew out around her like a cape. Seth didn't so much catch her as ease her to the ground in a sort of awkward embrace. Right before he released her, she felt his beard softly brush her cheek.

"Ugh," Seth groaned.

"Sorry. Did I kick you?"

"*Neh,* you're just a lot heavier than you look."

"Coming from you, that's a compliment." Trina giggled.

Seth was so close she could smell the peanut butter on his breath. He lifted his hand and Trina actually thought he was going to caress her cheek but instead he picked a leaf from her hair. "You have vegetation in your mane," he gibed.

Trina giggled again. "*Denki* for helping me down. I'll stay here awhile, so you and Fannie and the *kinner* will have privacy on your outing."

As Seth opened his mouth to reply, in the distance Fannie yelled, "Seth, I can't find Tanner."

A panicked look crossed Seth's face, but Trina said, "It's alright, I know where they probably are. I'll go this way, you go check up the hill." She broke into a hard run, knowing where the boys pretended elephants lived. It was a reedy place close to the creek where it wasn't always possible to tell where the embankment ended and the water began. Trina never allowed them to go anywhere near it unless they were holding her hand.

Sprinting past Fannie, her daughters and Timothy, Trina called, "Tanner! Where are you? Say my name!"

When her command was met with silence, Trina charged into the reeds, shouting, until she reached the water's edge. Then she slogged through that, too. Her shoes and socks were wet and the hem of her skirt was weighted down with water, sticking to her legs. "Tanner! Tanner!" she shouted, feeling lightheaded. She waded deeper and deeper until she was up to her thighs in the frigid water. The current was moving at a quick clip and she struggled to remain upright.

"Trina, we found him," Seth yelled from far away. "Trina?"

Denki, she prayed. *Denki, Lord.* She splashed back toward the embankment and up the hill where the others were calling her. "Here I am," she squawked, her throat too dry for her voice to be heard.

"Trina!" Tanner called when he finally spotted her. He barreled straight for her. The force almost knocked her over as he hugged her legs. "Are you okay?"

Nearly sobbing from exertion and relief, she bent to kiss his head multiple times. "*Jah*, I'm fine. Are you okay?"

He looked up at her, tipping his head so far back she could see his nostrils. "*Jah.*"

Just then Seth clambered down the hill. "I'm so sorry about that, Trina," he said. His eyes were blazing. "Tanner was in one of their make-believe dens and he couldn't hear Fannie calling him. She was worried he fell into the creek."

"But, *Daed,* you told me I should never go near the creek by myself," Tanner said as his round eyes sprang tears. "I wouldn't disobey."

"We know you wouldn't," Trina said. "It's okay, Tanner. Everyone's okay."

Fannie came loping down the hill with her hand pressed to her mouth. "That had me so worried," she lamented.

Placing her hands on her hips, Hope told Trina, "I think you may be taking things a little too far in telling them about animals."

In all of Trina's years of teaching children, she'd encountered some inappropriate language, but no child had ever had the nerve to admonish her as Hope was doing now. Trina kept silent so she wouldn't embarrass Seth's guests by speaking her mind, but she felt like telling the girl to show some respect or go home immediately.

"You've got to be freezing," Seth said. "Let's get you to our house. We've got a nice fire going. Martha's making cookies and she'll give you dry clothes while Fannie puts on a kettle."

"*Denki*, but I just want to go home and dry off there," Trina said. Her head was really pulsating now and her legs were tottery as she started toward her house.

"Funny, isn't it?" Fannie tittered. "Both times I've seen you so far you've been soaking wet."

That was the last thing Trina remembered before everything went dark.

Seth had been walking behind Trina and he noticed something was off about her gait and the way she was speaking, so when she staggered he was right there to keep her from falling and hitting her head. She collapsed backward into his arms and he gently lowered her to the ground. Kneeling beside her, he forcefully jiggled her arm.

"Trina, wake up. Trina, open your eyes," he said loudly. She immediately blinked and lifted her hand to rub her eyes. She couldn't have been out for more than a few seconds, but he needed to be sure she was alright. "Trina, who am I? Can you tell me my name?"

"You don't know?" she asked, a wry smile flickering across her pale face. "Seth Helmuth," she said to his satisfaction. "I'm alright. I have a *koppweh*, that's all." She groaned when she tried to sit up. This time, Seth didn't ask permission to take her home. He simply swept her up in his arms and carried her to his house, despite her protests and Fannie's pouting. He didn't set her down until he'd settled her into a rocking chair near the fire in his parlor.

"What happened?" Martha asked as she followed them from the kitchen, wringing her hands. The house smelled of cookies, not of smoke. That was at least one good thing. Seth relayed what had occurred while the children added their comments and Fannie remained silent, warming her hands by the stove as if she'd been the one who'd waded through the water to rescue Tanner.

"I'm fine," Trina said when they finished talking. "I think Seth wanted to prove to Fannie how strong he is by carrying me, that's all."

Seth knew Trina was attempting to smooth things over between him and Fannie, and he appreciated the gesture, especially considering how rude Fannie had been to her. He suggested Fannie should take the children into the kitchen to have some cookies and put on tea. Then he told his grandmother, "Trina needs something dry to wear."

"I'll say she does," Martha said, pressing her hand to Trina's forehead. "This *maedel* is cold and clammy. How long was she unconscious? We ought to take her to the doctor."

Seth was hesitant. On a Sunday, the only doctor they could take her to was in the ER at the hospital in Highland Springs. Ever since Freeman ran off with Kristine and she resumed her job as a nurse, Seth worried he might bump into one of their friends at the hospital, even though Freeman and Kristine had long since moved out of the area. Seth didn't want anyone to inquire about his brother and stir up sad memories.

"*Neh,* no doctor," Trina insisted. "I'm fine, really. I just need some sleep."

Seth was relieved but still felt concerned. "What about your friend Ethan? Can we ask him to take a look at you? I'll use the phone shanty to call him, unless you know where he lives."

"I do, but please don't bother yourself," Trina said weakly. "I've already spoiled your afternoon."

"It's not a bother. I'll stop at Ethan's on the way back from taking Fannie and her *meed* home."

"Please let him, Trina. Otherwise I'm going to worry about you all night and I won't get any sleep," Martha said. Like most people, Trina couldn't refuse the older woman's wishes, but she did insist on going home and putting her own clothes on and climbing into her own bed. Martha said she'd go with her.

After Seth escorted them to Trina's house and got

the fire roaring, he took everyone, including his boys, to drop Fannie off in Elmsville. He left the boys in the buggy while he walked the others to the door. After the girls had gone inside, Fannie frankly stated, "I don't think you and I are a match, Seth."

After a startled pause, he said, "*Denki* for your honesty, Fannie. I wish you *Gott*'s best in finding a suitable spouse."

Fannie crossed her arms and furrowed her eyebrows. "Don't you even want to know why I don't think we're a match?"

Feeling as if it would be rude to say it wasn't necessary since he had come to the same conclusion, Seth said, "Please tell me."

"I don't think we're a *gut* match because I wouldn't ever agree to be courted by a man who is inappropriately friendly with an *Englisch* woman."

He didn't know what to say. The problem was, there was nothing he *could* say. Like it or not, she was right.

Fannie waited for a second and when Seth didn't deny it, she closed the door in his face.

Chapter Seven

Martha propped the pillows up behind Trina and urged her to drink a glass of water. Then she said, "You rest. I'll be right in the parlor if you need anything."

"Please, don't go," Trina requested, so Martha sat down on the end of the bed. Trina closed her eyes. Feeling like a child, she said, "My *mamm* used to sit on the end of the bed when I was sick. I always felt comforted by the weight of her body on the mattress near my feet."

"*Jah*, she used to tuck her feet beneath me when she was sick," Martha said.

Martha had been there to comfort her mother when she was sick? Trina was glad to know that. "Sometimes I wondered how she became such a *gut mamm* since her own *mamm* died when she was so young. *Denki*, Martha, for teaching her."

"Oh, I can't take credit for that, dear. Your *groossmammi* was as loving as anyone could be. Even if Patience was too young to remember, those things still leave an impression on a *kin*."

"Mmm," Trina murmured. She felt comfortably

drowsy but she didn't want Martha to stop talking to her. She forced herself to open her eyes. "Speaking of *kinner*, what did you think of Fannie's *dechder*?"

"Judging from the fact you have to ask, I probably think the same thing you think." Martha chuckled. "But Seth is determined to find a wife, so I try to keep my mouth shut and be supportive. What that young man doesn't seem to realize is it might be better if…"

Trina drifted off until two people, a man and a woman, began speaking in hushed tones at the end of her bed. She dreamed it was her father and mother. Or maybe she was remembering the Christmas her father came to visit and she'd had chicken pox. It was one of the only times she heard genuine concern in his voice as he asked her mother how she was doing…

But no, it was Ethan talking to Martha, who was recounting what happened at the creek.

"I'm not a *kin*," she said aloud, realizing she wasn't dreaming after all.

Ethan chuckled. "That's okay, just because I'm a pediatrician doesn't mean I can't determine the state of your health."

Trina tried to say that's not what she meant, but her mouth wouldn't cooperate. Martha supported Trina's head and lifted a glass of water to her lips. The room seemed to come into focus again. After taking her vital signs and asking a few questions, Ethan said he thought she might be suffering from shock. And possibly anemia, since she was so thin and pale.

"I want to take your blood and run a few tests, but you had quite a scare. You're also dehydrated, which could have given you the headache originally," he explained. "You'll need plenty of fluids and lots of rest for the next three days."

Trina smiled wanly. "I'm not sure how much rest Timothy and Tanner will let me have, but maybe if we—"

Ethan was suddenly very serious. "You won't be able to take care of Timothy and Tanner."

"But—"

"You need to take care of yourself, Trina. In fact, someone else needs to help take care of you."

"But I don't—"

"I'll contact one of the women from church. I know several people who will be happy to stay with you for a few nights."

"Nonsense!" Martha declared. "We'll take care of Trina ourselves."

Ethan seemed to sense he'd better not contradict her. He took a vial of Trina's blood and was pressing cotton against her arm when they heard footsteps on the porch, followed by a tentative knock and then Seth calling, "Hello? May we *kumme* in?"

"We're in here," Martha answered, removing her shawl and draping it modestly around Trina's shoulders.

"My hair," Trina said, suddenly self-conscious about how she looked.

"You're fine," Martha answered.

"She's fine?" Seth repeated hopefully, apparently thinking Martha was referring to Trina's condition.

"She will be, after a few days' rest," Ethan replied. "And lots of fluids."

"Oh, *gut*." Seth sighed, looking straight at Trina instead of at Ethan. She felt woozy again.

"Is Trina alright?" Tanner or Timothy piped up from the hall in squeaky voices.

"*Jah*, but she won't be if you two *buwe* don't allow her to rest," Martha told them. "*Kumme* in and say hello and then you need to go back home with your *daed*."

Watching Ethan tape a piece of gauze over the spot on her arm where he'd drawn blood, Timothy's eyes bulged. "Did you have to get a shot, Trina?"

"Um, sort of. Dr. Gray had to use a needle to draw blood."

"Did it hurt?"

Ethan responded, "Trina was so brave she deserves two sugar-free lollipops." He held up the candy.

"I'm not hungry, but maybe you can give them to the *buwe*. They're usually pretty brave, too," Trina answered.

"Okay," Ethan agreed, "but first you have to promise me something, Timothy and Tanner. You have to be very helpful to whoever cares for you while Trina's asleep because she needs lots and lots of rest."

"Kind of like she's hibernating?" Timothy asked.

"Exactly like that." Ethan laughed, extending a lollipop to each of the boys.

"Starting now," Martha said. "It's time to hightail it, *buwe*."

"I'll be right out," Seth said as the others left the room.

He nervously pulled a chair to the side of Trina's bed so his face was at the same level as hers. "I'm so sorry this happened," he said. The shadows beneath his eyes were so dark he looked as grim as she felt. Trina was overwhelmed by the depth of his concern.

"*You're* sorry? If you hadn't had to help me down from the rock, none of this would have happened. I'm the one who panicked about Tanner and ran into the water."

"That's what I love abo—" Seth coughed and started again. "That's what I appreciate. You put Tanner's welfare above your own. I can't ever express how much that means to me."

Was he going to say that's what he loved about me? Trina wondered. Or was she dreaming again? She must have been. After all, her eyes were closed and it seemed like she was floating. She hadn't felt this calm since before her mother got sick and if it was a dream, she didn't want to wake up from it for a long while.

When Seth exited Trina's room, Ethan was still in the kitchen with the others. He asked Seth if he'd walk to his car with him so they could talk and Seth obliged. He didn't know whether the serious look on Ethan's face was because he was concerned about Trina as a doctor, as a friend or possibly as a boyfriend.

"Are you sure she's going to be okay?" he asked anxiously before Ethan had a chance to speak.

"Trina? Yes, she should be fine. I'm running a few blood tests to make sure and I'll stop to check on her tomorrow. But I wanted to talk to you about your grandmother."

Seth was so surprised he repeated the *Englisch* term. "My grandmother?"

"Yes. I had a chance to speak with her about her

vision and I believe she may have cataracts. There's a simple surgery she can have that will help restore her vision. It's important she has it soon, before the damage becomes irreversible."

Seth was taken aback. Who did Ethan think he was, questioning his grandmother about her health? Martha had accepted long ago she'd eventually go blind. For one thing, she believed it was God's will. For another, she was terrified of surgery. But a pushy *Englisch* doctor wouldn't understand that.

"*Denki* for caring for Trina on such short notice," Seth said pointedly ignoring Ethan's advice.

Ethan's features went slack. "As I said, I'll stop by tomorrow to see how she's doing. On Tuesday I won't be able to visit, since I'll be picking up my fiancée at the train station. She's coming from Philly during a break from her graduate studies. Her family lives close by so I'll get to spend some time with her, too."

His fiancée? Seth was more thrilled than he should have been to discover Ethan was engaged. The doctor gave him his card and said to call him or the hospital if Trina seemed confused, had a fever or was difficult to wake up.

When Seth returned to the house, Martha was sitting at the kitchen table with the boys, very quietly telling them the Bible story about Daniel in the lions' den. She tried to persuade Seth she'd be fine taking care of Trina overnight by herself, but this time he got the last word. He didn't want to have to worry about both her and Trina until morning.

"Maybe I can ask Emma Lamp if she'll spend the

night tending to Trina. I could pay her for her assistance," he suggested.

Martha clucked and shook her head. "*Suh,* what you don't know about women could fill a book."

"What do you mean? Emma's helpful and capable, and there's a spare room here, so—"

"You know how word gets around in Willow Creek. Emma surely knows by now you chose to go out with Fannie again. Don't you think her feelings are hurt?"

"Why would Emma's feelings be hurt? Fannie didn't seem to mind I considered becoming Emma's suitor. I was very clear I wasn't making any definite commitments."

"Trust me, you can't ask Emma over." Martha paused and then instructed, "Here's what you need to do. Go to Pearl Hostetler's house and see if she'll *kumme* for the night. I'll bring the *buwe* back here with me in the morning. We'll do something quietly indoors for the day."

Seth had every intention of staying home the next day to watch the boys and help Martha with Trina's needs, but he didn't want to fight that battle at the moment. First, he had to secure help for that night. He felt funny burdening Pearl with assisting an *Englischer*, but he knew she wouldn't say no, in deference to Martha. Having been friends for over seventy years, the two women were like sisters and they'd do anything they could for each other.

After taking books and drawing paper back to Trina's house for the boys and stoking the fire, Seth left for Pearl's house. He worried she might be out visiting people instead of receiving visitors herself, so he was relieved when he arrived and Pearl answered the door.

"Seth, do *kumme* in. We were just talking about you. Rather, about your neighbor, Trina," Pearl bubbled, ushering him to the parlor without letting him get a word in edgewise. He wished she'd let him speak privately to her in the kitchen—this matter wasn't something he wanted to discuss in front of anyone else.

"Kate Dienner meet Seth Helmuth. You knew his *groossmammi*, Martha Helmuth, when you lived in Willow Creek. You might even remember his *daed,* Moses Helmuth, who lived here before he got married and moved to Ohio."

The woman, who looked to be a bit younger than his parents would have been, set down her cup and clasped her hands beneath her chin. "How *gut* to meet you, Seth. I do remember your *groossmammi,* but your *daed* was quite a few years older than I was, so I think by the time I went to school, he'd already moved to Ohio to marry your *mamm.* But Pearl tells me Patience Kauffman's daughter is living here now?"

Sometimes Seth wished everyone in Willow Creek didn't know everything about everyone else. No wonder Trina once told him living in the city afforded a person a certain amount of anonymity, which was sometimes beneficial. *"Jah,"* he said, wondering what else Pearl had told Kate.

"Patience and I were as thick as thieves until the summer I moved away when I was thirteen," Kate explained. "I haven't been back to Willow Creek since then, but this week my husband has business in town. He's friends with Pearl and Wayne's son, so when they agreed to host us as while we're in town, we were delighted. Anyway, I'd love to meet Trina."

Seth waffled, "Um, I'm not sure that's a *gut* idea."

"It's alright," Kate assured him. "I know about how her *mamm* went *Englisch*. I'm not going to judge."

"*Neh*, it's not that," Seth said and then told them about their predicament. Kate insisted she should stay with Trina so Pearl could stay home to host both of their husbands. This actually seemed like a good idea to Seth, who was concerned about the older woman's stamina. Since Kate had only arrived the night before, she hadn't fully unpacked yet, so it only took a minute for her to gather her things and bid her husband goodbye at the barn where he was chatting with Pearl's husband, Wayne.

Back at Trina's house, Martha was just as glad to see Kate as Kate was to see her, and the older woman seemed relieved it was Kate, not Pearl, who would be staying the night with Trina.

"I'm here all week, so I can stay as long as you'd like," Kate said, but Seth supposed they'd only need her assistance for a night or maybe two.

Since Kate was so capable, the next day Seth decided that, rather than staying home, he'd take the boys with him to work so they'd be out of the women's way. It wouldn't be easy having them underfoot at the shop, but he had three *Englisch* customers coming to pick up their specialty orders and he didn't want to fail them if at all possible. First, he took Martha to Trina's house so she could keep Kate company, or more accurately, so Kate could keep an eye on Martha. While the boys waited outside, he popped in to ask about Trina.

"She had a slight fever last night, but nothing alarming. She's so exhausted I don't think she's even registered who I am. I'd like to stay another day, so if you could let Pearl and my husband know, I'd appreciate it."

"Will do," he agreed. "Is there anything I can bring you from town?"

"There sure is," Martha interrupted. "Half a dozen fry pies from the bakery."

When Seth raised an eyebrow, Martha said, "Unless you want me to bake, instead…" So he agreed to purchase the goodies.

As soon as the third customer had picked up her attaché case at two thirty, Seth closed shop. When he and the boys reached Trina's house, he noticed Ethan's car in the lane. Kate and Martha greeted them in the kitchen, just as Ethan emerged from Trina's room. He informed everyone that Trina's vitals seemed fine and her color was better now that she had rested.

"She's awake?" Seth asked.

"She sure is. She's hungry, too. You can go through and see her if you'd like. She's dressed and she wants to come out for something to eat and to sit by the fire. She might need a hand for balance."

The door was ajar but Seth knocked anyway and slowly pushed it open when Trina told him to come in. She was sitting on the edge of the bed, which was made, with a hairbrush in her hand, but her tresses were still loose.

"Hi, Trina. How are you?" he asked.

"Seth! You're home early. It's because you couldn't get someone to care for the *buwe*, isn't it?"

"Well, I wouldn't blame anyone for not wanting to. After all, look what happens when someone does care for them," he said, gesturing toward her in reference to her illness.

But she must have misinterpreted his comment, because she tucked her hair behind her ear. "I know I look a mess. I can't believe a simple thing like combing my hair requires so much energy today."

"*Neh*, I meant, look what happens to your health, not to your hair," Seth protested. Then, although he knew he shouldn't give voice to his thoughts, he didn't stop himself from adding, "Your hair always looks pretty, whether it's around your shoulders or pulled up in a horse's tail."

Trina threw back her head. Seth wasn't sure how she'd take the compliment, but he hadn't expected her to laugh at it. "You mean a *pony*tail," she said, and then he had to laugh, too.

"Everyone is in the kitchen preparing sweets and waiting to see you. Can I help you up?" Seth offered his arm and Trina grasped it as she pulled herself into a standing position. Then she let go and took a few wobbly steps. Seth immediately held out his hand again and she interlocked her fingers with his. They simultaneously lowered their arms between them as if they were holding hands while out for a stroll. The sensation made *him* feel unsteady but he ambled with her down the hallway like that. Then, squeezing their fingers in silent agreement, right before entering the kitchen they released each other's hand so no one would see.

Seth's steady, masculine fingers gripping hers for a few fleeting seconds was worth every hour of feeling lousy the past night and day. Trina hadn't glanced at him while they were walking hand in hand from her room down the short hallway and through the parlor because she hadn't wanted to discover she was having another feverish dream. But once the warmth of his skin against hers slipped away and she entered the brightness of the kitchen, she knew it had been real and she wished she had walked slower. Or stopped walking altogether—anything to prolong their closeness.

She'd been close to Seth before, of course, such as when he'd helped her down from the rock or up from her bed, but this time was different; this time there was no questioning whether there was something more than helpfulness or friendliness between them. Right before dropping her hand, Seth had given hers a squeeze and she'd squeezed back in secret acknowledgment of their mutual affection.

So when Martha told her she looked dazed, Trina replied, "I'm fine. It's just I'm not used to the bright sunlight," and the woman introduced as Kate Dienner quickly drew the shade.

After the boys had given her drawings of lions they made while they were at Seth's shop, Kate poured tea for the adults and milk for the boys, and then served apple fry pies.

"What about me? Don't I get one?" Trina sounded like a disappointed child when she wasn't offered a piece of dessert.

"I don't know if that's wise, dear," Martha said. "I think you should start slowly, maybe have a piece of dry toast."

Trina wrinkled her nose. "Dry toast?" she repeated,

as if she'd been offered a dead skunk. "I've been exhausted, not sick to my stomach."

Seth interjected, "Before he left, Dr. Gray—I mean, Ethan—didn't say she couldn't have regular food, so I don't see any harm in it."

Trina glanced at him and said, "*Jah*, please listen to the man who thinks I need to fatten up." The second the words were out of her mouth she worried her comment indicated they'd been bantering in a way that might not have been considered appropriate for an Amish man and an *Englisch* woman.

Fortunately, Timothy piped up. "*Jah, Groossmammi.* When bears *kumme* out of hibernation, they're hungry, too, and they forage for food."

"You don't have to forage, Trina." Tanner offered, "You can have mine."

Clearly the darling boy still felt guilty for Trina's incident at the creek and her heart expanded to near bursting from his sentiment.

Martha chuckled. "Alright, alright. But don't blame me if you get a tummy ache," she said as if Trina were a youngster.

The fry pies were so delicious Trina said, "This is the best thing I've ever tasted. And that's not just because I'm ravenous." As she licked icing from her upper lip, she caught Seth looking at her and he quickly glanced away again.

"We should go, *buwe*," he said when they'd all finished eating, and Martha agreed.

After they left, Kate insisted Trina sit down in the parlor and Trina was suddenly so tired again that she didn't argue. After Kate finished washing the cups and glasses, she brought Trina a drink of water, urging her to increase her intake of liquids.

"*Denki* for staying with me," Trina said. "I don't know how to express my appreciation that you'd do this for a stranger."

"Anyone who lives in Willow Creek isn't a stranger," Kate replied, settling onto the sofa opposite. "And you especially aren't a stranger. I grew up with your *mamm*. At least, until I was about thirteen and we moved away."

Trina's concentration must have been off due to her illness because she couldn't place the woman in the stories her mother shared. The only childhood friend she mentioned had the last name of Stuckey, not Dienner. And her first name was Katrina, not Kate. Suddenly, it dawned on Trina, "What was your name before you married?"

"Stuckey," Kate said.

Trina leaped up so quickly she felt unsteady again. "You're Katrina Stuckey!" she exclaimed.

Kate moved to Trina's side and eased her onto the sofa beside her. *"Jah,"* she said. "Although Patience was the only person I ever allowed to call me by my full name, Katrina. Everyone else calls me Kate."

"My *mamm* thought the world of you. That's why she named me Trina." Trina didn't know if it was because she'd been sick, but she was suddenly overwhelmed with emotion and she began to weep into her hands.

Kate wrapped her arm around Trina's shoulder. "I know. I know," she said soothingly, until Trina caught her breath again. Then she told her, "Patience was such a dear *maedel*, my closest friend. How I regret losing touch with her after I moved..."

It was Trina's turn to comfort the older woman. "*Mamm* understood. She said she figured you were probably adjusting to life with your new friends in a new place and she wanted you to be happy there." After a pause, Trina confided, "My *mamm* left the Amish, you know."

"I do know. I probably even know why," Kate said. "I might not agree with her decision, but I really do understand why she made it."

Trina changed the subject to something happier. "One of *mamm*'s favorite memories was when the two of you went ice skating on her thirteen birthday at Wheeler's Pond the winter before you moved."

"Mine, too! Our teeth were chattering and our toes were frozen, but we didn't want to leave. Not as long as the *buwe* were still playing broom hockey."

"What?" Trina's mother hadn't told Trina about that.

"*Jah*—we were awfully young, but your *mamm* was smitten with a boy named Hannes Kinnell and I liked Jethro Bechler. That's why Patience decided the perfect birthday would be spent trying to capture their attention. We even brought a thermos of cocoa to entice them to chat with us." Kate shook her head, remembering.

"Did they?"

"Only long enough to drink the cocoa." Kate giggled. "Now I don't blame them. They were a *gut* five years older than we were. Mind you, they were decent *buwe* and kind in their own way, but they weren't interested in us romantically at all. But, at the time, we were devastated. I think both of them eventually married *meed* from Ohio. And I married a man from Indiana."

"And my *mamm* married an *Englischer* from New York," Trina said sadly.

"I always hoped she had met someone like Hannes," Kate said. "I'm sure if she'd met a man like that, she never would have left the Amish."

"That may be true," Trina agreed. "Sometimes, growing up, I felt like she didn't leave the Amish— she only left the geography. I mean, she was still true to her faith. She was true to me, as her family. And she passed down so many Amish ideals and traditions." Trina laughed. "She tried to, anyway. Some of them I didn't want to learn. Like how to wash the windows until they sparkled."

"To tell you the truth, I still don't like washing windows," Kate said, laughing.

The conversation was bittersweet and Trina felt worn out with emotion and from the increase in activity, so she decided to turn in early that evening. Kate helped her get ready for bed and brought her a glass of water.

"I always wondered what your *mamm* would look like if I saw her again as an adult," she confessed. "I used to wonder if I'd recognize her. Now that I've seen you, I know I would have. There's a lot of her in you, Trina. As much as you miss her, you have so many of her ways."

Trina was glad it was too dark for Kate to see her tears. *"Denki,"* she murmured.

But when the door closed behind Kate, Trina couldn't sleep. She thought about how Kate had said that if Trina's mother had found a kind and honest man like Hannes Kinnell, she probably wouldn't have left the Amish. Seth was a kind and decent man, but Trina couldn't become Amish to have a romantic relationship with him. Being Amish was about a commitment to God, first and foremost. Yet she kept thinking, *But I already have that commitment to the Lord. It would just be a different way of demonstrating it.* Then she asked herself, if Seth continued to court and even married Fannie, would Trina still want to become Amish? She wasn't quite sure, although there was definitely something about being among the *leit* of Willow Creek that made her feel as if she'd come home.

Which in turn made her feel guilty. Like a traitor. How could she think of returning to the place her mother fled from? What kind of daughter was she? No, in her weakened state, her mind was playing tricks on her. She knew she needed rest, and before she could even roll over in bed, she'd fallen asleep again.

Because Martha absolutely wouldn't take no for an answer, Seth reluctantly agreed to leave the boys home with her the following day.

"I promise not to use the stove or oven," she said. "If I want tea, I'll drop in on Kate. This will mean you'll have to get a pizza for dinner."

"Pizza!" Timothy and Tanner cheered. Take-out pizza was a rare treat in their house and he was glad his sons were so happy about it. Tanner had seemed unusually out of sorts since Trina's creek incident, even though Seth repeatedly assured him it wasn't his fault.

"*Daed*, I told Fannie where I'd be," he explained. "I don't know why she said she couldn't find me."

Seth had suspected as much. Fannie had probably beckoned Seth because she didn't want him to be alone with Trina any longer than he had been. Seth sighed, knowing she probably had good reason to be wary of the two of them dawdling behind. Every fiber of his being had wanted to take Trina's hand and run in the opposite direction that day.

Thinking about Trina's fingers interlocked with his in the hallway of her house made Seth sore with yearning. There was no denying they had joined hands the way a couple would and held on until the last possible second. It was so romantic how, as they let go, her fingers delicately trailed along his palm and his trailed along hers until just their fingertips were touching before they'd parted contact completely. Ordinarily, the Amish didn't prohibit handholding before marriage. But a baptized Amish man handholding with an *Englischer*, when marriage wasn't even possible, was another story. Seth knew he was in a precarious position, but at that moment he hadn't cared. If he had to do it all over again, he would have.

A deep ache harried him all through the morning in his shop. It was a mix of longing and guilt, as well as a strange new understanding of his brother. For the first time since Freeman left, Seth experienced an inkling of empathy toward him, even though he didn't agree with the choices his brother ultimately made. It was bad enough that Freeman brought pain to their family, but if Seth were to leave, it would be that much worse because he had children. He couldn't imagine tearing them away from their Amish roots—making a choice for them he hoped they'd never make for themselves.

What was wrong with him to even entertain the notion of leaving the Amish? *I could never do that*, he thought. *I've got to put these feelings about Trina aside.* That's all they were—feelings. Emotions. Whims. Besides, she was leaving soon. Was Seth going to ruin his reputation by flirting with an *Englischer* who was just passing through?

Of course he wasn't. But try as he might, he still couldn't get thoughts of Trina out of his mind. He thought of her telling him she'd always have the memory of her mother and herself at the Cape to hold on to. Likewise, Seth would always have the memory of holding hands with Trina, as forbidden as it was. But no, that wouldn't do. It would be wrong to harbor such a thought.

Instead, he decided to help Trina safeguard *her* memory of her mother in a material sense. He wanted to fashion a picture frame made of leather. But first he walked to the library on his dinner break and checked out a book on birds. Using the index, he located the page that contained a picture of sandpipers. Yes, that's what he'd etch into the leather along the border of the frame: two sandpipers scurrying along the edge of a wave. One for Trina and one for her mother. Far, far from here.

It would be his parting gift to Trina, so she wouldn't forget him, since she wasn't forbidden to dwell on the memories of their time together. As for him, he had to put thoughts of her out of his mind for good.

"Can Trina eat supper with us?" Timothy asked when Seth arrived home that night carrying a big square box of pizza.

"*Neh*, she's eating with Kate at her house tonight."

"Pearl stopped by to check on Trina and Kate. Since Ethan visited today and said Trina was much better, Pearl took Kate back to her house. So I think Trina would *wilkom* a chance to eat with us," Martha suggested.

"This pizza isn't very big," Seth argued.

"What has gotten into you, *suh*?" Martha asked. When he didn't answer she said, "Alright, fine. I'll go over to Trina's house and make supper for her there."

"Neh!" Seth barked the word at his grandmother. Why couldn't she just leave well enough alone? It was futile; she'd never change. "I'm sorry. I didn't mean to snap, *Groossmammi*. I mean *neh*, it's dark. I'll walk over and get her. I don't want you to fall."

Martha looked dubious but since she'd gotten her way, she said, "*Kumme*, *buwe*, help me put plates and napkins on the table."

"Pizza sounds *appenditlich*," Trina said, accepting Seth's invitation after he knocked on her door. Her hair was neatly arranged in a bun and she was wearing the skirt she'd been sewing with Martha's guidance.

"I see you're wearing the skirt you made," he said and immediately regretted it. She might think he was too preoccupied with her appearance. Which he was.

"*Jah*, but I had to move the button. In fact, I've had to move the buttons on all of my skirts," she said. "I've actually gained a few pounds since I arrived here."

"That's *gut*," he said as he hurried down the porch steps and along the walkway, not wishing to get too close to her again.

From behind, Trina called, "I'm sorry. I'm still a little weak. I can't keep up."

Seth slowed his pace. He couldn't look at her for fear the hole in his heart would grow even bigger.

"Is something wrong?" she asked when she caught up. "You seem distracted."

Seth stopped to face her. He loved how tall she was, how he could look her in the eyes. "I'm sorry, Trina. For yesterday. I shouldn't have and I'm sorry."

"Shouldn't have what?" she asked. Was she being coy? Or hadn't she felt what he felt? No, he couldn't believe that, even if she was going to make him say it aloud.

"I'm sorry for holding your hand like I did. I shouldn't have done that and I promise you it won't ever happen again."

Trina stumbled backward as if she'd been struck and her mouth fell open. Then she turned on her heel.

"Trina, wait!"

She whirled back around and in the dimming light he noticed her cheeks suddenly glistened with tears. "I understand, Seth, why you and I can never be... I understand that you're Amish and I'm *Englisch*. But I'm not sorry about the affection you've shown me. And I'm not sorry you know I feel the same way about you."

Watching her dash back toward her house, Seth fought the impulse to follow her and profess his affection—his *love*—too. Letting her go was the most difficult thing he'd ever done and when the door closed behind her, he dropped to his knees, covered his face with his arm and groaned in a way he hadn't since he was in mourning.

Chapter Eight

In the weeks following her illness, Trina went out of her way to avoid Seth, and it appeared he was avoiding her, too. It would have been painful enough if they'd kept their distance because they were having an argument, but this time, Trina knew it was because they *weren't* having an argument. They were keeping their distance because they both knew how dear they were to each other and they couldn't act on those feelings.

Trina tried to force herself into cheerfulness, but even her best experiences with the boys were tinged with the awareness she'd soon leave them. Of course, the change in her mood didn't escape Martha's notice, nor did the change in her relationship with Seth. One Friday night when Trina and Seth were alone in the kitchen after having supper—Martha had insisted Trina eat with them since Seth had returned home so late that day—he handed her a plate by the sink. He was in such a rush to get away from her he didn't wait until her fingers had wholly grasped the dish and it slipped and shattered on the floor.

Martha flew into the kitchen, nearly toppling a chair one of the boys had pulled away from the table so he could sweep the floor beneath it. "What is going on?" she demanded.

"I'm sorry. I dropped a dish," Seth said before Trina could take the blame for it.

"I'll clean it up," Trina quickly offered.

"*Neh*, you'll do no such thing," Martha scolded. She had an edge to her voice Trina hadn't heard directed at her before. "The two of you will clean up whatever disagreement you've had before you'll tend to a few bits of broken glass."

"We haven't had a disagreement," Seth objected.

"Don't give me that. You've both been sulking like wet *katze*. The tension is almost unbearable. I can't stand it in my house a moment longer and neither can the *buwe*. So go outside until you can *kumme* back reconciled and smiling." Martha pointed to the door. She meant business.

Trina quietly dried her hands and lifted her light sweater from the peg by the door. The mid-April evening air was just chilly enough for her to need it, although Seth didn't bother to put on his jacket. Trina walked to the railing and burst into tears. She didn't mean to, but Martha was right; the tension was unbearable. She couldn't contain it any longer.

"Trina, please don't cry," Seth said, but he didn't draw near. His tone was so kind it made her cry even harder. "I wish I could make this better, but I don't know what to do," he said, walking to the railing but staying at least four feet away from Trina. What was he afraid of? It was insulting that he didn't even trust her enough to stand by her side. Or maybe it was himself he didn't trust. Maybe, instead of bridging the distance between them, they needed to increase it even more—for his good, as well as hers. Clearly he was hurting, too.

"I do," she sighed, drying her eyes on the edge of her apron. "It's only a couple more weeks until my time here is up. I'd considered staying until the house is sold and watching the *buwe* until school lets out at the end of May, but I think I should leave on May first, instead."

Seth ran his hand through his hair and tipped his head toward the sky. Was that a tear he wiped from his face when he brought his hand down to his side again? "*Jah*, that's probably for the best," he admitted. In a lower voice he said, as if speaking to himself, "Even though it feels like it's for the worst."

Just hearing him acknowledge how difficult it was to separate moved Trina deeply. He was obviously upset and she wished she could allay his suffering. They were both silent, observing the dusky spring sky. It would have seemed romantic under any other circumstances but this evening Trina had to concentrate on practical matters. "Until I leave, we've got to convince Martha there's nothing wrong between us."

Seth shrugged. "I don't know if we can. Nothing gets by her."

"Nonsense!" Trina declared, sounding just like Martha herself. "If your *buwe* can pretend they're wolves, then you and I can pretend nothing's wrong."

"It would be easier to pretend I'm a wolf," Seth muttered, and then he quietly howled toward the rising moon, causing them both to laugh.

"*Kumme,*" Trina said, motioning toward the door. "We can do it. For the *buwe*'s sake. I don't want them to remember our time together as being tense."

Seth agreed and when they opened the kitchen door, Martha was standing there with a broom. "All better?" she demanded.

"All better," they both claimed at the same time.

"*Gut.* Then Seth can sweep up the glass and Trina, you serve dessert. The *buwe* want to play Noah's Ark again. I think it's time for you to teach them a new game, Trina. I'm getting tired of guessing they're bears, wolves or tigers."

So when they finished eating dessert, Trina told Timothy and Tanner that Martha would be Noah and the boys had to be Noah's sons, while Seth and Trina acted out the animals. Their imitations were humorously awful and everyone laughed so hard Trina's smile came naturally again.

The next day was Saturday, and after Seth returned from work, Trina went home to call the realtor from church Sherman and Mabel had recommended. She forgot she'd put the phone back in Abe's old bedroom and she was glad to discover it was set on vibrate. She would have regretted if it had rung while Kate was sleeping there. Exiting the room, Trina noticed a Bible on the nightstand. Was that Abe's or did Kate forget hers there? She picked it up to see whose name was inscribed in it; it was her grandfather's. As she was putting the Bible back on the nightstand, an envelope fell from its pages. TRINA it said in big letters. It must have been from Kate; perhaps she'd written down more memories of Patience she wanted to share with Trina.

Deciding she'd be too emotional to make her phone call if she read the letter first, Trina set the envelope on the end table in the parlor and then turned her attention to her cell phone. It logged thirteen unanswered calls. Thirteen! All from Kurt, the realtor. Suddenly, she was infuriated. Seth was right, *Englischers* were pushy. Kurt just wouldn't take no for an answer. Trina pressed his number in her call history setting and paced while she was waiting for him to pick up. When he did, she didn't give him any time to work his sales pitch on her.

"This is Trina Smith and I want you to stop calling me," she spouted. "I will never, ever sell my house to a land developer. If I have to, I'll make it a stipulation of sale that any new owner can only resell to an Amish resident for the next one hundred years!" She was about to disconnect but she wanted to wait until Kurt confirmed he'd heard her loud and clear.

"You're saying you wouldn't sell to anyone who isn't Amish?" he asked.

Trina didn't know if such a stipulation was even legally allowed, but she confirmed, "That's exactly what I'm saying."

"Not even if the buyer is your father, Richard Smith?"

Trina staggered backward and dropped onto the sofa. "My father? Is this some kind of joke?"

"It's not a joke at all, Trina. How do you think I knew you had a house for sale? Your father contacted me and told me all about it."

"How did *he* know?" Trina asked suspiciously.

"He tried to track you down after your mother died and eventually his inquiries led him to Willow Creek, where rumors spread like wildfire."

Trina couldn't deny how quickly gossip traveled through the tiny community. "Why would my father want to buy a house—my *mother's* house—here?"

"He wants to reconnect with you, Trina. He wants to be part of your life again. Taking the house off your hands would be a way for him to help you out."

That didn't sound like her father. He had never tried to help her when she was a child and at her most vulnerable. Why would he help her now? "What's in it for him?" she asked.

Kurt coughed. "Well, he's sort of taken a hit recently, with the economy and the stock market... He sees this as an opportunity to get back on his feet. He's afraid he's going to lose his own house and wind up on the street."

Trina hadn't known that, but hearing it now filled her with conflicting emotions. Her first thought was of her mother. It didn't seem fair that her father was griping about losing his house when Trina's mother had never owned a house herself. Half the time, she'd struggled just to pay rent.

Yet Trina was also choked up to learn her father might be on the brink of homelessness. She didn't want to turn her back on him, even though he had neglected to help Trina and her mother for years. Regardless, Patience had frequently urged Trina not to bear a grudge against him. "God is forgiving and he wants us to be forgiving, too," she'd say. "For our sake as well as for the other person's sake. Remember, bitterness harms us more than it harms anyone else."

"My father wants to move here?" Trina asked Kurt. It didn't make sense. She couldn't imagine her father living next door to Seth. More importantly, she couldn't imagine her father living in her mother's childhood home. It wasn't right; somehow, it seemed like a betrayal.

"Not exactly." From the length of his pause Trina knew Kurt was going to tell her something she didn't want to hear. "Uh, remember the developer I told you about? Well, the developer is actually your father. And he's, um, partnering with a business associate who can front the cost of buying your house…"

Trina felt as if she'd been knocked flat to be told her father was the one behind the proposal to use the property for a liquor store. She didn't even have to think about her response. "No. Absolutely not."

"Don't you care if your father ends up bankrupt and homeless?"

"Of course I care," Trina said. "But that doesn't mean I'll sell him the house and land. Please don't call me again. This matter is closed."

Her emotions roiling, Trina's hands trembled as she disconnected the call. She knew her refusal to sell to her father might mean he'd suffer financial hardship. No matter what he'd done—or what he *hadn't* done— in the past, Trina still regretted letting him down now. As her mother had always reminded her, for better or worse, he was the only father she had.

But she couldn't in good conscience allow the property to be used for a liquor store. To do so would add insult to injury in regard to her mother's past. Not to mention, the presence of a wine and spirits store in a residential location would be a violation of the values of Willow Creek's Amish community, especially the Helmuths. Suspecting Kurt would continue to hound her despite her refusal,

Trina figured the only way to get him to back off would be to sell to someone else as soon as possible. Picking up the phone, she called the realtor from her church as quickly as her fingers could tap the numbers.

Seeing Emma Lamp at church always made Seth feel that much worse about his future. He knew he couldn't court Trina, for obvious reasons. But each time he saw Emma he realized he couldn't court her or Fannie or anyone else for a reason that had now become crystal clear: he couldn't imagine himself growing to love another woman. Rather, he knew he'd never be *in* love with anyone the way he was in love with Trina. Knowing her had changed what was acceptable to him for a marriage relationship. Loving her had been effortless; it was *not* loving her that was going to be a struggle. From now on, he'd stay single and pay a nanny to mind the boys and help Martha rather than marry someone he didn't love.

"Can we ask Trina to walk to the creek with us?" Tanner asked when they arrived home after church and Martha had turned in for a nap.

"*Jah*, she hasn't caught a frog yet," Timothy pleaded. "She hasn't even seen any tadpoles."

"Okay," Seth agreed. It was exactly two weeks before May first, the day Trina would move, and he realized the boys wanted to spend as much time with her as possible. "You go knock on her door and invite her and I'll wait here beneath the willow."

The yard had come alive; green buds decorated the willow, yellow daffodils shone like sunshine along the lane and Martha's tulips had overtaken the garden in a variety of purples, pinks and reds. But Seth's appreciation of spring dimmed in comparison with how he felt when he glimpsed Trina walking toward him, her long hair loose and glinting in the sun, the boys frolicking at her side. But when she came close, Seth saw her nostrils were pink and she was wearing the mirrored glasses she'd loaned Martha so long ago.

"*Buwe*, you run to that big rock over there and climb up on it to make sure you don't see any birds of prey around, okay? I need to talk to your *daed*."

Seth held his breath. If Trina cried in front of him one more time, he might break down and take her into his arms.

"I have to tell you something about my *daed*," she began, and he released his breath. So it wasn't about him—about *them*—after all. Yet, as she told him about her father contacting the realtor and how he was the developer who wanted to build a liquor store, Seth had to fight twice as hard not to embrace her. He could hear how distressed she was that her father might be facing financial ruin. How could a father manipulate his daughter's emotions for financial gain?

"My *daed* never honored a single commitment to help provide for me when I was a *kin*," Trina confided. "My *mamm* had to scrimp and save and work two or three menial jobs at a time. As I've mentioned, we were often very poor. I didn't care about that as much as I cared about my *daed* never following through with his promises. He'd say he'd *kumme* visit me and I'd get my hopes up, but then he wouldn't show…and other things like that. After a while, I lost faith in him altogether. But *mamm* was never bitter. Before she died, she told me if my *daed* ever tried to reconcile with me, she hoped I'd give him another chance. She said she didn't want my relationship with him to be estranged like hers was with her own *daed*."

Seth's fingers were curled into fists. "But your father hasn't actually asked for your forgiveness, has he?"

"*Neh*, not exactly. But the realtor said he wanted to reconnect with me. I don't know if he's sincere or if he's just after my inheritance. But that's not the point. The point is it was important to my *mamm* that I allow him back into my life if he wants to reconcile. And the Lord desires us to be forgiving, too."

"I understand," Seth said solemnly, marveling at Trina's willingness to honor her mother's wishes, as well as to obey God's word about forgiveness.

"Of course, forgiving him and allowing him back into my life doesn't mean selling the property to him," Trina clarified. "If he's truly desperate, perhaps I can help him financially so he doesn't end up homeless. I've contacted a realtor from church and I've asked about making a quick sale so no one can pressure me. We also discussed putting conditions on ownership, so no one can turn around and sell the house to anyone except residents in the future, too."

The gravity of what Trina had done sank in for Seth. Not only was she honoring her mother's memory, but she'd rejected her father's offer in favor of the Amish. She no doubt would have profited greatly from selling the property to him, but she'd said no in part because she understood the adverse effect a liquor store in that area would have on Seth and his family, as well as on the rest of the Amish community. Just when he thought he couldn't love her any more…

"Trina," he said, touching her arm gently. "Please take off those sunglasses and look at me. I need to see your eyes."

Trina did as he asked and gazed at him, droplets collecting on her lashes.

"I can never repay what you've done for my family and me. For all of Willow Creek's Amish. What you're doing takes courage and—" Seth's voice cracked and he abruptly stopped talking and tried to regain his composure.

"Denki," Trina uttered, blinking. Then she cleared her throat and said pointedly, "It was the right decision, but sometimes even making the right decision is difficult. It's excruciating."

Seth nodded, knowing what she meant. She was talking about the two of them parting ways because it was the right thing for each of them to do.

"Trina! *Daed!* Why are you just standing there like that?" Tanner called from atop of the large rock in the distance.

Timothy was more polite. "Please *kumme*! If you don't hurry all the tadpoles will be grown up by the time we get to the creek."

The two adults chuckled, in spite of themselves. Trina glanced sideways at Seth and taunted, "I'll beat you there."

"Don't be so sure about that," Seth retorted, breaking into a run.

Several paces later, Trina passed him, her hair flying out behind her as Timothy and Tanner cheered them on. She tagged the rock before Seth did and then collapsed onto her back on the new grass, laughing and clutching her stomach. The boys scrambled down to pull her up by her hands, just as they had that first day. It was the only moment in his life when Seth ever wished he had a camera so he could capture the sight on film as well as in his memory.

Trina had been so distraught about Kurt's phone call on Saturday that she completely forgot about the envelope with her name on it until midway through the week. She was cleaning her house on Wednesday morning because the realtor, Dianne Barrett, had said she'd come over later that day while Martha watched the boys. The meeting with Dianne was really just a formality since Trina had already spoken to her about making a quick sale and about the stipulation of the property being family owned for any sales within the next fifty years.

Trina tucked the envelope into her nightstand drawer so she could read it at bedtime and then she surveyed the house. Aside from the surface cracks Seth had fixed, it was a sturdy, well-built home and she hoped the realtor could find a nice, quiet but friendly couple or small family to make it their home. Seth had said he'd ask Amish families to spread the word to their relatives in neighboring districts. Perhaps one of them would want to relocate to Willow Creek. *As long as it's not Fannie Jantzi*, Trina thought. *Because I don't believe she's given up on Seth so easily.*

Trina should know; she was still having a hard time letting go of him herself. She was so depressed about it her appetite vanished again and she spent more time awake than asleep at night. Despite her insomnia, Trina forced herself to go through the motions of a regular routine, just as she had after her mother died. For the

sake of the boys—and to make things easier on Seth—
she was determined to keep her feelings about leaving to herself, too. There would be enough time to cry
after she returned to Philadelphia.

But who would help comfort her there? Missing
her mother had been more bearable when Trina was
surrounded by people who knew her and could bring
memories of her to mind. But because Patience and
Trina had moved around so frequently and her mother
tended to keep to herself, there was no one in the *Englisch* world who could comfort Trina as well as the
Amish had comforted her, even if their memories were
only of Patience when she was a girl.

By the time Seth returned home that evening, Trina
was beat and she declined Martha's invitation to eat
supper with them. Remembering the envelope from
Kate and hoping it contained memories about her
mother, Trina went to bed early so she could savor
reading it beneath the covers. She delicately tore the
envelope open and unfolded the paper. The letter was
longer than she expected and as she scanned the page,
she was aghast to realize the signature was Abe Kauffman's. Her hands trembled as she read.

Dear Trina,
You probably know a little about me from stories your mother told you. Regrettably, they're all
true. I was exactly the kind of father she said I
was. Actually, knowing her kindness, I was probably much worse than Patience ever described.

It's not an excuse for my behavior, but after
your grandmother died, part of me died, too. In-

stead of cherishing my daughter and relying on Gott for comfort, I turned to drinking, may the Lord forgive me.

You're probably also aware that your mother sent me a photo of you with a brief letter every year until you turned eighteen. What you don't know is how much her messages meant to me. I've kept them and the photos in the drawer in my nightstand if you want them.

Trina sat straight up in bed. It felt as if her world was tipping on its axis. She had no idea her mother had communicated with Abe for eighteen years, much less sent him photos of Trina. She didn't know what to make of this new information. Why wouldn't her mother have told her she'd done that? She continued reading.

Her sweet letters might be of consolation now that Patience is with the Lord instead of with you, just as they were a comfort to me when she was in the *Englisch* world instead of with the Amish community.

This part of the letter made Trina so furious she would have liked to rip the letter to shreds. The nerve of him! He was the very reason Trina's mother left the Amish. What right did he have to claim he missed her?

As you'll read, after your father divorced her, your mother asked me each year to say the word and she'd return with you to Willow Creek. But I couldn't. I wouldn't. And I want you to know why because it had nothing to do with her or you or with being Amish.

Now Trina started to cry. Was Abe lying? She felt as if she didn't even know her mother anymore. She'd had no idea Patience had so much as thought about returning home, much less asked for Abe's approval to do so. Every time she'd talked to her mother about going back to Willow Creek, her mother said they were better off where they were. Why would Patience lie to her about something so important?

Then Trina realized her mother hadn't actually ever said she wasn't in contact with her family. Whenever Trina asked her if she wanted to go back, her mother had replied, "You don't understand, honey. That's just not done under circumstances like mine."

"It isn't? Not ever?"

"Well, there is a process which allows a person to repent and return. But for someone who is divorced… well, there's a great deal of shame in that."

Trina had always assumed her mother was talking about her own shame. Now it was dawning on her that Patience had longed to return, but she wouldn't because she wanted to spare Abe the shame of having a divorced runaway daughter. Trina sat there weeping for some time before she could read any further.

To say I wanted my daughter to come back would be to admit I was the reason she left in the first place. That would mean coming to terms with my drinking, which I was unwilling to do.

As contradictory as this sounds, I was ashamed

of myself. I read Patience's letters and saw the photos of you and I knew your mother was raising you far better than I ever raised her. I thought you'd be happier in the *Englisch* world with her than you'd ever be within a one-hundred-mile radius of me.

It wasn't until I stopped drinking four years ago that I began to take responsibility for my wrongdoings. By then, the letters had stopped coming and I figured Patience no longer wanted to return home. I tried several times to locate you two, but my letters were returned with a stamp indicating you'd moved. Smith is a common name so I couldn't track you down after that.

I didn't hear about you and Patience again until your father contacted me and informed me of her passing.

So, Trina's father *had* known about Patience's death. Why hadn't he at least gotten in touch with Trina to offer consolation? Hadn't he been able to find her, either?

To say how grieved I was would be an insult to your own grief.

That's for sure! Trina thought and then she kept reading.

But I want you to know I am so sorry for your loss. Your mother loved you dearly and I'm sure you loved her dearly, too.

People often said Patience made the decision

to leave the Amish, but in truth, I didn't give her much of a choice. I feel like I've stolen an opportunity from you as well as from her, which is why I put the stipulation on the inheritance that you have to stay here for sixty days. I want you to decide for yourself whether you want to live in Willow Creek.

Your mother gave you the best parts of being Amish—her faith and her love. But she couldn't give you the community. For what it's worth, I want to give you that now.

Whether or not you choose to stay in Willow Creek, I pray you'll forgive me. I wish I had said those words to your mother, too, but I trust we'll be reconciled in heaven, through God's grace.

Abraham Kauffman

PS: I've had a problem with mice. The next-door neighbor, Seth Helmuth, might be able to trap them for you if you're squeamish.

Despite her heartache, Trina laughed aloud at the postscript, but the laughter twisted deep within her chest, like a sob. Too distraught get up and retrieve the photos and letters from the drawer in Abe's old room, she curled up in a ball, alternately thinking, weeping and praying for guidance until the sun came up.

When Seth returned from milking the cow on Thursday morning, he noticed the kitchen lamp on and he smelled something baking in the oven, but his grandmother wasn't present.

"Groossmammi?" he said quietly, wiping his boots

on the rag rug by the door. When she didn't answer, he walked toward the parlor, but she wasn't there, either.

"I'm here," a muffled voice cried from the hall.

When Seth came around the corner, he spotted her sitting on the floor with her back against the wall and he rushed to her side. "Are you hurt?"

"I don't think so. Help me up, slowly, please."

Seth cautiously eased her to a standing position and she moaned as she limped toward the sofa with his assistance. Then he settled her onto a cushion.

"That's better," she said. "I'll sit here awhile. Will you bring me my *kaffi*?"

Seth retrieved the steaming cup and only then did he ask what happened.

"I don't know. I slipped on something, I guess."

Seth walked to the hall and looked. One of the boys' library books lay on the floor. How many times had he told them to put their books away at night? Yet he wasn't really angry at them; he was upset that such a small thing could have resulted in a big accident for his grandmother.

"Are you certain you're okay?" he asked again. "You didn't bump your head, did you?"

"*Neh*. I caught myself before my head hit. My arm hurts a little, but it was probably from the impact."

But Seth continued to worry about her until Trina arrived and he pulled her aside to tell her what happened.

"Oh, *neh*!" she exclaimed, which elicited a scolding from Martha in the other room.

"You two need to stop talking about me in there. I told you I'm fine."

Trina whispered, "She probably *is* fine but should we take her to the hospital to get checked out?"

"She hates hospitals. She wouldn't go," Seth answered. He didn't add, "And I wouldn't, either."

"Perhaps you could ask Ethan if he'd take a look. She seems to like him alright."

Seth agreed but instead of using the phone shanty he decided on his way to the shop he'd stop and talk to Ethan in person at his home. The doctor seemed glad to help before going to the clinic. "I want to see Trina as often as I can before she goes back to Philly, anyway."

His reminder that Trina was leaving soon was like a punch to Seth's gut, but he thanked Ethan and continued toward work. It was pouring and it took him longer than usual to get there. On the way he thought about what could have happened to Martha. He couldn't put it off: he definitely needed someone to keep her safe as much as he needed someone to watch the boys. What was he going to do in between the time Trina left, and school let out and a local *maedel* was available? Would it really be so offensive if he asked Emma Lapp to help? His understanding was she didn't have a full-time job until the summer when her family sold produce at their roadside vegetable stand.

Inside the shop, he examined the leather frame he'd made for Trina. He just had to burn a few more details of the etching before it would be ready to give to her, but since it was a parting gift he delayed finishing it, as if that would mean she wasn't leaving. Once again, thinking about her departure made his stomach hurt and he was unusually irritable with a customer because her coat dripped rain onto one of the suede purses he had on display.

Then, as if his day couldn't get any worse, at two o'clock Fannie Jantzi came by with Hope and Greta. "We were buying cupcakes for Greta's birthday at the bakery," she explained.

Seth was surprised—Elmsville to Willow Creek was a long way to travel for cupcakes. Faith Schwartz's were the best around, but they were considered specialty items, not something the Amish would ordinarily buy for a child's birthday.

"I see," he said noncommittally.

"So the *Englischer* is leaving Willow Creek soon, *jah*?"

Through clenched teeth, Seth replied, "As you know, her name is Trina, but *jah*, she's moving the Sunday after this one, on May first."

"Who will care for the *buwe* until school lets out?" Fannie asked.

Seth didn't know why it was any of Fannie's business, but he was too tired to point that out to her. "I don't know," he said with a heavy sigh. "I thought I'd ask Emma Lamp."

"Emma Lamp? You haven't heard?"

"Heard what?"

"She broke her ankle chasing that scamp brother of hers, Thomas."

Seth tried not to show the disappointment he felt. "I guess I'll have to make other arrangements." But who would he ask? Pearl and Ruth couldn't keep up with the boys. Iris might be able to, but she was already occupied tending to Ruth.

"I suppose I could help," Fannie volunteered, "since my sister-in-law lives right next door to me and her *kinner* are in school, too, I could take the *meed* to her house in the morning and pick them up when I return from your house toward evening."

I suppose now that Trina is leaving, Fannie isn't avoiding me any longer, Seth thought. As unpalatable as the idea of having her as a nanny was, he didn't have any other options. It would only be for a few weeks until school let out. As long as Fannie understood he wasn't interested in any other kind of relationship with her, he decided to accept her offer.

"I'd appreciate it," he said. Then, to emphasize it was an employment arrangement, he added, "I'll pay a fair wage, especially considering you'll have to *kumme* from Elmsville."

"*Gut.* I'll see you bright and early on Monday, May second. *Mach's gut*, Seth."

After she exited the shop, Seth shook his head. He knew he should have been grateful the Lord had provided him a solution to his problem, but all he could think about was that when Trina first arrived, he'd wished time would pass quickly until she left. Now he wished it would stand still.

Chapter Nine

While the boys were napping, Trina brought cups of tea into the parlor for herself and Martha. Ethan had arrived that morning before he headed to his office and looked Martha over. He'd said she seemed fine, but if she developed pain anywhere, she'd need to get X-rays. Apparently people didn't always realize how they landed when they fell and sometimes they broke their bones without knowing it.

Before leaving, he urged Martha to reconsider visiting an ophthalmologist. "It could change the quality of your life. Wouldn't you prefer to be more independent than you are now?"

Martha pretended her hearing was as poor as her vision and she didn't respond to his question, but Trina wanted to get to the bottom of the matter and find out why she refused to consider surgery. She also wanted to talk to Martha about the letter from Abe.

After taking a seat across from the older woman, Trina decided an indirect approach was best. "Martha," she started, "there's something I'd like to ask about

Willow Creek's Amish *leit*. Does the *Ordnung* here prohibit modern *Englisch* medication and technology?"

"In other words, you want to know why I'm refusing to have eye surgery," Martha replied bluntly. Subtlety was lost on her. She explained, "I had an emergency removal of my gall bladder when I was in my fifties. The doctors botched the procedure and I needed a second surgery. I was in the hospital for a week. So, plain and simple, I'm scared to death of hospitals."

"Really?" Trina was stunned. She didn't think there was anything Martha was frightened of. "Is Seth afraid, too? He seems as reluctant to consult a medical doctor as you are."

"*Neh*. His aversion comes from something else... I told you how his brother left the Amish to marry an *Englischer*? Well, she was a nurse. Ever since then, Seth hasn't wanted to go anywhere near the hospital. He's afraid he'll bump into Kristine's old friends and seeing them will stir up memories he'd rather let rest. I think he's also developed a bias toward medical personnel. Seth doesn't trust them because he felt Kristine fooled him. He says if they'd deceive people in their personal lives, they'd lie to patients in their professional lives, too."

"That's *lecherich*—" Trina protested.

"*Jah*, it is. But it's probably ridiculous for me to be afraid, too, just because I had one bad operation when I was younger. Our perceptions and fears shape our truths and they shouldn't, because often they're wrong."

"You're right about that," Trina agreed. Then she delved into how she'd found the letter from her grandfather and what he'd written about her mother wanting to come back. "All this time I thought my *mamm* resented living in Willow Creek. I never knew she wanted to return. Every time I asked her about it, she said we were better off in the *Englisch* world."

"She was probably protecting you from knowing how much she wanted to return because she knew it wasn't a possibility. She didn't want you to feel sad on her behalf."

Trina's eyes overflowed. She'd ended up feeling sad on her mother's behalf anyway.

"Would you ever think about staying in Willow Creek?" Martha asked quietly.

"I've considered it," Trina replied as she dabbed her cheeks with a tissue. "But I don't know what I'd do for a living around here."

"The schoolteacher, Katie Yoder, is resigning at the end of the school year. I probably shouldn't mention this, but she's going to have a *bobbel* soon."

Trina's mood brightened. "Would the school board accept an *Englisch* schoolteacher?"

"They've done it in the past. Of course, they'd give preference to an Amish teacher."

Trina was afraid to voice the question she'd mulled over and prayed about all night, for fear of the answer. "Do you think…do you think there's any possibility I might become Amish?"

Martha pushed the rocker back and forth a few times before answering. "Ordinarily, I'd be doubtful. Most *Englischers* can't adjust to our lifestyle. There are too many obstacles in the way. The language, for one. Giving up modern conveniences, for another. And many of them are drawn to the lifestyle but they don't accept the faith that's at the core of everything we do."

Trina waited with bated breath to hear what Martha would say next.

"But given your background, as well as your faith and your demonstrated ability to forfeit modern conveniences, I think there's a *gut* likelihood the bishop would allow it, through conversion and convincement…if it's what you really want. But do you understand you'd be making the change for yourself and for the Lord, not for anyone else?"

Trina exhaled loudly. Now that the possibility was open to her, she knew it was exactly what she wanted. And she didn't want to become Amish simply because her mother had wanted it for her, nor because she was in love with Seth—although both had influenced her decision. Trina wanted it for herself. "I do," she said, as solemnly as if she were taking a wedding vow.

Martha was radiant. "Then we'll make an appointment to meet with the deacons and the bishop. You'll need an Amish woman to take you under her wing—I'll volunteer, if you agree."

"Of course I agree! I'd be so grateful," Trina said. From what she could tell, Martha had been mentoring her since she arrived. She asked the older woman not to tell Seth yet. Trina wanted to deliver the news herself for the pleasure of seeing his initial response in person.

"I won't say a word. Now, don't you think this calls for a celebratory funny cake?"

Trina laughed. Her days of feeling like a funny cake herself—unsure of whether she wanted to be Amish or *Englisch*—had come to a close. She had no question what she wanted to be. "I think you should teach me a new Amish recipe. I'm ready to try custard pie now."

The two women spent the rest of the afternoon baking. It was raining again so the boys were stuck inside but Trina was so elated she didn't even mind playing Noah's Ark another time. She positioned herself so she could see the lane, and when Seth's buggy appeared she ran outside without an umbrella to tell him about her decision.

"What's wrong? Is it my *Groossmammi*?" he asked when she burst into the stable—a place she'd tried to avoid because she was skittish around the livestock.

"*Neh*. Ethan said she checked out just fine," she quickly assured him. "Please, *kumme* closer to the door so I can see your face in the light. I have something *wunderbaar* to tell you."

Seth took a few steps closer. His hat was dripping so he removed it with one hand and raked his fingers through his hair with the other. He looked so handsome Trina almost forgot to speak and then the words rushed out. She told him about the letter and how she'd spoken to Martha and that she was going to stay in Willow Creek and join the Amish for good.

At first, Seth's expression was serious and Trina knew he was taking it all in. But instead of growing happier, it seemed he grew graver, not uttering a word. When she finished speaking, he walked a few paces toward a post, then turned around and looked at her. Then he crossed to the other side of the stable and leaned against the opposite post, staring down at the hay strewn across the floor as if it were the most fascinating thing he'd ever seen.

She was on the brink of tears. "Aren't you going to say something?"

He slowly looked at her and asked, "What is it you want to hear, Trina?"

"I want to hear how you feel," she said, but suddenly, she wasn't so sure she did.

Seth's heart was making a racket in his ears. How he felt? On one hand, he was thrilled because this was too good to be true. And on the other hand—well, he was dubious because this was too good to be true. So which feeling should he tell her about?

"I'm surprised. I'm—I'm shocked, really..." he stammered.

Trina's chin was quivering. "That's it? That's your response?"

"How do you expect me to respond?" Seth snapped. Thunder rumbled in the distance; a spring storm was approaching.

"I don't know." Trina's beautiful voice had gone monotone. "Forget I asked."

"Wait." He pulled her arm and she stopped but wouldn't face him. He looked at the delicate swirl of her ear as he spoke. She might not be happy with what he was about to say but she deserved his honesty. "I'm apprehensive, Trina. I guess I'm—I'm afraid."

"Afraid?" Trina repeated. "You're *afraid*? Of what?"

Seth walked to a bale of hay and sat down. "I'm terrified I might believe you. Terrified you'll change your mind. Terrified of what that would do to the *buwe* and Martha." Choking, he added, "And to me. I've been down this road before. I've seen what it can do to a family…"

"Oh, Seth," Trina said and sat down next to him, their knees separated by the thinnest slice of space. "I'm not like Kristine. I won't change my mind. I want this more than anything. And I—wait, I'm probably saying the exact things she said, right?"

Seth nodded miserably. Kristine *had* said the same things. Over and over again. But in the end, she still changed her mind.

"I understand why you'd have your doubts. If I were in your shoes, I probably would, too," Trina said. "So I won't ask you to trust me. Instead, I'll keep showing you—and all the *leit* in Willow Creek—that I *am* trustworthy. I *am* true to my word. Time will prove it. You'll see."

Seth's heart ballooned because Trina was so understanding about the source of his disbelief. The truth was, he *wanted* to trust her and at least that was a strong step in the right direction. He turned his face toward hers and took in her earnest eyes and winsome expression. He wished he could allow himself one kiss on those lips, which he imagined would feel as velvety soft as the petals of a rose. Just one kiss before he said what he had to say, because once he said it, he couldn't take it back.

"You have to understand," he carefully began. He didn't want to sound presumptuous, but he needed her to know where he stood. "Even though your intention is to become Amish, until you've actually been baptized into the church, you're still *Englisch*."

"I understand," she whispered, tilting her chin toward him. Their mouths were even closer now and he looked at her from beneath lowered eyelids as he spoke.

"Which means an Amish man in Willow Creek wouldn't be allowed to court you. He wouldn't be able to kiss you." Seth's mouth felt parched and he had to lick his lips before continuing. "He wouldn't be allowed to tell you he loved you, no matter how much he wanted to."

"I understand. And I would respect him for that, no matter how much I wanted all those things, too," Trina stated seriously. "I would expect him to stay true to his beliefs and I wouldn't tempt him to violate them in any way." As if to prove it, Trina pulled her head back, stood up and walked toward the door.

Come back. Come closer, Seth thought, contradicting the very words he'd just spoken. But by moving away from him, Trina was demonstrating the sincerity of her intention to follow Amish practices and he loved her even more for that.

A sheet of rain fell outside the door but instead of exiting, Trina pivoted and said, "You know, Seth, I'm afraid, too. I'm afraid now that I've admitted how much I want this, I'm going to be turned down by the bishop. Martha said most people aren't successful at converting."

Seth had little fear of that and he said so. "You're not most people, Trina. You're different. You're the most unique *Englischer* I've ever met. And I'll support you through the convincement process however I can."

"Denki," Trina said, her skin aglow. "Now all I have to do is tell the realtor I've changed my mind about selling the house."

"You'll eventually have to get over your fear of barn animals, too," Seth joked.

Trina giggled. "I've conquered my fear of *hinkel*. Next, my fear of mice. Eventually I'll work my way up to horses and cows."

"It won't be easy," Seth said, and suddenly he wasn't joking anymore. "Not any of it." He was referring to himself waiting to see if she was really going to stay.

"But it will be worth it. You'll see," Trina said, again erasing his fears.

"Oh, *neh!*" Seth smacked his palm against his forehead. "I just remembered. Today I made arrangements for Fannie to watch the *kinner* starting on May second until school lets out."

Trina put her hands on her hips. "Fannie? That's who you chose to replace me?"

"I didn't want to, but there wasn't anyone else. I was worried about my *groossmammi.*"

"Perhaps it's for the best. Martha agreed to mentor me, so now we can spend time alone together without waiting for the *buwe* to take their naps. Fannie will keep them occupied."

"More likely *they'll* keep *her* frustrated."

Trina giggled. "As long as no one winds up in the creek, I think you should be grateful."

Seth laughed. He reveled in their rapport; at least he wouldn't have to refrain from talking to her until she was baptized into the Amish church. Trina excitedly told him Martha was going to help her refine her *Deitsch,* sew an Amish wardrobe and learn to cook more Amish meals.

"Can I make a suggestion?" Seth asked and when

Trina said yes, he continued, "Forget about refining your *Deitsch.* Instead, ask her to give you additional bread-making lessons. The loaves you make are like leather."

Now Trina cracked up. "*Jah,* but you love leather."

"I enjoy working with it, not chewing it."

"You'd make a terrible lion," she jested and they darted through the rain toward the house. Once he followed Trina inside, Seth shook his hair like a dog all over Timothy and Tanner, who were waiting for them at the door. They screeched with hilarity at his antics.

"It smells like custard pie in here," Seth noticed immediately. "If dessert smells this *appenditlich,* I can't imagine what we're having for supper."

"Actually, I haven't put supper together yet," Trina confessed. "Martha and I were so focused on baking the pie and talking about—"

"That's okay," Seth interjected. "I'm treating all of us to supper at Browns' Diner on Main Street. *Buwe,* go tell *Groossmammi,*" he instructed and the boys raced down the hall.

"Are you sure?" Trina asked coyly. "Browns' Diner is *Englisch,* isn't it?"

"*Jah,* but there's no rule against eating there and tonight is a special occasion," Seth said, winking at her. "Besides, since you're not returning to Philadelphia, you'd better get used to our local version of a Philly cheese-steak sandwich."

"That's probably the only thing I'm going to miss about Philadelphia," she said. "Everything else about living there pales in comparison to my life in Willow Creek."

Seth knew exactly what she meant because he felt like every other woman paled in comparison to Trina.

Dianne Barrett was very understanding about Trina changing her mind. In fact, the realtor said she'd been hoping Trina would reconsider, since a quick sale wouldn't work in Trina's favor, given how much property she owned. To add to Trina's joy, Martha arranged to have the bishop and one of the deacons call on them a few days later on the Sabbath, since it was an off Sunday. While Seth discreetly disappeared with the boys to the creek, Trina and Martha discussed Trina's conversion with the two clergymen, who gave tentative approval of her efforts to begin the convincement process. There would be many formal requirements for her to meet before she was accepted into the church, but the deacon said he'd announce her intention the following Sunday, May first, when the *leit* gathered again for church.

Trina sailed through the week, as well as the following weekend. On Monday, May second, the lawyer visited her and finalized the paperwork for her to take ownership of her grandfather's house, just as they'd arranged from the beginning. Since it was Fannie's first day watching the *buwe*, Trina was free to meet with the attorney alone at home.

"Congratulations," he said, handing her the deed. "The house is yours to sell."

"I'm not selling. I'm staying," Trina replied with a huge grin on her face.

That evening, right after she spied Fannie's buggy heading back down the lane, Trina hurried next door to tell Martha and Seth it was official: she owned the house. The boys greeted Trina from where they were stomping in puddles in the lane. Seth must have permitted them to engage in their favorite activity in order to burn off a little energy before bedtime.

"Trina, *Groossmammi* said she's going to your house tomorrow by herself. Why can't we *kumme*, too?" Tanner questioned.

"Fannie said we're not allowed," Timothy told him. "Remember? She said Trina might be able to wash *Daed*'s brain but she wasn't going to let her wash our brains."

"Is that true?" Tanner asked Trina. "I don't think I want my brain washed."

Trina was appalled. Had Timothy not heard right or did Fannie really say that? Because Seth didn't want the boys to accidentally tell other people about Trina's intention to convert, she'd agreed not to let Timothy and Tanner know until it had been announced in church on Sunday. Although Trina hadn't been able to attend the service, Seth informed her on Sunday evening the boys hadn't been present when the announcement was made. He suggested he'd sit down with Timothy and Tanner to talk about it when he had time to explain it thoroughly and answer any questions they had. Meanwhile, apparently word had spread to Fannie's district within hours.

"I think Fannie heard wrong because I'm not washing anyone's brains, I promise," Trina assured Tanner. "And if your *groossmammi* says you may *kumme* to my house with her tomorrow, then you may. I'll go talk to her about it now."

The boys whooped and resumed puddle jumping as Trina knocked on the kitchen door. There was no answer but Seth approached from the stable and warned the boys they had five more minutes to play. He let Trina inside, telling her Martha was resting because her head hurt.

"Because of her eyes again?"

"Maybe. Or maybe it was because of the kind of day she had."

Trina thought the latter was more likely the cause. Seeing dirty dishes piled in the sink, Trina felt a twinge of complacency knowing Fannie wasn't able to manage the household as well as Trina had. "I'm here to tell you and Martha it's official—the house is mine!" she exclaimed.

"That's *wunderbaar*," Seth said. "You made it two months. Now let's see if you can make it two years."

His comment reminded Trina of when she first met him and she wasn't sure if he was teasing or not, but she shrugged it off, retorting, "From the looks of it, you should be more worried about if your new nanny can make it here two *days*." Then she told him about Fannie's remark and asked when he was going to tell Timothy and Tanner that Trina was staying.

Seth hesitated, and this time Trina was insulted. She knew he still didn't fully believe she was here for good. It pained her, but considering all he'd been through with Freeman and Kristine, she understood. "Seth, I know it's difficult for you to believe, but I assure you I've already put every last *Englisch* thing out of my life. I even donated my *Englisch* Bible to my church. I'll use my *groossdaadi*'s German one, instead. From this moment forward, I'm going to live as an Amish person would, except when taking liberties would be inappropriate."

Seth remained silent so she continued. "If you don't want to tell the *buwe* yet, I understand and I'll respect that. But since the rest of the community found out during church yesterday, eventually the boys will, too. We have to tell them something, otherwise they'll be confused that I'm still here. And I don't want Fannie's explanations to take root in their minds."

Seth noncommittally offered, "Maybe I'll tell them tonight before putting them to bed."

"Oh, okay." Once again, Trina was disappointed by his reluctance, but she reminded herself she'd committed to showing him, however long it took, that she would honor her word.

The next day at five in the morning she woke to rapid knocking and she sat up straight, panicking. Had Martha's headache worsened?

"What's the matter?" she asked Seth at the door as the *buwe* cavorted behind him.

"Nothing. It's time for milking. If you're serious about living like the Amish, you need to learn how to milk a cow. No more milk from a plastic jug."

Was he challenging her or trying to be helpful? Trina couldn't decide, but either way, she was willing to learn. "Great. Maybe later in the week you'll teach me to hitch the horse, too."

Even in the dreary early morning light, Trina caught his sparkling smile. "You were going to take it slowly," he reminded her. Then, as the boys ran to the stable ahead of them, Seth explained, "They were so excited to find out you're staying here they woke up before I did."

Seth must have told them the previous night! Trina was so delighted she nearly skipped to the barn like a child herself. After Seth gave her a preliminary demonstration of how to milk the cow, she returned home to make breakfast. While she was eating, Seth knocked on her door yet again, informing her Martha wouldn't be coming that day. Her head still hurt.

Although she was disappointed, Trina decided to give her home a more thorough spring cleaning than she had before Dianne visited. Now that the house was hers, she realized she couldn't keep Abe's door shut forever. She'd probably want to host overnight guests eventually, so she stood in the doorway trying to decide how to brighten the room yet keep the furnishings modest and plain, in accordance with the *Ordnung*. That's when she remembered she still hadn't looked at the letters and photos in Abe's nightstand, so she pulled open the drawer and removed the folder.

Sure enough, it contained a letter and photo for each year from the time Trina was born until she turned eighteen. She couldn't bear to read the letters in which her mother asked Abe if she could return, but flipping through the photos was like seeing a movie of her life. In one picture, she was crawling. In another, she was smiling broadly, showing off the gap where her tooth had fallen out. There was a photo of her riding a bicycle and another one of her standing primly in a new dress beneath a blossoming dogwood tree at Easter time. Filled with a mix of nostalgia and loneliness for her mother, Trina slid the items back into the folder.

Since photographs weren't permitted, she'd have to get rid of them and rely on the images she knew by heart, instead.

Just then, something buzzed loudly in the room. At first she thought a fat housefly had gotten into the house, but then she realized it was her cell phone, still sitting on the windowsill. The last time she'd used it was to finalize a meeting time with Dianne—or was it when she entered Ethan's phone number into it after finding the business card he'd left behind? In any case, she'd forgotten all about it. Making a mental note to cancel her service before discarding the phone, she briefly glanced at the screen and noted a text. It said:

It's me, your father. I'm about to call you. Please pick up. It's urgent.

She had just finished reading the text when the phone vibrated in her hand again. Fearful something was wrong, she felt compelled to answer her father's call.

"It's Trina," she said into the receiving end of the phone.

"Hello, Trina. Thank you for answering. I'm here in town and I need to talk to you. Will you meet with me? I'll pick you up and take you to lunch."

Her father was in Willow Creek? Trina was silent, her mind reeling.

"Trina, please. You're the only child I have. I don't want anything to come between us. I know I haven't been in touch, but I'd like to change that now."

Trina thought of how her mother had never gotten to

reconcile with Abe. She didn't want that to happen with her father, too, especially since her mother had urged her not to turn him away if he wanted a relationship. Trina knew she had to listen to what her father had to say and to forgive him if he asked. She wanted to tell him about her choice to become Amish, too.

That's when she had an idea; she'd give the photos to her father, since he'd missed seeing Trina during so many of the years her mother had caught on camera. He'd probably be as delighted to get them as Abe had been. Trina separated them from the letters and took the folder with her to her room, where she changed into a fresh top and skirt, and then went out onto the porch to wait for her father there.

To her surprise, not one but two cars were already parked in the lane by her house. Because it was drizzling, she slipped the folder inside her coat so it wouldn't get wet and then sprang across the lawn and found both vehicles were empty. Twirling around to scan the yard, Trina spotted two men walking up from the creek. She didn't know one of them, but the other one was definitely her father. Although Trina hadn't seen him in years, she'd recognize him anywhere, even though he was balding now and had developed a bit of a paunch.

When he came near, he kissed her cheek and said, "You look exactly like your mother did at your age. Beautiful." After a pause, he added, "I'm sorry she's gone, Trina."

He really did look sorry, too, and Trina felt a pang of guilt for being so resentful she couldn't locate him in time for her mother's funeral. She extended her hand to the short, dark-haired man accompanying her father and said, "I'm Trina."

"Oh, sorry," Richard apologized. "Trina, this is my business associate, Drex Watson—"

It suddenly dawned on Trina what her father and this man were doing down by the creek; they'd been scoping out the property. Drex was probably there to help persuade—no, to *pressure*—Trina to reconsider selling the land to her father. Trina's temper flared and she didn't give her father a chance to finish making introductions. "I've already told the realtor I have no intention of selling the property for development purposes. So there's no need for you to accompany us, Mr. Watson." She deliberately used a formal address to indicate they weren't on friendly terms.

"Trina, wait. Just consider—" Drex began to protest, but Trina's father interrupted him.

"It's okay, Drex. My daughter wants to speak with me alone. I'll catch up with you later."

Drex's eyes darted from Richard to Trina and then back to Richard before he shrugged and said, "Alright. Catch you later."

After Drex drove away, Richard said, "Come on, Trina, it's raining. Let's go get some lunch in town, okay?"

Trina hesitated. On one hand, she wanted to hear him out. On the other hand, she didn't want him pressuring her to change her mind about selling to him. She slowly walked to the car and accompanied him to Browns' Diner. As they drove, Trina realized his vehicle was worth a fortune and she wondered if Kurt had been exaggerating how broke her father actually was.

At the diner Richard chose a booth by the front window and while they waited for their meals, Trina told him about her decision to become Amish. He looked surprised but didn't say anything as she described the process she'd undergo before being baptized into the church.

When she was done speaking, her father said, "So, while you're going through this—what did you call it, convincement process?—you'll live with your mentor?"

Trina cocked her head. "No. I'll live in my own house. Why?"

Her father's cheeks broke out in ruddy patches. "I just wondered, that's all."

"Dad," Trina said firmly, although the term felt strange to her ears, "I'm *not* going to sell the house. To anyone."

"I understand," he said, but his mouth sagged. Trina waited for him to change the subject—specifically, to talk about his desire to reconcile with her, but he stayed silent until the server brought them their meals. By that time, Trina had realized he never truly intended to come back into her life, except to purchase her house. She poked at her fries but didn't take a bite since she wouldn't have been able to swallow.

After her father paid the check, Trina summoned the last of her grace and reached over to clasp his hand. "Dad, even though I'm becoming Amish, I'll always welcome you into my home as a guest," she said. "And I'll always welcome you into my life as my father."

He glanced up. *Green eyes. Is that all we have in common?* Trina wondered as she waited for him to speak, but he didn't say a word. Then the server returned with his change and her father pulled his hand out from under Trina's to pocket the bills.

Trina decided she'd walk home and her father didn't object even though it was raining harder now. Before she stood to leave she remembered the folder of photos and she pushed it across the table toward him. "I want you to have these memories from my childhood. Even though it was difficult sometimes and I wished you were with us, Mom and I were happy together." Rising, she leaned over the table to kiss his head before saying, "Take care, Dad."

Then she stepped outside, where raindrops and teardrops rolled steadily down her face.

Shortly before Seth was going to leave for the day, Joseph Schrock stopped in to report the south end of Willow Creek was blocked off because the creek had overflowed its banks and Meadow Road was submerged.

"I'll walk home on West Street, instead," Seth said. "*Denki* for telling me. Otherwise I would have had to double back once I got to Meadow Road."

"I only found out myself when I returned from an appointment in Highland Springs this afternoon. Otherwise, I would have warned Trina, too. Poor *maedel*, it must have taken her over an hour to get home from the diner."

"Trina was in the diner?" Seth wondered why she had ventured out in the inclement weather.

"*Jah*, I saw her eating with an *Englischer*. He looked old enough to be her *daed*. Anyway, *mach's gut*, Seth."

Joseph gave a brief wave of his hand and slipped back out the door.

As Seth trudged home, he was so consumed with wondering who Trina met at the diner he didn't notice the rain had soaked through his coat to his shirt until he arrived at the house and Fannie handed him a towel.

"Where's my *groossmammi*?" he asked, patting his sleeves dry.

"She's in her room with the door closed. I think her *koppweh* might have gotten worse. Probably from the *buwe*—they've been very loud today."

"And where are they?"

"In the basement. I'll start to make supper now that you're home."

The last thing Seth wanted was for Fannie to stay any longer. "That's alright. I'm sure your daughters are waiting to see you. We'll just have sandwiches."

Fannie's shoulders drooped in disappointment, so Seth quickly offered, "I'll hitch your buggy for you and bring it around so you won't get wet."

"*Denki*. I'd appreciate that," she replied. Ever so casually, she added, "Unlike Trina and her two *Englisch* guests, I have no interest in strolling around in the rain."

Seth couldn't help taking her bait. "Trina had guests today?"

"*Jah*. She was walking around her yard with two men. It seemed as if they were surveying the property."

Seth's stomach lurched as he briefly wondered if Trina was reconsidering selling. He just as quickly dismissed the notion. Trina would never do that. But why was she showing anyone the property, especially in the rain? Seth could hardly wait for the boys to go to sleep so he could go talk to her. First, he checked on Martha, who refused anything to eat, and then he made sandwiches for the boys, gave them baths and tucked them into bed.

"Is everything okay?" Trina asked as she let him in.

"I don't know. Maybe you'd like to tell me," he said, crossing the threshold.

"What do you mean?" Her face was puckered with confusion.

He wasn't in the mood for their usual repartee. "Don't play games, Trina."

"What are you talking about, Seth?" Now her hands were on her hips. "And why do I suspect Fannie is at the bottom of whatever's troubling you?"

"Maybe it's because you know she knows you had men here looking at your property."

"Oh, that." The scowl faded from Trina's face as she sat down at the table, waving her hand dismissively. How could she be so casual? "*Jah*, my *daed* and his business associate came here and, *jah*, they were looking at the land. But I made it clear to them I wasn't interested in selling."

"Was this before or after you ate lunch with them in the diner?"

Trina's head jerked back. "Wow. I know Willow Creek is a small community, but I didn't realize just how many people are interested in my business."

"So it's true, you had dinner with them?"

"Not with *them*. I ate dinner with my *daed*. Alone. Is that a crime?"

"Was it your idea?" Seth was annoyed he had to grill

her for details. If she had nothing to hide, why wasn't she being more forthcoming?

"I don't know why that matters, but *neh*, he was the one who texted me. He wanted to get together and I felt I owed him that much. I wanted to tell him I'd always—"

"He *texted* you? You still have your cell phone?" Seth was astounded.

"*Jah*. I'd forgotten all about it until I heard the text notification go off."

Seth paced the length of the kitchen. This was exactly how things had started to unravel with Kristine's plans to join the Amish. First, it was her cell phone she couldn't give up. Then it was her favorite pieces of jewelry. Next, it was her laptop. She always had a compelling excuse for keeping whatever it was she wanted to keep—including Freeman. Now here was Trina, making similar excuses just one day after she promised him she'd put every last *Englisch* thing out of her life. Worse, it was just one day after he'd told his young, vulnerable sons about her plan to convert! Seth was seething.

"Your cell phone. Your father. Your father's business associate." He counted on his fingers, listing her offenses. "What other parts of your *Englisch* life are you still holding on to?"

"Are you kidding me?" Trina asked with knives in her voice. "After everything I've given up, do you really believe there's any aspect of *Englisch* life I'm deliberately hanging on to?"

"Clearly there is," Seth barked. His volume rose as he continued, "I just wish you would have recognized you weren't fully committed to leaving your *Englisch* life behind before I told the *buwe* you were converting. It will devastate them if you change your mind."

"You know I understand that better than anyone!" Trina countered, her nostrils flaring. "I'd never break such an important promise to Timothy and Tanner because I remember exactly how destructive it was when my *daed* didn't keep his promises to me."

"That's exactly what I'm worried about." Seth glowered back at her. "Maybe it's like *daed*, like *dochder*. Can't trust him, can't trust you."

Trina slapped her palms against the table and jumped to her feet, leaning forward to glare directly into his eyes. "The problem isn't that I'm untrustworthy—it's that *you're* untrusting. So if you want to live the rest of your life distrustful and afraid, go right ahead. But you're not the only one who's going to miss out—your attitude is going to harm your *buwe*, too. And that's as unfair to them as my *daed* was to me."

She twirled and stormed out of the room at the same time Seth stomped outside into the rain. As angry as Trina was, he was twice as livid. He didn't regret it one iota that he'd challenged her commitment. No matter what she said about his so-called distrustful attitude affecting Timothy and Tanner, if there was even an inkling of doubt Trina wasn't going to stay, it was Seth's parental duty to protect his sons from becoming even more attached to her. He resolved from then on to keep them away from her—and to keep himself away from her, too.

Chapter Ten

Trina waited until she was sure Seth had left before she emerged from her room, slamming the door behind her. Who did he think he was, acting as if she'd committed a crime by meeting with her father? And who did he think *she* was to suggest she didn't want to let go of her *Englisch* life? She circled the parlor, ranting aloud, "If I wanted to hold on to my *Englisch* life, I wouldn't have forfeited a half a million dollar sale in order to stay here!"

Her anger gave her a surge of energy. She pulled a sack of flour from the pantry and yeast from the fridge and began making bread. Nothing ever felt as good as kneading the dough hard and punching it down. She made four loaves in succession while flashes of lightning illuminated the sky and thunder raged outside as tempestuously as she did.

She realized she was sick and tired of trying to prove herself to Seth. She was almost grateful he'd said such awful things because it showed her he wasn't going to change. What good would it do for him to trust her after she'd become Amish? That wasn't trust; that was proof. She wanted him to trust her now, before she converted. She wanted him to have faith in the best, not to always suspect the worst.

And what about *him* keeping *his* word? He'd said he'd support her however he could during her convincement process. What hypocrisy! He accused *her* of being like her father, but he was more like Richard Smith than she'd ever be. She was crushed to discover he was like every man who'd ever left her when she most needed help, and suddenly her anger completely fizzled out, leaving her feeling dejected and alone. Desperate for consolation, she read and reread the letters her mother sent Abe until the accounts of happier times soothed her heartache enough that she could finally go to sleep.

The next day, when Timothy and Tanner knocked on the door, Trina pushed her lips into a smile to conceal the sadness that had returned. "Hello, *buwe*. Did you *kumme* over here alone?"

"*Jah.* Fannie said we had to scamper quickly. She's waiting over there." Timothy turned and pointed to Fannie, who was standing out of the rain beneath a willow in the Helmuths' yard. Why wasn't she accompanying the boys? Was she afraid she'd become tainted by visiting someone who was still an *Englischer*? Trina took a small measure of satisfaction in lifting her hand in a friendly wave, but Fannie just looked at her shoes.

"Would you like to *kumme* in?" she asked the boys. "I made sweet bread last night."

"*Neh, Daed* said we're not allowed," Tanner said. "But Fannie told us we have to visit you this one time."

Trina suppressed a gasp, outraged that Seth was using the boys to take out his anger at her. "Why did Fannie want you to *kumme* here?"

"We're supposed to tell you *Groossmammi* can't visit you today. Her head is splitting," Tanner reported.

"Oh, dear, do you mean she has a splitting *koppweh*?"

"*Jah*. And *Daed*'s getting a blue face."

"A what?" Trina didn't think she'd heard correctly.

Timothy said, "*Groossmammi* told *Daed* he could talk about it until his face turns blue but she wasn't changing her mind. And *Daed* said he wasn't changing his mind, either. He said he couldn't stop *Groossmammi* from visiting you but he could stop his *buwe* from visiting you."

"And *Groossmammi* cried and went to her room because of her head splitting," Tanner added. Scrunching his nose, he asked, "Will it hurt when *Daed*'s face turns blue?"

For the boys' sake, Trina fought to keep her ire at Seth in check. "I don't think your *daed*'s face is really going to turn blue," she explained carefully. "Sometimes people use funny words called idioms but the words aren't really what they mean. Like if I say yesterday it rained cats and dogs, there weren't really cats and dogs falling from the sky. I just mean it rained hard."

"Like when Fannie told *Daed* he was as strong as an ox she didn't mean it? Because an ox is really strong and *Daed* is really strong but *Daed* can't pull a plough."

It just figures Fannie would appeal to Seth's mas-

culinity like that, Trina thought. To Tanner she said, "Exactly like that. So don't you worry about your *daed*. What you ought to do is be especially kind to your *groossmammi* today. Can you do that?"

"Jah," the boys readily agreed, as Trina knew they would. She ducked into the kitchen, slipped two loaves of bread into separate bags and returned to hand one to each of them.

"Timothy can carry the cinnamon-raisin bread and, Tanner, you carry this sweet bread. If Fannie says it's okay, you may have a piece. And guess what? It's not even tough like carrion!"

Pleased she'd elicited a smile from the boys' serious faces, she kissed their heads and sent them off with a reminder to tell Martha she'd see her when she was feeling better. The boys darted back to Fannie, who was already walking toward the Helmuths' house.

Trina couldn't help worrying about Martha's health. Whether her headaches had increased because of her vision problem or because of her "nanny problem," it seemed she'd benefit from a visit to the doctor. *But if I suggest that again, Seth will just tell her it's because I haven't let go of my* Englisch *ways*, Trina thought bitterly.

Knowing she needed to improve her German comprehension as well as her attitude, Trina sat down, picked up her Bible and began reading until there was a break in the rain. Then she walked into town to do her shopping and inquire about summer employment. She had to take the long way, avoiding both Meadow Road and the path along the creek because of the flooding, but she felt so listless she didn't mind. After picking up her groceries, she stopped at Schrock's Shop to ask about a job.

Joseph told her he didn't have any openings right then, but in another month he might need extra help, since so many tourists came through town once school let out. Before Trina left he asked if Meadow Road was still flooded. When she confirmed it was, he sympathized because her section of Willow Creek was cut off to traffic on three sides. To Trina, it hardly mattered since she traveled by foot, not by buggy. Also, now there was less of a chance that her father would return. Not that she expected him to.

The sky began pouring again on her way home and she was drenched by the time she reached her door. She was bending to unlace her shoes when she thought she heard her name being called from a distance. She straightened her spine, listening.

"Trina!" That was definitely Tanner outside her door. She flung it open. His face was bright red and he was panting.

Crouching down, she placed her hands on his shoulders. "Take a deep breath and then tell me what happened."

"Timothy fell off his bicycle in the basement. He was going real fast around a corner and his bike tipped and he went flying through the air and he landed like this," Tanner said, gesturing with his hands. "Fannie is crying and *Groossmammi* wants you to *kumme*."

Although her heart was drumming in her ears, Trina had the presence of mind to grab her cell phone before she ran across the yard and into the house with Tanner. When they reached the bottom of the basement stairs, she found Martha and Fannie kneeling beside Timothy, who was lying on the floor, moaning. As Trina leaned closer, she noticed his arm was swollen and positioned oddly.

"It's broken—his arm is broken!" Fannie seemed nearly hysterical. "And he might have a concussion, too!"

Under her breath, Trina hissed, "Shh! Calm down and don't move him." If Timothy had a head or neck injury, Trina didn't want to splint his arm. She quietly asked Timothy if he'd hit his head, but he didn't answer, so she gingerly parted his blond curls to examine his skull. There was no blood, but a large egg was already forming on the right side.

She quickly pulled her phone out of her pocket. She'd gladly suffer any consequences or shaming remarks from Seth for using her cell phone: Timothy's health was more important to her than anything else at that moment. She tapped in 911.

When the operator came on the line, Trina described their emergency. The operator said they'd dispatch an ambulance, but it might take a while for it to get there because of the flooding. He asked if there was anyone nearby with a car who could reach them quicker and bring Timothy to the hospital. Trina said no before suddenly remembering Ethan. The dispatcher wanted to stay on the line with her, so after Trina gave him Ethan's number, he told another dispatcher to contact Ethan, who confirmed he'd be there as soon as possible. Once Martha heard help was on the way, she stopped ringing her hands and pressed them together, praying, "*Denki*, Lord!" and Trina inwardly echoed her gratitude to God.

She instructed, "Tanner, I'd like you to lead your *groossmammi* upstairs by the hand and let Dr. Gray in when he arrives. Fannie, bring me a quilt to keep Timothy warm." Fannie looked so peaked Trina was afraid she might pass out, so in what she hoped was a convincing voice she added, "Timothy's going to be okay, Fannie. Really, he will."

As the others clambered up the stairs, Trina cooed to the boy, "I know it hurts but you're doing great. Could you say your name so I know you're okay?" When he continued to moan without answering her, she asked, "What's the fiercest animal you can think of right now?"

"A shark," he mumbled, to her relief. In order to keep him awake and to prepare him for what would happen at the hospital, she told him a story about a shark that broke its fin. "The fish doctor said the shark needed to get an X-ray, which is what you'll probably get and it won't hurt at all. An X-ray is like a drawing of the bones on the inside of your skin."

Without opening his eyes, Timothy argued, "But sharks don't have bones. They have cartilage."

Trina could have wept for joy at his remark—clearly his brain was functioning just fine! A few minutes later Ethan arrived and evaluated Timothy's pupils, head, neck and spine, and then made a temporary splint to immobilize his arm and lifted him up.

"Instead of waiting for the ambulance, it'll be quicker for us to take him to the hospital. They'll need to set his arm, which might involve surgery, depending on the fracture. We'll have to take West Street to avoid the flooded areas. When we pass through town we can pick up Seth since we'll need his permission to treat Timothy."

When they got to Main Street, Ethan pulled over in front of Seth's shop and left the car running as he dashed into the store. A few moments later, three *Englisch* shoppers spilled onto on the sidewalk and Seth and Ethan followed closely behind.

Seth slid into the back seat with Trina and Timothy, careful not to jostle his son. "Please, *Gott*, ease Timothy's pain and keep him well," he prayed aloud. Timothy's eyes briefly fluttered open at the sound of Seth's voice before closing again.

Seeing Seth's affliction, Trina wanted to comfort him. No matter how angry she'd been, she wouldn't wish the kind of distress he was experiencing on anyone. But she was deeply shaken, too, and her addled mind couldn't come up with anything encouraging to say. She remained silent until Ethan pulled into the emergency entrance area. They were met by two staff members with a gurney who eased Timothy out of the back seat. Seth and Ethan followed them inside, while Trina drove the car to the parking lot, her hands trembling on the steering wheel.

Seth felt as if he had rocks in his gut as the hospital staff wheeled his son away. Before Ethan joined them, he assured Seth that Timothy would be in good hands. After filling out the necessary paperwork at the front desk, Seth paced the hallway, too distraught to sit with the others in the main waiting room. He silently pleaded with the Lord to keep close watch on Timothy. His prayers quickly turned into self-admonishment. How could he have been so irresponsible as to let Fannie watch the boys after what had happened the day she was alone with them by the creek?

Timothy's suffering was his fault and Seth wished he could take his son's place. For the first time in a long while, he thought of Eleanor. "I'm sorry," he whispered, leaning his head against the wall. All she had asked of him was, if he remarried, to choose a woman who would take good care of the boys. He hadn't even found a nanny who would take good care of them. Other than Trina, that was. "I'm so sorry," he whispered again.

A hand rested flat against his back. "Seth?" It was Trina and her hair was dripping wet. He'd been too distraught to notice if she'd been wet in the car on the way, but for a moment his mind flashed to the Sunday when he'd first courted Fannie and he'd picked Trina up on the roadside. He wished he could turn the clock back to that day. He would have trusted his initial perspective that he and Fannie weren't a match.

"Let's sit." Trina motioned to a backless wooden bench farther down the hall. "It's quieter there, so we can pray."

But Seth couldn't form any words, so Trina petitioned the Lord on his behalf. They sat with their heads bowed for what seemed like hours until finally Ethan came to tell them Timothy was going to be fine. He said the fracture was an ugly one but it didn't require surgery. However, the doctors wanted to keep him overnight because of the swelling. After it subsided, they'd cast his arm. The really great news was that he didn't appear to have a concussion.

"*Denki,* Lord! *Denki!*" Seth exclaimed, looking heavenward as a few tears streamed from his eyes down his cheeks and into his sideburns. "Is Timothy awake? May I see him?"

"He's groggy from the medication they gave him before setting the bone but you can go in," Ethan replied. "Sorry, Trina, it's family only until they transfer him to a room."

Whatever Trina might have said in reply, Seth didn't hear it. All he could focus on was seeing his son. Tears again sprang from his eyes when he viewed Timothy's small form reclining on the white bed. He hurried to his child's side and kissed the top of his head, but Timothy was too drowsy to stir. As the nurse was making arrangements to secure a room for him in the pediatric wing, Seth returned to the hall where Ethan and Trina had been.

Finding Ethan there alone, he asked, "Where's Trina?"

"She's driving back to your house to tell your *groossmammi* Timothy is going to be okay. Then she'll return with a few things for you, since she figured you'll probably want to stay overnight with him here. She'll pick me up then, too."

Seth felt horrible. After all of the cruel things he'd said to Trina, she was repaying him with kindness. Seth was indebted to Ethan, too. "I can't tell you how grateful I am for your medical expertise," he told him.

Ethan clasped his shoulder. "I'm blessed the Lord enabled me to study medicine and gave me an aptitude for it," he said. "But all of my knowledge wouldn't have done much good if Trina hadn't had the 911 dispatcher call me as soon as she did. If they had contacted me even ten minutes later, I wouldn't have made it to your house because my road was flooding over. I had to drive through about eight inches of standing water as it was."

It dawned on Seth that since the phone shanty was on a road flooded by the creek, the only way Trina could have called 911 was by using her cell phone. He shuddered, thinking what could have happened. "She's been a blessing to my family in more ways than one," Seth told Ethan. Now he hoped he could find a way to express his appreciation to Trina—if she was even willing to talk to him. She'd been awfully quiet on the ride to the hospital, although Seth figured it was because she was worried about Timothy, too. He didn't think she could have been any more concerned if Timothy had been her own child.

By the time Trina returned to the hospital and located Seth in the pediatric wing, Ethan had gone to check on a patient who happened to have been admitted that day, too, and Seth was walking back to Timothy's new room after buying a coffee in the cafeteria.

Holding out a bag she said, "It's a change of clothes. And a sandwich for supper—Fannie made it."

"Denki," was all he could say even though he wanted to express so much more.

Averting her eyes, she asked how Timothy was and Seth grinned. Here was his chance. "He's terrific, thanks to you and Ethan. Ethan's visiting a patient, by the way. He said he'd be back soon. Listen, Trina, I—"

A nurse interrupted him as she exited Timothy's

room. "Oh, there you are. Timothy's awake and he's asking for you. He won't believe me that you didn't leave. Could you please go show him you're still here, Mr. and Mrs. Helmuth?"

Glancing at Trina, who had brushed her hair into a bun and changed into a dry skirt and a plain, modest blouse, Seth understood why the nurse mistook her for an Amish woman. But he had a feeling Trina was insulted to be referred to as his wife.

"Of course," she replied to the nurse and Seth's hope surged. Maybe she wasn't as disgusted by his recent behavior as he feared. Then she added, "I can't wait to see him again," and Seth realized she was willing to overlook the nurse's error if it meant she had access to Timothy's room.

They found him sitting up in his bed that was fitted with sheets that had monkeys printed on them. Timothy greeted Trina before saying, "I was scared, *Daed.* I thought you left."

"*Neh,* I'd never leave, *suh,*" Seth promised. The words seemed to catch in his throat. Hadn't Trina repeatedly offered Seth the same assurance? Realizing he'd been acting like a child himself, Seth almost wished Timothy would go back to sleep so he could apologize to Trina for his immature behavior, among other things.

"Timothy, did you paint those toucans on the walls?" she teased, pointing to the jungle motif wallpaper.

"*Neh.*" Timothy's giggle was music to Seth's ears—just as Trina's voice had so often struck him as musical. "Dr. Levine said they have an acqua...an acquar...um, a home for real, live fish I can see in the common room tomorrow morning. Can Tanner *kumme* see it, too?"

"If your *daed* says it's okay, I think I can arrange a way to get Tanner and your *groossmammi* here," Trina said. Inwardly, Seth cringed, recognizing how careful Trina was being to defer all decisions regarding the children to him. It was as if she was a stranger, unsure of whether her help would be welcomed, and Seth knew he was the one who'd created that distance between them.

After a couple of minutes, Ethan knocked on the door and, seeing Trina, asked if she was ready to go. Seth wished he could steal a moment to speak with her in private, but before he could think of a way to take her aside, she gently kissed Timothy on his cheek and was gone.

Timothy soon dozed off again and slumbered peacefully through the night, but Seth didn't sleep a wink. As he watched his son's chest rise and fall, he recognized how blessed he was to have his family and he thanked God for them. He again thought about Trina using her cell phone to call the emergency service dispatcher and how relieved he was she hadn't gotten rid of it after all. He was just as grateful for Ethan's car, which delivered Timothy to the emergency room. And for the knowledge of the doctors and nurses who tended to him.

Ultimately, Seth knew it was the Lord who'd saved his son from worse harm, but He'd done it through Ethan, Trina and a handful of other *Englischers*. Of course, Seth had no intention of relying on *Englisch* transportation or technology for his daily needs, but he was ashamed when he recalled the insulting things he'd said to Trina about *Englishers* in general, and about her in particular. His desire to put things right between them consumed his thoughts and coursed through his body, almost like a physical pain, until the sun rose and Timothy finally awoke again.

Thrilled to have his breakfast in bed, Timothy refused any help from Seth and deftly fed himself using his left hand, which pleased the nurses and doctor. As Timothy was eating, Tanner and Martha walked into the room and Tanner's eyes lit up when he noticed the wallpaper. He carefully crawled atop the adjustable bed so Timothy could give him a "ride" on it, and while the boys played, Seth asked Martha how she got there.

"Fannie brought us. She's waiting in the buggy lot. I think she's afraid to *kumme* in."

"She should be!" Seth sputtered.

"Seth, you've been through a hard night." Martha pointed her index finger at him. "But this accident could have happened under anyone's care. It could have happened if you were with the boys, or if I was or if Trina was. Instead of casting blame, you ought to be grateful the Lord watched over Timothy as He did."

Seth swallowed. Martha was right, of course. "That's very true, *Groossmammi.* And I am grateful. Especially for Trina and Ethan. And for your prayers, too, because I know they were as vital to Timothy's well-being as the physical care he received here was." To keep himself from tearing up, Seth teased, "I have to admit, though, I'm surprised you wanted to come anywhere near a hospital."

"I could say the same to you!" Martha joked and they both cracked up. She continued, "Sometimes, our thoughts are irrational. They're based on fear, not truth. This hospital—these doctors—played a role in Timothy's healing, by *Gott*'s grace. It's not right for me to be so mistrustful of them because some other doctor made a mistake in my past."

Seth recognized Martha was no longer talking about hospitals, but about him and Trina—and Freeman and Kristine. "You're right again," he said, knuckling his eyelids.

"You ought to go home and get some sleep," Martha directed. "I think Fannie would appreciate knowing you aren't angry with her. Tanner and I will stay here and you can pick us up this afternoon. The nurse at the station said Timothy wouldn't be discharged until four or five."

Seth hesitated. "I don't want to leave Timothy. He's scheduled to get his cast on at two thirty."

"*Kumme* back by two, then," Martha said. "It's time to exercise a little trust, Seth. I'll be here and the doctors will take *gut* care of him if anything goes wrong. It won't, but the Lord never minds if we pray about things that trouble us."

On that note, Seth conceded. After bidding goodbye to the boys and assuring Timothy he'd return before he got his cast on, Seth headed to the special parking lot equipped with hitching posts for the area's Amish population.

When he climbed into the buggy, Fannie burst into tears. "I'm so sorry, Seth," she cried.

Seth repeated his grandmother's words. "It's alright. It's not your fault. Timothy's accident could have happened while anyone was watching him."

Fannie twisted to face him. "I know *that*," she said with a sniff. "What I'm sorry about is that I can't take care of the boys any longer. They're just too rambunctious."

Seth could barely respond he was so flabbergasted. "I understand," he uttered and neither of them said anything else all the way to his home.

As she drove up the lane, Fannie said, "In a way, it's a *gut* thing this happened. Not that Timothy's suffering is *gut*, but the entire incident showed me our families won't ever be compatible. I hoped once the *Englischer* wasn't watching your *kin* any longer they'd take a liking to me, and if we worked at it, eventually our families would grow to understand and cooperate with each other. But my *meed* and I are just too different from you and your *buwe*."

Seth simply nodded and thanked Fannie for bringing him home. He was so weary he went into the parlor and collapsed onto the sofa and covered his eyes with his hands. He'd made such a mess of things with Trina. Between that and all his pent-up tension over Timothy's accident, Seth had never felt so low, and he allowed himself to shed a few more tears before pulling out a handkerchief and blowing his nose.

Then he stood up. Before catching a nap, he needed to milk the cow, otherwise her udders would become too full and she'd run the risk of infection. He lumbered to the stable as if his feet were made of lead and pulled the door open, his eyes adjusting to the light. What he saw was so unexpected at first he thought he imagined it.

* * *

Trina glanced toward the stable door. She had intended to finish milking Bossy before Seth arrived, but she hadn't even started. Each time she held out an apple slice, trying to entice the cow to move toward the stanchion, Bossy lifted her head and stuck out her tongue to accept the treat. Trina was so afraid of being bitten she dropped the fruit on the ground. She was down to her last slice when Seth arrived.

Now that the worst of Timothy's crisis was over, all of the comments Seth made to Trina the previous day came rushing back and she was immediately on guard. Dropping the last piece of apple to the ground, she muttered defensively, "I guess this is one more thing *Englischers* aren't good at doing." She tossed her chin in the air and tried to flounce around him, but he stepped into her path, blocking her exit. In her peripheral vision, she noted his nose and cheeks were red and raw, and his eyes were watery. He looked absolutely miserable.

"*Denki*, Trina," he said.

Without looking at him she shrugged and said, "As you can see, I couldn't even get her to *kumme* to the stanchion."

"Well, *denki* for trying. And *denki* for saving Timothy from further harm—" Seth's voice quivered and he swiped his hand across his eyes.

"I didn't save him. *Gott* did. All I did was make a phone call—on a cell phone," she pointed out.

"I'm so grateful you still had the phone."

Was that his idea of an apology? If he still thought

she'd intentionally held onto the phone, his gratitude was meaningless. "I'm glad I had it, too, but I didn't keep it deliberately, no matter what you think."

"I believe you and I'm sorry I ever doubted you. And I don't know if you'll believe me, but I trust you more than anyone. I didn't realize just how much I trusted you until...until Timothy's accident. But I trust you with the most important thing in my life—my *kinner*. I trust you with my family, Trina."

Now Trina gazed into his eyes. Not so she could read his expression, but so he would have to read hers. "I trusted you with the most important thing in my life, too, Seth. I trusted you with my heart."

A tear escaped the corner of his eye and then another from his other eye. He pushed them away before soberly promising, "I know you did. And I'm so sorry I didn't care for your heart as lovingly as you cared for my family. I will do anything to make it right. Please give me another chance to prove *I'm* trustworthy, Trina. Please don't leave Willow Creek."

Despite the seriousness of the moment, Trina snorted. "Ha! Do you really think I'd give up my plan to become Amish because of you?"

Seth looked taken aback.

"I cared about you—I still care—more than any man I've ever known, Seth. But I wasn't becoming Amish because of you and I'm not going to leave the Amish because of you. I'm doing it because I think it's the best way for me to live out my faith."

Seth looked chagrined. "I don't know whether to feel humbled or insulted by that," he admitted, "but actually, I just feel happy because it means you're going to stay here."

"There's something else you need to know. I was saying goodbye to my father at the diner. But first I wanted him to know I wasn't holding a grudge and the door to a relationship with me would always be open. I didn't want to wait until it was too late, the way my *groossdaadi* waited until it was too late to restore his relationship with my *mamm*. He waited until it was too late to tell her he loved her."

His chin quivering noticeably, Seth asked, "If I told you now that I love you, would it be too late?"

Trina caught her breath, aching from the near promise in his words. "*If* you told me now, it wouldn't be too late—but it would be inappropriate. I'm not Amish. Not yet."

Seth's eyes shone a pure pale blue. "Then I guess I'll just have to wait until you are. And while I'm waiting, I'll try to become the kind of trustworthy man you can love, too."

To Seth's delight, Trina grinned mischievously and stuck her hand out to shake his. "Deal," she said.

Her skin was silky but her grasp was strong, just as on the first day he met her, when they were still strangers. "Stay right there," he said. "I have something for you."

He ran to his workshop behind the barn and returned with the picture frame, which he had wrapped in brown paper. After opening it, she sighed as she traced the etched sandpipers with her finger.

"It's to replace the one I broke," he said nervously, unsure of what she was thinking.

"It's beautiful. So beautiful," she murmured and hugged it to her chest. Then she looked at it again and sighed, "But photographs are forbidden."

"I think in this case, it's probably alright if you save the photo of you and your mother, as long as it's not prominently displayed in your parlor or anything."

"But, Seth, I gave that picture to my *daed* yesterday, along with the photos from Abe."

"You did?" Seth was amazed and crushed at the same time. The very day he'd accused Trina of holding on to her *Englisch* life, she had already given up the most precious *Englisch* possession she owned.

"But maybe I can use it to frame a certificate listing the years of my mother's birth and her passing?"

Displaying such certificates was an acceptable practice in the Amish community and Seth agreed, although he felt disappointed, too. "That's a *gut* idea, but I really wanted to give you a special place to store your treasured photo."

"I know you did and I appreciate it. But I'm already storing the image in a special place," she said, placing her hand over her heart. "It's right here, next to the love I have for other cherished people in my life."

Seth nodded. She didn't have to say anything more. He knew what she meant because he felt exactly the same way.

"I'd better start the milking," he said. "I was going to get a couple hours of sleep and then head back to the hospital."

"May I *kumme*, too?" Trina asked.

"Of course. I'll even show you how to work the reins on the way, if you'd like."

"Don't I need a special license to drive a horse?"

Seth shook his head. "First of all, we don't call it 'driving' a horse. But *neh,* you don't need a special li—" Then he realized she was joking and he smiled until his insides throbbed from the sheer joy of having this *Englischer* as his neighbor.

Epilogue

Usually the convincement process in Willow Creek took at least three or four years, but in Trina's case, she was baptized into the church the following spring, along with several Amish youth. Afterward, there was a special potluck dinner and then Seth took them all home in his buggy. Even though it wasn't raining, he dropped Trina off right at her door before taking Martha and the boys home.

Timothy asked, "Will you watch us ride our bikes in the backyard, *Daed*?" The boys no longer needed training wheels but they were often reckless so Seth preferred they ride on the grass until they gained more control.

"*Neh*, your *daed* has to stable the horse and take care of a few other matters. I'll watch you as long as you don't do any of those *narrish* stunts," Martha said. "Just because Trina bought you helmets to protect your heads doesn't mean you can't break your arm. We can't have that happening again."

She winked at Seth, who shot her a grateful look,

knowing she could see his expression. Last year as a Mother's Day present he'd given her the gift of cataract surgery. Although both he and his grandmother had worried about the procedure, Trina and Ethan encouraged them every step of the way. The surgery had been a success; Martha's vision was restored, her headaches vanished and there was no slowing her down now.

There was no slowing Seth down today, either. He stabled his horse and raced next door to see Trina. The silver tabby American shorthair kitten the boys had given her as an honorary Mother's Day gift the previous year had grown into a fourteen-pound cat, thanks in part to Timothy and Tanner constantly supplying it with cream. Named Tabitha by the boys, the cat lounged on the porch railing and flicked her tail as Seth climbed the steps. When she wanted to, Tabitha could be a really good mouser, but apparently, she didn't want to at the moment. Either that, or she'd already completely rid Trina's house of mice.

It seemed to take Trina an eon to open the door after Seth knocked. When she did, he beheld her luminous eyes and was momentarily lost in their beauty, unable to speak. But then language returned to him and he couldn't express himself quickly enough, saying all of the things he'd been prohibited from saying until this moment.

"Trina, I love you. Wholeheartedly and unconditionally, with everything in me, I love you. Not only do I love you, I'm *in* love with you."

"I'm in love with you, too, Seth," she answered, her words tripping over his as if she, too, could no longer contain her emotion. "I always believed in romantic love as a concept, as something necessary for marriage. But until I met you, I never experienced the fullness of being in love. I never experienced—"

But she couldn't finish her sentence because Seth pulled her close and pressed his lips to hers. "You were right," he said breathlessly when they pulled away.

Her eyes were shining. "About what?"

"That was worth the wait." He drew her to him and kissed her again, this time softly and slowly, reluctantly parting only to say, "But I don't ever want to wait that long again."

She put her cheek against his and whispered into his ear, "Ach, the Amish are so impatient." He could feel her face curling into a smile and he smiled, too.

"Does that mean it's too soon for me to ask if you'll marry me?"

"*Neh*, it's not too soon. Of course I'll marry you!"

They simultaneously tilted their heads and gracefully found each other's lips a third time. Then Seth said, "The *buwe* will be thrilled once we're married and you're living with us. And selling your house should be easy, since you already know a *gut* realtor. Who knows, maybe an *Englisch* family will move in,"

"Actually, I was thinking if Martha wants to, she could have my house. It would be like living in a *daadi haus*. She'll have independence and peace and quiet, yet we'll be close enough to give her a hand if she needs it."

"That would be *wunderbaar*. So, when do you want to get married?"

"Well, Amish wedding season is in the fall, so I'd say sometime in late November? Early December?"

"Since I was already married once, technically, we don't have to wait until then. We could get married at any time. We could get married tomorrow, if you want to."

Trina encircled him with her arms. "As much as I'd love that, I'd actually prefer a traditional Amish fall wedding."

"Okay, if you insist," Seth said with an exaggerated groan to make her laugh. Then he added, "But if you change your mind and want to get married earlier…"

Trina tapped his nose with her fingertip. "I'm not going to change my mind."

"I know. You're always true to your word. It's one of the many things I love about you." There was no longer anything prohibiting them from holding hands, so Seth interlaced his fingers with hers and gently tugged her out onto the porch. "Let's stroll to the creek and on the way I'll tell you some of the other things…"

* * * * *

WE HOPE YOU ENJOYED
THIS BOOK FROM

LOVE INSPIRED
INSPIRATIONAL ROMANCE

Uplifting stories of faith, forgiveness and hope.

Fall in love with stories where faith helps
guide you through life's challenges, and discover
the promise of a new beginning.

6 NEW BOOKS AVAILABLE EVERY MONTH!

LIHALO20

Isaac, we have a visitor. This is Leah Porte. She's an *Englischer* friend of ours, staying with us a few months. Leah, this is Isaac Sommer."

For a moment Isaac was struck dumb by the newcomer. With her dark hair tamed back under a *kapp*, and her chocolate eyes, he barely noticed the ugly red scar bisecting her right cheek.

Leah stepped forward. "How do you do?"

"Fine, *danke*. Where do you come from?"

"California."

"Please, sit. Both of you." Edith Byler gestured toward the table.

Isaac found himself opposite Leah and gazed at her as the family gathered around the table. When all heads bowed in silence, he found himself praying he could get to know the visitor better.

At once, chatter broke out as the family reached for food.

"We hope you'll have a pleasant stay with us." Ivan Byler scooped corn onto his plate .

"I...I'm not familiar with your day-to-day life." The woman toyed with her fork. "I don't want to be seen as a freeloader."

"What is it you did before you came here?" Ivan asked.

"I was a television journalist," she replied. Isaac saw her touch her wounded cheek and glance toward him. "But after my...my car accident, I couldn't do my job anymore."

Journalist! What kind of God-sent coincidence was that? H smiled. "Maybe I should have you write some articles for m magazine."

"Magazine?"

Edith explained, "Isaac started a magazine for Plain people. H uses a computer to create it. The bishop gave him permission."

"An Amish man using a computer?"

"Many *Englischers* have misconceptions of how muc technology the *Leit* allows," Ivan intervened. "You won't fin computers in our homes, or cell phones. But while we try to live n *of* the world, we still live *in* the world, and sometimes technolog is needed to keep our businesses running. So, some bishops hav decided a little technology is allowed."

"What's the magazine about?" Leah asked.

"Whatever appeals to Plain people. Farming. Businesses. Lan management."

"And you want *me* to write for it?" she asked. "I don't kno anything about those topics."

"But that's what a journalist does, ain't so? Learn about ne topics," Isaac replied. Her opposition made him more determine "Besides, you're about to get a crash course while you stay her Maybe you'll learn something."

"I already said I had no intention of being a freeloader."

He nodded. "*Gut.* Then prove it. You can write me an articl about what you learn."

"Sure," she snapped. "How hard could it be?"

He grinned. "You'll find out soon enough."

Don't miss
The Amish Newcomer *by Patrice Lewis,*
available September 2020 wherever
Love Inspired books and ebooks are sold.

LoveInspired.com